About the Authors

Andrea Laurence is a[n] author who has been a[n] since she learned to re[ad] [tra]nsplanted into the De[develop a taste for sw[[he]r boyfriend and her old bulldog. You can contact [An]drea at her website: http://www.andrealaurence.com

[Tr]acy Madison is an award-winning author who makes [her] home in Northwestern Ohio. She fills her days with [lov]e, laughter, and many cups of coffee. Her nights are [oft]en spent awake and at the keyboard, bringing her [cha]racters to life and leading them toward their well-[des]erved happily-ever-after. Tracy loves to hear from [rea]ders! You can reach her at tracy@tracymadison.com

[Fio]na Brand lives in the sunny Bay of Islands, New [Zea]land. Now that both of her sons are grown, she [con]tinues to love writing books and gardening. After a [life]changing time in which she met Christ, she has [un]dertaken study for a Bachelor of Theology and has [beco]me a member of The Order of St. Luke, Christ's [heal]ing ministry.

Scandalous Secrets

Scandalous Secrets:
Secrets of
the Past

ANDREA LAURENCE

TRACY MADISON

FIONA BRAND

MIX
Paper from
responsible sources
FSC
FSC C007454

This book is produced from independently certified FSC™ paper
to ensure responsible forest management.

For more information visit: www.harpercollins.co.uk/green

Printed and bound in Spain
by CPI, Barcelona

MILLS & BOON

First Published in Great Britain 2020
By Mills & Boon, an imprint of HarperCollins*Publishers*
1 London Bridge Street, London, SE1 9GF

SCANDALOUS SECRETS: SECRETS OF THE PAST © 2020
Harlequin Books S.A.

Her Secret Husband © 2014 Andrea Laurence
Reid's Runaway Bride © 2014 Tracy Leigh Ritts
Needed: One Convenient Husband © 2016 Fiona Gillibrand

ISBN: 978-0-263-28171-2

HER SECRET HUSBAND

ANDREA LAURENCE

One

"**Y**our dad's heart attack was pretty serious this time."

The doctor's words did little to make Heath Langston feel better about his foster father's condition. He stood outside Ken Eden's hospital room, listening to the doctor's prognosis. He felt helpless, which was not the way he liked it. He might be the youngest of the "Eden boys," but he owned his own advertising firm on Madison Avenue. He'd single-handedly developed one of the most successful ad campaigns of the last year. He was used to everyone, from his secretary to his business partner, looking to him to make decisions.

But this was serious stuff. Life and death. Not exactly his forte. Ken and Molly Eden's only biological child, Julianne, hadn't stopped crying since she arrived. Heath preferred to keep things light and he'd much rather see Julianne smile, but even he couldn't find anything to make a joke about right now.

The Edens' five children had rushed to their family farm in Cornwall, Connecticut, the moment they'd gotten the call about Ken's heart attack. Heath had gotten into his car and bolted from New York City, not knowing if his foster father would be alive by the time he got to the hospital. His biological parents had died in a car accident when he was only nine years old. He was a grown man now, the CEO of his own company, but he wasn't ready to face losing another parent.

Heath and Julianne were the last to arrive and were receiving the report the others had already heard.

"He's stable now, but we were lucky," the doctor continued. "That aspirin Molly gave him may have made all the difference."

Julianne's tiny figure stood in front of him. Despite the doctor's serious words, Heath couldn't keep his eyes from going to her. She took after Molly, being petite but powerful. Today, she looked even smaller than normal, with her shoulders hunched over and her head dipped down to focus her eyes on the floor. Her blond hair had been long and loose when she'd first arrived, but after sitting forever in the waiting room, she'd clipped it up into a messy twist. She shivered at the doctor's words and tried to snuggle deeper into her green cashmere sweater.

Heath put a reassuring hand on her shoulder. His brothers each had their fiancées to hold for support, but he and Julianne were both alone. His heart went out to her. He hated seeing his feisty, confident artist looking so broken. Although they'd grown up in the same house, she had never been a sister in his mind. She had been his best friend, his partner in crime, and for a short time, the love of his life.

Knowing they had each other in this dark moment made him feel better. Tonight, he hoped they could put their tumultuous past behind them and focus on what was more important. Since Julianne didn't pull away, she had to feel the same. Normally, she would give him a playful shove and artfully dodge the physical contact, but not today.

Instead, her body slumped against him for support, her back pressing into his chest. He rested his cheek against the gold strands of her hair and deeply breathed in the scent that was imprinted on his brain. She sighed, sending a tingle of awareness traveling along his spine. The sensation turned the doctor's voice into a muffled mutter in the distance. For a moment, there was only him and her. It wasn't the most appropriate of times, but he would revel in the contact.

Touching Julianne was a rare and precious experience. She had never been a very physically demonstrative person, unlike Molly, who hugged everyone she met, but she kept an even greater distance from Heath. No matter what had happened between them all those years ago and who was to blame, in a moment like this he regretted the loss of his best friend the most acutely.

"He's going to need open-heart surgery. After that, he'll have to stay in ICU a few days until we can move him to a regular room."

"How long until he'll be able to come home?" Julianne asked, making Heath feel guilty for where his mind had strayed. Even as they touched, she was focused on something more important than the two of them and their history together. It was enough for him to straighten up and put some distance between their bodies once again. He opted to focus on the doctor's answer instead.

The doctor frowned. "I don't like to set expectations on this kind of thing, but as I told the others, he's going to be with us a week at least. He might need to go into a rehab center for a while. Maybe he could be at home if there's a bed downstairs and a nurse could be brought in. After that, he's going to have to take it easy for a few months. No lifting, no climbing stairs. He won't be cutting down pine trees this Christmas, that's for sure."

That decided it. With everything else that was going on, Heath had already been thinking of taking a few months off to return to his foster parents' Christmas-tree farm. A body had been discovered on former family property last Christmas and it had recently been identified as Tommy Wilder, a foster child who had stayed briefly on the farm. Heath and the other Eden children knew that Tommy had been dead nearly sixteen years, but the police investigation was just now heating up.

Heath had been torn between wanting to keep up with every news story on television about Tommy and wishing he could just pretend the bully had never existed. Unfortunately, he knew well that ignoring issues wouldn't make them go away.

As much as he hated to admit it, it was time for Heath to come home and answer for what he'd done. It was just Ken and Molly on the farm now, and although they knew nothing about the truth behind Tommy's disappearance, they were having to deal with the police investigation on their own. According to his only biological brother, Xander, the stress of Sheriff Duke threatening to arrest Ken had put him into the hospital today.

It was bad enough that one person was dead because of Heath's mistakes. He couldn't bear it if someone else, especially someone innocent like Ken, also fell victim.

The doctor disappeared and he and Julianne made their way back to the waiting room area, where the rest of the family was assembled. His three brothers and their fiancées were scattered around the room. Some were reading magazines, others were focused on their phones. All looked tired and anxious. "I'll be coming to stay at the farm until Dad is better," he announced to the group. "I can handle things."

"I know it's only the beginning of October, but Christmas will be here before you know it," his oldest foster brother, Wade, pointed out with a frown furrowing his brow. "The last quarter of the year is always a nightmare. You can't take all that on by yourself."

"What choice do we have? All of you are busy. My business partner can run Langston Hamilton for a few months without me. And I've got Owen," Heath added, referring to the Garden of Eden Christmas Tree Farm's oldest and most faithful employee. "He can help me with the details. When Christmas comes, I'll hire some of the high school and college boys to bag and haul trees."

"I'm coming home, too," Julianne announced.

The whole family turned to look at her. She'd been fairly quiet since she had arrived from the Hamptons, but only Heath seemed to realize the significance of her decision. She was volunteering to come home, even knowing that Heath would be there. While she visited the farm from time to time, it was very rare that the boys were there aside from Christmas celebrations. Volunteering to spend months with Heath was out of character for her, but she wasn't exactly in a good headspace.

Despite how small and fragile she looked, there was a sternness in her eyes. Unfortunately, Heath knew that look well. The hard glint of determination, like emeralds, had set into her gaze, and he knew she wouldn't be dissuaded from her decision. Once Julianne's mind was made up about something, there was no changing it.

Even without Heath there, her coming to the farm was a big deal. Julianne was a sculptor. Both her studio and her boutique gallery were in the Hamptons. It wasn't the kind of job where you could just pick up your twelve-hundred-pound kiln and work wherever you like.

"What about your big gallery show next year?" Heath said. "You can't afford to lose two or three months of work to come down here."

"I'm looking to set up a new studio anyway," she said.

Heath frowned. Julianne had a studio in her home. The home she shared with her boyfriend of the last year and a half. It was a personal record for her and everyone thought Danny might be a keeper. Looking for a new studio meant looking for a new place to live. And possibly a new relationship.

"Has something happened with you and Danny?" their brother Brody asked, saving Heath the trouble of nosing into her love life.

Julianne frowned at Brody, and then glanced around at her protective older brothers with dismay. She obviously didn't want to talk about this now, or ever. "Danny and I are no longer 'Danny and I.' He moved out about a month ago. I needed a change of scenery, so I've sold the house and I'm looking for something new. There's no reason why I can't move back for a few months while Dad recuperates. I can help around the farm and work on my art pieces when we're closed. When Dad's feeling better, I'll look for a new place."

Heath and the other boys looked at her dubiously, which only made the color of irritation flush her pale, heart-shaped face. "What?" she said, her hands going to her hips.

"Why didn't you say anything about your breakup with Danny? And selling your house? You two were together a long time. That's a pretty big deal," Xander noted.

"Because," Julianne explained, "three of you guys have gotten engaged recently. It's bad enough that I'll be going stag to all of your weddings. I wasn't exactly looking forward to telling all of you that I've got yet another failed relationship under my belt. Apparently I'm doomed to be the old maid in the family."

"That's hardly possible, Jules," Heath said.

Julianne's cool, green gaze met his. "Point is," she continued, deliberately ignoring his words, "I'm able to come home and help, so I will."

Heath could tell by her tone that the discussion was over for now. Taking her cue, he turned to the rest of his siblings. "Visiting hours are about over, although you'll pay hell to get Mom from Dad's bedside. The rest of us probably need to say good-night and head back to the farm. It's been a long, stressful day."

They shuffled into Ken's hospital room, the dark, peaceful space ruined by the beep of Ken's heart monitor and the low rumble of the voices on his television. There was one light on over the bed, illuminating Ken's shape beneath the off-white blanket. He was nearly as pale as the sheets, but it was a big improvement over the blue-tinged hue his skin had taken on earlier. His light blond, nearly white hair was disheveled from constantly pulling out his oxygen tube and putting it over the top of his head like a pair of sunglasses. Molly had obviously forced it back into his nose recently.

She was sitting in a reclining chair beside him. It was the kind that extended into a bed and that was a good thing. Molly wasn't going anywhere tonight. Her normally cheery expression was still pasted onto her face, but that was more for Ken's benefit than anything. Heath could tell there wasn't much enthusiasm behind it. They were all struggling just to keep it together for Dad's sake.

Ken shifted his gaze from his favorite evening game show to the group of children huddled at his bedside. Heath realized they must look ridiculous standing there. Five rich, successful, powerful people moping at their father's hospital bed, unable to do anything to help. All their money combined couldn't buy Ken a new heart.

At least, not *legally*. Since they'd already done their fair share of dancing on the wrong side of the law and had enough police lurking around their property to prove it, they'd stick with the doctor's recommendations for now.

"There's not much happening here tonight," Ken said. He tried to cover the fact that speaking nearly winded him, but he had to bring his hand to his chest and take a deep breath before saying anything else. "You kids get on home and get some rest. I'll be here. I'm not going anywhere, anytime soon."

Julianne stepped to his side and scooped up his hand. She patted it gently, careful not to disturb his IV, and leaned in to put a kiss on his cheek. "Good night, Daddy. I love you."

"I love you too, June-bug."

She quickly turned on her heel and moved to the back of the group so others could take their turns. She'd let the tears on her cheeks dry, but Heath could see more threatening. She was trying to hold them in and not upset Ken.

One by one, the rest of them said good-night and made their way out to the parking lot. The hospital was a good distance from Cornwall, so they merged onto the highway and made the long, dark drive back to their parents' farm.

Wade and Tori returned to their nearby home, but the rest of the family continued on to the farm. The boys each parked at the bunkhouse, leaving an impressive display of luxury vehicles out front. Heath was last, pulling his Porsche 911 Carrera in between Xander's Lexus SUV and Brody's Mercedes sedan.

Twenty-five years ago, the old barn had been converted into a guest house of sorts, where the foster children who came to live at the Garden of Eden would stay. It had two large bedrooms and baths upstairs and a large common room with a small kitchenette downstairs. It was filled with old, but sturdy furniture and all the comforts teenage boys needed. Heath was the youngest of the four boys who had come to the farm and stayed until adulthood. These days they spent their time in multimillion-dollar mansions and apartments, but this farm was their home and when they returned, the boys always stayed in the bunkhouse.

Heath watched Julianne pull her red Camaro convertible up closer to the main house. The old Federal-style home was beautiful and historic, but it didn't have enough space for a large crew of children. Ken and Molly had a bedroom, their daughter, Julianne, had a room and there was one guest room.

She stood on the porch, fumbling with her keys and looking lost. Heath didn't like that at all. Normally, Julianne was a woman who knew exactly what she wanted from life and how to get it. But tonight she looked anything but her normally spunky self. Nearly losing Ken right after things went south with Danny must have been more than she could take.

Heath grabbed his overnight bag from the trunk of his Porsche and followed the group into the bunkhouse. He set his duffel bag on the old, worn dining room table and looked around. The downstairs common room hadn't changed much since he'd moved in, aside from the new flat-screen television Xander had purchased during his recent stay.

There was a sense of comfort in being back home with his family. He imagined that wouldn't be the same for Julianne, who would be returning to an empty house. Heath might not be the person she'd choose to stay with her tonight, but he wasn't going to argue with her about it. He wasn't leaving her alone.

"Hey, guys," he said to his brothers and their fiancées as they settled in. "I think I'm going to sleep in the big house tonight. I don't like the idea of Jules being alone. Not after the day we've had."

Xander nodded and patted him on the shoulder. "That's a good idea. We'll see you in the morning."

Heath picked up his bag, stepped out and then jogged across the grass and gravel to the back door.

Julianne knew she should go to bed; it had been a very long day with unexpected twists and turns, but she wasn't sleepy. She'd woken up worried about her work and the fallout of her latest failed relationship. Then the phone rang and her world turned upside down. Her previous worries were suddenly insignificant. She'd dropped everything, thrown some clothes in a bag and hit the road.

Even now, hours later, she was still filled with nervous energy. There was a restless anxiety in her muscles, the kind that urged her to go to her workshop and lose herself in the clay. Usually, immersing herself in her work helped clear her mind and solve her problems, but all the pottery in the world wouldn't fix this.

She settled for a cup of chamomile tea at the kitchen table. That might bring her brain down a few notches so she could sleep. She was sitting at the table, sipping the hot tea, when she heard a soft tap at the door. The door almost immediately opened and before she could get up, Heath was standing in the kitchen.

"What is it?" she said, leaping to her feet. "Did the hospital call? Is there a problem?"

Heath frantically shook his head, making one curl of his light brown hair dip down into his eyes. He held up his hands in surrender and she noticed the duffel bag on his shoulder. "No, no problem. Dad's fine," he insisted. "I just didn't want you to be alone in the house tonight."

The air rushed out of her lungs in a loud burst. Thank goodness Dad was okay. Her heart was still racing in her chest from her sudden panic as she slipped back down into her chair. She took a large sip of the scalding tea and winced. After the day she'd had, she didn't need Heath hovering nearby and the distracting hum of his presence in her veins. An hour after they had left the hospital, she could still recall the weight of his hand on her shoulder and the comforting warmth of his chest pressed against her. The contact had been innocent, but her eyes had fluttered closed for a moment to soak in the forbidden contact. She'd immediately snapped herself out of it and tried to focus on her father's health.

"I'll be okay alone," she said.

Heath dropped his bag onto the wooden floor and flopped in the chair across from her. "No, you won't."

She sighed and pinched the bridge of her nose between her thumb and middle finger. She could feel a headache coming on and that was the last thing she needed. Of course, she could take one of her migraine pills and knock herself out. That was one sure way to get to sleep tonight, but what if something happened to Dad?

When she looked up at her guest, she found herself getting lost in the light hazel depths of his eyes. Heath was always happy, always ready with a joke or a smile. But tonight, his expression was different. There was a softness, a weariness, that lined his eyes. He looked concerned. Worried. But not for Ken. At least not entirely. He was concerned about her.

As always.

Julianne wouldn't make light, even in her own mind,

of Heath's protectiveness of her. He had gone to extraordinary lengths to keep her safe. She knew that anytime, day or night, she could call him and he would be there. But not just because they were family and he cared about her. There was a great deal more to it than that and tonight was not the night she was willing to deal with it.

"Thank you," she said at last. She wasn't going to put up a fight and force him into the bunkhouse. She didn't have the energy to argue and frankly, it would be nice to have someone in the big, creaky house with her. No matter what had happened between them over the years, she always knew she could count on him to respect her boundaries.

"It feels weird to be in the house without Mom and Dad," he said, looking around at the large, empty kitchen. "Mom should be fussing at the sink. Dad should be tinkering with farm equipment outside."

He was right, but she didn't want to think about things like that. Those thoughts would require her to face the mortality of her aging parents. Dad would come home this time, but eventually, he wouldn't. She'd rather pretend they were immortal, like she had believed as a child. "Would you like some tea?" she asked, ignoring his words.

"No, I'm fine, thanks."

She wished he would have accepted the tea. That would have given her something to do for a couple of minutes. Instead, she had to sit idly and wait for the questions she knew were coming. They hadn't been alone together and able to really talk since before she had left for college eleven years ago. That had been by design on her part. There were so many thoughts, so many feelings she didn't want to deal with. Looking into Heath's eyes brought everything back to the surface. The burning attraction, the anxiety, the overwhelming feeling of fear…

"So, what happened with you and Danny? That seemed kind of sudden."

Julianne sighed. "We decided we wanted different things, that's all. I wanted to focus on my art and building my career. Things have really taken off and I want to strike while the iron is hot. Danny wanted to take our relationship to the next level."

A spark of interest flickered in Heath's light eyes, his full lips pursing with suppressed amusement. "He proposed?"

"Yes," she said, trying not to let the memories of the uncomfortable moment flood into her mind. She'd told him repeatedly that she wasn't interested in marriage right now, and kids were far, far on the horizon. And yet he'd asked anyway. He seemed to mistake her hesitation as her playing hard to get or using reverse psychology with him. She wished she knew why. She'd given him no signals otherwise. "I refused, as politely as I could, but he didn't take the rejection very well. After that, we decided if we weren't moving forward, we were stagnating. So he moved out."

Danny had been a great guy. He was fun and exciting and sexy. At first, he hadn't seemed interested in settling down. Given her situation, he was the perfect choice. She didn't want to get too serious, either. They wouldn't have even moved in together if he hadn't needed a new place on short notice. He must have seen that as a positive relationship step, when in fact it was simply practicality and economics. In time, it was just easier to stay together than to break things off and cause an upheaval.

"You didn't want to marry him?" Heath asked.

Julianne looked up at him again and shook her head in exasperation. That was a ridiculous question. He knew full well why she'd turned him down. "No, I didn't. But even if I *did*, what was I going to say to him, Heath?"

There was a long, awkward silence before Heath spoke again. "Jules?"

"Listen, I know I brought it up, but I really don't want to talk about it tonight." Julianne sipped the last of her tea and got up from the table. "With Dad and the stuff with Tommy, I can't take any more drama."

"That's fine," he said as he leaned back into the wooden chair and watched her walk into the kitchen. "But considering we're going to be spending the next few months together, you need to come to terms with the fact that we need to talk about it. We've swept the issue under the rug for far too long."

She knew when she made the decision to come home that this would happen. No matter how uncomfortable it might be, she knew they needed her help on the farm, so that was where she would be. There wasn't anywhere else for her anyway. She had sold her house. Closing was next week, and then she was officially homeless. She had to come back here. And she had to deal with her past once and for all.

Julianne looked over at the funny, charming man that had stolen her heart when she was too young and messed up to know what to do about it. Even now, the soft curve of his lips was enough to make a heat surge through her veins and a longing ache in her belly. It took almost no effort at all to remember how it felt when he'd kissed her the first time in Paris. The whisper of his lips along her neck as they admired the Sagrada Família in Barcelona…

Her parents thought they were sending their two youngest children on an exciting graduation trip through Europe. Little did they know what freedom and romantic settings would ignite between their daughter and their youngest foster child. Heath wasn't her brother. She'd known him before his parents died and had never thought of him like a brother. He was her best friend. But if she ever wanted him to be something more, she had to deal with the past.

"Agreed," she said. "Once Dad is stable and we have some time alone to talk, I'm ready to deal with it."

Heath narrowed his gaze at her and she knew instantly what he was thinking. He didn't believe her. She'd been feeding him excuses and dragging her feet for years. He probably thought she got some sort of sick pleasure from drawing all this out, but that was anything but true. She was stuck between not wanting to lose him and not knowing what do with Heath if she had him.

A lifetime ago, when they were eighteen and far, far from home, he'd wanted her. And she'd wanted him. At least, she thought she had. She was young and naive. Despite the attraction that burned at her cheeks when he touched her, she'd found she couldn't fully give herself to him in the heat of the moment.

"It's been easy to ignore while both of us were in school and building our careers," Heath said. "But it's time. Your recent breakup is one of several signs we can't disregard any longer. Whether you like it or not, eventually you and I are going to have to face the fact that we're still married."

Two

He'd laid his cards out on the table. This would end, and soon. After several minutes spent in silence, waiting for her to respond to his declaration, Heath finally gave up. "Good night, Jules," he said, pushing up from his seat.

With Ken's attack, he understood if she couldn't deal with this tonight, but he wasn't waiting forever for her. He'd already wasted too much time on Julianne. He picked his bag up off the floor, and carried it down the hall and up the stairs to the guest bedroom.

The guest room was directly across the hall from Julianne's room and next to the bathroom they would share. He could count on one hand how many times he'd slept in the big house over the years. It just wasn't where he was drawn to. The big house was beautiful and historic, filled with antiques and cherished knickknacks. Most anyone would be happy to stay here, but Heath always felt like a bull in a china shop when he was in the house.

As kids, the bunkhouse was the ideal boy zone. They could be rowdy because the furniture was sturdy but old, there were no breakable antiques and downstairs was all wood flooring, so they could spill and not stain the carpet. There was a big television, video games, a foosball table and an inexhaustible supply of soda and other snacks to fuel growing boys. Things had changed over the years, but being there with his brothers again would make it feel just the same.

Tonight, he made an exception and would stay in the big house for Julianne's sake, but it would be a mistake for her to confuse his gesture as weakness where she was concerned. Any love he had for her had fizzled away when she'd slammed her dorm room door in his face.

For years, he'd been as patient as he could stand to be. He knew now that he had been too nice. He'd given her too much space and let her get too contented. There was no incentive for her to act. That was going to change. He had no intention of being easy on her while they were here. Whatever it took, no matter how hard he had to push her out of her comfort zone, he would leave this farm a happily divorced man. Heath knew he shouldn't enjoy watching Julianne squirm, especially tonight, but he did.

Eleven years of marriage without his wife in his bed could do that to a guy.

He opened the door to the guest room and put his bag down on the white eyelet bedspread. The room was intricately decorated, like the rest of the house, with antique furniture, busy floral wallpaper, lacy curtains and shelves filled with books and framed pictures. As he kicked out of his Prada loafers, he noticed a portrait on the wall in a carved, wooden frame.

It was of Julianne. One of her elementary school pictures, although he couldn't be sure what year. Her golden hair was pulled up into a ponytail, a sprinkle of freckles across her nose. She was wearing a pink plaid romper with a white turtleneck underneath it. She looked just as he remembered her.

He had fallen in love with Julianne Eden the first time he'd seen her. They were in Mrs. Henderson's fourth-grade class together. The cheerful blonde with the curly pigtails and the bright smile had sat right next to him. Whenever he forgot his pencil, she would loan him one of hers. They were pink and smelled like strawberries, but he didn't care. He left his pencil at home on purpose just so he could talk to her.

He'd fabricated childish plans to marry Julianne one day. It seemed like a pipe dream at the time, but one day on the playground, she kissed him—his very first kiss— and he *knew* that she was meant to be his. He'd even made her a Valentine's Day card to tell her how he felt.

He never gave her the card. The weekend before their class party, his parents were killed in a car accident. Heath had been in the car at the time, but his injuries, while serious, had not been fatal. When he was finally discharged from the hospital, both he and his brother, Xander, had found themselves in the care of Family Services. The next thing he knew, they were living at the Christmas-tree farm on the edge of town and the beautiful golden-haired girl of his dreams was supposed to be his "sister."

He had outright rejected that idea right away. They might live in the same home, but not once in twenty years had he ever referred to her as "sis" or "my sister." She was Jules, usually; Julianne when he was speaking about her to the uninitiated.

He'd given up the dream of ever marrying his child-hood love soon after coming to the Garden of Eden. Julianne never kissed him on the playground again. They were friends, but that was all. It wasn't until they were seniors in high school and the only kids left on the farm that things started to change between them. The trip to Europe had been the tipping point. Unfortunately, it hadn't tipped in his favor for long.

That seemed to be Julianne's M.O. Since they'd broken up, she had dated, but from what he could tell, never seriously and never for long. None of the brothers had ever met a boyfriend. She never brought one home to the farm. Danny had come the furthest, moving in with Julianne. She didn't really let any man get close, but Heath wasn't certain what was the cause and what was the effect. Did their marriage fail because she didn't do relationships, or did her relationships fail because she was married?

He had unpacked a few things and was halfway undressed when he heard a soft tap at his door. "Come in," he called out.

Julianne opened the door and stuck her head in. She started to speak, and then stopped, her gaze dropping from his face to his bare chest. He tried not to move, fighting the urge to puff up his chest and suck in his stomach. He liked to think he looked pretty good without all that, but it was such a reflex. He jogged the High Line every morning and lifted weights. As a child, he was always the smaller, scrappier of the boys, but no longer. He might be the shortest, at six feet, but he could take any of his brothers and look good doing it.

The dumbstruck Julianne seemed to agree. A crimson flush rose to her delicate, porcelain cheeks. Her full bottom lip hung, useless, until her tongue shot across it and her mouth slammed shut.

If Heath had known strutting around shirtless would get this kind of reaction from her, he would have done it a long time ago. Nothing made her more uncomfortable than the topic of sex. If he'd pushed the issue, perhaps he'd be happily single or happily married right now. Watching her reaction, he thrust his hands in his pockets. His Dolce & Gabbana slacks rode lower with the movement, exposing the trail of hair beneath his navel and the cut of his muscles across his hips.

Julianne swallowed hard and then shook her head and shifted her gaze away to the nearby armoire. "I'm s-sorry," she stuttered. "I didn't realize you were…"

"It's okay," Heath said with a sly smile, enjoying her discomfort. "I'm not bashful and it's nothing you haven't seen before."

She shook her head, sending a wave of the luxurious golden strands over her shoulders. "I don't remember you looking like *that*," she said, quickly bringing her hand up to cover her mouth. She looked embarrassed to share her observation aloud.

Heath glanced down at the display of his own body and shrugged. "I'm not eighteen anymore."

He supposed he would be struck just as hard to see her topless after all this time. Hell, he'd barely seen her naked back then. Sometimes when he was feeling particularly masochistic, he would allow himself to imagine what she looked like now beneath her sweaters and her jeans. The teenage girl he loved had become a very sexy and gifted woman. Any gangliness had been replaced with lush curves and soft, graceful movements. Beautiful and aggravating.

She stood awkwardly in the doorway, nodding, not looking at him, not saying anything for a few moments.

"Did you need something?" Heath prompted at last.

Her green gaze shifted back to his, her purpose suddenly regained. "Yes. Well, I mean, no. I don't *need* anything. I, uh, just wanted to say thank you."

"Thank you? For what?"

"For staying here with me tonight. I know you'd rather be laughing and chatting with Xander and Brody. You guys never get to see one another."

"I see them more than I get to see you," Heath said before he could stop himself. It was true. As children, they had been inseparable. She was his best friend. The marriage that should have brought them even closer together had driven them apart and he still didn't understand why. "I miss you, Jules."

A sadness crept into her eyes, a frown pulling down the corners of her mouth. "I miss you, too, Heath."

"Be honest. You avoid me. Why?" he asked. "Even if we divorced, I get the feeling that you'd still be uncomfortable around me."

"I'm not uncomfortable," she said, but not convincingly.

"Am I being punished for what happened between us?"

Julianne sighed and slumped against the door frame. "It's not about punishing you. And no, it's not about what happened in Europe, either. There are just things in our past that I don't like thinking about. It's easier to forget when I don't see or talk to you."

"Things in our past? Wait…" he said. "Are you blaming me for what happened with Tommy Wilder?"

"No!" she spoke emphatically, raising her palm up to halt him. "You are my savior. The one who protected me when no one else could."

"But you think of that horrible night when you look at me?" Heath was almost nauseated at the thought.

"No," she insisted again, but less forcefully. "If that were true, I never could've fallen for you. It's just easier for me to focus on the future instead of dwelling in the past. Our relationship is in my past."

"Not according to the public records office. It is very

much current and relevant. Ignoring things won't change them. It just makes it worse."

Julianne chuckled and crossed her arms over her chest. "Believe me, I know. I just don't know what else to do about it."

"We get divorced. We can't just stay married forever."

"It's worked okay so far."

Now it was Heath's turn to laugh. "Says the woman that just broke up with her boyfriend when he proposed."

"I didn't…" she began to argue, and then stopped. "This conversation has strayed from what I'd intended when I knocked. Thank you, again," she repeated. "And good night."

Heath watched her slip through the doorway. "Good night," he replied just as the door shut. Once he was certain she was settled in her room, he cast off the rest of his clothes and crawled into bed in his boxer shorts. The bed was soft and inviting, the sheets smelling like the lavender soap Molly used for linens and towels. The bed very nearly forced him to relax, luring him to the edge of sleep faster than he ever thought possible.

Things hadn't worked out between him and Julianne, but he wasn't stupid. He had long ago set aside any idea that their farce of a marriage might become something real. They'd never even consummated it. He'd thought she would come around eventually. It was her first time, perhaps she was just nervous. But then she left for her art program in Chicago without even saying goodbye. He chased after her, driving all night to figure out what was going on. He'd imagined a romantic moment, but instead, she'd told him their marriage was a mistake, he needed to forget it ever happened and practically shut her dorm room door in his face.

He'd been devastated. Then the devastation morphed

into anger. Then indifference. After that, he'd decided that if she wanted a divorce so badly, she could be the one to file. So he'd waited.

Eleven years.

As she'd mentioned, it hadn't been a problem. At least, logistically. He hadn't met a single woman that made him want to walk down the aisle again, but it was the principle of the thing. She didn't want him, and yet she was resistant to let him go. Julianne always seemed to have an excuse. They were broke. They moved around too much after school to establish residency. They were busy starting their businesses. Her appointment with her divorce attorney was rescheduled, and then rescheduled again.

After a while, he began to wonder if she would rather stay married and keep it a secret than file for divorce and risk people finding out she'd married *him*. Her big mistake.

He'd known her since they were nine years old and he still didn't understand what went on in that beautiful blond head of hers.

Julianne sat in a rocking chair on the back porch clutching a big mug of steaming coffee. She had barely slept last night and she desperately needed the infusion of caffeine to make it through today. She'd lain in bed most of the night thinking about Heath and how he was so close by. Her mind had wandered to their first trip together and how wonderful it had been. Even as young as they were, he'd known just how to touch her. With the backdrop of Europe, so romantic and inspiring, behind them, she thought she might be able to overcome the fear. She'd been wrong.

The familiar ache of need had curled in her belly, but she'd smothered her face in the pillows until it faded. It didn't matter how much she'd loved him back then. How much she wanted him. It didn't stop the fear from nearly strangling her with irrational panic. If she couldn't give herself to Heath, the one who protected her, the one she was closer to than anyone else… When it came down to it, she had been too messed up back then to be with anyone.

Heath was right, though. They needed to move on. She'd dragged her feet. Hoping the words would come easier after all this time, she made excuses. If the years had taught her anything, it was that the truth could be more painful than a lie. She lied for everyone's sake, including her own. To have a real, honest relationship with Heath, she would have to tell him the truth about their wedding night. And she just couldn't do it.

That meant that all there was left to do now was clean up the tattered remains of their relationship.

And there would be time for that soon. Other more pressing issues had to be addressed first, like arranging her move and seeing her father through his heart surgery, but even those could wait until after she'd had her coffee and settled into her day. It was early. The sun had just come up. Heath was still asleep and there was no sign of life from the bunkhouse. For now, it was just her, the cool air and the pine forest that spread out in front of her.

At one time in her life, those trees had been her sanctuary. Whenever something was troubling her, she could walk through row after row, losing herself in them. And then Tommy Wilder came to the farm. She never imagined someone could hurt her so badly and not kill her. The physical scars healed, but the emotional ones lingered. The trees had turned their backs on her that day, and she'd refused to go out there any longer. The boys had gladly picked up her share of chores in the field and she took on more responsibility in Molly's Christmas store. Her mother thought that it was Julianne's budding artistic spirit that drove her out of the trees and into the shop.

That was so far from the truth. It was actually the other way around. Her refuge in the shop had fueled an artistic creativity in her she didn't know she had. She started helping Molly decorate and make wreaths, but soon she was painting the windows and molding Nativity scenes out of clay. She was keeping so many painful, confusing things inside; it was easy to give her mind over to the intricacies of her art. It was only her good fortune that she was talented at what she did and was able to turn her therapy into a career.

The rumble of car tires across the gravel caught her attention. A moment later, Molly's Buick rounded the house and parked beside her Camaro.

Julianne got up and walked to the stairs to meet her. "Morning, Mama. Is Daddy doing okay?"

Molly nodded. "He's fine. Feeling well enough to shoo me home for a while. His surgery is tomorrow morning, so he wants me to take a break now, while I can."

That sounded like Daddy. He hated to be fussed over, just like she did. "I've made some coffee."

"Thank goodness," Molly said, slowly climbing up the stairs. "That sludge at the hospital hardly qualified."

They went inside and Julianne poured her a large mug with a splash of cream and one spoon of sugar. She joined her mother at the kitchen table, where she and Heath had had their uncomfortable conversation the night before. Looking at the weary, worn-out woman across from her, Julianne knew she just couldn't let her parents find out she'd eloped with Heath right out of high school.

It wasn't because of *whom* had she married, or even *how*. If Julianne hadn't been such a mess and things worked out, Molly wouldn't have been happy about them eloping, but she would have come around. The problem was explaining what went wrong between them and why she wasn't willing to work things out. Everyone would want to know how they could marry and break up in an instant. She couldn't even tell *Heath* that. How could she tell her parents, who had no clue that Tommy had ever laid a hand on her, much less ruined their daughter?

Julianne refused to be anything other than the cool and confident daughter of Ken and Molly. She supposed it was growing up as the only child of parents who desperately wanted more children. They loved her without question, but at the same time, they were always vocal about their disappointment in having only one. When they started taking in foster children, it made it even harder to get attention. At first, she tried to excel in school to prove to them that she was good enough to make up for being the only one. She was well-behaved, polite and never caused the tiniest problem for her parents.

It had worked. To a point. They were always quick to praise her, but her parents continued to bring in foster children. Perfection became her way to stand out and get noticed. It wasn't until after the incident with Tommy that she threw an uncharacteristic fit and demanded her parents stop bringing in other children and pay attention to her for once. It was selfish. And she felt horrible doing it. But she couldn't risk another boy coming to the Garden of Eden who might look at her the way Tommy did.

"Are you doing okay this morning?" Molly asked her.

"Yeah. Heath stayed in the guest room so I wouldn't be alone. We talked last night and a couple of us are going to come stay here for a few months. Through the New Year, at least, to help with Christmas and such."

Molly's chin shot up—her mother was ready to argue—but she stopped herself and nodded. They both knew she couldn't run the farm alone. Her petite frame and increasingly stiff fingers couldn't haul Christmas trees twice her size. Having the kids here would take the pressure off of her and keep Ken resting the way he should. "Which of you are coming up?"

"Heath and I. He's taking a few months away from the advertising agency. I've sold my house in Sag Harbor and I'm moving here until Dad is better, then I'll find someplace new."

"What about you and, uh…" Molly's voice trailed off.

Her mother couldn't remember the name of her boyfriend. That said volumes about her ill-fated relationship history. "Danny," Julianne offered. "We've broken it off."

"Oh," Molly said. "I'm sorry to hear that."

"Liar," Julianne said, smiling into her coffee mug as she took a sip.

Molly shrugged, but didn't argue with her on that point. "I've been speaking with a private medical care company about bringing your father home to recuperate instead of putting him in a nursing home. They recommended moving a bed downstairs, and they could provide a live-in nurse for a few weeks."

"That sounds perfect." She wanted her father to have the best possible care, but she hated the idea of him in a nursing home, even if temporarily.

"Well, except that you'd have to stay in the bunkhouse. We'd need to move one bed downstairs and have the other for the nurse. Is that okay?"

"Absolutely," Julianne responded, although the idea of close quarters with Heath didn't thrill her. Last night was bad enough. "It will give me some room to store my equipment, too."

"Speaking of which, what about your studio? And your gallery showing? You have to keep working, don't you?"

"The store is fine without me. My place in the Hamptons does too well to move and my staff there run it beautifully. As for my studio, I'm thinking I can work here and it wouldn't impact the show. Since I'm staying out there, maybe I can use part of the bunkhouse."

"You know," Molly said, "the storage room there hasn't been used in ages. We could clean that out and you could use it."

"Storage room?"

"Yes. You know what I'm talking about. In the bunkhouse, under the staircase. It's about twelve by twelve, I'd say, with a window and its own door to the outside. That's where we used to hide your Christmas presents when you all were small. Right now, I think it might just have some boxes of the boys' old toys and sporting equipment."

Honestly, she hadn't given much thought to the nook under the stairs. Her time in the bunkhouse was usually spent watching television or messing around with the boys, not surveying the property. "Now I remember. If it's as big as you say, that would be perfect."

"If Heath is staying," Molly continued, "perhaps he can help you get the space ready. There should be some time before the holiday rush begins."

"What am I helping out with?" Heath stumbled sleepily into the kitchen in jeans, a casual T-shirt and bare feet. His light brown hair was tousled. It was a far cry from his expensive tailored suits and perfectly styled hair, but it impacted Julianne even more powerfully. This morning, he looked more like the Heath she'd fallen in love with. The successful, powerful advertising executive was a stranger to her.

"We need you to help clean out the old storage room in the bunkhouse," Molly answered.

He located a mug and made his own cup of coffee. "The one where you hid our Christmas presents?"

A light flush of irritation rose to Molly's cheeks. Julianne had her mother's same pale, flawless complexion. It was always quick to betray their feelings. They blushed bright red at the slightest provocation.

"You knew about that?" Molly asked.

Heath smiled and took a step farther from his mother under the guise of looking in the cabinet for something to eat. "We've always known, Mom. We just didn't have the heart to tell you."

"Well, hell," Molly said, smacking her palm against the table. "Just as well we turn it into a studio, then."

"Mom says that Dad's surgery is tomorrow," Julianne added, steering the conversation in another direction.

Heath pulled down a box of cereal and nodded. "Once we're certain that he's doing okay after surgery, I'll probably head back to New York for a few days and get my things. I need to make arrangements with work and such, but I can probably be back up here in two or three days."

Julianne nodded. She had plenty of things to take care of, too. "Same here. I've got to close on the house. Most of my things are already boxed up. I'll put what I can in storage somewhere and bring the rest."

"How are you going to get all your stuff into that little bitty sports car?" Heath asked.

"The Camaro is bigger than your Porsche," she countered.

"Yeah, but I'm not hauling all your sculpting supplies and tools. What about your kiln?"

"I'm selling it locally," Julianne said, although she didn't know why he was so concerned. "I wanted a new one anyway, so I'll get it delivered here."

Heath frowned at her and crossed his arms over his chest in irritation. She tried not to focus on the way the tight fabric stretched across his hard muscles when he moved, but her eyes were instantly drawn to it. She followed the line of his collar to the lean cords of his neck and the rough stubble along his jaw. Her gaze stopped short when she noticed his amused smirk and arched eyebrow. He'd caught her. At that, she turned her attention back to her coffee and silently cursed herself.

"You need movers," he persisted. "And a truck. I can get you one."

Julianne scoffed at the suggestion. This was so typical of the way the last few years had gone. They avoided the big issues in their relationship and ended up quibbling about stupid things like moving trucks. She supposed to others, they seemed like bickering siblings, when in fact they were a grumpy, married couple. "I might need a truck, but I don't need you to pay for it. I'm capable of handling all that myself."

"Why won't you—"

"We'll discuss it later," she interrupted. She wasn't going to argue with him in front of Molly. She eyed her mother, who was casually sipping her coffee and sorting through her mail.

As if she could feel the tension in the room, Molly set down her stack of bills and stood up. "I'm going to go take a shower," she announced. She took the last sip of her coffee and went upstairs, leaving the two of them alone.

Heath took Molly's seat with a bowl of cereal in one hand and a mug of coffee in the other. "It's later."

"You paying for my movers looks suspicious," she complained. And it did. She made decent money. She didn't need someone to handle it for her, especially Heath playing knight in shining armor.

"I wasn't planning on paying for it. My agency handles the Movers Express account. The CEO owes me a favor. I just have to make a call. Any why is it suspicious? If Wade or Xander offered the same thing, you'd take them up on it without question."

"Because I understand their motives," Julianne said.

Heath's brows went up in surprise. "And what are my motives, Jules? Do you think I'll demand my rights as a husband in exchange for it? Sex for a moving truck? That's certainly a new one on me. Shoot. I should have made that part of the deal up front." His light hazel eyes raked over her, a devious smile curling his lips. He leaned across the table and spoke in a low, seductive tone. "I saw the way you were looking at me just now. It isn't too late to rene-gotiate, Jules."

The heat of his gaze instantly warmed the blood pump-ing through her veins. He very quickly made her aware of every inch of her body and how she responded to him. She wished he didn't have that power over her, but the moment she'd looked at him as something more than a friend, it was like a switch had flipped and she hadn't been able to reverse it. She also hadn't been able to do anything about the attraction.

"Yes, it is," she said, dropping her gaze to her coffee mug in the hopes she could suppress her stirring libido. "Way, way too late."

"Well then, I guess I'm just trying to be nice."

He made her reluctance to accept his offer seem child-ish. "Of course," she said, but a part of her still wondered. There were too many undercurrents running between their every interaction. Whenever Heath was nice to her, when-ever he did something for her, she couldn't help but won-der why. He had every reason to be angry with her. She'd treated him terribly, practically throwing his love back in his face.

On their trip to Europe, they had lain on the grass at the base of the Eiffel Tower and watched the lights twinkling on the hour. There, he'd confessed to her that he had been in love with her since the fourth grade. Swept up in the moment, she told him that she loved him, too. Their relationship had begun in Paris. The marriage started and ended in Gibraltar just three days later. She'd pushed him away for his own good, but he'd never understand that. All he saw was that she turned her back on him and wouldn't tell him why.

For a while he was angry with her. He didn't talk to her for their entire freshman year of college. Then he avoided her, doing internships instead of coming home for the summer. Their interactions were short, but polite. It took years, but eventually, he went back to the funny, easygoing Heath she'd always loved.

The light banter and humor covered up their issues, however. They had both been apart for so long, most days it was easy to ignore what happened between them on the graduation trip. But now they were looking at months together. In close quarters.

Julianne had the feeling that the pressure cooker they'd kept sealed all this time was about to blow.

Three

Ken's surgery went perfectly the next day. He spent twenty-four hours in ICU, and then he was moved to a regular room. Once he was off the ventilator and able to talk, Ken demanded everyone go home and stop hovering over him like it was his deathbed.

As instructed, Brody and his fiancée, Samantha, drove back to Boston. When Ken had his attack, Xander had been in Cornwall to move his ten-year-old son and new fiancée, Rose, to D.C. to live with him. He'd sent them along without him, so he gathered up the last of their things and met up with them back in D.C. Wade and Tori lived nearby and agreed to watch the farm while Heath and Julianne went home to make arrangements and make the transition to their new, temporary home.

Heath had offered to drive with Julianne and help with her move, but of course, she'd declined. He didn't know if she just didn't trust him, or if she felt too guilty to accept things from him after she'd broken up with him. He liked to think it was guilt.

The drive to Manhattan was quick, about two and a half hours. He called his business partner as he reached Chelsea and asked Nolan to meet him at his place to go over details while he packed. He found a metered spot on the street as he got off the phone. It was a great spot, considering how much he needed to load into the car. Some days he wasn't so lucky and wished he'd gotten a place with parking.

He hadn't been looking for a condo in this area when he first started shopping, but he'd fallen in love with the modern feel and large rooftop terrace that was bigger than his first New York apartment. Everything else, including parking, fell to the wayside. It was close enough to the office, near a subway stop and one of his favorite restaurants was a block up the street. He couldn't pass it up.

Heath had cleaned all the perishables out of his refrigerator and had his largest suitcase packed when he heard the buzzer for the outer door of the building. He hit the release to let Nolan in and waited there for him to come out of the elevator. "Hey, man. Thanks for coming by."

Nolan smiled and straightened his tie as he walked down the hallway. It was the middle of the week, so he was dressed more for work than Heath, who was in his jeans and NYU alumni sweatshirt.

"How's your dad doing?" Nolan asked.

Heath urged him inside and shut the door. "He's stable. I think he's going to pull through fine, but as I mentioned earlier, I'm going to be gone a few months while he recovers."

"Totally understandable. I think everything will go smoothly at the office. The only account I worry about with you gone is J'Adore."

Heath went to the refrigerator and pulled out two bottles of sparkling water. He opened them both and handed one over to Nolan. "The cosmetics account? Why do they worry you?"

"Well—" Nolan shrugged "—it has more to do with the owner's preference for *Monsieur Langston*."

"Oh," Heath replied. Now he understood. The French cosmetics company was a great account. They'd helped J'Adore break into the high-end American cosmetics market in the last year. Thanks to his company's marketing campaign, J'Adore was the trendiest new product line for the wealthy elite. The only issue was the owner, Madame Cecilia Badeau. She was in her late fifties, wealthy and eccentric, and she had Heath in her sights. For a while he was concerned they would lose the account if he didn't make himself...*available* to her.

"Thank goodness you're married, man," Nolan said, flopping down onto the sleek, white leather couch.

There was that. It was the first time he was thankful to have that stupid piece of paper legally binding him to Julianne. In order not to offend Madame Badeau, Heath had to tell her he was married. It came as quite a shock to her, as well as Nolan, who was also in the room at the time. They were the only other people who knew he and Julianne were married. He explained that Julianne traveled for her work and was always out of town when he was asked about her. Madame Badeau had immediately backed off, but she still insisted the account be personally handled by Heath.

"I think she'll understand that I've taken a leave of absence."

Nolan looked at him, his dark brows pointedly drawn together with incredulity. "I sincerely hope so, but don't be surprised if you get a call."

"After a month on the farm, I might be happy to answer." Heath hadn't spent more than a few days back at the Garden of Eden Christmas Tree Farm since he'd graduated from college. Avoiding Julianne had meant avoiding his family, although he was beginning to think that was the wrong tactic. He was out of sight, out of mind with her. From now on, he was going to be up close and personal.

"Are you going to be running that huge place all by yourself?" Nolan asked.

"No," Heath said, sliding onto the other end of the couch. "Julianne is going back for a while, too."

Nolan sputtered, obviously trying not to choke on his sip of water. "Julianne? Your *wife*, Julianne?"

Heath sighed. "Technically, yes, but I assure you it means nothing. I mean, I told you we never even slept together, right?"

"I still don't know what you could've done to ruin a marriage within hours of your vows."

Heath had wondered that same thing a million times. One moment, he had achieved his life's dream and married his glorious Julianne. The next, she was hysterically crying and screaming for him to stop touching her. The moment he let her go, she ran into the bathroom of their hotel room and didn't come out for two hours.

"I don't know. She never would tell me what changed. She was happy. The perfect, beautiful blushing bride. She responded to me, physically. Things were going fine until they weren't. All she would ever say was that she was sorry. She thought she could be with me, but she just couldn't do it."

"Was she a virgin? My high-school girlfriend was a nervous wreck our first time."

"That's what I thought. I never asked her directly, that felt weird, but that was my assumption. I kept thinking she'd warm up to the idea. She didn't." When he'd first told his partner about his crazy marriage, Heath hadn't elaborated and Nolan had been kind enough not to press him for details. Now, facing months with Julianne, he was glad he had someone to talk to about it.

Nolan scoffed. "What about when you got home?"

"I was trying not to push her. She asked not to tell anyone about the marriage right away and I agreed. I thought she needed time, and we had a few weeks before we both went to school. One morning, I came in from the fields and her car was gone. She'd left early to go to Chicago and didn't tell me or say goodbye."

"What did you do?"

"I followed her up there. She wouldn't even let me into her room. I'd never seen such a hard, cold expression on her face before that day. She told me getting married was a mistake. She was so embarrassed, she couldn't bear to tell anyone about it. Then she told me to go home and forget it ever happened."

"Do you think there's more to it than what she told you?"

"Some days, yes, some days no. I do think she was ashamed to tell people that she married me. Especially our parents. She's always been too concerned with what people think. Jules had to have Molly and Ken's approval for everything. Maybe she didn't think she would get it for our marriage."

"Or?"

That was the big question. Something just didn't add up. If she had been so concerned about their parents finding out what happened, she either wouldn't have married him at all or she would have panicked when they returned home and had to face telling them. But she had panicked on their wedding night without any warning that his eighteen-year-old self could pick up on. They had kissed and indulged in some fondling in the days before the wedding and again that night. It wasn't until all the clothes came off that the mood shifted.

Then there was fear in her eyes. Sudden terror. And he'd barely touched her, much less hurt her. He'd had eleven years to live that night over and over in his mind and still didn't know what he did wrong.

"I have no idea. I just know that whatever the issue is, she doesn't want to talk about it."

"Why are you two still married, then? You're not still in love with her, are you, Heath?"

"I'm not," Heath assured him. "That boyhood crush died a long time ago, but it's more complicated than that."

"Enlighten me."

"At first, I thought she would change her mind. We had broken up, but I was certain she would realize she was overreacting about the sex and after being apart for a while she would miss me and decide she really did love me and want to be with me." He sighed, remembering how many nights he'd lain in bed naively fantasizing about her revelation. "But she didn't. She just pretended it never happened and expected me to do the same. She wouldn't talk about it."

"Then divorce her," Nolan suggested. "Be done with it."

Heath shook his head. "I know that I should, but there's no way I'm letting her off the hook that easily. I definitely think it's time to wrap the whole thing up between us, but she left me. I'm going to make her finish the job."

Nolan didn't look convinced. "That hasn't worked so well for you so far."

"I just think she needs a little incentive. Something to push her to make a move."

"What have you got in mind?" Nolan asked, his eyes

lighting up with his wicked imagination. He was the perfect business partner for Heath. They were both devious to a fault, but Heath had the creativity and Nolan had the business smarts.

He could still picture her flushed cheeks and stuttering speech when she was faced with his half-naked body. That really was the key. "I'm going to go back to the house and help Jules set up her new studio there. I'll do everything I need to around the farm. But I'm not going to pretend like nothing ever happened between us. I'm not going to sit on my hands and ignore that we're still attracted to one another."

"You're still into her? After everything that has happened? That's kinda twisted, man."

Heath shrugged. "I can't help it. She's even more beautiful than she was back then. I've always been attracted to her, and if she was honest with herself, she'd have to admit she's still got a thing for me, too. I'm going to try to use it to my advantage. Sex was always our problem, so I intend to push the issue and make her so uncomfortable, she will be all too happy to file for divorce and put this behind her. By the time I come back to New York, I expect to be a free man."

Nolan nodded slowly and put his bottle of water onto the coffee table. "And that's what you want, right?"

Heath wasn't sure what his business partner meant by that. Of course he wanted this to be over. And it would be. There was no way that Julianne would take him up on his sexual advances. She'd run, just like she always did, and he could finally move on. Just because he was still attracted to Julianne didn't mean that anything would come of it.

"Absolutely." Heath smiled wide, thinking of all the ways he could torture his bride over the next few weeks.

When it was all said and done, he would get his divorce and they would finally be able to move on.

But he sure as hell wasn't going to make it easy on her.

No one was around when Julianne arrived in her small moving truck. She wouldn't admit it, but Heath had been right. She needed help moving. There was more than she could fit in the car, so she decided to skip the storage rental and just bring it all with her. By the time she had that realization, she was already in Sag Harbor staring down the piles of stuff she didn't remember accumulating, so she ended up renting a truck one-way and towing her Camaro behind it the whole way.

She pulled the truck up behind the bunkhouse, where it would be out of the way until she could unload everything. Her clothes and personal things could go into her bedroom, but all the supplies for her studio would have to wait. She'd scoped out the storage room before she left and knew it would take time to clean it out. She'd considered doing it then, but Heath had insisted she wait until he was back from New York and could help her.

She opened the door to the storage room to give it a second look. The room was dim, with only the light coming in from one window, so she felt around until she found a light switch. A couple of fluorescent bulbs kicked on, highlighting the dusty shelves and cardboard boxes that filled the space. Molly was right—with a little elbow grease it would be the perfect place for her to work.

The hardwood floors continued into the storage room. There were several sturdy shelving units and open spaces for her to put her equipment. The brand-new, top-of-the-line kiln she ordered would fit nicely into the corner. She couldn't wait to get settled in.

Julianne grabbed her large rolling suitcase and threw

a duffel bag over her shoulder. She hauled them slowly up the stairs and paused at the landing between the two bedrooms. She wasn't sure which one to use. She'd never slept in the bunkhouse before. Whenever she came home, she used her old room, but that was going to be unavailable for a few weeks at least until Dad was able to climb the stairs again. She reached for the doorknob on the left, pushing the door open with a loud creak.

It was a nice, big space. When she was younger the rooms had been equipped with bunk beds that would allow the Edens to take in up to eight foster children at a time. Wade, Brody, Xander and Heath had stayed at the Garden of Eden until they were grown, but there were a dozen other boys who came and went for short periods of time while their home situations straightened out.

She was relieved to see the old bunks had been replaced with two queen-sized beds. They had matching comforters and a nightstand between them. A large dresser flanked the opposite wall. She took a step in and noticed the closet door was ajar and a suitcase was lying open inside it. And a light was coming from under the bathroom door. Heath was back. She hadn't noticed his car.

Before she could turn around, the bathroom door opened and Heath stepped out. He was fresh from the shower. His hair was damp and combed back, his face pink and smooth from a hot shave. The broad, muscular chest she caught a glimpse of a few days before was just as impressive now, with its etched muscles and dark hair, only this time his skin was slick. He had a towel wrapped around his waist, thank goodness, but that was the only thing between her and a fully naked Heath.

Once upon a time, the sight of her naked husband had launched her into a complete panic attack. The cloud of confused emotions and fear had doused any arousal she might have felt. Eleven years and a lot of therapy later, only the dull ache of need was left when she looked at him.

Heath wasn't startled by her appearance. In fact, her appraising glance seemed to embolden him. He arched an eyebrow at her and then smiled the way he always seemed to when she was uncomfortable. "We've really got to stop meeting like this."

A flush rushed to her cheeks from a mix of embarrassment and instant arousal. She knew Heath could see it, so that just made the deep red color even worse. "I'm sorry. I've done it again." Julianne backed toward the door, averting her eyes to look at anything but his hard, wet body and mocking grin. "I parked the moving truck out back and didn't realize you were here. I was trying to figure out which room I should use."

"You're welcome to use this one," Heath said. He sat down on the edge of one of the beds and gave it a good test bounce. "That would prove interesting."

"Uh, no," she said, slipping back through the doorway. "The other room will be just fine."

Her hands were shaking as she gripped the handle of her luggage and rolled it to the opposite bedroom. When she opened the door, she found it to be exactly the same as the other one, only better, because it didn't have her cocky, naked husband in it.

She busied herself hanging up clothes in the closet and storing underthings in the dresser. Putting things away was a good distraction from the sexual thoughts and raging desire pumping through her veins.

Julianne was setting out the last of her toiletries in the bathroom when she turned and found Heath in her doorway, fully clothed.

"Do you need help bringing more things in?"

"Not tonight. Tomorrow, maybe we can work on clearing out the storage room and then I can unload the rest of my supplies there. There's no sense piling up things in the living room. I don't have to return the truck for a few days."

"Okay, good," he said, but he didn't leave.

Julianne stood, waiting for him to speak or do something, but he just leaned against her door frame. His hazel gaze studied her, his eyes narrowing in thought. A smile curled his lips. She had no idea what he was actually thinking, but it was unnerving to be scrutinized so closely.

Finally, she returned to putting her things away and tried to pretend he wasn't inspecting her every move. There was something about the way he watched her that made her very aware of her own body. It happened every time. He didn't have to say a word, yet she would feel the prickle of awareness start up the back of her neck. Her heart would begin pounding harder in her chest. The sound of her breath moving rapidly in and out of her lungs would become deafening.

Then came the heat. What would start as a warmness in her cheeks would spread through her whole body. Beads of perspiration would start to form at the nape of her neck and the valley between her breasts. Deep in her belly, a churning heat would grow warmer and warmer.

All with just a look. She tried desperately to ignore him because she knew how quickly these symptoms would devolve to blatant wanting, especially if he touched her. Eleven years ago, she was too frightened to do anything about her feelings, but she'd come a long way. There was nothing holding her back now. Whether or not Heath still wanted her, he seemed happy to push the issue. How the hell would she make it through the next few months with him so close by? With no brothers or other family here to distract them?

"I'm surprised you're staying in the bunkhouse," Heath said at last.

"Why is that?" Julianne didn't turn to look at him. Instead, she stuffed her empty duffel bag into her luggage and zipped it closed.

"I would've thought you'd want to stay as far away from me as possible. Then again," he added, "this might be your chance to indulge your secret desires without anyone finding out. Maybe you're finally ready to finish what we started."

Julianne turned to look at him with her hands planted on her hips. Hopefully her indignant attitude would mask how close to the truth he actually was. "Indulge my secret desires? Really, Heath?"

He shoved his hands into the pockets of his gray trousers and took a few slow, casual steps into the room. "Why else would you stay out here? I'm sure things in the big house are much nicer."

"They are," she replied matter-of-factly. "But Daddy will be coming home soon and there won't be a room for me there. Besides, being out here makes me feel more independent. My studio will be downstairs, so it's convenient and I'll be less likely to disturb Mom and Dad."

"Yes," he agreed. "You can stay up late and make all the noise you want. You could scream the walls down if you felt inclined."

Julianne clenched her hands into fists at her sides. "Stop making everything I say into a sexual innuendo. Yes, I will be staying out here with you, but that's only because it's the only place to go. If there were an alternative, I'd gladly take it."

Heath chuckled, but she could tell by the look on his face that he didn't believe a word she said. "You're an awfully arrogant bastard," she noted. "I do not want to sleep with you, Heath."

"You say that," he said, moving a few feet closer. "But I know you better than you'd like to think, Jules. I recognize that look in your eye. The color rushing to your cheeks. The rapid rise and fall of your breasts as you breathe harder. You're trying to convince yourself that you don't want me, but we both know that you hate leaving things unfinished. And you and I are most certainly unfinished."

He was right. Julianne was normally focused on every detail, be it in art or life. She was an overachiever. The only thing she'd found she couldn't manage was being a wife. Just another reason to keep their past relationship under the covers.

A tingle of desire ran down her spine and she closed her eyes tightly to block it out. Wrong choice of words.

"Were you this arrogant when we eloped?" she asked. "I can't fathom that I would've fallen for you with an ego this large."

Heath looked at her, the smile curling his lips fading until a hard, straight line appeared across his face. "No, I wasn't this arrogant. I was young and naive and hopelessly in love with a girl that I thought cared about me."

"Heath, I—"

"Don't," he interrupted. He took another step forward, forcing Julianne to move back until the knobs of the dresser pressed into her rear end. "Don't say what you were going to say because you and I both know it's a waste of breath. Don't tell me that you were confused and scared about your feelings for me, because you knew exactly what you were doing. Don't bother to tell me it was just a youthful mistake, because it's a mistake that you refuse to correct. Why is that, I wonder?"

Julianne stood, trapped between her dresser and Heath's

looming body. He leaned into her and was so close that if she let out the breath she was holding and her muscles relaxed, they might touch. Unable to escape, her eyes went to the sensual curve of his mouth. She didn't care for what he was saying, but she would enjoy watching him say it. He had a beautiful mouth, one that she'd secretly fantasized about kissing long before they'd gone to Europe and long after they came back.

"Maybe," he added, "it's because you aren't ready to let go of me just yet."

It was just complicated. She'd wrestled with this for years. She wanted Heath, but the price of having him was too high for both of them to pay. And yet giving up would mean letting go of the best thing that ever happened to her. "Heath, I—"

"You can lie to everyone else," he interrupted. "You can even lie to yourself. But you can't lie to me, Jules. For whatever reason, the time wasn't right back then. Maybe we were just too young, but that's no longer the case. You want me. I want you. It's not right or wrong, black or white. It's just a fact."

His lips were a whisper away from hers. Her own mouth was suddenly dry as he spoke such blunt words with such a seductive voice. She couldn't answer him. She could barely think with him this close to her. Every breath was thick with the warm scent of his cologne and the soap from his shower.

Heath brought his hand up to caress her cheek. "It's time for you to figure out what you're going to do about it."

Julianne's brow drew down into a frown. "What I'm going to do about it?"

"Yes. It's pretty simple, Jules. You either admit that you want me and give yourself freely and enthusiastically to your husband at last. Or…you get off your hind end and file for divorce."

Julianne's mind went to the last discussion she'd had with her attorney. He could draw up the paperwork anytime. It was a pretty cut-and-dried arrangement with no comingled assets. She just had to tell him to pull the trigger. It was that simple and yet the thought made her nearly sick to her stomach. But what was her alternative? Staying married wouldn't solve their problems. And if marriage meant sleeping with Heath, there would just be sex clouding their issues.

"Why can't this wait until we're both back in New York and can work through the paperwork privately? Don't we have enough going on right now? I'm not really interested in either of your options."

A wicked grin curled Heath's full lips, making her heart stutter in her chest. "Oh, you will be. There's no more stalling, Jules. We've both lived in New York long enough to have addressed it privately, if that was what you really wanted. If you don't choose, I'll make the decision for you. And if *I* file for divorce, I'll go to Frank Hartman."

Frank Hartman was the family attorney and the only one in Cornwall. Even if Heath didn't spread the news she had no doubt that their parents would find out about their marriage if he filed with him. That would raise too many questions.

"Your dirty little secret will be out in the open for sure. I'll see to it that every single person in town finds out about our divorce." His lips barely grazed hers as he spoke, and then he started to laugh. He took a large step back, finally allowing her a supply of her very own oxygen.

"You think on that," he said, turning and walking out of her bedroom.

Four

Heath stumbled downstairs the next morning after pulling on some clothes. He could smell coffee and although still half-asleep, he was on a mission for caffeine. He'd slept late that morning after lying in bed for hours thinking about Julianne. After he'd walked out of her room, he'd shut his door, hoping to keep thoughts of her on the other side. He'd failed.

It would take a hell of a lot more than a panel of wood to do that. Not after being so close to her after all this time apart. Not after seeing her react to him. She was stubborn, he knew that, but she'd gotten under his skin just as he'd gotten under hers.

Part of him had enjoyed torturing her a little bit. He wasn't a vindictive person, but she did owe him a little after what she'd done. He wasn't going to get a wife or an apology out of all this. He'd just be a lonely divorced guy who couldn't tell the people he was closest to that he was a lonely divorced guy. His brothers, whom he typically turned to for advice or commiseration, couldn't know the truth. Poor Nolan would end up with the burden of his drama. He could at least watch her squirm a little bit and get some satisfaction from that. The whole point was to make her so uncomfortable that she would contact her lawyer.

But what had bothered him the most, what had kept him up until two in the morning, had been the look in her eyes when he'd nearly kissed her. He'd been close enough. Just the slightest move and their mouths would have touched. And she wanted him to kiss her. She'd licked her lips, her gaze focused on his mouth with an intensity like never before. It made him wonder what she would have done if he had.

He hadn't kissed Julianne since their wedding night. Heath never imagined that would be the last time he would kiss his wife. They'd been married literally a few hours. Certainly things wouldn't go bad that quickly. Right?

With a groan, he crossed the room, his gaze zeroing in on the coffeepot, half the carafe still full. He poured himself a cup and turned just in time to see Julianne shuffle into the kitchen with a giant cardboard box in her arms.

Despite the chilly October weather outside, she had already worked up a sweat moving boxes. She was wearing a thin tank top and a pair of cutoff jean shorts. Her long blond hair was pulled up into a messy bun on the top of her head with damp strands plastered to the back of her neck.

Heath forced down a large sip of hot coffee to keep from sputtering it everywhere. Man, she had an amazing figure. The girl he'd married had been just that—a girl. She'd been a tomboy and a bit of a late bloomer. She had still been fairly thin, a tiny pixie of a thing that he sometimes worried he might snap when he finally made love to her.

Things had certainly changed since the last time he'd run his hands over that body. He'd heard her complain to Molly about how she'd gained weight over the years, but he didn't mind. The tight little shorts she was wearing were filled out nicely and her top left little to his imagination. His brain might not be fully awake yet, but the rest of his body was up and at 'em.

"What?"

Julianne's voice jerked him out of his detailed assessment. He was staring and she'd caught him. Only fair after her heavy appraisal of him over the last few days. "You're going to hurt yourself," Heath quickly noted. He tried leaning casually against the kitchen counter to cover the tension in his body.

Her cool green gaze regarded him a moment before she dropped the box by the staircase with a loud thud and a cloud of dust. It joined a pile of four or five other equally dusty boxes. "I'm supposed to be helping you with that," he added when she didn't respond.

She turned back to him, rubbing her dirty palms on her round, denim-clad rear end. "I couldn't sleep," she said, disappearing into the storage room. A moment later she came back out with another box. "You weren't awake."

"I'm awake now."

She dropped the box to the floor with the others. "Good. You can start helping anytime then." Julianne returned to her chores.

"Good morning to you, too," he grumbled, drinking the last of his coffee in one large sip. Heath put his mug in the sink and walked across the room to join her in the storage room.

He looked around the space, surveying the work ahead of them. Clearing out the room would be less work than figuring out what to do with all the stuff. He plucked an old, flattened basketball out of one box and smashed it between his hands. Just one of a hundred unwanted things left behind over the years. They'd probably need to run a couple loads to the dump in Ken's truck.

"Is there a plan?" he asked.

Julianne rubbed her forearm across her brow to wipe away perspiration. "I'd like to clear the room out first. Then clean it so we can move my things in and I can return the truck. Then we can deal with the stuff we've taken out."

"Fair enough." Heath tossed the ball back into the box and picked it up.

They worked together quietly for the next hour or so. After the previous night's declarations, he expected her to say something, but he'd underestimated Julianne's ability to compartmentalize things. Today's task was cleaning the storeroom, so that was her focus. She'd used the same trick to ignore their relationship for other pursuits over the years. He didn't push the issue. They'd get a lot less cleaning done if they were arguing.

When the room was finally empty, they attacked the space with brooms and old rags, dusting away the cobwebs and sweeping up years of dust and grime. Despite their dirty chores, he couldn't help but stop and watch Julianne every now and then. She would occasionally bend over for something, giving him a prime view of her firm thighs and round behind. The sweat dampened her shirt and he would periodically catch a glimpse as a bead of perspiration traveled down into the valley between her breasts.

He wasn't sure if it was the hard work or the view, but it didn't take long for Heath to get overheated. As they were cleaning the empty room, he had to whip his shirt off and toss it onto the kitchen table. He returned to working, paying no attention to what was going on until he noticed Julianne was watching him and not moving any longer.

Heath paused and looked up at her. She had her arms crossed over her chest, suggestively pressing her small, firm breasts together. He might enjoy the view if not for the irritated expression puckering her delicate brow. "Is something wrong, Jules?"

"Do you normally run around half-naked or is all this just a show for my benefit?"

"What?" Heath looked down at his bare chest and tried to determine what was so offensive about it. "No, of course I don't run around naked. But I'm also not usually doing hard, dirty labor. Advertising doesn't work up much of a sweat."

Julianne was frowning, but he could see the slight twist of amusement in her lips. He could tell she liked what she saw, even if she wouldn't admit that to herself.

"It seems like every time I turn around, you're not wearing a shirt."

Heath smiled. "Is that a complaint or a pleasant observation?"

Julianne planted her hands on her hips, answering him without speaking.

"Well, to be fair, *you've* barged into my bedroom twice and caught me in various states of undress. That's not my fault. That's like complaining because I don't wear clothes into the shower. You make it sound like I've paraded around like a Chippendales dancer or something." Heath held out his arms, flexing his muscles and gyrating his hips for effect.

Julianne brought her hand to her mouth to stifle a giggle as he danced. "Stop that!" she finally yelled, throwing her dust rag at him.

Heath caught it and ended his performance. "You're just lucky I left my tear-away pants in Manhattan."

She shook her head with a reluctant smile and turned

back to what she'd been cleaning. They finished not too long after that, then piled their brooms and mops in the kitchen and went back in to look around.

"This isn't a bad space at all," Julianne said as they surveyed the empty, clean room. "I think it will make the perfect studio."

Heath watched her walk around the space, thinking aloud. "Is it big enough for all of your things?"

"I think so. If I put the new kiln over here," she said, "my big table will fit here. I can use this shelf to put my pieces on that are in progress. My pottery wheel can go here." She gestured to a space below the window. "And this old dresser will be good to store tools and supplies."

She seemed to have it all laid out in her mind. They just had to bring everything in. "Are you ready to unload the truck?"

Julianne shook her head and smoothed her palm over the wild strands of her hair. "Maybe later this afternoon. I'm exhausted. Right now, all I want to do is take a shower and get some lunch."

Heath couldn't agree more. "I'll probably do the same. But proceed with caution," he said.

"Caution?" Julianne looked at him with wide, concerned eyes.

"Yes. I *will* be naked up there. And wet," he added with a sly grin. "You've been forewarned."

Julianne was certain this was going to be the longest few months in history.

She'd quickly taken her shower and sat down on the edge of the bed to dry her hair. She could hear the water running in his bathroom when she was finished, making her think of his warning. He was wet and naked in the next room. She was determined to miss out on that event this time. Running into him once was an accident. Twice could be considered a fluke. A third time was stalking. Julianne wasn't about to give Heath the satisfaction of knowing she enjoyed looking at him. She did; he had a beautiful body. But she'd already gotten her daily eyeful of his hot, sweaty muscles as they worked downstairs.

That was more than enough to fire up her suppressed libido and set her mind to thinking about anything but cleaning. She shouldn't feel this way. It had been over a month since Danny moved out. Not a tragic dry spell by any means and she was more than capable of managing her urges. But somehow, the combination of Heath's friendly eyes, charming smile and hard body made her forget about all that.

It had been like that back in high school. She had gone years having Heath live with her family, trying to keep her attraction to him in check. Heath had been the first boy she'd ever kissed. She liked him. But somehow, once he came to the farm, it seemed inappropriate. So she tried to ignore it as he got older and grew more handsome. She tried to tell herself they were just friends when they would talk for hours.

By their senior year, they were the only kids left on the farm and it was getting harder for her to ignore the sizzle of tension between them. After what had happened to her five years earlier, she hadn't really dated. She'd kissed a boy or two, but nothing serious and nothing remotely close enough to hit her panic button. It was easy. Heath was the only one who got her blood pumping. The one who made her whole body tingle and ache to be touched. So she avoided him.

But it wasn't until they were alone in Paris that she let herself indulge her attraction. There, with the romantic twinkling lights and soft music serenading them, he'd told her he loved her. That he'd always loved her. This had to be the right thing to do. She loved him. He was her best friend. Heath would never hurt her. It was perfect.

Until her nerves got the best of her. Kissing was great. Roaming hands were very nice. But anything more serious made her heart race unpleasantly. Heath thought maybe she was saving herself for marriage and that would remove the last of her doubts. So they got married. And it only got worse.

Julianne sighed and carried the blow-dryer back into the bathroom. Funny how the thing that was supposed to bring them together forever—the ultimate relationship step—was what ended up dooming them.

It was easy to forget about her problems when her brushes with Heath were few and far between. They were both busy, and usually he didn't want to talk about their issues any more than she did. That did not seem to be the case any longer. She could tell that something had gotten into him, but she didn't know what. Perhaps Ken's second heart attack made him realize life was too short to waste it married to someone who didn't love him like she should. Or maybe he'd found someone else but hadn't told anyone about it yet.

That thought was enough to propel her out of the room and downstairs for some lunch. She didn't like thinking about Heath with someone else. That called for an edible distraction. It was a terrible habit to have, but she was an emotional eater. It had started after Tommy attacked her and it became a constant battle for her after that. Her therapist had helped her recognize the issue and to stop before she started, but when things weren't going well, it was nothing a cheeseburger and a Diet Coke wouldn't fix. At least for an hour or so.

At the top of the staircase, Julianne paused. She could

hear Heath's voice carrying from the kitchen. At first, Julianne thought he might be talking to her. She started down the stairs but stopped when she heard him speak again. He was on the phone.

"Hey, sweetheart."

Sweetheart? Julianne held her breath and took a step backward so he wouldn't see her on the stairs listening in. Who was he talking to? A dull ache in her stomach that had nothing to do with hunger told her she'd been right before. He hadn't mentioned dating anyone recently, but that must be what all the sudden divorce talk was about. Why would he tell her if he were seeing someone special? She was a slip of paper away from being his ex-wife, all things considered.

"Aww, I miss you, too." Heath listened for a moment before laughing. "I know it's hard, but I'll be back before you know it."

There was a tone to his voice that she wasn't used to hearing—an intimacy and softness she remembered from the time they spent together in Europe. This woman obviously had a special place in Heath's life. Julianne was immediately struck with a pang of jealousy as she listened in. It was stupid. They'd agreed that if they weren't together, they were both free to see other people. She'd been living with Danny for a year and a half, so she couldn't complain.

"You know I have to take care of some things here. But look on the bright side. When all this is handled and I come home, we can make that Caribbean vacation you've been dreaming about a reality. But you've got to be patient."

"Hang on, baby," Julianne muttered to herself with a mocking tone. "I gotta ditch the wife, then we can go frolic on the beach." And to think he'd been acting like he had been interested in something more between them. When he'd pressed against her, she was certain he still wanted her—at least short-term. He apparently had longer-term plans with someone else.

"Okay. I'll call again soon. 'Bye, darling."

Julianne choked down her irritation and descended the stairs with loud, stomping feet. When she turned toward the kitchen, Heath was leaning casually against the counter, holding his cell phone and looking pointedly at her. He had changed into a snug pair of designer jeans that hugged the thick muscles of his thighs and a button-down shirt in a mossy green that matched the color of his eyes. This was a middle-of-the-road look, a comfortable median between his sleepy casual style and his corporate shark suits. He looked handsome, put together and, judging by the light in his eyes, amused by her irritation.

"Something the matter?" he asked.

"No," she said quickly. There wasn't anything wrong. He could do whatever and whomever he wanted. That wasn't any concern of hers, no matter how spun up she seemed to be at the moment.

It was just because she'd never been faced with it before. That was it. Neither she nor Heath had ever brought anyone home to meet the family. They both dated, but it was an abstract concept that wasn't waved in her face like a red cape in front of a bull.

"I know you were listening in on my conversation."

She took a deep breath and shrugged. "Not really, but it was hard to ignore with all that mushy sweetheart nonsense."

The corners of Heath's mouth curled in amusement. "What's the matter, Jules? Are you jealous?"

"Why on earth would I be jealous?" she scoffed. "We're married, but it doesn't really mean anything. You're free to do what you want. I mean, if I wanted you, I could've had you, so obviously, I wouldn't be jealous."

"I don't know," Heath said, his brow furrowing. "Maybe you're starting to regret your decision."

"Not at all."

She said the words too quickly, too forcefully, and saw a flash of pain in Heath's light hazel eyes. It disappeared quickly, a smile covering his emotions the way it always did. Humor was his go-to defense mechanism. It could be maddening sometimes.

"You seem very confident in your decision considering you still haven't filed for divorce after all this time. Are you sure you want rid of me? Actions speak louder than words, Jules."

"Absolutely certain. I've just been too busy building my career to worry about something that seems so trivial after all this time."

Heath's jaw flexed as he considered her statement for a moment. He obviously didn't care for her choice of words. "We've never really talked about it. At least not without yelling. Since it's so *trivial*, care to finally tell me what went wrong? I've waited a long time to find out."

Julianne closed her eyes and sighed. She'd almost prefer his heated pursuit to the questions she couldn't answer. "I'd really rather not, Heath. What does it matter now?"

"You left me confused and embarrassed on my wedding night. Do you know how messed up it was to take my clothes off in front of a girl for the first time and have you react like that? It's ego-crushing, Jules. It may have been more than a decade ago, but it still matters."

Julianne planted her hands on her hips and looked down at the floor. This was no time for her to come clean. She couldn't. "I don't have anything more to tell you than I did before. I realized it was a mistake. I'm sorry I didn't correct it until that inopportune time."

Heath flinched and frowned at her direct words. "You seemed happy enough about it until then."

"We were in Europe. Everything was romantic and exciting and we were so far from home I could forget all the reasons why it was a bad idea. When faced with…" Her voice trailed off as she remembered the moment her panic hit her like a tidal wave. He was obviously self-conscious enough about her reaction. How could she ever explain to him that it wasn't the sight of his naked body per se, but the idea of what was to come that threw her into a flashback of the worst day of her life? She couldn't. It would only hurt him more to know the truth. "When faced with the point of no return, I knew I couldn't go through with it. I know you want some big, drawn-out explanation as though I'm holding something back, but I'm not. That's all there is to it."

"You are so full of crap. I've known you since we were nine years old. You're lying. I know you're lying. I just don't know what you're lying about." Heath stuck his hands in his pockets and took a few leisurely steps toward her. "But maybe I'm overthinking it. Maybe the truth of the matter is that you're just selfish."

He might as well have slapped her. "Selfish? I'm selfish?" That was great. She was lying to protect him. She'd left him so he could find someone who deserved his love, but somehow she was selfish.

"I think so. You want your cake and you want to eat it, too." Heath held out his arms. "It doesn't have to be that way. If you want me, I'm right here. Take a bite. Please," he added with emphasis, his gaze pinning her on the spot and daring her to reach out for him.

Julianne froze, not certain what to do or say. Part of her brain was urging her to leap into his arms and take what he had to give. She wasn't a scared teenager anymore. She could indulge and enjoy everything she couldn't have before. The other part worried about what it would lead to. Her divorce attorney's number was programmed into her phone. Why start something that they were on the verge of finishing for good?

"Maybe this will help you decide." Heath's hands went to her waist, pulling her body tight against him. Julianne stumbled a bit, colliding with his chest and placing her hands on his shoulders to catch herself. Her palms made contact with the hard wall of muscle she had seen so many times the last few days but didn't dare touch. The scent of his shower-fresh skin filled her nose. The assault on her senses made her head swim and her skin tingle with longing to keep exploring her newfound discovery.

She looked up at him in surprise, not quite sure what to do. His lips found hers before she could decide. At first, she was taken aback by the forceful claim of her mouth. This was no timid teenager kissing her. The hard, masculine wall pressed against her was all grown up.

In their youth, he had never handled her with less care than he would a fragile piece of pottery. Now, he had lost what control he had. And she liked it. They had more than a decade of pent-up sexual tension, frustration and downright anger between them. It poured out of his fingertips, and pressed into her soft flesh, drawing cries of pleasure mingled with pain in the back of her throat.

Matching his ferocity, she clung to his neck, pulling him closer until his body was awkwardly arched over hers. Every place he touched seemed to light on fire until her whole body burned for him. She was getting lost in him, just as she had back then.

And then he pulled away. She had to clutch at the countertop to stay upright once his hard body withdrew its support.

His hazel eyes raked over her body, noting her undeniable response to his kiss. "So what's it going to be, Jules? Are the two of us over and done? Decide."

There were no words. Her brain was still trying to process everything that just happened. Her body ached for him to touch her again. Her indecisiveness drew a disappointed frown across his face.

"Or," he continued, dropping his arms to his side, "do like you've always done. A big nothing. You say you don't want me, but you don't want anyone else to have me, either. You can't have it both ways. You've got to make up your mind, Jules. It's been eleven years. Either you want me or you don't."

"I don't think the two of us are a good idea," she admitted at last. That was true. They weren't a good idea. Her body just didn't care.

"Then what are you waiting for? End it before you sink your next relationship." Heath paused, his brow furrowing in thought. "Unless that's how you like it."

"How I like what?"

"Our marriage is your little barrier to the world. You've dated at least seven or eight guys that I know of, none of them ever getting serious. But that's the way you want it. As long as you're married, you don't have to take it to the next level."

"You think I like failing? You think I want to spend every Christmas here watching everyone snuggled up into happy little couples while I'm still alone?"

"I think a part of you does. It might suck to be alone, but it's better than making yourself vulnerable and getting hurt. Trust me, I know what it's like to get your heart ripped out and stomped on. Being lonely doesn't come close to that kind of pain. I'm tired of you using me, Jules. Make a decision."

"Fine!" Julianne pushed past him, her vision going red as she stomped upstairs into her room. He'd kissed her and insulted her in less than a minute's time. If he thought she secretly wanted to be with him, he was very, very wrong. She snatched her cell phone off the bed and went back to the kitchen.

By the time she returned, the phone was ringing at her attorney's office. "Hello? This is Julianne Eden." Her gaze burrowed into Heath's as she spoke. "Would you please let Mr. Winters know that I'm ready to go forward with the divorce paperwork? Yes. Please overnight it to my second-ary address in Connecticut. Thank you."

She slammed her phone onto the kitchen table with a loud smack that echoed through the room. "If you want a divorce so damn bad, fine. Consider it done!"

Five

The rest of the afternoon and most of the next day were spent working. They focused on their chores, neither willing to broach the subject of their argument and set off another battle. The divorce papers would arrive at any time. They had things to get done. There was no sense rehashing it.

They were unloading the last of her equipment from the rental truck when Heath spied Sheriff Duke's patrol car coming up the driveway.

Julianne was beside him, frozen like a deer in the oncoming lights of a car. He handed her the box he'd been carrying. "Take this and go inside. Don't come out unless I come get you."

She didn't argue. She took the box and disappeared through the back door of the storage room. He shut the door behind her and walked around the bunkhouse to where Duke's Crown Victoria was parked beside his Porsche.

Duke climbed out, eyeballing the sports car as he rounded it to where Heath was standing. "Afternoon, Heath."

Heath shook his hand politely and then crossed his arms over his chest. This wasn't a social call and he wouldn't let his guard down for even a second thinking that it was. "Evening, Sheriff. What can I do for you?"

Duke slipped off his hat, gripping it in his left hand. "I just came from the hospital. I spoke with your folks."

Heath tried to keep the anger from leaching into his voice, but the tight clench of his jaw made his emotions obvious as he spoke. "You interviewed my father in the hospital after open-heart surgery? After he had a heart attack the last time you spoke? Did you try to arrest him this time, too?"

"He's not in critical condition," Duke said. "Relax. He's fine. Was when I got there and was when I left. The doctors say he's doing better than expected."

Heath took a deep breath and tried to uncoil his tense muscles. He still wasn't happy, but at least Ken was okay. "I assume you're not here to give me an update on Dad as a public service to the hospital."

A faint smile curled Duke's lips. "No, I'm not. Would you care to sit down somewhere?"

"Do I need a lawyer?" Heath asked.

"No. Just wanting to ask a few questions. You're not a suspect at this time."

"Then no, I'm fine standing." Heath wasn't interested in getting comfortable and drawing out this conversation. He could outstand the older officer by a long shot. "What can I help you with?"

Duke nodded softly, obviously realizing he wasn't going to be offered a seat and some tea like he would if Molly were home. "First, I wanted to let you know that Ken and

Molly are no longer suspects. I was finally able to verify their story with accounts of others in town."

"Like what?" Heath asked.

"Well, Ken had always maintained he was sick in bed all that day with the flu. I spoke to the family physician and had him pull old records from the archives. Ken did come in the day before to see the doctor. Doc said it was a particularly bad strain of flu that year. Most people were in bed for at least two days. I don't figure Ken was out in the woods burying a body in the shape he was in."

"He was sick," Heath added. "Very sick. Just as we've told you before."

"People tell me a lot of things, Heath. Doesn't make it true. I've got to corroborate it with other statements. We've established Ken was sick that day. So, how did that work on the farm? If Ken wasn't working, did the whole group take the day off?"

"No," Heath answered with a bit of a chuckle. Sheriff Duke obviously hadn't grown up on a farm. "Life doesn't just stop when the boss is feeling poorly. We went on with our chores as usual. Wade picked up a few of the things that Ken normally did. Nothing particularly special about it. That's what we did whenever anyone was sick."

"And what about Tommy?"

"What about him?" Heath wasn't going to volunteer anything without being asked directly.

"What was he doing that day?"

Heath sighed and tried to think back. "It's been a long time, Sheriff, but if I had to guess, I'd figure he was doing a lot of nothing. That's what he did most days. He tended to go out into the trees and mess around. I never saw him put in an honest afternoon's work."

"I heard he got into some fights with the other boys."

Heath wasn't going to let Duke zero in on his brothers

as suspects. "That's because he was lazy and violent. He had a quick temper and, on more than one occasion, took it out on one of us."

Sheriff Duke's dark gaze flicked over Heath's face for a moment as he considered his answers. "I bet you didn't care much for Tommy."

"No one did. You know what kind of stuff he was into."

"I can't comment on that. You know his juvenile files are sealed."

"I don't need to see his files to know what he'd done. I lived with him. I've got a scar from where he shoved me into a bookcase and split my eyebrow open. I remember Wade's black eye. I know about the stealing and the drugs and the fights at school. You can't seal my memories, Sheriff." Some days he wished he could.

Duke shuffled uncomfortably on his feet. "When was the last time you saw Tommy?"

"The last time I saw him…" Heath tried to remember back to that day. He spent most of his time trying not to think about it. The image of Tommy's blank, dead stare and the pool of blood soaking into the dirt was the first thing to come to mind. He quickly put that thought away and backed up to before that moment. Before he heard the screams and found Tommy and Julianne together on the ground. "It was just after school. We all came home, Molly brought us some snacks to the bunkhouse and told us Ken was sick in bed. We finished up and each headed out to do our chores. I went into the eastern fields."

"Did you see Tommy go into the woods that day?"

"No." And he hadn't. "Tommy was still sitting at the kitchen table when I left. But that's where he should've been going."

"Was he acting strangely that day?"

He had been. "He was a little quieter than usual. More

withdrawn. I figured he'd had a bad day at school." Tommy had also been silently eyeing Julianne with an interest he didn't care for. But he wasn't going to tell Duke that. No matter what happened between the two of them and their marriage, that wouldn't change. He'd sworn to keep that secret, to protect her above all else, and he would. Even if he grew to despise her one day, he would keep his promise.

"Had he ever mentioned leaving?"

"Every day," Heath said, and that was true. "He was always talking big about how he couldn't wait to get away. He said we were like some stupid television sitcom family and he couldn't stand any of us. He said that when he was eighteen, he was getting the hell out of this place. Tommy didn't even care about finishing school. I suppose a diploma didn't factor much into the lines of work he was drawn to. When he disappeared that day, I always figured he decided not to wait. His birthday was coming up."

Duke had finally taken out a notepad and was writing a few things down. "What made you think he ran away?"

This was the point at which he had to very carefully dance around the truth. "Well, Wade found a note on his bed. And his stuff wasn't in his room when we looked the next morning." The note and the missing belongings were well-documented from the original missing-persons report. The fact that they never compared the handwriting to any of the other children on the farm wasn't Heath's fault. "It all added up for me. With Ken sick, it might have seemed like the right day to make his move." Unfortunately, he'd made his move on Julianne when she was alone in the trees.

"Did he ever talk to you about anything? His friends or his plans?"

At that, a nervous bit of laughter escaped Heath's lips. "I was a scrawny, thirteen-year-old twerp that did nothing but get in his way. Tommy didn't confide in anyone, but especially not in me."

"He didn't talk to your brothers?"

Heath shrugged. "Tommy shared a room with Wade. Maybe he talked to him there. But he was never much for chatting with the rest of us. More than anything he talked *at* us, not *to* us. He said nothing but ugly things to Brody, so he avoided Tommy. Xander always liked to keep friendly with everyone, but even he kept his distance."

"And what about Julianne?"

Heath swallowed hard. It was the first time her name had been spoken aloud in the conversation and he didn't like it. "What about her?"

"Did she have much to do with Tommy?"

"No," Heath said a touch too forcefully. Sheriff Duke looked up at him curiously. "I mean, there was no reason to. She lived in the big house and still went to junior high with me. If they spoke, it was only in passing or out of politeness on her part."

Duke wrote down a few things. Heath wished what he'd said had been true. That Tommy hadn't given the slightest notice to the tiny blonde. But as much as Julianne tried to avoid him, Tommy always found a way to intersect her path. She knew he was dangerous. They all did. They just didn't know what to do about it.

"Were they ever alone together?"

At that, Heath slowly shook his head. He hoped the sheriff didn't see the regret in his eyes or hear it in his voice as he spoke. "Only a fool would have left a little girl alone with a predator like Tommy."

Heath had been quiet and withdrawn that night. Julianne expected him to say *something*. About what happened with Sheriff Duke, about their kiss, about their argument or the divorce papers…but nothing happened. After Duke left, Heath had returned to unloading the truck. When that was done, he volunteered to drive into town and pick up a pizza.

While he was gone, the courier arrived with the package from her attorney. She flipped through it, giving it a cursory examination, and then dropped it onto the kitchen table. She wasn't in the mood to deal with that today.

Heath's mood hadn't improved by the time he got back. He was seated on the couch, balancing his plate in his lap and eating almost mechanically. Julianne had opted to eat at the table, which gave her a decent view of both Heath and the television without crowding in his space.

There was one cold slice of pizza remaining when Julianne finally got the nerve to speak. "Heath?"

He looked startled, as though she'd yanked him from the deep thoughts he was lost in. "Yes?"

"Are you going to tell me what happened?"

"You mean with Sheriff Duke?"

"I guess. Is that what's bothering you?"

"Yes and no," he replied, giving her an answer and not at the same time.

Julianne got up and walked over to the couch. She flopped down onto the opposite end. "It's been a long week, Heath. I'm too tired to play games. What's wrong?"

"Aside from the divorce papers sitting on the kitchen table?" Heath watched her for a moment before sighing heavily and shaking his head. "Sheriff Duke just asked some questions. Nothing to worry about. In fact, he told me Ken and Molly are no longer suspects."

Julianne's brow went up in surprise. "And that's good, right?"

"Absolutely. The conversation was fine. It just made me think." He paused. "It reminded me how big of a failure I am."

It didn't matter what happened between them recently. The minute he needed her support she would give it. "You? A failure? What are you talking about?" Every one of her brothers was at the top of their field with millions in their accounts. None were failures by a long shot. "You're the CEO of your own successful advertising agency. You have a great apartment in Manhattan. You drive a Porsche! How is that a failure?"

A snort of derision passed his lips and he turned away to look at the television. "I'm good at convincing people to buy things they don't need. Something to be proud of, right? But I fail at the important stuff. When it matters, it seems like nothing I say or do makes any difference."

She didn't like the tone of his voice. It was almost defeated. Broken. Very much unlike him and yet she knew somehow she was responsible. "Like what?"

"Protecting you. Protecting my parents. Ken. Saving our marriage…"

Julianne frowned and held her hands up. "Wait a minute. First, how is a nine-year-old boy supposed to save his parents in a car crash that he almost died in, too? Or keep Dad from having another heart attack?"

"It was my fault we were on that road. I pestered my father until he agreed to take us for ice cream."

"Christ, Heath, that doesn't make it your fault."

"Maybe, but Dad's heart attack *was* my fault. The second one at least. If I'd come clean to the cops about what happened with Tommy, they wouldn't have come here questioning him."

He was being completely irrational about this. Heath had been internalizing more things than she realized. "And what about me? How have you failed to protect me? I'm sitting right here, perfectly fine."

"Talking with Sheriff Duke made me realize I should've

seen it coming. With Tommy. I should've known he was going to come for you. And I left you alone. When I think about how bad it could've been…" His voice trailed off. "I never should've left you alone with him."

"You didn't leave me alone *with* him. I was doing my chores just like you were, and he found me. And you can't see the future. I certainly don't expect you to be able to anticipate the moves of a monster like he was. There's no reason why you should have thought I would be anything but safe."

He looked up at her at last, his brow furrowed with concern for things he couldn't change now. "But I *did* know. I saw the way he was looking at you. I knew what he was thinking. My mistake was not realizing he was bold enough to make a move. What if you hadn't been able to fight him off? What if he had raped you?" He shook his head, his thoughts too heavy with the possibilities to see Julianne stiffen in her seat. "I wish he had just run away. That would've been better for everyone."

The pained expression was etched deeply into his forehead. He was so upset thinking Tommy had attacked her. She could never ever tell Heath how successful Tommy had been in getting what he'd wanted from her. He already carried too much of the blame on his own shoulders and without cause. Nothing that happened that day was his fault. "Not for the people he would have hurt later."

Heath shrugged away what might have been. "You give me credit for protecting you, but I didn't. If I had been smart, you wouldn't have needed protecting."

Julianne scooted closer to him on the couch and placed a comforting hand on his shoulder. "Heath, stop it. No one could have stopped Tommy. What's important is everything you did for me once it was done. You didn't have to do what you did. You've kept the truth from everyone all this time."

"Don't even say it out loud," he said with a warning tone. "I did what I had to do and no matter what happens with Sheriff Duke, I don't regret it. It was bad enough that you would always have memories of that day. I wasn't about to let you get in front of the whole town and have to relive it. That would be like letting him attack you over and over every time you had to tell the story."

It would have been awful, no question. No woman wants to stand up and describe being assaulted, much less a thirteen-year-old girl who barely understood what was happening to her. But she was strong. She liked to think that she could handle it. The boys had other ideas. They—Heath especially—thought the best thing to do was keep quiet. Unlike her, they had to live with the fear of being taken away. They made huge sacrifices for her, more than they even knew, and she was grateful. She just worried the price would end up being far higher than they intended to pay.

"But has it been worth the anxiety? The years of waiting for the other shoe to drop? We've been on pins and needles since Dad sold that property. If you had let me go to the police, it would be long over by now."

"See…" Heath said. "My attempt to protect you from the consequences of my previous failures failed as well. It made things worse in the long run. And you knew it, too. That's why you couldn't love me. You were embarrassed to be in love with me."

"What?" Julianne jerked her hand away in surprise. Where the hell had this come from?

Heath shifted in his seat to face her head-on. "Tell the truth, Jules. You might have been intimidated by having sex with me or what our future together might be, but the nail in the coffin was coming home and having to tell your parents that you'd married *me*. You were embarrassed."

"I was embarrassed, but not because of you. It was never about you. I was ashamed of how I'd let myself get so wrapped up in it that I didn't think things through. And then, what? How could we tell our parents that we eloped and broke up practically the same day?"

"You're always so worried about what other people think. Then and now. You'd put a stranger ahead of your own desires every time. Here you'd rather throw away everything we had together than disappoint Molly."

"We didn't have much to throw away, Heath. A week together is hardly a blip in the relationship radar." How many women had he dated for ten times as long and didn't even bother to mention it to the family? Like the woman on the phone packing her bags for the Caribbean?

"It makes a bigger impact when you're married, I assure you. What you threw away was the potential. The future and what we could have had. That's what keeps me up at night, Jules."

It had kept her up nights, too. "And what if it hadn't worked out? If we'd divorced a couple years later? Maybe remarried and brought our new spouses home. How would those family holidays go after that? Unbelievably awkward."

"More awkward than stealing glances of your secret, estranged wife across the dinner table?"

"Heath…"

"I don't think you understand, Jules. You never did. Somehow in your mind, it was just a mistake that had to be covered up so no one would find out. It was an infatuation run awry for you, but it was more than that for me. I loved you. More than anything. I wish I hadn't. I spent years trying to convince myself it was just a crush.

It would have been a hell of a lot easier to deal with your rejection if it were."

"Rejection? Heath, I didn't reject you."

"Oh, really? How does it read in your mind, Jules? In mine, the girl I loved agreed to marry me and then bolted the moment I touched her. Whether you were embarrassed of me or the situation or how it might look…in the end, my wife rejected me and left me in her dust. You went off to art school without saying goodbye and just pretended like our marriage and our feelings for each other didn't matter anymore. That sounds like a textbook definition for rejection."

Julianne sat back in her seat, trying to absorb everything he'd said. He was right. It would have been kinder if she'd just told him she didn't have feelings for him. It would have been a lie, but it would have been gentler on him than what she did.

"Heath, I never meant for you to feel that way. I'm sorry if my actions made you feel unwanted or unloved. I was young and confused. I didn't know what to do or how to handle everything. I do love you and I would never deliberately hurt you."

He snickered and turned away. "You love me, but you're not *in love* with me, right?"

She was about to respond but realized that confirming what he said would be just as hurtful as telling him she didn't love him at all. In truth, neither was entirely accurate. Her feelings were all twisted where Heath was concerned. They always had been and she'd never successfully straightened them out.

"Go ahead and say it."

Julianne sighed. "It's more complicated than that, Heath. I do love you. But not in the same way I love Xander or Brody or Wade, so no, I can't say that. There are other feelings. There always have been. Things that I don't know how to…"

"You want me."

It was a statement, not a question. She raised her gaze to meet his light hazel eyes. The golden starbursts in the center blended into a beautiful mix of greens and browns. Heath's eyes were always so expressive. Even when he tried to hide his feelings with a joke or a smile, Julianne could look him in the eye and know the truth.

The expression now was a difficult one. There was an awkward pain there, but something else. An intensity that demanded an honest answer from her. He knew she wanted him. To tell him otherwise would be to lie to them both. She tore her eyes away, hiding beneath the fringe of her lashes as she stared down at her hands. "I shouldn't."

"Why not? I thought you weren't embarrassed of me," he challenged.

"I'm not. But we're getting a divorce. What good would giving in to our attraction do?"

She looked up in time to see the pain and worry vanish from his expression, replaced by a wicked grin. "It would do a helluva lot of good for me."

Julianne was hard-pressed not to fall for his charming smile and naughty tone. "I'm sure you'd be pleased at the time. So would I. But then what? Is that all it is? Just sex? Is it worth it for just sex? If not, are we dating?"

"Running off with me was very much out of character for you," he noted. "You can't just do something because it feels good and you want to. You have to rationalize everything to the point that the fun is stripped right out."

"I'm trying to be smart about this! Fun or not, you want us to get divorced. Why would I leap back into your bed with both feet?"

"I didn't say I wanted us to get divorced."

That wasn't true. He'd had her pressed against the dresser when he'd made his ultimatum. He'd demanded it yesterday. The papers were three feet away. "I distinctly recall you—"

"Saying you needed to make a choice. Be with me or don't. No more straddling the fence. If you don't want me, then fine. But if you do…by all means, have me. I'm happy to put off the divorce while we indulge in our marital rights."

Julianne frowned. "Do you even hear yourself? Put off our divorce so we can sleep together?"

"Why not? I think I deserve a belated wedding night. We've had all of the drama of marriage with none of the perks."

"You just want to catch up on eleven years of sex."

"Maybe." He leaned in closer, the gold fire in his eyes alight with mischief. "Do you blame me?"

The low, suggestive rumble of his voice so close made her heart stutter in her chest. "S-stop acting like you've lived as a monk this whole time. Even if you did, eleven years is a lot to catch up on. We do still have a farm to run and I have a gallery show to work on."

"I'm all for making the most of our time together here. Give it the old college try."

Julianne shook her head. "And again, Heath, what does that leave us with? I want you, you want me. I'm not about to leap into all this again without thinking it through."

"Then don't leap, Jules. Test the waters. Slip your toe in and see how it feels." He smiled, slinking even closer to her. "I hear the water is warm and inviting." His palm flattened on her denim-covered thigh.

The heat was instantaneous, spreading quickly through her veins until a flush rushed to her cheeks. She knew that all she had to do was say the word and he would do all the things to her she'd fantasized about for years. But she wasn't ready to cross the line. He was right. She did strip the spontaneity out of everything, but she very rarely made decisions that haunted her the way she had with him. She didn't want to misstep this time. She had too many regrets where Heath was concerned. If and when she gave herself to him, she wanted to be fully content with making the right choice.

"I'm sure it is." She reached down and picked up his hand, placing it back in his own lap. "But the water will be just as warm tomorrow."

Six

Julianne rolled over and looked at the clock on the dresser. It was just after two in the morning. That was her usual middle-of-the-night wake-up time. She'd gone to sleep without issue, as always, but bad dreams had jerked her awake about thirty minutes ago and she'd yet to fall back asleep.

She used to be a fairly sound sleeper, but she woke up nearly every night now. Pretty much since Tommy's body was unearthed last Christmas. As much as they had all tried to put that day out of their heads, there was no escaping it. Even if her day-to-day life was too busy to dwell on it, her subconscious had seven to eight hours a night to focus on the worries and fears in the back of her mind.

As much as he wanted to, Heath couldn't protect her forever. Julianne was fairly certain that before she left this farm, the full story would be out in the open. Whether she would be moving out of the bunkhouse and into the jailhouse remained to be seen. Sheriff Duke smelled a rat and he wouldn't rest until he uncovered the truth. The question was whether the truth would be enough for him. A self-defense or justifiable homicide verdict wouldn't give him the moment of glory he sought.

With a sigh, Julianne sat up in bed and brushed the messy strands of her hair out of her face. Tonight's dream had been a doozy, waking her in a cold sweat. She had several different variations of the dream, but this was the one that bothered her the most. She was running through the Christmas-tree fields. Row after row of pine trees flew past her, but she didn't dare turn around. She knew that if she did, Tommy would catch her. The moment his large, meaty hand clamped onto her shoulder, Julianne would shoot up in bed, a scream dying in the back of her throat as she woke and realized that Tommy was long dead.

You would think after having the same nightmares over and over, they wouldn't bother her anymore, but it wasn't true. It seemed to get worse every time. Most nights, she climbed out of bed and crept into her workshop. Something about the movement of the clay in her hands was soothing. She would create beauty and by the time she cleaned up, she could return to sleep without hesitation or nightmares.

For the last week, she'd had no therapeutic outlet to help her fall back asleep. Instead she'd had to tough it out, and she would eventually drift off again around dawn. But now she had a functioning workshop downstairs and could return to the hypnotizing whirl of her pottery wheel.

She slipped silently from the bed and stepped out into the hallway. The house was quiet and dark. She moved quickly down the stairs, using her cell phone for light until she reached the ground floor. There, she turned on the kitchen light. She poured herself a glass of water, plucked an oatmeal raisin cookie from the jar on the counter and headed toward her new studio.

The fluorescent lights flickered for a moment before turning on, flooding the room with an odd yellow-white glow. Heath had worked very hard to help her get everything in place. A few boxes remained to be put away, and her kiln wouldn't be delivered for another day or two, but the majority of her new workshop was ready to start work.

Julianne finished her cookie and set her drink on the dresser, out of the way. One of the boxes on the floor near her feet had bricks of ready-to-use clay. She reached in to grab a one-pound cube and carried it over to her wheel. A plate went down on the wheel, then the ball of soft, moist gray clay on top of it. She filled a bucket with water and put her smoothing sponge in it to soak.

Pulling up to the wheel, she turned it on and it started to spin. She plunged her hands into the bucket to wet them and then closed her slick palms over the ball of clay. Her gallery showing would be mostly sculpted figurines and other art pieces, but the bread and butter of her shop in the Hamptons was stoneware pieces for the home. Her glazed bowls, mugs, salt dishes and flower vases could be found in almost any home in the area.

When she woke up in the night, vases were her go-to item. Her sculptures required a great deal of concentration and a focused eye. At three in the morning, the creation of a vase or bowl on her spinning wheel was a soothing, automatic process. It was by no means a simple task, but she'd created so many over the years that it came to her as second nature.

Her fingers slipped and glided in the wet clay, molding it into a small doughnut shape, then slowly coaxing it taller. She added more water and reached inside. The press of her fingertips distorted the shape, making the base wider.

Cupping the outside again, she tapered in the top, creating the traditional curved flower-vase shape. She flared the top, forming the lip.

With the sponge, she ran along the various edges and surfaces, smoothing out the rough and distorted areas. Last, she used a metal tool to trim away the excess clay at the base and turned off the wheel.

She sat back with a happy sigh and admired her handiwork. When she first started sculpting, a piece like that would have taken her five tries. It would have collapsed on itself or been lopsided. She would press too hard and her thumb would puncture the side. Now, a perfect piece could be created in minutes. She wished everything in her life was that easy.

"I've never gotten to watch you work before."

Julianne leapt at the sound of Heath's voice. She turned around in her rolling chair, her heart pounding a thousand beats a minute in her chest. She brought a hand to her throat, stopping just short of coating herself in wet clay. "You shouldn't sneak up on a girl like that."

He smiled sheepishly from the doorway. "Sorry. At least I waited until you were done."

Heath was leaning against the door frame in an old NYU T-shirt and a pair of flannel plaid boxer shorts, and for that, she was thankful. She would lose her resolve to resist him if he came down in nothing but a pair of pajama pants. As it was, the lean muscles of his legs were pulling her gaze down the length of his body.

"Did I wake you?" she asked.

"I don't recall hearing you get up, but I woke up for some reason and realized I forgot to plug my phone into the charger. I left it in the kitchen accidentally." He took a few steps into the workshop. "I can't believe how quickly you did that. You're amazing."

Julianne stood up from her stool and took her metal spatula out of the drawer beside her. Uncomfortable with his praise, she lifted the metal plate and moved the wet vase over onto the shelf to dry. "It's nothing."

"Don't be modest," he argued. "You're very talented."

Julianne started the wheel spinning again and turned away to hide her blush. "Would you like to learn to make something?"

"Really?"

"Sure. Come here," she said. She eyed his large frame for a moment, trying to figure out the best way to do this. "Since I'm so short, it's probably easiest if you stand behind me and reach over. I can guide your hands better that way."

Heath rolled the stool out of the way and moved to her back. "Like this?"

"Yes." She glanced back at the position she had deliberately put them in and realized how stupid it was. Perhaps she would be smarter to talk him out of this. "You're going to get dirty. Is that okay?"

He chuckled softly at her ear, making a sizzle of awareness run along the sensitive line of her neck. "Oh, no, I'd better change. These are my good flannel boxers."

Julianne smiled at his sharp, sarcastic tone and turned back to the wheel. No getting out of this now. "Okay, first, dip your hands in the water. You have to keep them good and wet."

They both dipped their hands in the bucket of water, then she cupped his hands over the clay and covered them with her own. "Feel the pressure I apply to you and match it with your fingers to the clay."

They moved back and forth between the water and the clay. All the while, Julianne forced herself to focus on the vase and not the heat of Heath's body at her back.

The warm breath along her neck was so distracting. Her mind kept straying to how it would feel if he kissed her there. She wanted him to. And then she would realize their sculpture was starting to sag and she would return her attention to their project.

"This feels weird," Heath laughed, gliding over the gray mound. The slippery form began to take shape, their fingers sliding around together, slick and smooth. "And a little dirty, frankly."

"It does," she admitted. On more than one occasion, she'd lost herself in the erotic slip and slide of the material in her hands and the rhythmic purr of the wheel. That experience was amplified by having him so close. "But try to control yourself," she said with a nervous giggle to hide her own building arousal. "I don't want you having dirty thoughts every time you see my artwork."

Heath's hands suddenly slipped out from beneath hers and glided up her bare arms to clutch her elbows. The cool slide of his clay-covered hands along her skin was in stark contrast to the firm press of heat at her back. It was obvious that she was not the only one turned on by the situation.

"Actually, the artwork isn't what inspires me...."

A ragged breath escaped her lips, but she didn't dare move. She continued working the vase on her own now, her shaky hands creating a subpar product. But she didn't care. If she let go, she would touch Heath and she wasn't sure she would be able to stop.

Easing back, Heath brushed her hair over the other shoulder and, as though he could read her mind, pressed a searing kiss just below her ear. She tipped her neck to the side, giving better access to his hungry mouth. He kissed, nibbled and teased, sending one bolt of pleasure after the other down her spine.

She arched her back, pressing the curve of her rear

into the hard ridge of his desire. That elicited a growl that vibrated low against her throat. One hand moved to her waist, tugging her hips back even harder against him.

"Jules…" he whispered, sending a shudder of desire through her body and a wave of goose bumps across her bare flesh.

She finally abandoned the clay, letting it collapse on itself, and switched off the wheel before she covered his hands with her own. Their fingers slipped in and out between each other, his hands moving over her body. "Yes?" she panted.

"You said the waters would be just as warm tomorrow. It's tomorrow," he said, punctuating his point with a gentle bite at her earlobe.

That it was.

Julianne had been wearing a flimsy little pajama set when he walked in, but Heath was pretty sure it was ruined. The thin cotton camisole and matching shorts were sweet and sexy at the same time. The clothes reminded him of the girl he'd fantasized about in high school, and the curves beneath it reminded him of the ripe, juicy peach of a woman she was now.

He couldn't stop touching her, even though he knew his hands were covered in clay. Gray smears were drying up on her arms and her bare shoulders. The shape of his hand was printed on the cotton daisy pattern of her pajamas. A streak of gray ran along the edge of her cheek.

And he didn't care.

It was sexy as hell. Julianne was always so put together and mature. He loved seeing her dirty. He was so turned on watching her skilled hands shape and mold the clay. He wanted those hands on himself so badly, he had to bite his own lip to keep from interrupting her before she was finished. Even now he could taste the faint metallic flavor of his own blood on his tongue.

When Julianne finally turned in his arms to face him, he had to stop himself from telling her she was the most beautiful thing he'd ever seen in his life. Messy hair, dirty face and all. He'd already made the mistake of telling her too much before. It was a far cry from a declaration of love, but he intended to play this second chance much closer to the vest.

Julianne looked up at him, her light green eyes grazing over every inch of his face before she put her hands on each side of his head and tugged his mouth down to hers. The instant their lips met, colored starbursts lit under his eyelids. A rush of adrenaline surged through his veins, making him feel powerful, invincible and desperate to have her once and for all.

Their kiss yesterday hadn't been nearly enough to quench his thirst for her. It had only made his mouth even drier and more desperate to drink her in again. She was sweet on his tongue, her lips soft and open to him. The small palms of her hands clung to him. The moist, sticky clay felt odd against his skin as it started to dry and tighten, but nothing could ruin the feel of kissing her again.

It was like a dream. He'd stumbled downstairs, half-asleep, to charge his phone. He never expected to find her there at her wheel, looking so serene and focused, so beautiful and determined. Having her in his arms only moments later made him want to pinch himself and ensure he really was awake. It wouldn't be the first dream he'd had about Julianne, although it might be the most realistic.

Julianne bit on his lip, then. The sharp pain made him jerk, the area still sensitive from his previous self-inflicted injury. He pulled away from her, studying her face and coming to terms with the fact that she was real. After all these years she was in his arms again.

"I'm sorry," she said, brushing a gentle fingertip over his lip. "Was that too hard?"

Heath would never admit to that. "You just startled me, that's all."

Julianne nodded, her gaze running over the line of his jaw with a smile curling her lips. Her fingertip scraped over the mix of stubble and clay, making the muscles in his neck tighten and flex with anticipation. "I think we need a shower," she said. "You're a very, very dirty boy."

A shower was an awesome idea. "You make me this way," he replied. With a grin, Heath lifted Julianne up. As tiny as she was, it was nothing to lift her into the air. She wrapped her legs and arms around him, holding him close as he stumbled out of the workshop and headed for the stairs.

When they reached the top of the staircase, her mouth found his again. With one eye on his bedroom up ahead, he stumbled across the landing and through the door. He prayed there weren't any clothes or shoes strewn across the floor to trip him and he was successful. They reached into the bathroom and he pulled one hand away from a firm thigh to switch on the lights.

He expected Julianne to climb down, but she clearly had no intention of letting go of him. Not even to take off their clothes. She refused to take her mouth off of his long enough to see what she was doing.

She reached into the shower, pawing blindly at the knobs until a stream of warm, then hot, water shot from the nozzle. Julianne put her feet down onto the tiles and then stepped backward into the stall, tugging Heath forward until he stumbled and they both slammed against the tile, fully dressed. Their clothes were instantly soaked, and were now transparent and clung to their skin.

Her whole body was on display for him now. Her rosy nipples were hard and thrusting through the damp cotton top. His hands sought them out, crushing them against his palms until her moans echoed off the walls. His mouth dipped down, tugging at her tank top until the peaks of her breasts spilled out over the neckline. He captured one in his mouth, sucking hard.

The hot water ran over their bodies as they touched and tasted each other. Most of the clay was gone now, the faint gray stream of water no longer circling the drain. Their hair was soaking wet, with fat drops of water falling into his eyes as he hovered over her chest. It was getting hard to breathe between the water in his face and the steam in his lungs, but he refused to let go of Julianne long enough to change anything.

A rush of cold air suddenly hit his back as Julianne tugged at his wet shirt. She pulled it over his head and flung it onto the bathroom floor with a wet *thwump*.

"I thought you were tired of me running around without my shirt on," he said with a grin.

"You said it was okay in the shower, remember?"

"That I did." Leaning down, he did the same with her top and her shorts. She was completely exposed to him now, her body a delight for his eyes that had gone so long without gazing upon it. He wanted to take his time, to explore every inch and curve of her, but Julianne wasn't having it. She tugged him back against her, hooking her leg around his hip.

Lifting her into his arms once again, he pressed her back into the corner of the shower, one arm around her waist to support her, the other hand planted firmly on her outer thigh. The hot spray was now running over his back and was no longer on the verge of drowning them.

Julianne's hands reached between them, her fingers finding the waistband of his boxers and pushing them down. He wasn't wearing anything beneath. Without much effort, she'd pushed the shorts low on his hips and exposed him. He expected her to touch him then, but instead, she stiffened slightly in his arms.

"Heath?"

Julianne's voice was small, competing with the loud rush of the shower and the heavy panting of their breaths, but he heard her. He stopped, his hands mere inches from the moist heat between her thighs.

She wasn't changing her mind again, was she? He wasn't sure he could take that a second time. "Yes?"

"Before we…" Her voice trailed off. Her golden brown lashes were dark and damp, but still full enough to hide her eyes from him. "I don't want to tell anyone about us. *This*. Not yet."

Heath tried not to let the hard bite of her words affect him. She kept insisting she wasn't embarrassed of him and yet she repeatedly went out of her way to prove otherwise. He wanted to ask why. To push her for more information, but this wasn't exactly the right moment to have an in-depth relationship discussion. What was he going to say? He was wedged between her thighs, his pants shoved low on his hips. Now was not the time to disagree with her. At least not if he ever wanted to sleep with his wife.

"Okay," he agreed and her body relaxed. He waited only a moment before sliding his hand the rest of the way up her thigh. His fingers found her slick and warm, her loud cry more evidence that she wanted him and was ready to have him at last. He grazed over her flesh, moving in sure, firm strokes, effectively ending the conversation.

Julianne arched her back, pressing her hips hard into his hand and crying out. Her worries of a moment ago vanished and he intended to plow full steam ahead before she changed her mind, this time for good.

Heath braced her hips in his hands, lifting her up, and then stopping just as he pushed against the entrance to her body. He didn't want to move at this snail's pace; he wanted to dive hard and fast into her, but a part of him kept waiting for her to stop him. He clenched his jaw, praying for self-control and the ability to pull away when she asked.

"Yes, Heath," she whispered. "Please. We've waited this long, don't make me wait any longer."

Heath eased his hips forward and before he knew it, he was buried deep inside her. That realization forced his eyes closed and his body stiff as a shudder of pleasure moved through him. Pressing his face into her shoulder, he reveled in the long-awaited sensation of Julianne's welcoming heat wrapped around him.

How many years, nights, days, had he fantasized about the moment that had been stolen away from him? And now he had her at last. He almost couldn't believe it. It was the middle of the night. Maybe this was all just some wild dream. There was only one way to test it.

Withdrawing slowly, he thrust hard and quick, drawing a sharp cry from her and a low growl of satisfaction from his own throat. He could feel Julianne's fingers pressing insistently into his back, the muscles of her sex tightening around him. He was most certainly awake. And there was no more reason to hold back.

Heath gripped her tightly, leaning in to pin her securely to the wall. And then he moved in her. What started as a slow savoring of her body quickly morphed into a fierce claiming. Julianne clung to him, taking everything he had to give and answering his every thrust with a roll of her hips and a gasp of pleasure.

Everything about this moment felt so incredibly right. It wasn't romantic or sweet. It was fierce and raw, but that was what it needed to be. After eleven years of waiting… eleven years of other lovers who never quite met the standard Julianne had set. He was like a starving man at a buffet. He couldn't get enough of her fast enough to satiate the need that had built in him all these years.

Yet even as he pumped into her, his mind drifted to that night—the night they should have shared together in Gibraltar. They should have been each other's first. It would have been special and important and everything he'd built up in his mind. Instead, he'd given it up to some sorority girl whose name he barely remembered anymore. He didn't know who Julianne finally chose to be her first lover, but even all these years later, he was fiercely jealous of that man for taking what he felt was his.

He was going to make himself crazy with thoughts like that. To purge his brain, he sought out her mouth. He focused on the taste of her, instead. The slide of her tongue along his own. The sharp edge of her teeth nipping at him. The hollow echo of her cries inside his head.

His fingers pressed harder into the plump flesh of her backside, holding her as he surged forward, pounding relentlessly into her body. Julianne tore her mouth from his. The faster he moved, the louder Julianne's gasps of "yes, yes" were in his ear. He lost himself in pleasure, feeling her body tense and tighten around him as she neared her release.

When she started to shudder in his arms, he eased back and opened his eyes. He wanted to see this moment and remember it forever. Her head was thrown back and her eyes closed. Her mouth fell open, her groans and gasps escalating into loud screams. "Heath, yes, Heath!" she shouted.

It was the most erotic sound he'd ever heard. The sound went straight to his brain, the surge of his own pleasure shooting down his spine and exploding into his own release. He poured into her, his groans mixing with hers and the roar of the pounding water.

At last, he thought as he reached out to turn off the water. He'd waited years for this moment and it was greater than he ever could have anticipated.

Seven

He signed them.

Well, if that wasn't the cherry on top, Julianne didn't know what was. She didn't know exactly when it happened, but as she sat down at the kitchen table the next morning, she noticed the divorce papers were out of the envelope. She flipped through the bound pages to the one tabbed by her attorney. There she found Heath's signature, large and sharply scrawled across the page beside yesterday's date.

Well, at least he had signed it *before* they had sex.

That didn't make her feel much better, though. She had already woken up feeling awkward about what happened between them. She'd crept out of his bed as quietly as she could and escaped to the safety of downstairs.

Their frantic lovemaking in the middle of the night certainly wasn't planned. Or well-thought-out. It also wasn't anything she intended to repeat. He'd caught her in a vulnerable moment. Somehow, at 3:00 a.m., all the reasons it seemed like a bad idea faded away. Well, they were all back now. Eleven years' worth of reasons, starting with why they'd never had sex in the first place and ending with that phone call to his "sweetheart" the other night. They weren't going to be together. Last night was a one-time thing.

But even then, coming downstairs and finding their signed divorce papers on the table felt like a slap across the face somehow.

This was why she'd asked him to keep this all a secret. There was no sense in drawing anyone else into the drama of their relationship when the odds were that it would all be over before long. No matter what happened between them last night, they were heading for a divorce. He'd said that he didn't want a divorce, he wanted her to choose. Apparently that wasn't entirely true. For all his sharp accusations, he seemed to want to have his cake and eat it as well.

With a sigh, she sipped her coffee and considered her options. She could get upset, but that wouldn't do much good. She was the one who had the papers drawn up, albeit as a result of his goading. She couldn't very well hold a grudge against him for signing them after she'd had them overnighted to the house.

As she did when she got stuck on one of her sculptures, she decided it was best to sit back and try to look at this situation from a different angle. She and Heath were getting a divorce. It was a long time coming and nothing was going to change that now. With that in mind, what did sleeping with Heath hurt? She'd always wanted him. He'd always wanted her. Their unfinished wedding night had been like a dark cloud hovering overhead for the last eleven years.

When she thought about it that way, perhaps it was just something they needed to do. Things might be a little awkward between them, but they hadn't exactly been hunky-dory before.

Now that they'd gotten it out of their system, they could move forward with clear heads. But move forward into what? The divorce seemed to be a hot-button issue. Once that was official and they stopped fighting, what would happen? There was a chemistry between them that was impossible to deny. Now that they'd crossed the line, she imagined that it would be hard not to do it again.

What if they did?

Julianne wasn't sure. It didn't seem like the best idea. And yet, she wasn't quite ready to give it up. Last night had been…amazing. Eleven years in the making and worth the wait. It made her angry. It was bad enough that Tommy had attacked her and she had the shadow of his death on her conscience. But the impact had been so long-lasting. What if her wedding night with Heath had gone the way it should have? What if they'd been able to come home and tell their parents and be together? She felt like even long after he was dead, Tommy had taken not only her innocence, but also her future and happiness with Heath.

Back in college when her mind went down into this dark spiral, her therapist would tell her she couldn't change the past. All she could do was guide her future. There was no sense dwelling on what had happened. "Accept, acknowledge and grow" was her therapist's motto.

Applied to this instance, she had to accept that she'd had sex with Heath. She acknowledged that it was amazing. To grow, she needed to decide if she wanted to do it again and what the consequences would be. Why did there have to be negative consequences? It was just sex, right? They could do it twice or twenty times, but if she kept that in perspective, things would be fine. It didn't mean anything, at least not to her. Since he had signed the divorce papers first, she'd have to assume he felt the same way.

In fact... Julianne reached for the divorce decree and the pen lying there. She turned back to the flagged page and the blank line for her signature. With only a moment's hesitation, she put her pen to the paper and scrawled her signature beside his.

"See?" she said aloud to the empty room. "It didn't mean anything."

There. It was done. All she had to do was drop it back in the mail to her lawyer. She shoved the paperwork back in the envelope and set it aside. For a moment, there was the euphoria of having the weight of their marriage lifted from her shoulders. It didn't last long, however. It was quickly followed by the sinking feeling of failure in her stomach.

With a groan, she pushed away her coffee. She needed to get out of the bunkhouse. Running a few errands would help clear her mind. She could stop by the post office and mail the paperwork, pick up a few things at the store and go by the hospital to see Dad. Her kiln wouldn't be delivered until later in the afternoon, so why not? Sitting around waiting for Heath to wake up felt odd. There was no reason to make last night seem more important than it was. She would treat it like any other hookup.

She found it was a surprisingly sunny and warm day for early October. That wouldn't last. The autumn leaves on the trees were past their prime and would drop to the ground dead before long. They'd have their first snow within a few weeks, she was certain.

She took advantage of the weather, putting the top down on her convertible. There would still be a cold sting to her cheeks, but she didn't mind. She wanted the wind in her hair. Pulling out of the drive, she headed west for the hospital. With all the work on her studio, she hadn't been to see her father for a couple days. Now was a good time. Molly's car was at the house, so Dad was alone and they could chat without other people around. Even though her father didn't—and couldn't—know the details of what was bothering her, he had a calming effect on her that would help.

She checked in at the desk to see what room he was in now that he was out of intensive care, and then headed up to the fourth floor. Ken was sitting up when she arrived, watching television and poking at his food tray with dismay.

"Morning, Dad."

A smile immediately lit his face. He was a little thinner and he looked tired, but his color was better and they'd taken him off most of the monitors. "Morning, June-bug. You didn't happen to bring me a sausage biscuit, did you?"

Julianne gave him a gentle hug and sat down at the foot of his bed. "Dad, you just had open-heart surgery. A sausage biscuit? Really?"

"Well…" He shrugged, poking at his food again. "It's better than this stuff. I don't even know what this is."

Julianne leaned over his tray. "It looks like scrambled egg whites, oatmeal, cantaloupe and dry toast."

"It all tastes like wallpaper paste to me. No salt, no sugar, no fat, no flavor. Why did they bother saving me, really?"

Julianne frowned. "You may not like it, but you've got to eat healthier. You promised me you'd live to at least ninety and I expect you to hold up your end of the bargain."

Ken sighed and put a bite of oatmeal in his mouth with a grimace. "I'm only doing this for your sake."

"When do you get to come home? I'm sure Mom's version of healthy food will be better tasting."

"Tomorrow, thank goodness. I'm so relieved to skip the rehab facility. You and I both know it's really a nursing home. I might be near death, but I'm not ready for that, yet."

"I'm glad. I didn't want you there, either."

"Your mother says that you and Heath are both staying in the bunkhouse."

"Yes," she said with a curt nod. She didn't dare elaborate. The only person who could read her better than Heath was her dad. He would pick up on something pretty easily.

"How's that going? You two haven't spent that much time together in a long while. You were inseparable as kids."

Julianne shrugged. "It's been fine." She picked up the plastic pitcher of ice water and poured herself a glass. Driving with the top down always made her thirsty. "I think we're both getting a feel for one another again."

"You know," he said, putting his spoon back down on his tray, "I always thought you two might end up together."

The water in her mouth shot into different directions as she sputtered, some going into her lungs, some threatening to shoot out her nose. She set the cup down, coughing furiously for a few moments until her eyes were teary and her face was red.

"You okay?" he asked.

"Went down the wrong way," she whispered between coughs. "I'm fine. Sorry. What, uh…what makes you say something like that?"

"I don't know. You two always seemed to complement each other nicely. Neither of you seem to be able to find the right person. I've always wondered if you weren't looking in the wrong places."

This was an unexpected conversation. She wasn't entirely sure how to respond to it. "Looking in the family is frowned on, Dad."

"Oh, come on," he muttered irritably. "You're not related. You never even lived in the same house, really. It's more like falling for the boy next door."

"You don't think it would be weird?"

"Your mother and I want to see you and Heath happy. If it turns out you're happy together, then that's the way it is."

"What if it didn't work out? It's not like I can just change my number and pretend Heath doesn't exist after we break up."

Ken frowned and narrowed his eyes at her. "Do you always go into your relationships figuring out how you'll handle it when they end? That's not very optimistic."

"No, but it's practical. You've seen my track record."

"I have. Your mother told me the last one didn't end well."

He didn't know the half of it. "Why would dating Heath be any different? I mean, if he were even remotely interested, and I'm certain he's not."

Her father's blue-gray eyes searched her face for a moment, then he leaned back against the pillows. "I remember when you were little and you came home from school one day all breathless with excitement. You climbed into my lap and whispered in my ear that you'd kissed a boy on the playground. You had Heath's name doodled all over the inside of your unicorn notebook."

"Dad, I was nine."

"I know that. And I was twelve when I first kissed your mother at the junior high dance. I knew then that I was going to be with her for the rest of my life. I just had to convince her."

"She wasn't as keen on the idea?"

Ken shrugged. "She just needed a little persuading. Molly was beautiful, just like you are. She had her choice of boys in school. I just had to make sure she knew I was the best one. By our senior year in high school, I had won her over. I proposed that summer after we graduated and the rest is history."

Julianne felt a touch of shame for not knowing that much about her parents' early relationship. She had no idea they'd met so young and got engaged right out of school. They were married nearly ten years before they finally had her, so somehow, it hadn't registered in her mind. "You were so young. How did you know you were making the right choice?"

"I loved your mother. It might not have been the easy choice to get married so young, but we made the most of it. On our wedding day, I promised your mother a fairy tale. Making good on that promise keeps me working at our marriage every day. There were hard times and times when we fought and times when we both thought it was a colossal mistake. But that's when you've got to fight harder to keep what you want."

Julianne's mind went to the package of paperwork in her bag and she immediately felt guilty. The one thing she never did was fight for her relationship with Heath. She had wanted it, but at the same time, she didn't think she could have it. Tommy had left her in shreds. It took a lot of years and a lot of counseling to get where she was now and, admittedly, that wasn't even the healthiest of places. She was a relationship failure who had just slept with her husband for the first time in their eleven-year marriage.

Maybe if things had been different. Maybe if Heath's parents hadn't died. Or if Tommy hadn't come to the farm. Maybe then they could have been happy together, the way her father envisioned.

"I'll keep that in mind when I'm ready to get back in the saddle," she said, trying not to sound too dismissive.

Ken smiled and patted her hand. "I'm an old man who's only loved one woman his whole life. What do I know about relationships? Speaking of which—" he turned toward the door and grinned widely "—it's time for my sponge bath."

Julianne turned to look at the door and was relieved to find her mother there instead of a young nurse. "Well, you two have fun," she laughed. "I'll see you tomorrow at the house."

She gave her mom a quick hug and made her way out of the hospital. Putting the top up on the convertible, she drove faster than usual, trying to put some miles between her and her father's words.

He couldn't be right about her relationship with Heath. If he knew everything that had happened, her father would realize that it just wasn't meant to be. They would never be happy together and she had the divorce papers to prove it.

Julianne cruised back into town, rolling past Daisy's Diner and the local bar, the Wet Hen. Just beyond them were the market and the tiny post office. No one was in line in front of her, so she was able to fill out the forms and get the paperwork overnighted back to her lawyer's office.

It wasn't until she handed over the envelope and the clerk tossed it into the back room that her father's words echoed in her head and she felt a pang of regret. She hadn't fought. She'd just ended it. A large part of her life had been spent with Heath as her husband. It wasn't a traditional marriage by any stretch, but it had been a constant throughout the hectic ups and downs of her life.

"Ma'am?" the clerk asked. "Are you okay? Did you need something else?"

Julianne looked up at him. For a brief second, the words *I changed my mind* were on the tip of her tongue. He would fetch it back for her. She could wait. She wasn't entirely certain that she wanted this.

But Heath did. He wanted his freedom, she could tell.

She'd left him hanging for far, far too long. He deserved to find a woman who would love him and give him the life and family he desired. Maybe Miss Caribbean could give him that. That was what she'd intended when she broke it off with him originally. To give him that chance. She just hadn't had the strength to cut the last tie and give up on them.

It was time, no matter what her dad said. "No," she said with a smile and a shake of her head. "I'm fine. I was just trying to remember if I needed stamps, but I don't. Thank you."

Turning on her heel, she rushed out of the post office and back out onto the street.

Heath was not surprised to wake up alone, but it still irritated him. He wandered through the quiet house and realized at last that her car was not in the driveway. It wasn't hard to figure out that last night's tryst had not sat well with her. As with most things, it seemed like a good idea at the time.

They had been on the same page in the moment. It had been hot. More erotic than he ever dared imagine. They fell back to sleep in each other's arms. He'd dozed off cautiously optimistic that he might get some morning lovin' as well. That, obviously, had not panned out, but again, he was not surprised.

Frankly, he was more surprised they'd had sex to begin with. He dangled the bait but never expected her to bite. His plan had always been to push their hot-button issue, make her uncomfortable and get her to finally file for divorce. He never anticipated rubbing clay all over her body and having steamy shower sex in the middle of the night. That was the stuff of his hottest fantasies.

Of course, he'd also never thought she would cave so

quickly to the pressure and order the divorce paperwork the same day he demanded it. He expected spending weeks, even months wearing her down. She had already held out eleven years. Then the papers arrived with such speed that he almost didn't believe it. He'd wanted movement, one way or another, so he figured he should sign them before she changed her mind again.

Sleeping with her a few hours later was an unanticipated complication.

Heath glanced over at the table where he'd left the papers. They were gone. He frowned. Maybe she wanted this divorce more than he'd thought. He'd obviously given her the push she needed to make it happen, and she'd run straight to the post office with her prize.

He opted not to dwell on any of it. He signed, so he couldn't complain if she did the same. What was done was done. Besides, that's not why he was here anyway. Heath had come to the farm, first and foremost, to take care of things while Ken recovered. Dealing with Julianne and their divorce was a secondary task.

Returning to his room, he got dressed in some old jeans, a long-sleeved flannel shirt and his work boots. When he was ready he opted to head out to the fields in search of Owen, the farm's only full-time employee. It didn't take long. He just had to hop on one of the four-wheelers and follow the sound of the chain saw. They were in the final stretch leading up to Christmas-tree season, so it was prep time.

He found Owen in the west fields. The northern part of the property was too heavily sloped for people to pick and cut their own trees. The trees on that side were harvested and provided to the local tree lots and hardware stores for sale. Not everyone enjoyed a trek through the cold to find the perfect tree, although Heath couldn't fathom why. The tree lots didn't have Molly's hot chocolate or sleigh rides with carols and Christmas lights. No atmosphere at all.

Most of the pick-and-cut trees were on the west side of the property. The western fields were on flat, easy terrain and they were closest to the shop and the bagging station. He found Owen cutting low branches off the trees and tying bright red ribbons on the branches.

At any one time on the farm there were trees in half a dozen states of growth, from foot-tall saplings to fifteen-year-old giants that would be put in local shopping centers and town squares. At around eight years with proper trimming, a tree was perfect for the average home; full, about six to seven feet tall and sturdy enough to hold heavier ornaments. The red ribbons signified to their customers that the tree was ready for harvest.

"Morning, Owen."

The older man looked up from his work and gave a wave. He put down the chain saw and slipped off one glove to shake Heath's hand. "Morning there, Heath. Are you joining me today?"

"I am. It looks like we're prepping trees."

"That we are." Owen lifted his Patriots ball cap and smoothed his thinning gray hair beneath it before fitting it back on his head. "I've got another chain saw for you on the back of my ATV. Did you bring your work gloves and some protective gear?"

Heath whipped a pair of gloves out of his back pocket and smiled. He had his goggles and ear protection in the tool chest bolted to the back of the four-wheeler. "It hasn't been so long that I'd forget the essentials."

"I don't know," Owen laughed. "Not a lot of need for work gloves in fancy Manhattan offices."

"Some days, I could use the ear protection."

Owen smiled and handed over the chain saw to Heath. "I'm working my way west. Most of this field to the right will be ready for Christmas. Back toward the house still needs a year or two more to grow. You still know how to tell which ones are ready for cutting?"

He did. When he was too young to use the chainsaw, he was out in the fields tying ribbons and shaping trees with hedge clippers. "I've got it, Owen."

Heath went off into the opposite direction Owen was working so they covered more territory. With his headset and goggles in place, he cranked up the chain saw and started making his way through the trees. It was therapeutic to do some physical work. He didn't really get the chance to get dirty anymore. He'd long ago lost the calluses on his hands. His clothes never smelled of pine or had stains from tree sap. It was nice to get back to the work he knew.

There was nothing but the buzz of the saw, the cold sting of the air, the sharp scent of pine and the crunch of dirt and twigs under his boots. He lost himself in the rhythm of his work. It gave him a much-needed outlet as well. He was able to channel some of his aggression and irritation at Julianne through the power tool.

His mind kept going back to their encounter and the look on her face when she'd asked him to keep their relationship a secret. Like it had ever been anything but a secret. Did she think that once they had sex he would dash out of the house and run screaming through the trees that he'd slept with her at last? Part of him had felt like that after finally achieving such an important milestone in their marriage, but given he'd signed the divorce papers only a few hours before that, it didn't seem appropriate.

It irritated him that she wouldn't just admit the truth.

She would go through the whole song and dance of excuses for her behavior but refused to just say out loud that she was embarrassed to be with him. She wanted him, but she didn't want anyone to know it.

Up until that moment in the shower, he'd thought perhaps that wasn't an issue for them anymore. She might not want people to know they eloped as teenagers, but now? Julianne had been quick to point out earlier in the night just how "successful" he was. He had his regrets in life, but she was right. He wasn't exactly a bad catch. He was a slippery one, as some women had discovered, but not a bad one.

And yet, it still wasn't enough for her. What did she want from him? And why did he even care?

He was over her. Over. And he had been for quite some time. He'd told Nolan he didn't love her anymore and that was true. There was an attraction there, but it was a biological impulse he couldn't rid himself of. The sex didn't change anything. They were simply settling a long overdue score between them.

That just left him with a big "now what?" He had no clue. If she were off mailing their divorce papers, the clock was ticking. There were only thirty or so days left in their illustrious marriage. That was what he wanted, right? He started this because he wanted his freedom.

Heath set down the chain saw and pulled a bundle of red ribbons out of his back pocket. He doubled back over the trees he'd trimmed, tying ribbons on the branches with clumsy fingers that were numb from the vibration of the saw.

He didn't really know what he wanted or what he was doing with his life anymore. All he knew was that he wasn't going to let Julianne run away from him this time.

They were going to talk about this whether she liked it or not. It probably wouldn't change things. It might not even get her back in his bed again. But somehow, some way, he just knew that their marriage needed to end with a big bang.

Eight

Julianne returned to an empty bunkhouse. The Porsche wasn't in the driveway. She breathed a sigh of relief and went inside, stopping short when she saw the yellow piece of paper on the kitchen table. Picking it up, she read over the hard block letters of Heath's penmanship.

There's a sushi restaurant in Danbury on the square called Lotus. I have reservations there tonight at seven.

With a sigh, she dropped the note back to the table. Heath didn't ask her to join him. He wasn't concerned about whether or not she might have plans or even if she didn't *want* to have dinner with him. It didn't matter. This was a summons and she would be found in contempt if she didn't show up.

Julianne knew immediately that she should not have run

out on him this morning. They should have talked about it, about what it meant and what was going to happen going forward. Instead, she bailed. He was irritated with her and she didn't blame him. That didn't mean she appreciated having her evening dictated to her, but the idea of some good sushi was a lure. She hadn't had any in a while. Daisy's Diner wasn't exactly known for their fresh sashimi.

She checked the time on her phone. It was four-thirty now and it took about forty-five minutes to drive to Danbury. She'd never been to Lotus, but she'd heard of it before. It was upscale. She would have just enough time to get ready. She hadn't exactly gone all-out this morning to run some errands around town, so she was starting from scratch.

Julianne quickly showered and washed her hair. She blew it dry and put it up in hot rollers to set while she did her makeup and searched her closet for something to wear. For some reason, this felt like a date. Given they'd filed for divorce today, it also felt a little absurd, but she couldn't stop herself from adding those extra special touches to her makeup. After a week surrounded by nothing but trees and dirt, the prospect of dressing up and going out was intriguing.

Except she had nothing to wear. She didn't exactly have a lot of fancy clothes. She spent most of her time covered in mud with a ponytail. Reaching into the back of the closet, she found her all-purpose black dress. It was the simple, classic little black dress that she used for various gallery showings and events. It was knee length and fitted with a deep V-neck and three-quarter sleeves. A black satin belt wrapped around the waist, giving it a little bit of shine and luxury without being a rhinestone-covered sparklefest.

It was classic, simple and understated, and it showed off her legs. She paired it with pointy-toed patent leather heels and a silver medallion necklace that rested right in the hollow between her collarbones.

By the time she shook out the curls in her hair, relaxing them into soft waves, and applied perfume at her pulse points, it was time to leave.

She was anxious as she drove down the winding two-lane highway to Danbury. The fall evening light was nearly gone as she arrived in town. The small square was the center of college nightlife in Danbury and included several bars, restaurants and other hangouts. Lotus was at a small but upper-end location. She imagined it was where the college kids saved up to go for nice dates or where parents took them for graduation dinners and weekend visits.

Julianne parked her convertible a few spots down from Heath's silver Porsche. He was standing outside the restaurant, paying more attention to his phone than to the people and activities going on around him.

She took her time getting out of the car so she could enjoy the view without him knowing it. He was wearing a dark gray suit with a platinum dress shirt and diamond-patterned tie of gray, black and blue. The suit fit him immaculately, stretching across his wide shoulders and tapering into his narrow waist.

Heath had a runner's physique; slim, but hard as a rock. Touching him in that shower had been a fantasy come true after watching those carved abs from a distance day after day. Her only regret had been the rush. Their encounter had been a mad frenzy of need and possession. There was no time for exploring and savoring the way she wanted to. And if she had any sense, there never would be. Last night was a moment of weakness, a settling of scores.

It was then that Heath looked up and saw her loitering beside the Camaro. He smiled for an instant when he saw her but quickly wiped away the expression to a polite but neutral face. It was as though he was happy to see her but didn't want her to know. Or he kept forgetting he shouldn't be happy to see her. Their relationship was so complicated.

Julianne approached him, keeping her own face cautiously blank. She had been summoned, after all. This was not a date. It was a reckoning. "I'm here, as requested," she said.

Heath nodded and slipped his phone into his inner breast pocket. "So you are. I'm mildly surprised." He reached for the door to the restaurant and held it open for her to go inside ahead of him.

She tried not to take offense. He implied she was flaky somehow. After eleven years of artfully dodging divorce, it probably looked that way from the outside. "We've got weeks together ahead of us, Heath. There's no sense in starting off on the wrong foot."

The maître d' took their names and led them to their table. As they walked through the dark space, Heath leaned into her and whispered in her ear. "We didn't start off on the wrong foot," he said. The low rumble of his voice in her ear sent a shiver racing through her body. "We started off on the absolutely right foot."

"And then we filed for divorce," she quipped, pulling away before she got sucked into his tractor beam.

Heath chuckled, following quietly behind her. They were escorted to a leather booth in the corner opposite a large column that housed a salt water fish tank. The cylinder glowed blue in the dark room, one of three around the restaurant that seemed to hold the roof up overhead. The tanks were brimming with life, peppered with anemones, urchins, clown fish and other bright, tropical fish. They were the only lights in the restaurant aside from the individual spotlights that illuminated each table.

They settled in, placing their drink orders and coming

to an agreement on the assortment of sushi pieces they'd like to share. Once that was done, there was nothing to do but face why they were here.

"You're probably wondering what this is about," Heath said after sipping his premium sake.

"You mean you're not just hungry?" Julianne retorted, knowing full well that he had bigger motivations than food on his mind.

"We needed to talk about last night. I thought getting away from home and all *those people*," he said with emphasis, "that you worry about seeing us together might help."

Julianne sighed. He'd taken it personally last night when she asked to keep their encounter a secret. She could tell by the downturn of his lips when he said "those people." He didn't understand. "Heath, I'm not—"

He held up his hand. "It's fine, Jules. You don't want anyone seeing us together. I get it. Nothing has changed since we were eighteen. I should just be happy we finally slept together. Unfortunately, finding you gone when I woke up put a sour taste in my mouth."

"And going downstairs to find you'd signed the divorce papers left a bitter taste in mine."

Heath's eyes narrowed at her for a moment before he relaxed back against the seat. "I signed those last night after you left me on the couch, alone and wanting you once again. I assure you that making love to you in the shower at three a.m. was not in my plan at the time."

Julianne shook her head. "It doesn't matter, Heath. We both know it's what we need to do. What we've needed to do for a very long time. I'm sorry to have drawn it out as long as I have. It wasn't very considerate of me to put you through that. The papers are signed and mailed. It's done. Now we can just relax. We don't have to fight about it anymore. The pressure is off and we can focus on the farm and helping Dad recuperate."

He watched her speak, his gaze focused on her lips, but he didn't seem to have the posture of relief she expected. He had started all this after all. He'd virtually bullied her into filing. Now he seemed displeased by it all.

"So," she asked, "are you upset with me because I did what you asked? Because I'm confused."

Heath sighed. "I'm not upset with you, Jules. You're right, you did exactly as I asked. We filed. That's what we needed to do. I guess I'm just not sure what last night was about. Or why you took off like a criminal come morning."

Julianne looked at him, searching his hazel eyes. Having a relationship with him was so complicated. She wanted him, but she couldn't truly have him. Not when the truth about what had happened that night with Tommy still loomed between them. She didn't want anyone else to have him, either, but she felt guilty about keeping him from happiness. Letting him go didn't seem to make him happy. What the hell was she supposed to do?

"We shouldn't read too much into last night," she said at last. "It was sex. Great sex that was long overdue. I don't regret doing it, despite what you seem to think. I just didn't feel like psychoanalyzing it this morning, especially with our divorce papers sitting beside my cup of coffee."

"So you thought the sex was great?" Heath smiled and arched his brow conspiratorially.

"Is that all you got out of that?" Julianne sighed. "It was great, yes. But it doesn't have to change everything and it doesn't have to mean anything, either. We're attracted to each other. We always have been. Anything more than that is where we run into a problem. So can't it just be a fun outlet for years of pent-up attraction?"

Heath eyed her for a moment, his brows drawn together

in thought. "So you're saying that last night wasn't a big deal? I agree. Does that mean you're wanting to continue this…uh…*relationship?*"

When she woke up this morning, it didn't seem like the right thing to do. It would complicate things further in her opinion. But here, in a dark restaurant with moody lighting and a handsome Heath sitting across from her, it wasn't such a bad idea anymore. They were getting a divorce. The emotional heartstrings had been cut once and for all. If they both knew what they were getting into, why not have a little fun?

"We're both adults. We know that it's just physical. The things that held me back in our youth would not be in play here. So, perhaps."

The waiter approached the table with two large platters of assorted sushi. Heath watched only Julianne as things were rearranged and placed in front of them. The heat of his gaze traveled like a warm caress along her throat to the curve of her breasts. She felt a blush rise to her cheeks and chest from his extensive inventory of her assets.

When the waiter finally disappeared, Heath spoke. "You want us to have a fling?"

That's what she'd just suggested, hadn't she? Maybe that was what they needed. A no-strings outlet for their sexual tension. Perhaps then, she could sate her desire for Heath without having to cross the personal boundaries that kept them apart. He never needed to know about the night with Tommy or what happened during their botched honeymoon. She could make it up to him in the weeks that followed.

And why not? They were still married, weren't they?

Julianne smiled and reached for her chopsticks. She plucked a piece from the platter and put it into her mouth. Her eyes never left his even as she slipped her foot out of her shoe and snaked it beneath the table in search of his leg. His eyes widened as her toes found his ankle beneath the cuff of his suit pants. She slid them higher, caressing the tense muscles of his calves. By the time she reached his inner thigh, he was white-knuckling the table.

She happily chewed, continuing to eat as though her foot had not just made contact with the firm heat of his desire beneath the table. "You'd better eat. I can't finish all this sushi on my own," she said, smiling innocently.

"Jules," he whispered, closing his eyes and absorbing the feeling as her toes glided along the length of him. "Jules!" he repeated, his eyes flying open. "Please," he implored. "I get it. The answer is yes. Let's either eat dinner or leave, but please put your shoe back on. It's a long drive home in separate cars. Don't torture me."

The next few weeks went by easily. The uproar of the move and chaos of being thrown together after so long apart had finally dissipated. Dad was home and doing well under Nurse Lynn's care. Jules had a fully operational workshop with her new kiln. She had three new gallery pieces in various stages of completion that were showing a lot of potential and nearly a full shelving unit of stoneware for her shop. During the day, she worked with Molly in the Christmas store preparing for the upcoming holiday rush. They made wreaths, stocked shelves and handled the paperwork the farm generated. In the evenings, she worked on her art.

Heath had done much the same. During the day, he was out in the fields working with Owen. He'd sent out some feelers for teenagers to work part-time starting at Thanksgiving and had gotten a couple of promising responses. When the sun went down, he worked on his computer, trying to stay up-to-date with emails and other business issues. Things seemed to be going fine as best he could tell.

Most nights, Julianne would slip into his bed. Some encounters were fevered and rushed, others were leisurely and stretched long into the early hours of the morning. He'd indulged his every fantasy where she was concerned, filling his cup with Julianne so he would have no regrets when all of this was over.

He usually found himself alone come morning. Julianne told him she woke up with bad dreams nearly every night, although she wouldn't elaborate. When she did wake up, she went downstairs to work. When she returned to bed, she went to her own room. It was awkward to fall asleep with her almost every night and wake up alone just as often.

Despite the comfortable rhythm they'd developed, moments like that were enough to remind him that things were not as sublime as they seemed. He was not, at long last, in a relationship with Julianne. What they had was physical, with a strong barrier in place to keep her emotions in check. She was still holding back, the way she always had. Their discussions never strayed to their marriage, their past, or their future. She avoided casual, physical contact with him throughout the day. When nightfall came, they were simply reaping the benefits of their marriage while they could.

Given Heath had spent eleven years trying to get this far, he couldn't complain much. But it did bother him from time to time. When he woke up alone. When he wanted to kiss her, but Molly or Nurse Lynn were nearby and she would shy away. When he remembered the clock was ticking down on their divorce.

At the same time, things at the bunkhouse had certainly been far more peaceful than he'd ever anticipated going into this scenario. It was one of those quiet evenings when his phone rang. He'd just gotten out of the shower after a long day of working outside and had settled in front of his laptop when the music of his phone caught his attention from the coffee table.

Heath reached for his phone and frowned. It was Nolan's number and picture on the screen of his smartphone. He was almost certain this wouldn't be a social call. With a sigh, he hit the button to answer. "Hey."

"I'm sorry," Nolan began, making Heath grit his teeth. "I had to call."

"What is it?" And why couldn't Nolan handle it? He couldn't voice the query aloud. Nolan was running the whole show to accommodate Heath's family emergency, but Heath couldn't help the irritation creeping up his spine. He had enough to worry about in Connecticut without New York's troubles creeping in.

"Madame Badeau called today. And yesterday. And last week. For some reason, she must think your assistant is lying about you being out of the office. She finally threw a fit and insisted to talk to me."

Heath groaned aloud. Thank goodness only Nolan and his assistant had his personal number. The older French woman refused to use email, so if she had his personal number, she'd call whenever she felt the urge, time difference be damned. "What does she want?"

Nolan chuckled softly on the line. "Aside from you?"

"Most especially," Heath responded..

"She wants you in Paris this weekend."

"What?" It was *Wednesday*. Was she insane? He held her advertising account; he wasn't hers to summon at her whim. "Why?"

"She's unhappy with the European campaign we put together. You and I both know she approved it and seemed happy when we first presented it, but she's had a change of heart. It's a last-minute modification and she wants you there to personally oversee it. She wants the commercial reshot, the print ads redone—everything."

That wasn't a weekend task. Heath smelled a rat. Surely she wasn't just using this as an excuse to lure him to Paris. He'd told her he was married. She seemed to understand. "Why can't Mickey handle this?" Mickey was their art director. He was the one who usually handled the shoots. Redoing the J'Adore campaign fell solidly into Mickey's bucket.

"She didn't like his vision. She wants you there and no one else. I was worried about this. I'm sorry, but there's no dissuading her. I told her about your leave of absence for a family emergency, but it didn't make any difference to her. All she said was that she'd send her private jet to expedite the trip and get you back home as quickly as possible. A long weekend at the most, she insisted."

As much as Heath would like to take that private jet and tell Cecilia what she could do with it, they needed her account. It was hugely profitable for them. If she pulled out after they had spent the last two years making J'Adore the most sought-after cosmetic line in the market, it would be catastrophic. Not only would they lose her account, but others would also wonder why she left and might consider jumping ship. It was too high-profile to ruin. That meant Heath was going to Paris. Just perfect.

"So when is the plane arriving to pick me up?"

"Thursday afternoon in Hartford. Wheels up at four."

"I guess I'll pack my bags. I didn't really bring a lot of my suits to work on the farm. Thankfully it's only for a few days."

"You need to pack Julianne's bags, too."

"What?" he yelled into the phone. "How the hell did she get involved in this discussion?"

"Just relax," Nolan insisted, totally unfazed by Heath's tone. "When I was trying to talk her out of summoning you, I told her that your father-in-law had a heart attack and you and Julianne had gone to the farm. I thought reminding her about your wife and the serious situation you were dealing with would cool her off a little. I lost my mind and thought she would be a reasonable person. Instead, she insisted you bring Julianne to Paris as well."

"Why would I want to bring her with me?"

"Why wouldn't you want to bring your sweet, beloved wife with you to Paris? It's romantic," Nolan said, "and it would be suspicious if you didn't want to bring her. Between you and me, I think Madame Badeau wants to see her competition in the flesh. What can it hurt? Maybe she'll back off for good once she sees Julianne and realizes she's not just a made-up relationship to keep her at arm's length."

Heath groaned again. He'd never met a woman this aggressive. Had his mother not died when he was a child, she would be a year younger than Cecilia. It didn't make a difference to her. She was a wealthy, powerful woman who was used to getting what she wanted, including a steady stream of young lovers. Heath was just a shiny toy she wanted because she couldn't have him.

"Do you really think it will help to take her?"

"I do. And look at the bright side. You'll get a nice weekend in Paris. You'll be flying on a fancy private jet and staying in a fabulous hotel along the Seine. It's not the biggest imposition in the world. You're probably tired of staring at pine trees by now. It's been almost a month since you went up there."

Heath *was* tired of the trees. Well, that wasn't entirely

correct. He was tired of being cooped up here, pacing around like a caged tiger. If it weren't for the nights with Julianne to help him blow off steam, he might've gone stir-crazy by now. Perhaps a weekend away would give him the boost he needed to make it through the holidays. It was early November, so better now than in the middle of the holiday rush.

"Okay," he agreed. "You can let her know we'll be there."

"Thanks for taking one for the team," Nolan quipped.

"Yeah," Heath chuckled, ending the call.

Paris. He was going to Paris. With Julianne. Tomorrow. Even after the happy truce they'd come to, going to Paris together felt like returning to the scene of the crime, somehow. That's where he'd told her he loved her and kissed her for the first time since they were nine years old. They'd left Paris for Spain, and then took a detour to Gibraltar to elope.

With a heavy sigh, Heath got up from the kitchen table and tapped gently at the door to Julianne's studio. Now he had to convince her to go with him. And not just to go, but to go and act like the happy wife *in public*, one of the barriers they hadn't breached. To fool Madame Badeau, they had to be convincing, authentic. That meant his skittish bride would have to tolerate French levels of public affection. It might not even be possible.

The room was silent. She wasn't using her pottery wheel, but he knew she was in there.

"Come in."

Heath twisted the knob and pushed his way into her work space. Julianne was hovering over a sculpture on her table. This was an art piece for her gallery show, he was pretty certain. It was no simple vase, but an intricately detailed figure of a woman dancing.

Julianne's hair was pulled back into a knot. She was wearing a pair of jeans and a fitted T-shirt. There was clay smeared on her shirt, her pants, her face, her arms—she got into her work. It reminded him of that first night they'd spent together, sending a poorly timed surge of desire through him.

"I have a proposition for you, Jules."

At that, Julianne frowned and set down her sculpting tool. "That sound ominous," she noted.

"It depends on how you look at it. I need to take a trip for work. And it's a long story, but I need you to come with me. Do you have a current passport?"

Julianne's eyebrows lifted in surprise. "Yes. I renewed last year, although I haven't gone anywhere. Where on earth do you have to go for work?"

"We're going to Paris this weekend."

"Excuse me?"

Heath held up his hands defensively. "I know. I don't have a choice. It's an important account and the client will only work with me. She's a little temperamental. I know it sounds strange, and I hate to impose, but I have to take you to Paris with me. For, uh…public companionship."

A smile curled Julianne's lips. "I take it the French lady has the hots for you?"

He shook his head in dismay. "Yes, she does. I had to tell her I was married so she'd back off."

"She knows we're married?" Julianne stiffened slightly.

"I had to tell her something. Rebuffing her without good reason might've cost us a critical account. I had to tell my business partner, too, so he was on the same page."

Julianne nodded slowly, processing the information. She obviously didn't care for anyone outside of the two of them and their lawyers knowing about this. It was one thing for family to find out, but who cared if a woman halfway across the globe knew?

"She's insisting I come to Paris to correct some things she's unhappy with and to bring you with me on the trip. I think she wants to meet you, more than anything. It would look suspicious if I didn't bring you. We're supposed to be happily married."

"What does that mean when we get there?"

Heath swallowed hard. They'd gotten to the sticking point. "Exactly what you think it means. We have to publically act like a married couple. We need to wear our rings, be affectionate and do everything we can to convince my client of our rock-solid romance."

Heath looked down and noticed that Julianne was tightly clutching her sculpting tool with white-knuckled strength. "No one here will find out," he added.

Finally, Julianne nodded, dropping the tool and stretching her fingers. "I haven't seen you look this uncomfortable since Sheriff Duke rolled onto the property." She laughed nervously and rubbed her hands clean on her pants.

He doubted he had looked as concerned as she did now. "I can probably get Wade to step in and help while we're gone. Things are in pretty good shape around here. So can I interest you in an all-expense-paid weekend in Paris? We leave tomorrow. My personal discomfort will simply be a bonus."

Julianne nodded and came out from behind her work table. "I get to be a witness to your personal discomfort *and* experience Paris for free? Hmm…I think I can stand being in love with you for a few days for that. But," she added, holding up her hand, "just to be clear, this is all for show to protect your business. Nothing we say or do can be considered evidence of long-suppressed feelings for one another. By the time we get home, the clock will be up on the two of us. Consider this trip our last hoorah."

Nine

"Did you remember to bring your wedding ring?"

Julianne paused in the lobby of J'Adore and started searching in her purse. "I brought it. I just forgot to put it on. What about you?"

Heath held up his left hand and wiggled his fingers. "Got it."

Julianne finally located the small velvet box that held her wedding band. The poor, ignored gold band had been rotting in her jewelry box since the day they returned from their trip to Europe. They'd bought the bands from a small jewelry shop in Gibraltar. With a reputation for being the Las Vegas of Europe, there were quite a few places with wedding bands for last-minute nuptials. They hadn't been very expensive. They were probably little more than nickel painted over with gold-colored paint. Had they been worn for more than a week, the gold might have chipped off long ago, but as it was, they were as perfect and shiny as the day they'd bought them.

She slipped the band onto her finger and put the box away. It felt weird to wear her ring again, especially so close to the finalization of their divorce. Part of her couldn't help thinking this ruse was a mistake. It felt like playing with fire. She'd been burned too many times in her life already.

"Okay, are you ready? This is our first public outing as a married couple. Try to remember not to pull away from me the way you always do."

Julianne winced at his observation. She *did* pull away from him. Even now. Even with no one here having the slightest clue who they were. It was her reflex to shy away from everyone who touched her, at least at first. He seemed to think it was just him instead of a lingering side effect of her attack. She just didn't care to be touched very much. She wanted to tell him that it wasn't about him, but now was not the time to open that can of worms. "I'll do my best," she said instead. "Try not to sneak up on me, though."

Heath nodded and took her hand. "Let's go and get this over with."

They checked in at the front desk and were escorted to the executive offices by Marie, Madame Badeau's personal assistant. The walls and floors were all painted a delicate shade of pink that Heath told her was called "blush" after the company's first cheek color. When they reached the suite outside Madame Badeau's offices, the blush faded to white. White marble floors, white walls, white leather furniture, white lamps and glass and crystal fixtures to accent them.

"*Bonjour,* Monsieur Langston!"

A woman emerged from a frosted pair of double doors. Like the office, she was dressed in an all-white pantsuit. It was tailored to perfection, showing every flawless curve of the older woman's physique. This was no ordinary woman approaching her sixties. There wasn't a single gray hair in her dark brown coiffure. Not a wrinkle, a blemish, or a bit of makeup out of place. This woman had the money to pay the personal trainers and plastic surgeons necessary to preserve her at a solid forty-year-old appearance.

Heath reluctantly let go of Julianne's hand to embrace Madame Badeau and give her kisses on each cheek. "You're looking ravishing, as always, Cecilia."

"You charmer." The woman beamed at Heath, holding his face in her hands. She muttered something in French, but Julianne hadn't a clue what she said.

And then the dark gaze fell on her. "And this must be Madame Langston! Julianne, *oui?*"

At first, Julianne was a little startled by the use of the married name she'd never taken. She recovered quickly by nodding as the woman approached her. She followed Heath's lead in greeting the woman. "Yes. Thank you for allowing me to join Heath on this trip. We haven't been back to Paris since he confessed his love for me at the base of the Eiffel Tower."

Cecilia placed a hand over her heart and sighed. "Such a beautiful moment, I'm sure. You must have dinner there tonight!" The woman's accent made every word sound so lovely, Julianne would've agreed to anything she said. "I will have Marie arrange it."

"That isn't necessary, Cecilia. I'm here to work on the spring J'Adore campaign. Besides, it would be impossible to get reservations on such short notice."

Cecilia puckered her perfectly plumped and painted lips with a touch of irritation. "You are in Paris, Heath. You *must* enjoy yourself. In Paris we do not work twenty-four hours a day. There must be time for wine and conversation. A stroll along the Seine. If you do not make time for that, why even bother to be in Paris at all? *Non*," she said, dismissing his complaint with the elegant wave of her hand. "You will dine there tonight. I am good friends with the owner. Alain will make certain you are accommodated. Is eight o'clock too early?"

Julianne remembered how late Parisian evenings tended to go. Eating dinner at five in the evening was preposterous to them. "That would be lovely," she responded, before Heath could argue again. The last time she was in Paris, they couldn't even afford the ticket to the top, much less dining in their gourmet French restaurant. She would take advantage of it this time, for certain. "*Merci, madame,*" she said, using two of the five French words she knew.

Cecilia waved off Marie to make the arrangements. "Quickly, business, then more pleasure," she said with a spark of mischief in her dark eyes. "Heath, your art director has made the arrangement for a second photo shoot today. It should only take a few hours. While we are there, perhaps your *belle femme* would enjoy a luxurious afternoon in the spa downstairs?"

Julianne was about to protest, but the wide smile on Heath's face stopped her before she could speak. "That's a wonderful idea," Heath said. "Jules, the J'Adore spa is a world-famous experience. While I work this out, you can enjoy a few hours getting pampered and ready for dinner this evening. How does that sound?"

She thought for certain that Heath wouldn't want to be left alone with Cecilia, but this didn't seem to bother him at all. Perhaps her appearance had already made all the difference. "*Très bien,*" Julianne said with a smile.

Cecilia picked up the phone to make the arrangements and she and Heath settled at her desk to work on some details. Julianne sat quietly, sipping sparkling water and taking in the finer details of the office. A few minutes later, Marie reappeared to escort her to the spa.

Remembering her role as happy wife, Julianne returned to Heath's side and leaned in to give him a passionate, but appropriate kiss. She didn't want to overdo it. The moment their lips met, the ravenous hunger for Heath she'd become all too familiar with returned. She had to force herself to pull away.

"I'm off to be pampered," she said with a smile to cover the flush of arousal as one of excitement. "I'll see you this evening. *Au revoir*," she said, slipping out of the office in Marie's wake.

They returned to the first floor of the building, where a private entrance led them to the facility most customers entered from the street to the right of the J'Adore offices. Marie handed her over to Jacqueline, the manager of the spa.

"Madame Langston, are you ready for your day of pampering?" she said with a polite, subdued smile.

"I am. What am I having done?"

Jacqueline furrowed her brow at her for a moment in confusion, and then she laughed. "Madame Badeau said you are to be given all our finest and most luxurious treatments. You're doing *everything, madame.*"

Heath hoped everything went okay with Julianne. Had he not sent her to one of the finest day spas in the world, he might have been worried about working and leaving her alone like that. He'd thought perhaps that he would need her to stay with him all the time, but the moment Cecilia laid eyes on Julianne, the energy she projected toward him shifted. He knew instantly that she would no longer be in pursuit of him, although he wasn't entirely sure what had made the difference.

It wasn't until they were going over the proofs of the photo shoot several hours later that she leaned into him and said, "You love your Julianne very much, I can tell."

At first, he wanted to scoff at her observation, but he realized that he couldn't. Of course he would love his wife. That's how marriages worked. He tried to summon the feelings he'd had for her all those years ago so his words rang with an authenticity Cecilia would recognize. "She was the first and maybe the last woman I'll ever love. The day she said she would marry me was the happiest and scariest day of my life."

That was true enough.

"I see something between you two. I do not see it often. You have something rare and precious. You must treat your love like the most valuable thing you will ever own. Don't ever let it get away from you. You will regret it your entire life, I assure you."

There was a distance in Cecilia's eyes when she spoke that convinced Heath she knew firsthand about that kind of loss. But he couldn't see what she thought she saw in his relationship with Julianne. There might be passion. There might be a nostalgia for the past they shared. But they didn't have the kind of great love Cecilia claimed. A love like that would have survived all these years, shining like a bright star instead of hiding in the shadows like an embarrassing secret. Perhaps they were just better actors than he gave them credit for.

The conversation had ended and they'd finished their day at work. Julianne had texted him to let him know a car was taking her back to their hotel and she would meet him there to go for dinner. Cecilia had booked them a room at the Four Seasons Hotel George V Paris, just off the Chámps Élysées. He arrived there around nightfall, when the town had just begun to famously sparkle and glow.

Perhaps they could walk to the Eiffel Tower. It wasn't a long walk, just a nice stroll across the bridge and along the Seine. The weather was perfect—cool, but not too cold.

He opened the door of their hotel room, barging inside. He found Julianne sitting on the edge of their king-sized bed, fastening the buckle on the ankle strap of her beige heels. His gaze traveled up the length of her bare leg to the nude-colored lace sheath dress she was wearing. It hugged her every curve, giving almost the illusion that she was naked, it so closely matched the creamy ivory of her skin.

Julianne stood up, giving him a better view of the dress. She made a slow turn, showcasing the curve of her backside and the hard muscles of her calves in those sky-high nude pumps with red soles. The peek of red was the only pop of color aside from the matching red painted on her lips. "What do you think?"

"It's…" he began, but his mouth was so dry he had difficulty forming the words. "Very nice."

"When I got done a little early, I decided to go shopping. It's a Dolce & Gabbana dress. And these are Christian Louboutin shoes. I honestly can't believe I spent as much money as I did, but after all that pampering, I was feeling indulgent and carefree for once."

"It's worth every penny," Heath said. In that moment he wanted to buy her a hundred dresses if they would make her beam as radiantly as she did right now. "But now I'm underdressed. Give me a few minutes and I'll be ready to go."

Heath didn't have a tuxedo with him, but he pulled out his finest black Armani suit and the ivory silk dress shirt that would perfectly match her dress. He showered quickly to rinse away the grit and worries of the day and changed into the outfit.

"I was going to suggest we walk since it's so nice, but I'm thinking those shoes aren't meant for city strolls."

"Even if they were, Marie arranged for a car to pick us up at seven forty-five. Perhaps we can walk home." Julianne gathered up a small gold clutch and pulled a gold wrap around her shoulders.

Heath held out his arm to usher her out the door. In the lobby, a driver was waiting for them. He led them outside to the shiny black Bentley. They relaxed in the soft leather seats as the driver carried them through the dark streets and across the bridge to the left bank where the Eiffel Tower stood.

The driver escorted them to the entrance reserved for guests of the Jules Verne restaurant. The private elevator whisked them to the second floor in moments. Heath remembered climbing the over six hundred stairs to reach this floor eleven years ago. The lift entrance tickets were double the price, so they'd skipped it and walked up. The elevator was decidedly more luxurious and didn't make his thighs quiver.

They were seated at a table for two right against the glass overlooking Paris. Out the window, they could see the numerous bridges stretching over the Seine and the glowing, vaulted glass ceiling of the Grand Palais beyond it. The view was breathtaking. Romantic. It made him wish he'd been able to afford a place like this when they were kids. Proposing from the lawn had been nice, but not nice enough for their relationship to last. Caviar and crème fraîche might not a good marriage make, but it couldn't have hurt.

They both ordered wine and the tasting menu of the evening. Then they sat nervously fidgeting with their napkins and looking out the window for a few minutes. Pretending to be a couple in front of Cecilia was one thing. Now they were smack-dab in the middle of one of the most romantic places on earth with no one to make a show for.

They'd spent the last few weeks together. They shared a bed nearly every night. But they hadn't done any of that in Paris, the city where they fell in love. Paris was the wild card that scared Heath to death. He'd done a good job to keep his distance in all of this. Julianne's remoteness made that easier. He liked to think that in a few short days, he would be divorced and happy about that fact.

But Paris could change everything. It had once; it could do it again. The question was whether or not he wanted it to. He shouldn't. It was the same self-destructive spiral that had kept him in this marriage for eleven long years. But that didn't keep him from wanting the thing he'd been promised the day they married.

As the first course arrived, he opted to focus on his food instead of the way the warm lighting made her skin look like soft velvet. He wouldn't pay attention to the way she closed her eyes and savored each bite that passed her lips. And he certainly would ignore the way she occasionally glanced at him when she thought he wasn't looking.

That was just asking for trouble and he had his hands full already.

"We have to stay and watch the lights."

Julianne led Heath out from beneath the Eiffel Tower to the long stretch of dark lawn that sprawled beside it. The first time they had been here, they'd laid out on a blanket. Tonight, they weren't prepared and there was no way she would tempt the fabric of her new dress with grass stains, so she stopped at one of the gravel paths that dissected the lawn.

"We've seen them before, Jules."

She frowned at him, ignoring his protests. They were

watching the lights. "It's five minutes out of your busy life, Heath. Relax. The moment it's over, we'll head back to the hotel, okay?"

With a sigh, he stopped protesting and took his place beside her. It wasn't long before the tower went dark and the spectacular dance of sparkling lights lit up the steel structure. It twinkled like something out of a fairy tale. Heath put his arm around her shoulder and she slipped into the nook of his arm, sighing with contentment.

Heath might be uncomfortable here because this was where their relationship had changed permanently, but Julianne was happy to be back. This had been the moment where she was the happiest. The moment she'd allowed herself to really love Heath for the first time. She'd been fighting the feelings for months. Once he said he loved her, there was no more holding back. It had been one of those beautiful moments, as if they'd been in a movie, where everything is perfect and romantic.

It was later that everything went wrong.

The lights finally stopped and the high beams returned to illuminate the golden goddess from the base. Julianne turned and found Heath looking at her instead of the tower. There was something in his eyes in that moment that she couldn't quite put her finger on. She knew what she wanted to see. What she wanted to happen. If this *had* been a movie, Heath would have taken her into his arms and kissed her with every ounce of passion in his body. Then he would have said he loved her and that he didn't want a divorce.

But this was real life. Instead, the light in his eyes faded. He politely offered her his arm and they turned and continued down the path to the sidewalk that would lead them back to the Seine. Julianne swallowed her disappointment and tried to focus on the positives of the evening instead of the fantasy she'd built in her head.

As they neared the river, the cool night air off the water made Julianne shiver. The gold wrap was more decorative than functional.

"Here," Heath said, slipping out of his coat and holding it for her. "Put this on."

"Thank you," Julianne replied, accepting the jacket. "It's quite a bit cooler than it was when we went to dinner." She snuggled into the warm, soft fabric, the scent of Heath's skin and cologne comingling in the air surrounding her. It instantly brought to mind the hot nights they'd spent together over the last few weeks. The familiar need curled in her belly, urging her to reach for him and tell him to take her back to the hotel so she could make love to him.

Despite the night chill, her cheeks flooded with warmth. She no longer needed the coat, but she kept it on anyway. As much as she craved his touch, she wasn't in a hurry to end this night. The sky was clear and sparkling with a sprinkle of stars. The moon hung high and full overhead. After the emotionally trying few weeks they'd had, they were sharing a night together in Paris. She wouldn't rush that even to make love to Heath.

They stopped on the bridge and looked out at the moon reflecting on the water. It was such a calm, clear night, the water was like glass. In the distance, she could hear street performers playing jazz music. Heath was beside her. For the first time in a long time, Julianne felt a sense of peace. Here, there were no detectives asking questions, no family to accommodate, no unfinished art projects haunting her and no dead men chasing her in her dreams. It was just the two of them in the most romantic city in the world.

"Do you remember when we put the lock on the Pont des Arts bridge?"

Heath nodded. The bridge was farther down the Seine near the Louvre. It was covered in padlocks that had couples' names and dates written on them. Some couples came on their wedding day with special engraved locks. Others bought them from street vendors on the spur of the moment, like they had. The man had loaned them a marker to write "Heath and Julianne Forever." They'd put the lock on the bridge and threw the key into the river before heading to the train station and leaving Paris for Spain. The idea was that you were sealing your relationship forever. Perhaps that was why she couldn't fully let go of him.

"I wonder if it's still there."

"I doubt it," he said. "I read that they cut locks off or remove entire panels of the fence at night. It's been eleven years. I'm sure our lock is long gone."

Julianne frowned at the water. That wasn't the answer she was looking for. A part of her was thinking they would be able to walk down to the bridge and find it. That they might be overcome with emotions at seeing it firmly clasped to the fence, never to be unlocked, and they would finally be able to triumph over the obstacles that were keeping them apart.

Yes, because that's exactly what she needed to do when her divorce was virtually finalized. But if she were honest with herself, if she let her tightly clamped down emotions free like she did that night in Paris all those years ago, she had to admit nothing had changed. She still loved Heath. She had always loved him. It was her love for him that had forced her to push him away so he could have a real chance at happiness. And it was her love for him that wouldn't let her cut the cord that tied them together. She didn't need a lock to do that.

Heath had accused her of commitment-phobia, of using their marriage to keep men away. But that wasn't the whole truth. The whole truth was that she could never love any of those men. How could she? Her heart belonged to Heath and had since elementary school.

"That makes me sad," she admitted to the dark silence around them. "I was hoping that somehow our lock would last even though we didn't. Our love should still be alive here in Paris, just like it was then."

Heath reached for her hand and held it tight. He didn't say anything, but he didn't have to. The warm comfort of his touch was enough. She didn't expect him to feel the same way. She'd thrown his feelings back in his face and never told him why. He'd asked for a divorce, so despite their mutual attraction and physical indulgence over the last few weeks, that was all he felt for her. He'd carried the torch for her far longer than he should have, so she couldn't begrudge him finally putting it down. Telling Heath she had feelings for him *now*, after all this time, would be like rubbing salt in the wound.

Instead of focusing on that thought, she closed her eyes and enjoyed the feel of Heath's touch. In a few weeks, even that would be gone. Carrying on their physical relationship after the divorce wasn't a good idea. They were divorcing so Heath could move on with his life. Find a woman who could love him the way he deserved to be loved. Maybe take his mystery woman to the Caribbean. For that to happen, she couldn't keep stringing him along. She had to let him go.

She needed to make the most of the time they had left and indulge her heart's desires. And tonight, she intended to indulge in the fancy, king-sized bed of their hotel suite. She wanted the passionate, romantic night in Paris that she couldn't have when they were young and in love.

Julianne opened her eyes and turned to look at Heath. His gaze met hers, a similar sadness there although he hadn't voiced it. He probably thought they were mourning their marriage together in the place where it started. That was the smart thing for her to do. To appreciate what they had and to let it go once and for all.

She pressed her body to his side and with the help of her stilettos, easily tilted her head up to whisper into his ear. "Take me home."

Ten

Heath opened the door to their suite and Julianne stepped inside ahead of him. In a bucket by the seating area was a bottle of Champagne with a note. Julianne plucked the white card from the bottle and scanned the neat script.

"Madame Badeau has sent us a bottle of Champagne. She's not quite the cougar you warned me about, Heath."

Heath was slipping out of his coat jacket and tugging at his tie when he turned to look at her. "She told me earlier tonight that she could see we had a rare and precious love."

Julianne's eyes widened at him, but he didn't notice. He was too busy chuckling and shaking his head.

"Boy, did we have her fooled. I think she's finally given up on me."

She swallowed the lump in her throat and cast the card onto the table. A woman she'd known less than a day could see what Heath refused to see. "Spoils to the victor," she replied, trying to keep the bitter tone from her voice. "Open it while I change."

He walked over to take the bottle from her. When she heard the loud pop of the cork, she moved the two crystal flutes closer to him and took a few steps away to watch as he poured.

As many times as they had been together over the last few weeks, there hadn't been much fanfare to their love-making. No seduction. No temptation. It hadn't been as frantic as that first night in the shower, but they wanted each other too badly to delay their desires. But tonight she wanted to offer him a night in Europe they'd never forget, this time, for all the right reasons.

Heath set down the bottle and picked up the flutes filled with golden bubbly liquid. His gaze met hers, but instead of approaching him, she smiled softly and let her gold wrap fall to the floor. She reached for the zipper at her side, drawing it down the curve of her waist and swell of her hip. His gaze immediately went to the intimate flash of her skin now exposed and the conspicuous absence of lingerie beneath it.

Julianne knew the exact moment he realized she hadn't been wearing panties all evening. He swallowed hard and his fingers tightened around the delicate crystal stems of the glasses. His chest swelled with a deep breath before his gaze met hers again. There was a hard glint of desire there. He might not love her any longer, but there was no question that he wanted her. The intensity of his gaze stole the breath from her lungs.

Drawing in a much-needed lungful of cool air, she turned her back to Heath and strolled into the bedroom. Her fingertips curled around the hem of her dress, pulling it up and over her head. Her hair spilled back down around her shoulders, tickling her bare shoulder blades. She tossed the dress across the plush chaise and turned around.

Heath had followed her into the bedroom. He stood just

inside the doorway, clutching the glasses in an attempt to keep control. She was surprised he hadn't snapped the delicate stems in half. Julianne stalked across the room toward him, naked except for her gold jewelry and the five-inch heels she was still wearing. She stopped just in front of him. She reached past the glasses to the button of his collar. Her nimble fingers made quick work of his shirt, moving down the front until she could part the linen and place her palms on the hard, bare muscles of his chest.

He stood stone still as she worked, his eyes partly closed when she touched him. He reopened them at last when she took one of the glasses from him and held it up for a toast.

"To Paris," she said.

"To Paris," Heath repeated, his voice low and strained. He didn't drink; he just watched Julianne as she put the Champagne to her lips and took a healthy sip.

"Mmm…" she said, her eyes focused only on him. "This is good. I know what would make it better, though."

Leaning into Heath, she held up her flute and poured a stream of the Champagne down his neck. Moving quickly, she lapped at the drops that ran down his throat and pooled in the hollow of his collarbone. She let her tongue drag along his neck, meeting the rough stubble of his five o'clock shadow and feeling the low growl rumbling in his throat.

"You like that?" she asked.

Heath's arm shot out to wrap around her bare waist and tug her body close. Startled, Julianne smacked hard against the wall of his chest, pressing her breasts into him. She could feel the cool moisture of the Champagne on his skin as it molded to hers. When she looked up, he had a wicked grin across his face.

"Oh, yeah," he said. He took a sip of Champagne and then brought his lips to hers. The bubbly liquid filled her own mouth and danced around her tongue before she swallowed it.

Their mouths were still locked onto one another as Heath walked her slowly back toward the bed. With his arm still hooked around the small of her back, he eased Julianne's body down slowly until she met with the cool silky fabric of the duvet.

He pulled away long enough to look longingly at her body and whip off his shirt. Then he poured the rest of the Champagne into the valley between her breasts. He cast the empty flute onto the soft carpet with a thud and dipped his head to clean up the mess he'd made. His tongue slid along her sternum, teasing at the inner curves of her breasts and down to her ribcage. He used his fingertip to dip into her navel and then rub the Champagne he found there over the hardened peaks of her nipples. He bathed them in the expensive alcohol, then took his time removing every drop from her skin.

Julianne arched into his mouth and his hands, urging him on and gasping aloud as he sucked hard at her breast. Her own empty Champagne flute rolled from her hand across the mattress. She brought her hands to his head, burying her fingers in his thick hair and tugging him closer. He resisted her pull, moving lower down her stomach to the dripping golden liquid that waited for him there. His searing lips were like fire across her Champagne-chilled skin. She ached for him to caress every part of her and he happily complied.

Heath's hands pressed against her inner thighs, easing them apart and slipping between them and out of her reach. She had to clutch handfuls of the luxurious linens beneath them to ground herself to the earth as his mouth found her heated core. His tongue worked over her sensitive skin, drawing a chorus of strangled cries from her throat. He was relentless, slipping a finger inside of her until she came undone.

"Heath!" she gasped, her body undulating and pulsing with the pleasure surging through her. She hadn't wanted to find her release without him, not tonight, but he didn't give her the option. She collapsed back against the mattress, her muscles tired and her lungs burning.

She pried open her eyes when she felt the heat of Heath's body moving up over her again. He had shed the last of his clothing, his skin gliding bare along hers.

A moment later, his hazel eyes were staring down into her own. She could feel the firm heat of his desire pressing against her thigh. Eleven years ago this moment had sent her scrambling. The need and nerves in Heath's loving gaze had twisted horribly in her mind to the vicious leer of her attacker. Now there were only the familiar green and gold starbursts of the eyes she fantasized about.

She reached out to him, her palms making contact with the rough stubble of his cheeks. She pulled his mouth to hers and lost herself in him. Instead of fear, there was a peace and comfort in Heath's arms. When he surged forward and filled her aching body with his, she gasped against his mouth but refused to let go. She needed this, needed him.

Julianne drew her legs up, cradling his hips and drawing him deeper inside. She wanted to get as close to him as she could. To take in Heath and keep a part of him there inside her forever. The clock was ticking on their time together, but she could have this.

As the pace increased, Heath finally had to tear away from her lips. He buried his face in her neck, his breath hot and ragged as he thrust hard and fast. Her body, which had been exhausted mere moments ago, was alive and tingling with sensation once again. Her release built inside, her muscles tightening and straining like a taut rubber band as she got closer and closer. Heath's body was equally tense beneath her fingertips, a sheen of perspiration forming on his skin.

"I've never…wanted a woman…as much as I want you, Julianne."

His words were barely a whisper in her ear amongst the rough gasps and rustling sheets, but she heard them and felt them to her innermost core. Her heart stuttered in her chest. It wasn't a declaration of love, but it was serious. She couldn't remember the last time he'd used her full name when he spoke to her. And then it hit her and she knew why his words impacted her so greatly. When he'd said their wedding vows.

I take thee, Julianne Renee Eden, to be my lawfully wedded wife from this day forward.

The words from the past echoed in her mind, the image of the boy he was back then looking at her with so much love and devotion in his eyes. No one had ever looked at her like that again. Because no one had ever loved her the way he did. She might have ruined it, but she had his love once and she would cherish that forever.

"Only you," she whispered. "I've only ever wanted you."

There was the slightest hesitation in his movement, and then he thrust inside of her like never before. For a moment, she wondered what that meant, but before she could get very far with her thoughts, her body tugged her out of her own head. The band snapped inside and the rush of pleasure exploded through her. She gasped and cried into his shoulder, clutching him tightly even as he kept surging forward again and again.

"Julianne," he groaned as his whole body shuddered with his own release.

With Heath's face buried in her neck and their hearts beating a rapid tattoo together, she wanted to say the words. It was the right moment to tell him that she loved him. That she wanted to throw their divorce papers out the window and be with him. To confess the truth about what had happened on their wedding night and explain that it wasn't a lack of loving him, but that she was too damaged to give herself to anyone. It had taken years of therapy to get where she was now. She couldn't have expected him to wait for her.

But she knew telling him the whole truth would hurt him more than his imagined insults. All the boys carried a burden of being unable to protect her, but Heath most of all. If Heath knew that the end for Tommy had come too late…that he had already pillaged her thirteen-year-old innocence before he arrived, he would be devastated. Their marriage would no longer be his biggest regret; that moment would replace it and he would be reminded of it every time he looked at her.

Julianne wanted Heath to look at her with desire and passion. She didn't dare ask for love. But if he knew the truth, he would see her as a victim. He would know the full extent of the damage Tommy had caused and that would be all he would see. Could he make love to her without thinking about it?

Julianne squeezed her eyes shut and her mouth with them. She couldn't tell him. She couldn't tell anyone. No matter how much she loved Heath and how badly he deserved to know the truth, the price of voicing the words was too high. She'd rather he believe she was a flighty, spoiled little girl who couldn't decide what she wanted and stomped on his heart like a ripe tomato.

Heath rolled onto his side and wrapped his arm around her waist. He tugged her body against his, curling her into the protective cocoon to keep her warm. Even now, without realizing it, he was trying to protect her. Just like he always had.

Heath could never ever know that he'd failed that day.

The drive back to Cornwall from Hartford was long and quiet. Heath wasn't entirely sure what was going on with Julianne, but she'd barely spoken a word since they'd departed Paris earlier that morning. How was it that their relationship didn't seem to work on U.S. soil?

They pulled up at the bunkhouse and stumbled inside with their bags. It had been a long day, even traveling by private jet. The sun was still up but it was late into the night on Parisian time.

Heath was pulling the door shut behind him when he nearly slammed into Julianne's back. She had stopped short, her bags still in her arms, her gaze fixed firmly on the kitchen table.

"What is it?" he asked, leaning to one side to look around her. She didn't answer, but she didn't have to. Molly had brought in an overnighted package and left it on the table for them. The same type of packaging the divorce papers had originally arrived in. That only brought one option to mind. The thirty-day waiting period was up. A judge had signed the papers and her lawyer had mailed them.

They were divorced.

Just like that. After eleven years, their relationship was possibly better than it had ever been and they were divorced. Heath took a deep breath and closed his eyes. He wanted this. He had asked for this. He'd harassed her and demanded his freedom. And now he had what he wanted and he'd never felt so frustrated in his life.

He unceremoniously dropped his bags to the floor and

walked around Julianne to pick up the envelope. It had her name on it, but he opened it anyway. There was probably a similar envelope being held at the front desk of his building, waiting for him to return to Manhattan.

A quick glance inside confirmed his suspicions. With a sad nod, he dropped the papers back to the table. "Welcome home," he said with a dry tone.

"The time went by quickly, didn't it?"

He looked up, surprised at her first words in quite a while. "Time flies when you're having fun."

Julianne's eyes narrowed at him, her lips tightening as she nodded. She didn't look like she was having fun. She also didn't look pleased with him although he had no clue what the problem was.

"Julianne…" he began, but she held up her hand to silence him.

"Don't, Heath. This is what we wanted. I know the last few weeks have muddied the water between us, but it doesn't change the fact that we shouldn't be married. We aren't meant to be together long-term. As you said, we were having fun. But fun is all it was, right?"

Heath swallowed the lump in his throat. That was his intention, but it had started to feel like more. At some point, he had forgotten about the divorce and just focused on being with her. Was he the only one that felt that way? It didn't seem like it at the time. It seemed like she had gotten invested as well. Perhaps that was just Paris weaving its magic spell on their relationship again. "Fun," he muttered.

Julianne brushed past him and pulled her wedding ring off her finger. They were both still wearing them after their weekend charade for Madame Badeau. She placed it on top of the paperwork. "We won't need these anymore."

Even as she said the words, Heath got the feeling that

she didn't mean them. She was unhappy. Her, the girl who slammed the door in his face and told him to move on. When he finally tries, she takes it personally.

"So now what?" he asked. Heath wasn't sure how to proceed from here. Did getting a divorce mean their fling was over? They still had the crush of the Christmas season ahead of them. He wasn't looking forward to the long, cold nights in bed without her.

"I think it's time for me to move back into the big house," she said, although she wouldn't look him in the eye.

"Why?"

"When I spoke with Mom yesterday, she said the live-in nurse would be leaving tomorrow. They were able to move Dad's bed back upstairs since he's getting around well. That means I can have my room back."

"Your studio is out here."

She nodded. "But under the circumstances, I think it might be better if we put some distance between us."

Heath's hands balled into angry fists at his side. It was his idea to move forward with the divorce and yet it still felt like Julianne was breaking up with him all over again. "Why is it that whenever our relationship gets even remotely serious, you run away?"

Her eyes met his, a flash of green anger lighting them. "Run away? I'm not running away. There's nothing to run from, Heath. As I understand it, we were just having some fun and passing the time. I don't know if that qualifies as a relationship."

She was lying. He knew she was lying. She had feelings for him, but she was holding them back. Nothing had changed with her in all these years. She loved him then, just as she loved him now, but she refused to admit it. She always pulled away when it mattered. Yeah, he hadn't confessed that he had developed feelings for her, but what fool would? He'd done it once and got burned pretty badly.

"Why do I get the feeling that you're always lying to me, Jules? Then, now, I never get the whole story."

Her eyes widened. She didn't expect him to call her on it, he could tell. She sputtered a moment before finding her words again. "I-I'm not always lying to you. You know me too well for me to lie."

"You'd think so, and yet you'll look me in the eye and tell me we were just 'having fun.' We've had a lot of sex over the last few weeks, but that's the only barrier I've broken through with you, Jules. You're still keeping secrets."

"You keep your secrets, too, Heath."

"Like what?" he laughed.

"Like the reason why you really wanted a divorce."

Heath had no clue what she was talking about. "And what exactly did I say that was a lie?"

"It may not have been a lie, but you have certainly kept your relationship with that other woman quiet while you were sleeping with me the last few weeks. Now you're free to take her to the Caribbean, right?"

"What woman?"

"The so-called Sweetheart you were gushing at on the phone that day."

"You mean my sixty-three-year-old secretary?" He chuckled, although it wasn't so much out of amusement as annoyance. "I knew you were listening in on my phone call."

"You laid it on pretty thick. Do you really expect me to believe your sweetheart is a woman older than Mom?"

"You should. She likes to be flirted with, so I call her all sorts of pet names. I told her if she held down the fort while I was gone that I would give her a bonus big enough to cover the vacation she wants to take to the beach with her grandkids. Without *me*," he added. "Do you really think I would've pursued something with you while I had a woman on the side?"

Julianne's defiant shoulders slumped a bit at his words. "Then why did you really want the divorce, Heath? You came in here demanding it out of nowhere. I thought for sure you had another woman in mind."

"There's no other woman, Jules. How could there be? I'm not about to get serious with any woman while I'm married to you. That's not fair to her. Just like it wasn't fair to your almost fiancé. You just play with men's minds but you have no intention of ever giving as much as you take. You're right. It's a good thing this was just 'fun' to pass the time. It would be foolish of me to think otherwise and fall for your games twice."

"How dare you!" she said. "You don't know anything about my relationships. You don't know anything about what I've gone through in my life."

"You're right," he said. "Because you won't tell me anything!"

"I have always been as honest as I could be with you, Heath."

"Honest? Really. Then tell me the truth about what happened on our wedding night, Jules. The truth. Not some made-up story about you changing your mind. You were in love with me. You wanted me. The next minute everything changed. Why?"

Julianne stiffened, tears glazing her eyes. Her jaw tightened as though she was fighting to keep the flow of words inside. "Any question but that one," she managed to say.

"That's the only question I want answered. Eleven years I've spent wondering how you could love me one minute and run from me the next. Tell me why. I deserve to know."

Her gaze dropped to the floor. "I can't do that."

"Then you're right, Jules. We shouldn't be married. I'm glad we've finally gotten that matrimonial monkey off our backs. Maybe now I can move on and find a woman who will let me into her life instead of just letting me be a spectator."

"Heath, I—"

"You know," he interrupted, "all I ever wanted from you was for you to let me in. Over the years, I've given you my heart, my soul. I've lied for you. Protected you. I would've gone to jail before I let anyone lay a finger on you. And hell, I still might if Sheriff Duke comes back around. I'd do it gladly. Even now, although I really don't know why. I just don't understand you, Jules. Why do you keep me at arm's length? Even when we're in bed together, you've kept your distance, kept your secrets. Is it me? Or do you treat all men this way?"

Julianne looked back up at him and this time, the tears were flowing freely. It made his chest ache, even as he fought with her, to see her cry that way. But he had to know. Why did she push him away?

"Just you," she said. Then she turned and walked upstairs alone.

Eleven

Julianne sat on the edge of the bed staring at the bags she'd already packed. This morning, she would move back into the big house where she belonged. It broke her heart and made her cry every time she thought about it for too long, but she had to do it. They were divorced. No matter how much she loved him, Heath deserved to be happy. He deserved his freedom and a chance with a woman who could give him everything he wanted.

As much as she wanted to be, Julianne would never be that woman. She would always have her secrets. She would always have a part of herself that she held back from him. Even if she told him it was for his own good, he wouldn't believe her.

After the last few weeks together, she could tell he was confused. It was easy to feel like things were different when they were together so much, but that wouldn't last forever. They'd end up caught in the same circular trap where they'd spent the last eleven years. But she could get them out of it, even if he didn't seem to like it at the time.

He wanted his freedom and she would give it to him.

With a sigh, she stood up and extended the handle of her roller bag. She was nearly to the door of her room when she heard a loud banging at the front door.

She left her luggage behind and went downstairs. The low rumble of male voices turned into distinguishable words as she reached the landing.

"I'm going to have to bring her in for questioning."

"Why? You've asked a million questions. What do you want with her?"

Sheriff Duke was lurking in the door frame, looking larger and more threatening than ever before. "I need to talk to her. We also need a hair sample."

Heath glanced over his shoulder to see Julianne standing at the foot of the stairs. He cursed silently and turned back to the doorway. "Ask her your questions here. And get a warrant for the hair. Otherwise, you have to arrest us both."

"I can't arrest you just because you ask me to, Heath."

"Fine. Then arrest me because I killed Tommy."

Duke's eyes widened for a moment, but he didn't hesitate to reach for his handcuffs. "All right. Heath Langston, you're under arrest for the murder of Thomas Wilder. You have the right…"

The sheriff's voice faded out as the reality of what was happening hit her. Sixteen years' worth of karma was about to fly back in their faces. And to make things worse, Heath had confessed. Why had he confessed?

Duke clamped the cuffs on Heath's wrists and walked him to the back of the squad car.

"Don't say anything, Jules," she heard Heath say before the door slammed shut.

Returning to face Julianne, Duke started his speech again and reached for his second pair of cuffs. She stood silent and still, letting him close the cold metal shackles around her wrists. He took her to the other side of the squad car and sat her there beside Heath.

The ride into town was deadly silent. Anything they said could be used against them, after all. It wasn't until they were led into separate interrogation rooms that the nervous flutter of her stomach started up.

An hour went by. Then two.

She didn't have her watch on, but she was fairly certain that nearly four hours had passed before Sheriff Duke finally came in clutching a file of paperwork. Her stomach was starting to growl, which meant lunchtime had come and gone.

He settled down at the table across from her. No one else was in the room, but she had no idea how many people were gathered on the other side of the one-way glass panel. He flipped through his pages, clicked the button on his pen and looked up at her.

"Heath had a lot to say, Julianne."

She took a deep breath. "About what?" she replied as innocently as she could.

"About killing Tommy."

"I'm not sure why he would say something like that."

"I'm not sure, either. He had a pretty detailed story. If I didn't know better I'd lock him up right now and be done with it."

"Why don't you?"

A smirk crossed the policeman's face and Julianne didn't care for it. He was too pleased, as though he had everything figured out. He was probably already planning to use this big case to bolster his reelection.

"Well, as good a tale as he told me, it just doesn't match

up with the evidence. You see, Heath told me that he found Tommy on top of you and he hit him on the back of his head with a rock to stop him, accidentally killing him."

Julianne didn't blink, didn't breathe, didn't so much as shift her gaze in one direction or another.

"Problem is that the coroner says Tommy was killed instantly by a blow to his left temple."

"I thought they said on the news that Tommy had the back of his head bashed in." She tried to remember what she had seen on television. That's what the reports had said. Only she knew that injury came second. She didn't know if he was already dead by then or not.

"He did. But we don't release all the critical information to the news. Like the hair we found."

"Hair?" She hadn't heard anything about hair, either.

"You'd think that after all these years that any evidence would be destroyed, and most of it was, but we were lucky. Tommy died with a few strands of long blond hair snagged on the ring he was wearing. Hair and bone are usually all that's left after this length of time. It was as though he'd had a handful of a woman's hair in his hand shortly before he died."

"There are a lot of blondes in Cornwall."

"That's true, but Heath has already stated he saw Tommy on top of you, so that's narrowing it down for me."

"You said you didn't believe his story."

"I said it didn't match the coroner's report. And it doesn't. So that made me think perhaps he was protecting you. That made a lot of the pieces click together in my mind. Why don't you just save me the trouble and tell me the truth, Julianne. You don't really want me to charge Heath with Tommy's murder do you?"

"It wouldn't be murder," she argued. "It would be self-defense."

"Not exactly. He wasn't being threatened, just you. It might have been accidental, but his lawyers will need to prove it. There's nothing that says he didn't come up on Tommy in the woods and bludgeon him for no reason."

Julianne swallowed the lump in her throat. She wouldn't let Heath take the blame for this. She just couldn't. He'd always told her it wouldn't come to this, but if it did, he wouldn't be charged because he was protecting her. The sadistic gleam in Sheriff Duke's eyes made her think Heath might be wrong about that. Heath wouldn't spend a single day in jail protecting her. This had all gone on far too long. Keeping him out of prison was far more important than protecting his ego.

"I'm the one that killed Tommy. He…" She fought for the words she'd only said aloud a few times in her therapist's office. "He raped me," she spat out.

Sheriff Duke's eyes widened for a moment and he sat back into his chair. He didn't speak, but he reached over to check his voice recorder to make sure it caught everything.

She took a moment trying to decide where to go from there. "I was doing my chores after school. Same as any other day. The next thing I knew, Tommy was there, watching me. I was startled at first, but I thought I would be okay. Until he pulled out a switchblade and started walking toward me. I ran, but he grabbed my ponytail and yanked me back. I fell onto the ground and he was on top of me in an instant.

"He was so large. Bigger than my brothers. I was only thirteen and smaller than other girls my age. There was no way to fight him off. He had the knife at my throat so I couldn't scream. I kicked and fought at first, but he grabbed a fistful of my hair and yanked hard enough to bring tears to my eyes. He said if I didn't keep still, he'd cut my throat and leave my body naked for my daddy to find me."

Julianne's hands started trembling. The metal of the handcuffs tapped against the tabletop, so she pulled her arms back to rest in her lap. Her eyes focused on the table instead of the man watching her.

"I knew in the pit of my stomach that I was dead. No matter what he said, he wasn't going to let me run to my parents or the police. He would finish this and me before he was done. I tried to keep my focus and ignore the pain. It would've been so easy to tune everything out, but I knew that I couldn't. I knew that eventually, he'd get distracted and I would have my one and only chance to escape.

"I was able to slowly feel along the ground beside me. At first, there was nothing but pea gravel. I could've thrown that in his eyes, but it would have only made him angry. Then I found a rock. It was small but dense with a sharp edge I could feel with my fingertips. He still had the knife at my throat and if it wasn't enough to knock him out, I knew it was all over, but I didn't care. I had to do it. I brought the rock up and slammed it into the side of his head as hard as I could."

Julianne had seen this image in her dreams a thousand times so it was easy to describe even after all this time. "His eyes rolled into his head and he collapsed onto me. I struggled as quickly as I could to push him up and off of me. When I was finally able to shove him off, his head flung back and struck a rock sticking up out of the ground. That's when he started bleeding. I panicked. I kicked the knife away from him and started pulling my clothes back on. That's when Heath found me.

"We kept waiting for Tommy to get up, but he didn't. That's when we realized that hitting his head on the rock must have killed him. There was so much blood on the ground. He told me to sit tight while he went for help. He came back with the other boys. The rest was a blur, but I heard him tell the others that he'd hit Tommy with the rock when he saw him attacking me. There were so many times that we should've stopped and gone to the house to call the police, but we were so scared. In the end, all they wanted to do was protect me. And they did. None of them deserve to get in trouble for that."

"What about the note Tommy left? And all his things that were missing?"

"We did that," she said, not mentioning one brother or another specifically. "We were running on adrenaline, reacting faster than we could think. We hid the body, destroyed all his stuff and tried to pretend like it never happened."

"That didn't exactly work out for you, did it?"

Julianne looked up at the sheriff. He didn't seem even remotely moved by her story. He tasted blood and no matter what she said, she was certain he wasn't going to just close the case based on her testimony. "It's hard to pretend you haven't been raped, Sheriff Duke."

"And yet you waited all these years to come forward. It seems to me like you're hiding something. I think—"

A loud rap on the one-way glass interrupted him. Duke's jaw tightened and he closed the folder with his paperwork. "I'll be back," he said. He got up and left the room.

Julianne wasn't certain what had happened, but she was relieved for the break. It took a lot out of her to tell that story. Whether or not he backed down and dismissed the charges as self-defense, she knew she would have to tell that story again. And again. A part of her was terrified, but another part of her felt liberated. This secret had been like a concrete block tied around her neck. She knew it had to feel the same way to the others.

Maybe, finally, they could all stop living with the dark cloud of Tommy's death over their heads.

They sure were slow to book him. Heath had spent hours waiting for the inevitable. He'd told them he killed Tommy. Certainly the wheels of progress should be turning by now.

Not long after that, the door opened and Sheriff Duke's deputy, Jim, came through the door. "You can go."

"What?" He stood up from his chair. "I can go?"

Jim came over and unlocked the handcuffs. "Yes." He opened the door and held it.

Heath was thoroughly confused, but he wasn't about to wait for them to change their minds. In the hallway, he found several people waiting there. He recognized the woman as Tommy Wilder's sister, Deborah Curtis. Brody had sent them all the background report on her when she came to Cornwall asking about her brother. She was standing there with a man wearing an expensive tailored suit. He carried himself like he was important somehow, like he was her lawyer. Heath froze on the spot. Was she here to confront him for killing her brother?

Another door opened off the hallway and Julianne stepped out with a disgusted-looking Sheriff Duke at her side.

"What is going on?" Heath asked.

Julianne shook her head. "I have no clue. Duke said I was free to go."

The man beside Deborah stepped forward. "My name is Pat Richards. I'm a prosecutor for the state of Connecticut. With the evidence I have, your testimony and that of Mrs. Curtis, the state has opted not to press charges. This situation was tragic, but obviously in self-defense. I can't in good conscience prosecute Julianne after everything she went through."

Heath frowned. "Prosecute Julianne? I'm the one that confessed to killing him."

Pat smiled wide and nodded in understanding. "A noble thing, for sure, but it wasn't necessary. The charges have been dropped. You're both free to go."

Sheriff Duke shook his head and disappeared down the hallway into his office with a slam of his door.

"He disagrees, I take it?"

The prosecutor chuckled. "He fancied himself the hero cracking a huge case. There's not much crime around here for him to tackle, and this would give him the boost for his reelection. But even without Mrs. Curtis's testimony of her own attack, there was nothing for us to go forward on."

"What?" This time the question came from Julianne.

Deborah stepped forward, speaking for the first time. "I want you to know that I don't harbor any ill will against you or your family. You took Tommy in when no one else would and did only what you had to do to defend yourself. I completely understand that. My brother started displaying violent tendencies before he was even twelve years old. My parents tried to control him. They punished him, they put him in therapy. They even considered one of the boot camps for troubled teens. But it wasn't until my father came home early from work one day and caught him… attacking me…"

Julianne gasped, bringing her hand to cover her mouth. "Oh, god." Heath wanted to go to her side, but he resisted. Despite what had happened, she might still be upset with him.

"Tommy didn't succeed," Deborah said, "but he would've raped me if my father hadn't come home. I didn't want to press charges, I was too embarrassed. After that, he wasn't allowed to be alone with me. His close call didn't stop him from getting in trouble, though. He was constantly getting picked up for one thing or another. He even did a few weeks in juvie. Eventually the state removed him from the home as a repeat juvenile offender and I tried to forget it ever happened." She shook her head. "I never dreamed he would try to do it again. I feel awful."

"Mrs. Curtis's story was so similar to Julianne's that there was no reason to believe she wasn't telling the truth. The forensic evidence supported her version of his death. There's not a grand jury that would indict her. Anything that happened after the fact is well past the statute of limitations." Pat looked down the hall at the sheriff's office and shook his head. "Sheriff Duke might not be happy, but the only real crime here was committed by the deceased a long time ago. As much as I'd like to, I can't charge a dead man with second-degree sexual assault."

The words hung in the air for a moment. Heath let them sink into his mind. Pat meant *attempted* sexual assault, right? Attempted. Julianne had sworn that Tommy hadn't... And yet, why would a traumatized young girl want to tell him something like that? She wouldn't.

And then it hit him like he'd driven his Porsche into a brick wall. In an instant, every moment made sense. Every reaction Julianne ever had. Their wedding night...

How could he have missed this? It was so obvious now that he felt like a fool. And a first-class ass. He'd believed what she told him despite all the signs indicating otherwise. All these years he'd been angry with her while she'd carried this secret on her own.

"I'm going to have a talk with the local child services agency. There is a major breach in conduct if they didn't share the information about Deborah's assault with Mr. and Mrs. Eden before they placed Tommy there. They might not have taken him in if they'd known." The phone on Pat's hip rang and he looked down at the screen. "If you'll excuse me," he said, disappearing through the double doors.

After a few silent, awkward moments, Deborah spoke again, this time to Julianne. "Mr. Richards and I were listening in the observation room while you told your story," she said. "You are so much braver than I ever could have been. I'm sorry I wasn't stronger. If I had been, I would've pressed charges or talked to people about what happened and this might never have happened to you."

Julianne approached Deborah and embraced her. The two women held each other for a moment. "This is not your fault. Don't you ever think that. I've kept this a secret, too. It's hard to tell people the truth, even though you didn't do anything wrong."

When Julianne pulled away, Deborah dabbed her eyes with a tissue and sniffed. "You know, I came back to Cornwall to track down Tommy, but I wasn't looking for a happy family reunion. My therapist had recommended I find him so I could confront my fears and move on. He had vanished, but I expected him to be in jail or working at a gas station in the middle of nowhere. This," she said, waving her hand around, "was more than I ever planned to uncover. But it's better, I think. I don't have to be afraid of Tommy anymore. He's never going to show up on my doorstep and he'll never be able to hurt me or my little girl. I'm happy I was able to help with your case, too. It makes me feel like I have more power and control over my life than ever before."

Heath stood quietly while the two women spoke. He had so many things he wanted and needed to say to Julianne, but now wasn't the time. They eventually moved down the hallway, making their way out of the police station.

He was relieved to step outside. It was cold, but the sun

was shining. It was like an omen; Noah's rainbow signaling that all of this was finally over. They no longer had to worry about the police coming after them. It was in the past now, where it belonged.

At least most of it. With the truth out, the papers would no doubt pick up the story. They needed to sit down with Mom and Dad and tell them what had happened before some woman cornered Molly at the grocery store. Hopefully Ken's heart could withstand the news now that the threat of his children's incarceration was behind them.

Heath whipped out his phone to text his brothers, but found that wasn't enough. He needed to call them. He and Julianne both, to share the news. He wished he could give Julianne time to prepare, but the truth was out. They had protected her as well as they could over the years, but now she would have to tell her story. First to her family, then to the public. Perhaps after all this time, the blow of it would soften. He couldn't imagine the tiny, thirteen-year-old Julianne talking to police and reporters about killing her attacker. Her *rapist*.

His stomach still ached painfully at that thought. If he had only come across the two of them a few minutes sooner. He might have stopped Tommy before he could have... He sighed and shoved his hands into his pockets. He already believed he failed to protect Julianne, but he had no idea the extent of the damage that was caused. And by keeping Tommy's death a secret, they had virtually forced her to keep the rape a secret as well, and hadn't even known it. Had their attempt to protect her only made it worse?

The bile started to rise in the back of his throat. She should have been taken to the doctor. To a therapist. She should've been able to cry in her mother's arms and she was never able to do any of that.

His knees started to weaken beneath him, so Heath moved quickly to sit on the steps. He would wait there until Julianne and Deborah were done talking. Maybe by then, he could pull himself together.

After a while, Deborah embraced Julianne again, and then she made her way down the sidewalk to her car. Julianne watched her walk away and then finally turned to look at him. It was the first time she'd done that since they'd all gathered inside the police station. She walked over to the steps and sat down beside him.

Minutes passed before either of them spoke. They had shared so much together, and yet when it came to the important things, they knew almost nothing about each other.

"Thank you," she said at last.

That was the last thing he ever expected her to say. "Why on earth would you be thanking me right now?"

"Thank you for loving me," she elaborated. "No matter what we've said or done to each other over the years, when it was important, you were there for me. You probably don't think so, but the truth is that you would have gone to jail for me today. You've spent the last sixteen years covering for me, even lying to your own brothers about what happened that day. You looked Sheriff Duke in the eye and told him you killed Tommy, consequences be damned. How many people are lucky enough to have someone in their life that is willing to do that for them?"

"That's what families do. They protect each other." He watched the traffic drift by the main thoroughfare for a moment. He couldn't turn to face her while he spoke or he might give away the fact that his feelings for her ran much deeper than that. No matter what happened between them, he would always love Julianne. He couldn't seem to stop. Knowing the truth only made it harder not to love her more. All his reasons for keeping her at arm's length were nullified. But they were divorced. What did that matter now?

"You went far beyond family obligation, Heath."

"Why didn't you tell me what happened, Jules? You could've told me the truth."

"No," she said, softly shaking the blond curls around her shoulders. "I couldn't. You had me on this pedestal. I couldn't bear for you to know how flawed I was. How broken I was."

"As though what happened was your fault?"

"It wasn't my fault. I know that. But it wasn't your fault, either. If you knew, you would've blamed yourself. And you'd never look at me the same way again. I didn't want to lose that. You were the only person in my life that made me feel special. Mom and Dad loved me, but I always felt like I wasn't enough for them. You only wanted me. I wanted to stay that perfect vision in your mind."

"By making me despise you? You made me stay up nights wondering what I'd done wrong. Christ, I *divorced* you."

Julianne turned to look at him with a soft smile curling her lips. "I tried to push you away, but you still loved me. All this time, that was the one thing I kept hoping would change. I couldn't tell you the truth, so I knew there would always be a barrier between us. I kept hoping you'd move on and find someone who could love you the way you deserved to be loved. The way you loved me."

He shook his head. He didn't want anyone else to love him. All he had ever wanted was for Julianne to love him. And the way she spoke convinced him that she did. Maybe she had all this time, but the secret she kept was too big. It was easier to keep away than be subjected to his constant needling about why she left him. But to push him into another woman's arms *because* she loved him? "I still don't understand what you're thinking sometimes, Jules."

"I know." She patted his knee and stood up. "Let's go home. We have some long conversations to have with the family."

He got up and followed her to the street. She was right. And he had one important conversation with Ken in mind that she wouldn't be expecting.

Twelve

It was over. Good and truly over.

Julianne slipped into her coat and went out onto the porch to gather herself. The last hour had been harder than confessing the truth to Sheriff Duke. Looking her parents in the eye and telling them everything had been excruciating. Not for her, but she hated to burden them with the truth.

They had taken it better than she expected. Ken got quiet and shook his head, but his color was good and he remained stable. When it was over he'd hugged her tighter than he'd ever hugged her in her entire life. Molly cried a lot. Julianne expected that she would continue to for a while. Her mother was a mother hen. Knowing that had happened to her children under her watch would eat at her for a long time. Maybe always. But Julianne assured her that she was okay, it was a long time ago, and it seemed to calm her.

As she stepped onto the gravel lot behind the house, Julianne looked out at the trees. She had loved being out there once but hadn't set foot in the fields in sixteen years. The boogeyman was long gone. Most of her own personal demons had been set loose today. She took a deep breath and headed for the north field. That was where she'd been that day. If she were going to face this, she needed to go there.

It didn't take long to find the spot, but it took a while to walk out there. The trees were different, always changing as they were harvested and replanted. There were no monsters in the trees, no men to chase her, but she could feel the change in the weight on her chest as she got closer. While Wade had hidden the body and Brody took her to shower and change, Heath and Xander had cleaned up the scene. The rock she'd hit him with was flung into the far reaches of the property. The pool of blood was long gone. But when she looked, she could still see it all.

That's when the first snowflake drifted past her face. One flake became ten, became a thousand. In only a few minutes' time, the tree branches were dusted with white and the bloodstain in her mind slowly disappeared beneath a layer of snow.

It was a perfect moment. A pure, white cleansing of her past. She tipped her face up, feeling the tiny prickles of flakes melting on her cheeks, and sucked in a deep, cold breath.

Over.

Julianne turned her back to the scene of her attack, putting it behind her with everything else, and started walking in the opposite direction, through the fields. For the first time since she was thirteen, she could enjoy the moment. The snow was beautiful, drifting slowly down into fluffy clumps on the branches. The flakes were getting fatter, some larger than nickels. They would have several inches sticking before too long.

She climbed up the slope of the back property, looking for her favorite place on the farm. Somehow she expected it to have changed, but when she finally reached it, everything was just as she remembered. There, jutting out of the side of the hill, was a large, flat rock. She had come out here to sit and think when she was younger. The household was always full of kids and this was a place she could be alone.

Julianne dusted off the snow and sat down on the rock, turning to face the slope of the property laid out in front of her. To the left, she could see the roofline and lights of Wade and Tori's house over the hill. In front of her was the whole of the Garden of Eden. Her own little paradise.

It was nearing sunset, but the fat, gray clouds blocked out the color of the sky. The light was fading, but she could still make out the rows of trees stretching in front of her. The big house, with glowing windows and black smoke rising from the chimney, lay beyond it. Then the dark shape of the bunkhouse with Heath's silver Porsche out front.

Heath. Her ex-husband. Julianne sighed and snuggled deeper into her coat. With Sheriff Duke's unexpected arrival, she hadn't had much time to process her new marital status. While they had come clean about Tommy, they had deliberately opted not to tell anyone about the marriage. That was too much for one day. It might not be something they ever needed to tell. What would it matter, really? It only impacted the two of them since they were the only ones aware of it. And since it was done…it would only hurt her family to find out now.

But, like anything else in her life, keeping her feelings inside made it harder to deal with it.

Maybe if she hadn't come back to stay in Cornwall she

would feel differently about her freedom. If she hadn't made love to him. If they hadn't gone to Paris together. If the last month and a half never happened she might feel relieved and ready to move on her with life.

But it *had* happened. She had let herself get closer to Heath than she ever had in the eleven years of their marriage and then it was all done. How was she supposed to just walk away? How was she going to learn to stop loving him? Eleven years apart hadn't done it. Was she doomed to another eleven years of quiet pining for him?

In the gathering darkness, Julianne noticed a dancing light coming up the main tree lane from the house. The snow had let up a little, making it easier to see the figure was walking toward her with a flashlight. She tensed. She was at a tentative truce with the trees, but she wasn't sure if adding another person would work. It didn't feel as secure as being here alone.

Then she made out the distinctive bright blue of the coat and realized it was Heath. She sighed. Why had he followed her out here? She needed some time alone to mourn their relationship and deal with a hellish day.

Heath stopped a few feet short of the rock, not crowding into her space. "Your rock has missed you."

At that Julianne chuckled. Even Heath remembered how much time she had spent sitting in this very spot when they were kids. "Fortunately, time is relative to a rock."

"I still feel bad for it. I know I couldn't go that long without you in my life."

The light atmosphere between then shifted. Her gaze lifted to meet his, her smile fading. "Life doesn't always work out the way you plan. Even for a rock."

"I disagree. Life might throw obstacles in your path, but if you want something with your whole heart and soul, you have to fight for it. Nothing that's easy is worth having and nothing worth having is easy. You, Julianne, have been incredibly difficult."

"I'm going to take that as a compliment."

He smiled. "You should. I meant it as one. You're worth every moment of pain and frustration and confusion I've gone through. And I think, perhaps, that we might have weathered the trials. In every fairy tale, the prince and the maiden have obstacles to triumph over and strengthen their love. I think the evil villain has been defeated. I'm ready for the happy ending."

It sounded good. Really, it did. But so much had happened. Could they really ever get back to a happy ending? "Life isn't a fairy tale, Heath. We're divorced. I've never read a story where the prince and his princess divorce."

"Yeah, but they have angry dragons and evil wizards. I'll take a divorce any day because things can always change. We don't have to stay divorced. We can slay this dragon, if you're willing to face it with me."

She watched as his hand slipped into his coat pocket and retrieved a small box. A jewelry box. Her heart stilled in her chest. What was he doing? They'd been divorced for two days. He wasn't really…he couldn't possibly want this after everything that had happened.

"Heath…" she began.

"Let me say what I need to say," he insisted. "When we were eighteen, we got married for all the wrong reasons. We loved each other but we were young and stupid. We didn't think it through. Life is complicated and we were unprepared for the reality of it. But I also think we got divorced for all the wrong reasons."

Heath crouched down at the foot of the rock, looking up at her. "I love you. I've always loved you. I never imagined my life or my future without you in it. I was hurt that you wouldn't open up to me and I used our divorce to punish you for it. Now, I understand why you held back. And I realized that everything you did that hurt me was also meant to somehow protect me.

"You said at the police station today that I was willing to go to jail for you. And you were right. I was willing to take on years of misery behind bars to protect you. Just as you were willing to give me a divorce and face a future alone in the hopes that I could find someone to make me happy."

"That's not the same," she insisted.

"A self-imposed prison is just as difficult to escape as one of iron and stone, Jules." He held up the box and looked her square in the eye. "Consider this a jailbreak."

"Are you honestly telling me that between Parisian jet lag, getting divorced, getting arrested and spending all day at the police station, you had the time to go to the jeweler and buy an engagement ring?"

"No," he said.

Julianne instantly felt foolish. Had she misinterpreted the whole thing? If there were earrings in that box she would feel like an idiot. "Then what is going on? If you're not proposing, what are you doing?"

"I am proposing. But you asked if I went to a jeweler and I didn't. I went to talk to Ken."

Julianne swallowed hard. "We agreed we weren't going to tell them about us."

"Correction. We agreed not to tell them we were married before. You said nothing about telling him that I was in love with you and wanted his blessing to marry you. No one needs to know it's round two for us."

She winced, torn between her curiosity about what was in the box, her elation about his confession of love and how her daddy had taken the news. "What happened?" she asked.

Heath smiled wide, easing her concerns. "He asked me

what the hell had taken so long. And then he gave me this."
He opened the hinge on the box to reveal the ring inside.

It couldn't be. Julianne's jaw dropped open. The large round diamond, the eight diamonds encircling it, the intricate gold lacework of the dull, worn band… It was her grandmother's wedding ring. She hadn't seen this ring since she was a small child and Nanna was still alive.

Heath pulled the ring from the box and held it up to her. "The last ring I gave you was cheap and ugly. This time, I have enough money to buy you any ring you'd like, but I wanted a ring that meant something. Ken told me that they had been saving this ring in the hopes that one day it would be your engagement ring. He knew how much you loved your nanna and thought this would be perfect. I was inclined to agree.

"Julianne Eden, will you marry me *again*?"

Heath was kneeling in the snow, freezing and holding his breath. Julianne took far too long to answer. Her expression changed faster than he could follow. At first, she'd stared at that ring like he was holding up a severed head. Then her expression softened and she seemed on the verge of tears. After that, she'd gone stony and silent. Waiting more than a beat or two to answer a question like this was really bad form.

"Yes."

And then his heart leapt in his chest. "Yes?"

Julianne smiled, her eyes brimming with tears. "Yes, I will marry you again."

Heath scrambled to slip the ring onto her finger. It flopped around a bit. "I'm sorry it's too big. We'll get it sized down as soon as we can get to a jeweler."

"That's okay. Nanna was Daddy's mother and I take after Mama's side of the family. We're much tinier people." She looked down at the ring and her face was nearly beaming. "I love it. It's more than perfect."

She lunged forward into his arms, knocking him backward into the snow. Before he knew it, he was lying in the cold fluff and Julianne was on top of him, kissing him. Not so bad, after all. He ignored the cold, focusing on the taste of the lips he'd thought he might never kiss again. That was enough to warm his blood and chase off any chill.

Julianne was going to marry him. That just left telling Molly. Even though he now knew that Julianne had never kept their relationship a secret out of embarrassment, the idea shouldn't bother him, but he still felt a nervous tremble in his stomach. A part of him was afraid to say the words. "It's getting dark. Are you ready to head back to the house and tell everyone?"

He expected her to dodge the way she always did, to make some excuse, to say that she wanted to celebrate with just the two of them for now. A part of him would even understand if she wanted to wait until tomorrow after all the drama of the day.

"Absolutely," she said, smiling down at him. "I'm thrilled to give them some good news for a change."

Relief flooded through him, and the last barrier to total bliss was gone. They got up and held hands as they walked back through the trees to the house. When they came in together through the back door, Molly was in the kitchen cooking and Ken was in the living room reading a book.

"Mom, do you have a minute?"

Molly nodded, more focused on the boiling of her potatoes than the clasping of their hands. "Yes, these need to go for a bit longer."

"Come into the living room," Heath said, herding her ahead of them to sit down next to Ken by the fireplace.

Heath and Julianne sat opposite them. He was still holding Julianne's hand for support. She leaned into him, placing her left hand over their clasped ones and inadvertently displaying her ring.

"Mom, Dad..." Heath began.

"What is that?" Molly asked, her eyes glued on Julianne's hand. "Is that an engagement ring? Wait. Is that Nanna's ring?" She turned to Ken with an accusatory glare. "You knew about this and you didn't tell me!"

Ken shrugged. If he got wound up every time Molly did, he would have had twenty heart attacks by now. "He asked for my blessing, so I gave him the ring. That's what you wanted, didn't you? Saving the ring for Jules was your idea."

"Of course it's what I wanted." Molly's emotions seemed to level out as she realized she should be more focused on the fact that Heath and Julianne were engaged. A bright smile lit her face. "My baby is getting married!" She leapt from her chair and gathered Julianne into her arms.

She tugged Heath up from his seat to hug him next. "I didn't even know you two were seeing each other," she scolded. "A heads-up would have been nice before you dropped a marriage bomb on me! Lordy, so much news today. Is there anything else you all need to tell us?"

Heath stiffened in her arms. He was never good at lying to Molly, but Julianne was adamant that their prior marriage stay quiet, no matter what. "Isn't this enough?" he said with a smile.

"Wonderful news," Molly said, her eyes getting misty and far off as her mind drifted. "We'll have the wedding here at the farm," she declared. "It will be beautiful. Everyone in town will want to come. Please don't tell me you want a small affair or destination wedding in Antigua."

Julianne smiled and patted Molly's shoulder. "We'll

have it here, I promise. And it can be as big and fabulous as you can imagine it."

"This time," Heath added, "I think we need to have a grand wedding with the big cake and a swing band."

"This time?" Molly said, her brow furrowed.

Julianne turned to look at him, her green eyes wide with silent condemnation. It wasn't until then that Heath fully realized what he'd said. Damn it. With a shake of her head, Julianne held out her hand, gesturing for him to spill the last of their secrets. They might as well.

"Uh, Mom…" he began. "Julianne and I, uh, eloped when we were eighteen."

Both he and Julianne took a large step backward out of the blast zone. Molly's eyes grew wide, but before she could open her mouth, Ken stood up and clasped her shoulders tightly. It made Heath wonder if it was Ken's subtle restraining of his tiny wife hidden beneath the guise of supportiveness.

Molly's mouth opened, then closed as she took a deep breath to collect her thoughts. "When did this happen?"

"While we were on our European vacation after graduation."

"You two immediately went off to separate schools when you got home," she said with a frown.

"Yeah, we didn't plan that well," Heath admitted. Even if they'd had the perfect honeymoon and had come home blissfully in love they still would have faced the huge obstacles of where they went from there. They were heading to different schools a thousand miles apart. Not exactly the best way to start a marriage, but an ideal way to start a trial separation.

"And how long were you two married? I'm assuming you're divorced now, considering you're engaged again."

This time Heath looked at Julianne. It was her turn to

fess up since they were married that long due to her own procrastination.

"Eleven years. Our divorce was final a couple days ago."

Molly closed her eyes. "I'm not going to ask. I really don't think I want to know. You think you know what's going on in your kids' lives, but you have no clue. You two were married this whole time. Xander and Rose had a baby I never knew about. And to think I believed all of you were too busy with careers and I might never see everyone settled down!"

"We would've told you, Mama, but we pretty much broke up right after we married. We've been separated all this time."

"I think I've had about all the news I can take for one day, good or bad. This calls for a pot of tea, I think. You can let go of me now, Ken." Molly headed for the kitchen, then stopped in the entryway. "I might as well ask…you're not pregnant, are you?"

Julianne shook her head adamantly. "No, Mama. I promise we are not pregnant."

"All right," she said. "You two wash up. It's almost time for supper."

Molly disappeared. Ken clapped Heath on the shoulder as he passed by. In a moment, they were alone with all their secrets out on the table.

"I think it was better this way, don't you?" Heath asked.

"You only think that because you're the one that spilled the beans."

Heath turned to her and pulled Julianne into his arms. "Maybe. But I am happy to start our new life together with no more secrets. Everything is out in the open at last. Right? You've told me all of it?"

Julianne nodded, climbing to her toes to place a kiss on his lips. "Of course, dear."

Heath laughed. "Spoken like a wife filled with secrets she keeps from her husband."

She wrapped her arms around his neck, a naughty grin curling her lips as she looked up at him. "This *is* my second marriage, you'll remember. I'm an old pro at this now."

"Don't think I don't know all your tricks, woman. It's my second marriage, too," Heath noted. "And last."

Julianne smiled. "It better be."

Epilogue

It was a glorious spring day in northwestern Connecticut. The sun was shining on the farm. The delicate centerpieces of roses, hydrangeas, lilies and orchids were warming in the afternoon light, emitting a soft fragrance on the breeze. It was the perfect day for a wedding on the farm; the second in the last six months, with two more on the horizon.

Molly was absolutely beaming. She'd been waiting years to see her children marry and start families of their own. All of them had been more focused on careers than romance, much to her chagrin, but things had turned around and fast. It seemed like each of them had gone from single to engaged in the blink of an eye.

Today was Brody and Samantha's big day. It was the ceremony that she'd lain awake nights worrying she might never see. Molly had always hoped that Brody would find a woman who could look beyond the scars. She couldn't have imagined a more perfect match for him than Sam.

She had thought for certain that Brody and Sam would opt for a wedding in Boston. He'd promised her a huge ceremony with half the eastern seaboard in attendance, but when it came down to it, Sam had wanted something far more intimate at the farm, which thrilled Molly. That didn't mean a simple affair, by any stretch—this was still Sam's wedding they were talking about. Her new daughter-in-law imagined an event that was pink and covered in flowers and Swarovski crystals.

All of "her girls" were so different, and Molly was so pleased to be able to finally say that. She had four daughters now, and each of their weddings would be unique experiences that would keep the farm hopping all year.

When Ken had his heart attack, Wade and Tori had postponed their plans for a fall wedding. Since Brody and Sam were already planning a spring ceremony, they opted to wait until the following autumn and keep with the rustic theme they'd designed. Xander and Rose were marrying over the long Fourth of July weekend in an appropriately patriotic extravaganza.

And as for Heath and Julianne…they hadn't gotten very far into planning their second wedding when it all got chucked out the window. They'd promised Molly a big ceremony, but when they realized they'd come home from Paris with more than just souvenirs, they moved up the timeline.

Molly stepped away from her duties as mother of the groom to search for her daughter in the crowd. Julianne was sitting beneath the shade of the tent, absent-mindedly stroking her round, protruding belly. The delicate pink bridesmaid gown Sam had selected for her daughter to wear did little to hide the fact that she was extremely pregnant. Although Julianne had sworn she had no more secrets, in only two months, Molly would be holding her second grandbaby and she could hardly wait.

Julianne and Heath had had the first of the weddings on the farm—a small family ceremony while everyone was home for Christmas. It was the polar opposite of today's circus. Brody and Sam had a band, dancing, and a catered sit-down meal.

A new song began and Brody led Sam onto the dance floor. They might as well have been the only people here since Brody couldn't take his eyes off of her. His bride was beaming like a ray of sunshine. Her white satin gown was stunning against the golden tan of her skin. The intricate crystal and bead work traveled down the bodice to the mermaid skirt, highlighting every amazing curve of Sam's body. Her veil was long, flowing down her back to pool on the parquet dance floor they set up on the lawn. She was stunning.

Brody, too, was looking handsome. Molly had always thought he was a good-looking boy, but the first round of reconstructive surgery with the specialist had done wonders for his scars. There would be more surgeries in the future, but Molly could already see the dramatic change in the way he carried himself. She'd never seen Brody look happier than he did right now.

It wasn't long before Wade and Tori joined them on the dance floor. Then Xander and Rose. Julianne took a little convincing, but eventually Heath lured her out to dance, completing the wedding party.

The sight of all of them together brought a happy tear to Molly's eye. The last few years had been so hard with nearly losing Ken, the crippling financial burden of his medical bills and dealing with the police investigation. Even when all that was behind them, Molly and Ken had to work through their guilt over what had happened with

Tommy and how their children had suffered silently for all these years. It had been rough, but the Edens were made of stern stuff and they had survived and become stronger for it. The year of weddings at the Garden of Eden was a fresh start for the whole family.

Molly felt a warmth at her back, then the slide of Ken's arms around her waist. He hugged her to his chest, pressing a kiss against her cheek.

"Look at our beautiful family, Mama," he whispered into her ear.

Molly relished the feel of his still strong arms holding her and sighed with contentment. "It's hard to believe there was a time we thought we might not have any children," she said. "And here we are with a full house. And grandbabies."

"It's better than I ever imagined or could even have hoped for. I think the fairy tale I promised you on our wedding day is finally complete."

"Yes," Molly agreed. "We've reached our happily ever after."

* * * * *

REID'S RUNAWAY BRIDE

TRACY MADISON

This story is dedicated to a person who has become very important in my life. Thank you for your kindness, compassion, and seemingly endless support. I am eternally grateful.

Prologue

Less than two hours ago, Daisy Lennox had stood in front of her bedroom windows and breathed in the fragrant scents emanating from her mother's flower garden. The softest of breezes whispered against her cheek with the promise that Steamboat Springs, Colorado, would be blessed with a beautiful spring day. A perfect day, in fact, for a wedding.

For *her* wedding.

She'd closed her eyes and savored the anticipation, as the excitement strummed through her body. By nightfall, she would be Mrs. Reid Foster. It seemed…incredible that this day had finally arrived, that her dreams were so close to becoming reality.

Falling in love with Reid had happened naturally. Effortlessly. He'd been a part of her existence for almost as far back as she could remember, even if it had taken an absurd amount of time for him to view her as anything other than his best friend's little sister.

Once he had, though, neither of them questioned their connection. And when he'd proposed last year, on the evening of her graduation from the University of Colorado, she'd accepted without hesitation. She couldn't imagine her life without him.

With Reid, she felt whole. Reid's love chased off the persistent sensation of not belonging, of not fitting in, of being the odd person out, that she'd battled since childhood.

So, yes. When Daisy had awakened to sunny skies and a warm, fragrant breeze, with hope and delight bubbling in her veins, she had zero reason to believe that anything would—or *could*—interfere with her pure, soul-deep certainty of the future.

Unfortunately, fate had other ideas.

A broken, emotional confession from Daisy's mother had shifted everything she'd ever known to be true into a new reality. This—the story her mother told—was the fodder for bad television, and not the life of a woman who was about to be married.

None of this could be real. Yet…somehow, it was.

Emptiness, engulfing and complete, overtook her prior joy. Her breaths came in jagged gasps and her body shook as she attempted to process the unimaginable.

"I know this is a shock," her mother, Clara Lennox, said. She wrapped her arm over Daisy's shoulder and drew her close. "Are you okay?"

Okay? No, she was most definitely not okay. She pulled free from her mother's grasp, and as if on their own accord, her fingers reached for the wedding gown she'd laid out on her bed that morning. She crumpled the silky fabric in her fist and tried to bring Reid's face, his voice, his very presence, to mind. Tried to sink herself in his love for her, in hers for him.

"That was a silly thing to ask. Of course you're not okay," Clara said. "How could you be? But…do you think, once this settles some, you'll—"

"Settles? I can't imagine any of this settling in the near future." *Or ever.*

"I understand. I'm sorry for this, sorry for…all of it."

Lifting her chin, Daisy looked at her mother. Her pale

blue eyes were puffy from crying. Her fiery red hair—so like Daisy's own—had been nervously tucked behind her ears while she'd slowly, word by word, shredded the strands of Daisy's identity.

On the morning of her wedding.

"Why today? Why not yesterday or six months ago or when I was ten?" Daisy pushed out the questions, still unable to fully comprehend the magnitude of her mother's confession. "Why would you wait until what is supposed to be the happiest day of my life to tell me that…that—" she swallowed the sobs choking her throat "—I'm not the person I thought I was?"

"You are exactly the same person you have always been." Sighing, Clara ran her hands over her face. "But I shouldn't have waited for so long. I should have—"

"No, Mother. You shouldn't have waited until my wedding day to tell me that I'm the product of an affair!" *Selfish.* Wrong to feel this way, perhaps, but this confession and the timing of it came off as selfish to Daisy. What did this do for her now, other than cause inexplicable amounts of pain and confusion? Not one damn thing. "How could you do this to me?"

"I waited too long," her mother repeated. "I didn't mean to, darling. I just couldn't ever seem to find the right words or the right time or…I kept hoping your father would—"

"Which father?" Daisy's anger rolled in, coating the rest of her spinning emotions. "The man who raised me or the man I didn't even know existed until now?"

Clara reeled back, as if Daisy's words held the physical force of a slap. "Charles Lennox. The man who raised you. The man who accepted you when I admitted my… mistake to him."

"He has never accepted me," Daisy whispered. "And now, I know why."

"You're wrong. He loves you."

"Then why isn't he sitting here with us?"

"Because your father...that is, *we* decided this should come from me."

Not a surprise. If there was one aspect of her father's personality that Daisy understood, it was his reluctance to become embroiled in emotional scenes. Even so, she wished her father had chosen to be here, to offer his support, to give his assurances that he loved her, that he considered her his daughter through and through, and that he always had.

More than a want. She *needed* to hear this.

In that moment, though, with the glorious May sun dappling across her bedroom floor, Daisy didn't fool herself into believing she'd ever hear those assurances from Charles Lennox. If he hadn't been able to do so before, he certainly wouldn't today.

She'd always ached to have the close relationship with her father that her older brother, Parker, did. Over the years, she'd convinced herself that her father simply had more in common with his son than he did with his daughter, and that their relationship, while often distant and cool, had absolutely nothing to do with her. Some men, as her mother consistently said, related better with their male offspring. Some men just weren't able to develop a close connection with their daughters. And this belief, as much as it hurt, had also offered relief.

But this new information, the obvious absence of her father, along with the history of their relationship, painted an altered picture. One that stung in deep and intrinsic ways. She was not Charles Lennox's daughter; she was the product of an affair. What could she possibly mean to him, other than providing the visible proof that his wife had cheated?

In heartbreaking clarity, this understanding answered every question she'd ever had. It explained the distance, the awkward hugs and the lack of pride or enthusiasm whenever Daisy accomplished something. More than anything else, though, this knowledge brought an undeniable logic to her father's unwillingness to…love her the way he loved Parker.

Hell, she wasn't sure she could blame him.

"He isn't even in the house right now, is he?" she asked.

"He…thought we should be alone for this conversation." Clara let out a short breath. "But he said he'll return in time for the wedding."

There was more her mother wasn't saying. The truth of that was written all over her expression, in the tight way she held her body, in the subdued manner in which she spoke. And with sudden, sickening insight, Daisy thought she understood what that something was.

"Oh, my God." Nausea lurched in Daisy's stomach. "After twenty-three years of being my father, he doesn't want to walk me down the aisle, does he? That's why he isn't here. That's why you had to tell me today. He insisted, didn't he?"

"He'll change his mind," Clara said quickly, still not looking at Daisy. "I…hope he'll change his mind once he sees that you won't view him differently now that you know."

"He won't change his mind." This knowledge sat inside Daisy with total certainty, and somehow, the realization was more defeating than the rest. "You know it as well as I do."

Clara faced Daisy. "I *know* he loves you."

"I'm not sure I've ever believed that." Squeezing her eyes shut, Daisy attempted to slow her breathing, to quiet the stirred-up emotions. "Who is my father?"

"Charles Lennox," her mother said stubbornly.

"I wish that were the case." Daisy crumpled the silky fabric of her wedding gown tighter and asked again, "Who is my father?"

Releasing a sigh, Clara said, "What do you want to know?"

"Does he know about me?"

"No. It… We didn't have an actual relationship. Like I said, he was someone I dated in college. I…I knew him before I met Charles, and he was just passing through. Your fath—Charles was out of town so often, and your brother was so little. I was lonely, Daisy. And—" a small sob broke through "—I made a mistake."

That last statement carved into Daisy's heart with the force, the sharpness, of a samurai sword. All she heard was that *she* was the mistake. Not the poor choice her mother made in the heat of the moment, not the one-night stand itself, but that Daisy's very existence was some horrible blunder that could never be corrected.

Unaware of her distress—or, perhaps, just too lost in the past—her mother kept talking, repeating much of what she'd already said. This time, though, Daisy listened to every word, every nuance, every hesitation, and as she did, her sense of self—the person she believed herself to be—slowly and painfully disintegrated. None of what her mother shared eased the agony or the chaos or filled the gaps within. She didn't know who she was. Not really.

"Thank you," she said, interrupting her mother in midsentence, having heard enough. "I need to be alone. I need to think. I need to… Just leave for now. Please."

The second that Clara exited the room, Daisy curled up into a ball and allowed her tears free rein. They exploded from deep inside, ravaging through her body with a ferocious intensity. When they stopped, she lay motionless, trying to find meaning in that which held none. Despite how hard she searched, there was nothing to grasp on to for strength, for stability.

Desperate and alone, she thought of Reid and how his love had always given her that strength and stability, a sense of wholeness and security. How just being near him brought all the shady, uneven areas of her life into focus. He made her...real.

And God, she loved him. She did. But the rest of her world had ceased to exist—at least, the world she'd always known, had always believed in—and what remained seemed cloudy and off-balance and without oxygen. She couldn't breathe. Couldn't see the rest of today, let alone tomorrow or the next day or the one after that.

The sudden, frantic need to get away, to find a place she *could* breathe, hit her hard. *No, no, no.* She couldn't do that...couldn't leave Reid and the future she'd craved for so long. How could she do that? He made her real. Who would she be without him?

From the moment they became a couple, she had done everything in her power to show him that she could be exactly the woman he thought she was...the woman he wanted her to be. And unlike with her father, she'd succeeded with Reid. She didn't have to fight so hard to gain his acceptance, his affection or his approval.

Really, all she had done was follow the path he'd created, whatever that path was, whether that meant her—*their*—choice of colleges, the timing of their engagement, their wedding date, even the details of their wedding. Reid made everything, from the smallest hurdle to the largest, easy. He knew what he wanted, and Daisy loved him, so she wanted what he did.

Didn't she? Of course she did. Of course.

Another series of breathless sobs broke free. She wrapped her arms around her legs, pulling them closer to her chest. With Reid, she would always know who she was, where she belonged. She would never have to guess or struggle...or...

Oh, Lord. No. Just...no.

One by one, memories jabbed into her consciousness,

forcing her to confront the impossible. Throughout her life, she had attempted to become the daughter she believed Charles Lennox wanted. She'd formed her decisions, her interests, around him. And she had done so for the specific purpose of creating a loving relationship with her father.

Now she understood why she had continually failed. But with Reid, she hadn't failed. They were to be married that very afternoon. In front of family and friends, but without her father by her side. In a wedding ceremony that Reid had planned from beginning to end, without Daisy uttering one word of complaint or offering her opinion.

She would simply sit back, nod and smile. Happy to do whatever he wanted, however he wanted. Not his fault, she knew, but hers. He was, for all intents and purposes, a force of nature. She had grabbed on to his energy, his strength of will, and let the tide carry her.

By doing so, she had become the woman Reid Foster professed to love, and with that love came definition. An identity. She was *his* girlfriend, *his* fiancée, now…soon, *his* wife. Maybe in a year or two or three, the mother of his children.

Who would she be if she hadn't muted herself for her father, for Reid? Would Reid even love her if she hadn't morphed into the woman she believed he wanted?

An unrelenting pressure stole the air from Daisy's lungs, shuddered through her and stifled her sobs. She didn't know the answer to either of those questions. Didn't know if Reid would still want her, love her, and she couldn't see a version of herself that didn't include Reid.

He makes me real.

But…shouldn't she be real on her own? Shouldn't she know who she was, regardless if Charles Lennox were her father or not? Regardless if she were Reid's wife or not?

Shouldn't she be able to find some type of strength and security and confidence within herself?

The answer was swift and tragic and…honest. *Yes.*

Sitting up, Daisy stared at her wedding gown, unable to believe that she was on the cusp of making such an unbearable, heart-wrenching decision. But she was. She had.

Fresh tears filled her eyes. Oh, God…she had.

She wiped her cheeks, took in a fortifying breath, and the soothing stillness of calm certainty took control. Yes. She had made her decision. There would not be a wedding today.

Daisy reached for the phone, her intent to call Reid and have him come over. So she could explain the horrifying details of what she'd learned, of her decision and the reasons for it, the best she could, face-to-face. He deserved nothing less. She *knew* this.

In the end, she just couldn't do it. Seeing him now, when her emotions were so raw, when she felt lonelier than she ever had in her life, would do her in. She wouldn't cancel the wedding or leave Steamboat Springs. She wouldn't be able to say goodbye.

Reid's commanding presence, his love for her, his absolute surety that they belonged together, would convince her to ignore what her instincts were all but shouting. Far easier and less painful to follow in his wake and become his wife, than to trust her newfound convictions and…leave. Start over. Become real on her own, without her family. Without…Reid.

Even as she wrote the letter, even as she carefully folded the tearstained pages and removed her engagement ring, even as she packed her suitcase, and even as she quietly slipped out of the house she'd grown up in, she kept waiting for something—an inner voice, a sign, *anything*—to change her mind. To stop her from leaving the man she loved.

Nothing did.

Dear Reid,

This morning, my life shattered into a million unrecognizable pieces. As it turns out, my father is not my father, and therefore, he is unwilling to walk me down the aisle. And I don't know if you can understand this, but this information has made me feel lost, without balance, and I need to figure out how to fix this.

I can't believe, even now, that I have made this decision or that it feels so right. But I have, and it does. I'm sorry I don't have the strength or the courage to tell you this in person, but I have to leave. This is about me, not you. I know that sounds clichéd and awful. In this case, though, it's the complete truth.

My love for you hasn't disappeared. I doubt my love for you will ever disappear, and even as I write this, I still want to marry you.... Just not today. Maybe, if fate is on our side and you can find it within yourself to forgive me, we'll have another chance in the future. A second chance at forever.

Someday.

Please, please forgive me.

All my love,
Daisy

Chapter One

Snowflakes, plump as a cherub's cheeks, spewed and spat in the wind-soaked air, where they whirled in a mad, frenetic dance before they dropped to the ground and coated the world—this part of the world, anyway—in a thick, icy canopy of pure white.

Why *wouldn't* Steamboat Springs, Colorado, be in the middle of a roaring winter storm on the night of the runaway bride's return? Nothing else would've made any sense.

Gritting her teeth in concentration, Daisy attempted to see through the blinding snow as she navigated the last several miles to her brother's house. Truth be told, she should've stayed overnight in Grand Junction when she heard the weather report. She hadn't for the simple reason that she'd wanted to complete the last leg of her journey without delay.

She'd left her home in Los Angeles at the crack of dawn, and barring the intermittent stops to walk her dog, had made excellent time. Another four hours of driving—even with a winter storm warning in place—had seemed preferable to putting off the inevitable for another day. So, with the hope that she'd beat the worst of the storm, she'd pushed onward.

Well, four hours had turned into six-plus hours, and if what brewed outside her car wasn't the worst of the storm, then Daisy figured it was soon to come. Her only goal at this point was to be safely ensconced inside Parker's home when that moment arrived.

Sighing, she slid to a halt at a stop sign and tried to set aside the ridiculous notion that this storm was Mother Nature's way of warning her off, of reminding Daisy that she wouldn't be welcomed in her hometown after close to an eight-year absence.

And really, the thought *was* absurd.

It was the end of February, for crying out loud, so snowstorms in Colorado were far from unheard of. They were, in fact, more the norm than not. This bit of logic, however, didn't stop the anxiety from roiling in her stomach. Gripping the steering wheel tighter, she made a careful right-hand turn, just as the GPS instructed. How many folks would even remember her name, let alone her hotfooted retreat from the wedding altar and the man she was supposed to marry?

Couldn't be too many, she assured herself. Out of those who happened to remember both Daisy and the details of that long-ago May morning? The majority of that group would likely be a great deal more curious about her reappearance than they would be unwelcoming.

Unfortunately, she knew what rested at the center of her unease, and it wasn't the weather or the general population of Steamboat Springs. Nope, the reason for her pumped-up nerves and racing heart could be found in one man and one man only: Reid Foster.

The man she'd left behind.

Just the thought of seeing Reid again brought forth a slew of shivers and complicated, complex emotions. They hadn't spoken even once since the day she'd ended their relationship and had discarded their future in favor of a quickly packed suitcase and a bus out of town.

She'd wanted to. Had damn well yearned to speak with him, to fully explain why she'd behaved so cowardly and left him with a letter, instead of an honest conversation. Months had passed before she gathered enough courage to call.

When she finally did, Parker had answered Reid's phone. Unexpected, as Parker had lived in Boston then, but also— due to her brother's friendship with Reid—not terribly surprising. And he'd stated that she'd caused enough damage. That the best thing she could do for everyone was to leave well enough alone and forget about Reid.

If her brother had been unkind, she might not have listened. But in truth, he'd sounded sad and serious, rather than rude and blaming. She heard his deep concern, and in a flood of self-awareness, Daisy had understood—completely—the pain she'd caused.

So, because Parker's stance made sense and the last thing she wanted was to create any additional pain, she chose to live with her guilt and heed his advice. Good advice, as it turned out, since Reid hadn't attempted to contact her in all of these years, either.

But now, by the sole virtue of being back in Steamboat Springs, they'd bump into each other eventually. If not in some strange, random occurrence—such as at the grocery store—then either at the hospital, where Parker was recovering from a serious skiing accident, or at the house, where Daisy would be caring for her two young nieces, Erin and Megan, in the interim.

Regardless of the specifics, Daisy felt sure she'd find Reid in her line of vision sooner rather than later. Fate would demand nothing less. And she couldn't imagine what that scene would look like, sound like, feel like. And that meant she couldn't prepare.

Strange, really, how in some ways, the past eight years seemed as if an entire lifetime had elapsed, but in other ways, those exact same years were no more than a few seconds of a ticking clock. Or, perhaps more accurate in this scenario, a ticking bomb.

Over those years, she'd created a life. Had made friends and figured out how to work for herself, and now made a decent living. She'd even found her biological father, had spent a little time getting to know him, only to realize that he did not hold any answers for her. Only she could provide those. And, for the most part, she had.

She understood who she was. How she needed to live in order to survive, to remain true to herself, and seeing Reid again could potentially undo all of that.

So, yes, a ticking bomb was a fair and accurate comparison.

A strong gust of wind yanked the car to the side, catapulting Daisy to renewed awareness of her surroundings. Muttering a curse, she eased off the gas pedal and breathed in relief when the car returned to the road. None of what might or might not happen in the coming days mattered right now. All that did was getting off the road and to her brother's house.

Parker hadn't phoned her until almost a full week after his accident. Again, not unexpected. Her relationship with her entire family had remained distant and uncomfortable. If anything, she was surprised to be notified at all. By anyone.

But he'd been half-loopy from pain medications, and it had taken a while for Daisy to understand how serious his injuries were. Learning how close he had come to dying scared her, had made her realize how much time they had wasted. She'd already decided to return to her hometown when Parker asked if she would look after his daughters while he recovered.

Her sister-in-law—Parker's wife, Bridget—had died three years earlier from cancer, and Daisy and Parker's parents now lived in Florida. She had no doubt that if Charles Lennox weren't recovering from hip-replacement surgery, it would be her parents caring for the girls. So she supposed she was the obvious choice, but she'd still been surprised by Parker's request.

Naturally, she'd said yes.

But she hadn't considered that she barely knew her nieces, having only met them twice before. Once when Parker had brought his family to California, and then, at his wife's funeral in Boston, where the couple had met and made their home. Just short of a year after becoming a widower, Parker had returned to Steamboat Springs to raise his daughters.

And, other than the customary phone calls on birthdays and holidays, Daisy and Parker rarely spoke. So, no. She didn't know her nieces. She didn't know their likes or dislikes, what made them happy or sad, or any of the other myriad details that made up their lives.

A new rush of fear hit Daisy. How was she supposed to provide the security her nieces were sure to need when she'd spent so little time with them?

One way or another, she'd have to figure it out.

She also hadn't thought about what it would be like to breathe in the same air as Reid Foster, to look into his sinfully dark eyes or to listen to the slow, deep, evocative cadence of his voice again after so freaking long. Any of those occurences might prove to be her undoing.

"Everything will be fine," she said, forcing firmness into her tone. "Parker will make a full recovery. The girls and I will get to know each other. I'm their aunt, so they'll love me. Of course they will! And seeing Reid again won't be easy, but I'll survive."

Her dog, a rescue whippet whose brindle coat held varying shades of white, fawn and gray, whined plaintively from the backseat in a definite plea to get out of the car.

"Soon, Jinx," Daisy said in a soothing voice. "We're almost there."

Due to her shock at Parker's accident and her hurried departure, Daisy had forgotten to mention that she was bringing Jinx with her. Hopefully, neither of the girls was afraid of dogs, because she refused to kennel Jinx for however long her stay might last.

Whippets—a medium-size breed that originated from greyhounds—were intensely devoted to their owners, and since Jinx was a rescue dog, building the trust between them had taken close to six months. Not bringing her along was out of the question.

The GPS announced that Daisy had arrived at her destination. Slowing to a crawl, she located the proper house and parked the car as close to the side of the road as she could. She pulled in a fortifying breath and gave herself a few minutes to gather her bearings while staring at her brother's home. Between the darkness and the blowing snow, she couldn't see much, but the outside light was on, casting a friendly glow. A safe haven.

For now, at least.

Parker had stated that a few of his neighbors were pitching in until Daisy could take over, so she guessed the girls were safely tucked in for the night at one of the other houses dotting the street. She'd see them tomorrow. Her brother had also promised to have someone leave a key under the porch mat, so Daisy would have access to the house. She prayed he hadn't overlooked this not-so-small detail, otherwise, she'd be back on the road, searching for shelter.

"Well, Jinx," she said. "I guess we're here."

And, because there was nothing left to do other than go inside, Daisy leashed and picked up her dog, grabbed her overnight bag—the rest of her luggage could wait until morning—and pushed her way through the whipping snow toward the welcoming light.

"Ready or not," she whispered into the howling wind, "here I come."

Exhaustion, pure and complete, seeped through Reid Foster's body. He leaned against the wall in the Lennoxes' upstairs hallway, let out a bone-weary sigh and hoped the girls were as sound asleep as they'd appeared. The prior week and a half had taught him that one or the other—sometimes both—would fall victim to unquenchable thirst within minutes of their bedroom light going out. Sometimes, they just wanted another hug.

Either way, he figured he'd wait right here for a bit. Just in case.

Erin and Megan were scared, and rightly so. They'd already lost their mother, had already learned that even parents can get hurt, or sick, and go away forever. His heart wouldn't allow him to do anything other than care for them the best he could. Most days, that meant rushing from work to pick them up and bring them home, so they could exist in familiar surroundings, with their toys and their own beds to sleep in.

But Lord, he was tired.

During the winter months, his job as a ski patroller often demanded extended hours filled with physically draining, challenging work. Toss in the care and well-being of two frightened children, along with visiting Parker whenever he could, and Reid was running fairly scarce on energy. Especially tonight.

With forewarning of the storm, which was now raging outside, and completing the necessary preparations, work had started early and ended late. When he'd arrived at the next-door neighbor's house to collect the girls, he noticed they were more high-strung than normal. Soon enough,

Reid discovered that they'd watched some tearjerker of a family movie about several children who were unexpectedly orphaned.

The neighbor had clued in to Reid's disapproval and had apologized, stating she hadn't realized the plot of the movie until the girls were engrossed. At that point, she felt she would've done more damage by not allowing them to finish watching it. Reid didn't know about that, but the next hour of the evening had then been filled with one question after another.

Seven-year-old Erin, the elder of the two, who looked to be growing into a near replica of her aunt Daisy—both in personality and, other than the color of her eyes, appearance—had asked who would take care of her and Megan if their daddy died like their mommy had?

Initially, Reid was at a loss. Honesty, he decided, was the best route, so he'd—once again—explained that all indications stated that Parker was out of danger and on the road to a full recovery. And he was, though from what Reid understood, Parker had another surgery facing him, followed by months of physical therapy.

Five-year-old Megan hadn't said a word, just sat there and watched Reid with her sad, fearful brown eyes. She'd looked so lonely that he'd picked her up and put her on his lap, where she snuggled against his chest and gripped his shirtsleeve as if it were a life preserver.

Refusing to let the rest of her question go, Erin had jutted out her chin—a mannerism that, again, had Daisy written all over it—and asked, "But if something happened to Daddy, who would take care of us? I don't want to be in a f-foster home."

Damn that movie. "Sweet pea, that would never happen," Reid had said, and he'd meant it, but the truth was that he had no idea what Parker's plans were if such a crisis ever occurred. He could, however, guess at the likeliest candidates.

He started with Parker's parents, Charles and Clara Lennox, who had retired to Florida several years earlier, and then moved on to the girls' maternal grandparents, who lived in Boston. While he knew Erin and Megan had a good relationship with both sets of their grandparents, neither answer fully satisfied the elder Lennox daughter.

With a quietly contemplative expression, she'd asked, "What if they can't? Who then?"

Reid had fumbled for a second before naming their aunt Daisy, not fully believing that Parker would trust the care of his daughters to someone who was a virtual stranger, but unable to latch on to another person that would make sense.

Saying Daisy's name aloud—something he rarely did—caused him a fleeting spasm of pain, of loss…a little bewilderment, along with a good, solid dose of anger.

At Daisy, for not giving them a chance before taking off. At himself, too, for keeping silent on the very same news that had sent her running. He should've told her the truth about her paternity when he learned of it, and not decided to wait until after they were married.

Perhaps if he had, she would've leaned on him, trusted in him and their relationship, instead of bolting and never looking back. To this day, she had no idea that he could have saved her from her mother's ill-timed confession. No one, not even Parker, knew about the argument he'd overheard between Clara and Charles Lennox the week before the wedding.

That was a secret he still kept.

So, yeah, he'd kicked himself over his misguided actions. But he couldn't undo them. And Daisy had made the decision to leave him and their future without so much as a conversation. In his estimation, that made both of them wrong and neither of them blameless.

But Reid was a practical man, and as the years had piled up on one another, he'd learned to keep the past where it belonged. Mostly, this mindset had proven successful.

Mostly wasn't always, though, so mentioning Daisy as a possible guardian for the girls evoked the same mixed bag of reactions he'd become resigned to dealing with. As usual—at least for the last long while—those feelings dissipated as abruptly as they'd appeared, and Reid had returned his focus to the little girl on his lap and the one standing directly in front of him.

"Listen to me, angel," he'd said, purposely speaking in a slow and authoritative voice. "I will never let you live in a foster home. I will always be here for you and your sister."

Erin's pinched expression softened slightly. "Do you promise?"

"I promise."

That had done the trick, and shortly, the three were crowded around the tiny table in the girls' bedroom, having a tea party with their favorite stuffed animals. After which, he'd prepared dinner, and the rest of the evening had flown by with various activities. The highlight, of course, was speaking with their father, and the promise that they should be able to visit him soon.

Baths and tickling and bedtime stories—three of them—followed. Both girls had seemingly drifted off toward the end of the last, and Reid had tucked them in, kissed them on their cheeks and gone into the hallway to stand guard.

Deciding enough time had passed to believe they were good and truly out, Reid pushed himself off the wall and yawned. He'd straighten the kitchen, since he hadn't after dinner, shower and see if he could stay awake long enough to catch the news. Or…hell, maybe he'd skip all of it and just hit the sack, try to get up early enough to—

Muffled sounds that couldn't be what he thought drifted up the stairs from the living room. A barking dog? *In* the house? Had one of the girls turned on the television when he hadn't noticed? Had to be that, because he remembered locking the front door. Still, he took the stairs two at a time, and when he reached the landing, every damn hair on his arms stood up straight.

He didn't need to take another step to recognize the low, sultry voice emanating from around the corner. It didn't matter how many years had passed, that voice had been branded into his brain for all eternity. Without a doubt, Daisy Lennox—the woman he'd once envisioned spending the rest of his life with—had come home.

Dumbfounded, Reid froze and…just listened. She crooned to what he assumed was the dog he'd heard, saying something about kibble and a fresh bowl of water. One by one, each of his senses went on high alert, and his earlier mixed bag of emotions returned with a bang.

Part of him wanted to walk into the living room, pull her into his arms and take up where they'd left off—no questions asked. The other part wanted to go upstairs and hightail it out of a bedroom window, just so he'd never again have to look her in the eyes.

The first idea was foolhardy and beyond ludicrous. The second was gutless and as impossible as the first. Even if behaving cowardly were in Reid's DNA, he wouldn't sneak off while the girls were sleeping. He wouldn't disappear on them, now or ever. With or without a letter.

To Reid's way of thinking, that left him with a solitary option: man up and announce his presence, remain polite and calmly let Daisy know—since he had to assume her arrival was due to learning of Parker's accident—that he had everything under control.

Shouldn't take much to get her to leave, and this time, he'd be relieved—hell, happy—to send her on her way. Right. She'd be gone within two days. Certainly no more than three.

He could keep the peace for three days, couldn't he? Yup, that he could. Decision made, Reid relaxed his features into an emotionless mask and forced his leaden legs to carry him forward. As he walked, he focused on three words: *calm, polite* and *detached.*

Of course, those three words evaporated the second he rounded the corner into the archway that separated the house's entrance from the living room, the second his eyes settled on the woman he'd never been able to forget. She was still beautiful. Still…Daisy.

Seeing him, she gasped, but didn't speak. Neither did he.

At some juncture, she'd cut her long, coppery red hair into a short, wispy style that pulled attention to her arresting green-blue eyes and the delicate angles of her face. She was dressed inappropriately for February in Colorado, wearing a lightweight jacket over what appeared to be a summery dress and a pair of…clogs? Yeah, clogs. The woman was insane.

But achingly familiar. The Daisy he'd fallen for had lived in her own head, her own secret world, and had rarely taken notice of anything as practical as the weather. It seemed that some things, regardless of time, hadn't changed.

Reid's breath locked in his lungs as the past crept up and swarmed him with memories. In a split second, he was reliving the worst moment of his life, the moment he'd read that damn letter of hers and the sickening, unbelievable realization that she'd left. The anger, the sadness, the self-recriminations and wondering if he had behaved differently, if she would have, as well.

All of it was there, fresh and alive and…potent. The years spanning those many yesterdays with today vanished, and Reid forgot about remaining polite, calm and detached.

"Hello, darlin'," he drawled, ignoring the crazy rat-a-tat beat of his heart. "By my calculations, you're…oh, about seven years and nine months late for our wedding."

Chapter Two

"I can do better." Daisy kept her voice smooth and without inflection. Fate, it seemed, had decided not to waste a second in putting Reid Foster in her line of vision. "Seven years, nine months and four days. I can probably figure out the hours and minutes, if you'd like."

"Nah." Leveraging his right shoulder against the inner-archway wall, Reid angled his arms across his chest in a laid-back, nonchalant manner. Irritating that he seemed so at ease when Daisy had yet to catch her breath. "The broad strokes are more than sufficient."

Her brain tried to process a reply, but failed. How in heaven's name was she supposed to have a conversation with this man at this moment? Impossible. She couldn't think.

Somewhat regrettably, she also couldn't stop staring.

Naturally, he looked good. She wouldn't have expected anything less. He wore dark denim and a thick flannel shirt in shades of soft greens and dark blues. He had the same coal-black hair cropped close to his head, the same strong, lithely muscular form and the same ingrained power that all but sprang from every pore of his body.

The same Reid. Yet…not exactly. There was an aura of

toughness—a hardness, she supposed—that hadn't existed in *her* Reid. Had she done that to him? Maybe. Probably.

Guilt layered in, joining the already complex synthesis of her emotions, tying her tongue into knots and making her wish—desperately—that she'd stayed overnight in Grand Junction.

"I…um…didn't expect to find anyone here." One memory after another clicked into being. *Breathe. All I have to do is breathe.* "I expected the girls to be at a neighbor's house."

"They're at the neighbor's when I'm working," Reid said, maintaining his casual persona, as if seeing her again held zero effect. Lucky him. "Otherwise, they're with me."

Of course. Why hadn't she considered that Reid would be helping with Erin and Megan? She should have. He remained close friends with Daisy's brother, and the Reid she remembered had always been there for the people he cared about.

"That's…nice of you," she said, infusing brightness into her tone. "I'm here now to take up the slack. Exhausted after the long drive, but here."

An indefinable emotion darkened Reid's gaze. He appraised her quietly, his body tense, his jaw hard. "So… you're here to take up the slack, are you?"

"That's right." Reid continued to stare at her in that silent, steady way of his. To combat the silence and the stare, she pushed out the first words that entered her head. "How's life been treating you? I mean…um…are you doing well?"

"Oh, I'm friggin' fantastic," Reid muttered. "Life's a dream."

"That's really great to hear, and—"

"What about you, Daisy? How have you been since I saw you last…when was that, exactly?" Pausing, as if in deep reflection, Reid suddenly smiled and winked. "I got it. The last time I saw you was at our rehearsal dinner, correct? The night before you took off."

There it was, out in the open. "Yes, that would be correct," she said, matching his sarcasm, note for note. "I've been wonderful! Thanks so much for asking."

Heavy silence hung between them, layering the air with unsaid words and questions. All of which had to do with their past, with the decision Daisy had made on that long-ago day. And okay, she owed Reid what she hadn't been able to give him then, but having that particular discussion now seemed inappropriate and rushed and…far too painful.

Right or wrong, fair or unfair, she just wasn't ready.

Thankfully, Jinx decided the quiet was her opportunity to make herself known. She whined and tugged at the leash. While she only stood about twenty inches tall and weighed twenty-four pounds, she could be quite determined when she set her mind to it.

Relieved to have a millisecond to reel in her shock, Daisy unhooked the leash from the dog's collar. "There you go, sweets," she said to Jinx. "Explore to your heart's content."

Without delay, Jinx began to sniff the hardwood floor and whatever objects she came across. Daisy watched for a few minutes, using the break to gather her strength, her balance. And while she watched, she took in her surroundings.

Awash in vivid colors, the living room held a bright red sofa that stretched in front of a bay window, on which were a plethora of handicrafts likely created by her nieces. Next to the couch sat a sunny yellow chair that was large enough to hold two adults—or, Daisy imagined, a father and his young daughters—and had more in common with a puffy cloud than an actual piece of furniture. She could live in a chair like that.

Rounding out the room was a television, a pair of squat bookshelves filled with an array of children's books and a square, low-to-the-ground coffee table that was perfect for game nights, crafts or eating a meal while watching a favorite TV show or movie.

A comfortable place, filled with energy and life. Daisy could easily envision two little girls playing and laughing and growing up here. Somehow, that thought boosted her resolve.

She was here for a reason. A reason that had zip to do with Reid Foster.

And right now, even standing in the same room with him had annihilated her equilibrium. Therefore, her first order of business was claiming her brother's home as her territory.

Before she could proceed, Jinx's low, rumbling growl met Daisy's ears. A quick bolt of untimely humor cut into her anxiety. Biting the inside of her lip to stop the grin from emerging, she stood and pivoted so that she faced Reid. Yep, just as she'd thought.

Jinx's teeth were embedded in the cuff of Reid's jeans and, with her body buckled in concentration, her dog was valiantly attempting to tug him to the door and out of the house. While whippets were highly energetic dogs, most tended to be quiet with sweet and loving temperaments. When it came to men, however, Jinx defied the typical.

She flat-out disliked men. *All* men.

The rescue service through which Daisy had adopted Jinx hadn't been able to provide a specific reason as to why, though they had warned Daisy of the oddity early on in the process. Even after months of becoming acquainted with her few male friends, Jinx hadn't warmed up in the slightest. So, no, Daisy wasn't surprised by Jinx's behavior.

She was, however, highly amused by the dog's timing.

"Jinx!" Daisy said, hiding her laughter. "Stop beating up on the poor man."

The dog didn't hesitate. If anything, her tugging grew more exuberant, more purposeful. Enough so, that Reid had to give up his kicked-back pose in order to sustain his balance.

Standing straight, he glanced from Jinx to Daisy. "Dare I ask?"

"Don't take it personally," Daisy said, biting her lip harder. "She isn't a fan of men. And while she's very well-behaved in other areas, she…tends to ignore me when a man is around."

"You have a man-hating dog?" Reid gently jiggled his leg in a failed attempt to unhinge Jinx's teeth. "Did she come that way or did you train her?"

"Trained her, of course," Daisy said with a straight face. "After all, a single woman living in L.A. has to have some type of defense in today's world."

Reid's lips quirked in the beginnings of a smile, causing the rigid line of his jaw to relax a miniscule amount. Maybe Jinx had broken the ice. It was a nice, if overly hopeful, thought.

"I don't know," he said. "If protection was your goal, you might have considered choosing a larger, more menacing breed of dog."

"Oh, she does the job well enough. She has you good and cornered, doesn't she?"

"I'm humoring her," Reid said, his tone sandpaper-dry. "Until she loses interest."

"She's stubborn on this account."

"I'm fairly sure I can outwait a dog."

"You can try, but as long as you're here, she won't stop." Deciding to make her stance clear before the energy in the room shifted again, Daisy pulled every ounce of her strength to the surface and said, "Just be careful when you leave that you don't let Jinx out. She runs like the wind, and I don't relish the idea of chasing her down in this snow."

"Good to know." Reid shook his leg harder. All that did

was compel Jinx to grab on tighter, growl louder and pull with increased force. "But I'm not going anywhere."

"Um…of course you are," Daisy said firmly. "You're going home."

Dark, molasses-hued eyes met hers in a silent challenge. "Why would I do that?"

"Simple. I'm here now."

He looked at her with incredulity. Maybe with the slightest touch of annoyance, as well. "This isn't that simple, Daisy. Not by any stretch of the imagination."

"I disagree." On the basics, anyway, if not the complete picture. "The girls don't need two caregivers, and since I'm here, there isn't any reason for you to stay."

"There are plenty of reasons," he countered, his voice growing cooler with each syllable. "I've been here the entire time. You have not. The girls know me. They do not know you. Add in the difficulty of what they're going through, how scared they are about their father, and the last thing they need is for anything else to change in their worlds."

Valid points, all of them. And damn it, she even agreed with his take. Because no, she didn't want to upset her nieces or add yet another degree of turmoil into their lives. But she absolutely didn't want Reid here mucking with her emotions.

"I admit I haven't spent much time with Erin and Megan, but we talk on the phone every now and again, and I send them gifts throughout the year," Daisy said, forcing authority into her voice, her demeanor. "I am not a stranger to them."

"Not being a stranger is a hell of a lot different than knowing someone enough to feel comfortable or safe." Reid swore again, this time under his breath. Whether at the still frantic Jinx or at Daisy's statement, she couldn't speculate. Probably both. "And let's face the facts here. You don't know them any better than they know you."

Hurt by his words, by the truth of them, Daisy removed her wet coat and kicked off her shoes. No, she didn't know her nieces, and she hated that it had taken something as horrible as her brother's accident to propel her to change the status quo. But she was here now.

"That doesn't mean we won't get to know each other, or that they won't eventually become comfortable. I'm their family, Reid."

"Family? Depends on your definition. Mine has to do with being present, available, for the people you love." Reid gave his leg another jerk, this one somewhat stronger than the last. Jinx, bless her heart, held on tight. "I'm not entirely sure my definition applies here."

Wow. Just…wow. The need to offer a defense came on strong, but why bother? Yes, she'd kept her distance from her family, but Parker and her parents had done the same with her. The culpability—in this regard, anyway—did not wholly rest on her shoulders. More to the point, she didn't owe Reid any explanations on this aspect of her life. Not a one.

"Seeing how I'm standing in my brother's home right this very instant, I'm fairly sure your definition does apply," she said, managing to hold her temper in check. "I don't know what your expectations are, but—"

"My expectations," Reid said, slowing his words to a crawl, "are that you'll visit with your brother, assure yourself of his health and future prognosis, spend a little time with your nieces and go back home. That will take two, maybe three days. Four on the outside."

"Hold on here. Are you asking me to leave?" Daisy took one step forward, stopped and planted her hands on her hips. "Or are you *ordering* me to leave?"

"Neither." His shoulders tensed in frustration. "And my goal isn't to sound rude, but no one here is counting on you, Daisy. There isn't any need for *you* to hang around."

Ouch. "Guess what, Reid? You don't get to shoo me off as if I'm some pesky bug." Sudden moisture dotted her eyes, threatening tears. "And in case you're wondering, Parker asked me to come, so I'd say *he* is counting on me."

"Parker—" Shaking his head in disbelief, Reid said, "I can't fathom a reasonable scenario where your brother would ask for your help. He knows I have everything under control."

"Of course you have everything under control, that's your mantra, isn't it?" *Whoa.* Unfair in this circumstance. Unfair, Daisy admitted, in *any* circumstance. Reid—his current level of rudeness notwithstanding—had never pushed for control, he'd just…stepped into the role with ease. "That was uncalled for and I apologize. But this is not about us."

"Nope, this isn't about us." Reid gave Jinx—who hadn't yet relented in her growl-and-tug approach—an exasperated, are-you-kidding-me-just-stop-already sort of scowl. "This is about Erin and Megan and what is best for them."

"Which is what I just said!"

"Not really, no." Now his eyes were flat, almost…cold. "You state that I should leave, without asking one question about the well-being of your nieces. What's going on with them, how they're doing, if there is anything you should know before you give their primary caregiver a boot out the door. Tell me, how is any of that what's best for Erin and Megan?"

"I'm their aunt, whether you like that fact or not." She counted to three, then to five. Unfortunately, her frustration didn't subside. It grew larger. "Parker asked for my help," she repeated. "I'm here for my brother and my nieces, and I don't want—"

"Put yourself in their place, if you can," he said, interrupting Daisy. "Try to imagine how they would feel to wake up in the morning and find you here and me gone.

Without any warning or explanation." Reid snapped his fingers. "Just gone."

She stifled a gasp as Reid's full inference hit home. He wasn't only speaking of Erin and Megan's feelings, but a reflection of his own from when he read her goodbye letter. Traversing that pothole-ridden road now wouldn't solve anything, though. Not when their emotions, their shock at seeing one another again, remained so high.

Better, easier, to focus on the issue of who would stay to watch the girls and who would leave. And, at the end of the day, only one person had the authority to send Daisy packing. That person, no matter how much he might wish it to be so, was not Reid.

Lifting her chin, she said, "I'm not going anywhere. I'm staying for the duration, however long that might last. Unless Parker says different."

"Is that so?"

"That's so." She raised her chin another notch. "You'll have to find a way to deal with my being here, because that is not changing. I'm taking over the girls' care from here on out."

"Oh, I can deal. But, sweetheart—" Jinx's antics finally proved too much. Bending at the waist, Reid disengaged the dog from his jeans, swept her into his arms and muttered, "Behave." To Daisy, he said, "You are not taking over and I am most certainly not leaving."

"We both can't stay. That would mean…"

"That's right. As of now, we're living together." Reid's long legs ate up the space between them in mere seconds. Passing Jinx from his arms into hers, he said, "This will be cozy, don't you think? Why, we'll almost be like one big, happy family."

Oh, hell, no. "You're crazy. That won't work."

"Trust me, I'm not overly fond of the idea, but there isn't another viable option."

"You leave. I stay. There, problem solved."

"Sure. If you can answer three questions about Erin and Megan, I'll pack up and leave tonight. We'll even start with a simple one," he said. "What are their favorite colors?"

Ten…twenty…thirty seconds ticked by. Pink? Probably for one of them, if not both. Purple, maybe. But she didn't want to guess. She wanted to *know*.

Swallowing, she gave a short nod of concession. "Point made. But I don't see how this… We can't just…" Daisy searched for another solution. Just one. And came up lacking. "Supposing I agree, how long will this living-together thing last?"

"No clue. Later, once the three of you are better acquainted, we can reassess. For now, as much as I hate to admit it—" he looked upward, as if praying for divine intervention "—we're in this together. Lock, stock and barrel."

Damn it. Damn *him*. He was right.

Here she was, almost eight years later, being pulled along by the force of Reid Foster. She had no defense against his bulletproof logic. Nothing she could do or say to get out of this ridiculous situation. Other than turn around and get back in her car and return home.

And she couldn't—wouldn't—do that. "Fine," she said stiffly. "We can discuss the details tomorrow. I'm exhausted. Is there a guest room I can use?"

Her agreement eased the lines of tension creasing Reid's forehead. Stroking his jaw as if in thought, he said, "Good question. There are only two bedrooms. The girls share one, and the other is Parker's. I've been bunking there. And I'd be happy to sleep on the sofa, but…"

"But…?"

"The girls sometimes drift in at night if they've had a bad dream, or if they wake in the morning before I do. If you're there instead of me, they won't know what to think."

His words were reasonable, as was typical. But something about the way he spoke sent a trickle of awareness down the nape of Daisy's neck. It might have been the deepening of his tone or the slowing of his cadence or even the close proximity of his body to hers, but all at once, the air around them became charged. Not with shock or anger or unsaid questions. With…heat.

"I'm happy to take the sofa," she said quickly, before he could start the game she was sure he was set on embarking. "That isn't a problem."

"Yup, that's a possibility." With another wink, this one far more devilish than sardonic, he stepped closer. "Or… we could bunk together. Just to sleep, you understand."

Oh, she understood. She wondered, briefly, what his reaction would be if she called him on his…offer. Hmm. Maybe she should. If he wanted to play with fire, why not hand him the match? "You know, that's a great option. As long as you're certain it won't be too awkward."

"What's awkward about sleeping?" he asked in apparent innocence. "That is, if we're still talking about *only* sleeping?"

"We are." Narrowing the space between them by another inch, so they were only separated by the dog she held, and were close enough to—potentially, of course—kiss, she said, "The thing is, I've recently developed this small… idiosyncrasy, I'd guess you'd call it, and I'd hate for you to get the wrong impression."

Interest, amusement and, unless she missed her guess, desire flickered over him in varying degrees of intensity. "Keep talking," he said. "I can't wait to hear this."

"It's just that I find clothing so…restrictive." Fluttering her lashes, Daisy dropped her voice to a near whisper and looked him straight in those sexy-as-hell eyes of his. "I can't seem to sleep if I have anything at all covering me. So as long as you're okay with—"

Reid blinked once. Twice. "You sleep in the…?"

"Every single night." He seemed unable to talk, so being the kind and sensitive soul she was, she helped him out. "I think the sofa will be perfect. Don't you?"

"Right. The sofa."

"Though I could use a pillow and a few blankets."

"Right," Reid repeated. "I…ah…can get those for you."

"Thank you," she said in her best sweet-as-pie voice. "I would appreciate that."

He stayed put and continued to appraise her, his eyes slowly narrowing in contemplation. "Nice one, Daisy," he said after an abbreviated pause. "You almost had me."

Without uttering another syllable, Reid strode from the room. Daisy waited a full minute before collapsing on the sofa, before allowing the trembles to ripple along her skin and overtake her body. Her throat tightened and her stomach swam. How would she survive this?

She'd won this round due purely to surprise. That wouldn't happen again. If there were a next time, Reid would be fully prepared to call her on her bluff.

"I'm in trouble, Jinx," she whispered. Her dog's ears perked at the sound of her name and she butted her nose against Daisy's hand, begging for attention. Complying, Daisy stroked Jinx's head. "And not just your average type of trouble, either."

Nope. What she had was the cataclysmic, in-over-her-head, lucky-to-walk-away-in-one-piece type of trouble. And every speck of that trouble began and ended with Reid Foster.

The man she'd spent years trying to forget. The man who, despite her belief to the contrary, still claimed some part of her heart, her soul. She couldn't let him in again. Couldn't yield so much as an ounce of what she'd worked so hard to achieve, to become.

So, yeah. Trouble. In every which way that Daisy could see.

Chapter Three

Far too early the next morning, Reid rolled over and stared at the clock, trying to decide if there were any point in attempting to get a little more shut-eye. He should. The day ahead promised to be challenging on myriad fronts, but he doubted he'd have any more luck in turning off his brain now than he had throughout the long, long night.

A certain flame-haired woman had occupied his thoughts, along with vivid—and unwanted—images of her asleep on the living room sofa in nothing but her birthday suit. He knew better, of course. Her parting shot, while an excellent and creative maneuver in putting an end to the juvenile game he'd stupidly started, was entirely false. This knowledge, however, hadn't stopped the images of a naked, prone Daisy from interfering with his ability to sleep.

He remembered her body with full and absolute clarity.

Reid groaned and punched his pillow. Why the hell had he stated they would live together? There were other options. Namely, he could have continued to be a presence in the girls' daily lives without the added difficulty of sleeping here. Easy enough to stop in after work, spend some time with Erin and Megan and return to his house when the girls were tucked into bed for the night. *That* would've been the sane option.

But no. The words *as of now, we're living together* had flown from his mouth, and once they had, he'd obstinately stuck to his guns. And even now, after a full night of considering the insanity of coexisting with Daisy, he wouldn't back out. The lines had been drawn.

He'd have to be careful, though. Within minutes of her arrival, he'd realized that whatever immunity he'd developed in regard to Daisy had weakened. She still held power over him. This concerned him. Unfortunately, it also fascinated him.

If she managed to squirrel in past his remaining defenses—if he made the almighty mistake of loving her again—he wasn't confident he'd recover when she left. The first go-round had nearly destroyed him. It had taken far too many months to locate the smallest, most fragile foothold in which to begin building the rest of his life on.

The idea of having to rebuild that foothold from scratch petrified him to the bone.

Frustrated with his seeming inability to push Daisy out of his mind for more than a few minutes, Reid chose to focus on the practicalities of what needed to occur. Due to the weather, he had—at minimum—an unexpected morning off.

Since the prior night's storm hadn't abated, and the high-velocity winds combined with the unrelenting snowfall had resulted in blizzard conditions, the mountain passes were closed. Later, once the weather calmed some, he and his fellow ski patrollers would sweep the mountain to determine the level of damage and where avalanche-control measures were required.

For now, though, he was relieved to have some additional personal time in which to help the girls grow more comfortable with their aunt. Also, he needed to apprise

Daisy of Erin and Megan's schedule and a few of their individual quirks.

Every now and again, Megan would decide she'd only wear clothes and eat foods of a certain color. Reid hadn't yet determined a reason for this behavior, but a few days ago she'd chosen blue. Most of her menu had revolved around blueberries.

Perhaps not the most balanced diet, but for one day, it had worked well enough.

And Erin, ever since her mother's death, often required something to hug whenever she was emotional or sitting for an extended length of time. A pillow or a stuffed animal or, once or twice, her backpack or her coat. Typically, this was handled without too much of a problem.

But if such an item wasn't close at hand at the wrong moment, she'd become fretful. To combat this, Reid unobtrusively ascertained that a stuffed animal was always nearby.

Major obstacles? No. But Daisy needed to be made aware of them, nonetheless.

Reid pushed out a long breath and tried to relax his muscles. If he fell asleep right this instant, he'd get an hour before the girls woke and the day began. Using a centering technique, he envisioned being on top of the mountain in perfect ski weather. The sun shone, the sky held the color of a robin's egg and the powder was…glorious.

In his head, he inhaled a lungful of cold, fresh air, felt the bite of the wind against his cheek and prepped his body for takeoff. He was a few short seconds from the push and the exhilarating ride down when the scene blinked out and Daisy appeared.

A naked and prone Daisy, on the sofa downstairs. The deep red hue of her hair in stark contrast with the pale warmth of her skin. Her blue-green eyes—filled with desire and love, need and longing—were directed at him. And a soft, seductive smile played upon her lips.

God. That look—that smile—had always done a number on him.

Forcing his eyes open, he gave up on the idea of sleep. His agenda now consisted of a cold shower and a pot of hot, strong coffee. Then he'd get started on breakfast and hope that today was one of Megan's "rainbow" days, which basically meant zero color preferences.

After that...well, he'd figure out the rest as needed.

Reid made the bed and grabbed a selection of clean clothes, including a pair of heavy work jeans and a thick forest-green cable-knit sweater, and headed for the upstairs bathroom. He'd no more than entered the hallway when a blur of color sped toward him with a...well, he didn't quite know what to call this particular canine noise.

Not a growl or a howl. Not really a bark, either. *Yip* was too small of a word, and didn't come close to the note of exuberant challenge erupting from the animal's throat.

"Really?" he said when Jinx collided with his ankles. Bare ankles, at that, since he wore a pair of boxer shorts. "This is the way it's going to be, huh? Every time you see me?"

The dog growled in reply and latched on to his left ankle in a surprisingly gentle grasp, as if searching for the pant leg she knew should be there. She didn't hurt him, didn't come close to actually biting, just grumbled and huffed with a few light gnaws tossed in for good measure.

More amused than annoyed, he let this go on for a good thirty seconds or so before deciding enough was enough. Walking carefully, to avoid squashing the crazy dog, he made his way down the hallway until he reached the bathroom.

"That's it," Reid said, as he turned on the light and put

his clothes on the counter. "The end of the road. Go find a ball or, I don't know, something to sniff."

Not to be deterred, Jinx trailed into the bathroom with him, darting around his legs as he moved and bounding toward his ankles whenever possible. If it weren't for the incessant growling, he'd think the beast just wanted to play.

"Listen up," he said, feeling somewhat idiotic for trying to reason with a dog. "I really hope it's only men you don't like, because two little girls live in this house. If you're this ornery around them, your visit will be awfully short."

Since Jinx seemed unimpressed by this morsel of logic, Reid guided the dog to the hallway using his ankles as bait. She was quicker than he was, though, and managed to squeeze back into the room the second he started closing the door.

Obviously, another tactic was called for.

Shaking his head, he picked up the dog. Jinx wiggled in his grasp and began growling in an elongated manner that damn near sounded as if she were trying to form the necessary words to talk to him. Ludicrous thought. He blamed his lack of sleep.

He hefted the dog up, so they were eye to eye. "Pay attention, pooch. We can do this the easy way and become friends or you can remain miserable for however long you're here. I guarantee you a happier visit if we're friends. A visit that might just include table scraps and belly rubs. Your choice. Friends or miserable living companions? Let me know."

And if a dog's eyes could narrow in deliberation, Reid would've sworn Jinx's did. Nonsensical, of course, but hell…that was what it looked like.

"That's right, you consider that." Petting the dog, he moved into the hallway and halfway down the stairs, where he put her down. "Find something to do. Or…I know, why don't you wake up Daisy and tell her to make breakfast. And coffee. Strong coffee."

He then retraced his steps without looking over his shoulder.

Thirty minutes later, showered and dressed but no more comfortable with his new living arrangements, he cautiously peered into the hallway. No sight or sound of Jinx.

Hell, if he could get a man-hating, irrational pooch to leave him alone, then he could certainly handle being around Daisy without repeating old patterns. Yesterday had been a shock to the system, that was all. Of course he'd reacted strongly.

Today was a different matter. She wouldn't be able to get to him on the same level that she had last night. Besides which, his memories were of a woman—no more than a girl, really—who likely no longer existed. He'd changed in the past eight years. Surely, she had, as well.

The tight, suffocating pressure encasing his chest lightened. Perhaps he should view this…madness as a blessing in disguise. He and Daisy could finally have the conversation they should have had years earlier. She could fully answer his questions and…well, ask her own once he confessed that he'd known the truth about her paternity before reading her letter.

He'd tell her all of it. The overheard argument. His decision to keep what he'd learned to himself until after their wedding. How his past self couldn't bear to see her hurt, couldn't allow her to go through even a second of what that knowledge would do to her in the days before they were to be married. How he'd wanted that moment of their lives to remain unmarred and whole.

Good enough reasons, Reid supposed, for keeping such a secret. But well-meaning didn't equate to what was right or just or honorable. And hell, he hadn't saved her from a damn thing.

She'd likely be spitting mad by his admittance. That was fine. Due and deserved, even. And he had his own brew to get off of his chest, over the way she'd ended their relationship and had just…walked into the sunset. *Without him.* Yeah. He had a lot to say on that front.

A difficult conversation for both of them, no doubt. But…restorative, too? Should be.

Confidence settled in, replacing every other sentiment he'd warred with throughout the night. His defenses were solid. His heart was safe.

His immunity, thank the Lord, remained intact.

Reid held this belief, this confidence, for the length of time it took to reach the kitchen from the upstairs hallway. She was there, dressed in an oversize purple flannel shirt worn as a nightgown, her elbows planted on the counter and her chin in her hands, while she stared at the slowly brewing coffeepot. And he was…mesmerized.

A simple scene. Nothing overtly sexy or out-of-the-ordinary about it. But his heart seemed to stop beating. His lungs seemed to stop taking in air. Every last muscle seemed to lose the ability to move. He was, for the next several seconds, frozen in time. Nothing but a statue, really—gifted with sight, thought and emotion.

In a rush of sensation, of raw awareness, his body started functioning again. His prior arguments fell away. They were meaningless and false. Nothing more than the desperate ramblings of a man who recognized he was a goner but wasn't prepared for surrender.

But now, Reid understood that a choice had never really existed. Without any further hesitation or the slightest whisper of doubt, he surrendered. And he knew that he would do whatever it took, whatever was in his power, to make certain that he saw this scene—Daisy, soft and rumpled from sleep—every morning for the rest of his life.

Well, hell.

Reid shook his head and swallowed a silent groan. Nope, he didn't have to worry about falling in love with Daisy again. That would be impossible.

He'd never stopped loving her to begin with.

There were men who could enter a room, not say a word, not do anything but stand in stillness, and every other person in that space would pause, turn and look. Reid Foster was such a man. He'd always had this quality, this…charismatic, magnetic aura, even as a boy.

So, despite her tiredness or the fact that she faced the opposite direction, Daisy sensed Reid's presence the instant he entered the kitchen. She didn't move or greet him or show any sign that she knew he stood behind her. Rather, she just waited.

For the coffee, which she desperately needed. For him, to set the tone, the cadence, of how they were going to start the day. In polite resignation or veiled hostility? With sexual innuendo or calm solidarity? She hoped for the solidarity. That somehow they would find a way to cross the minefield to band together, for the sake of Parker and her nieces, and become a…team.

But she wasn't holding her breath.

"Darlin', you must be a psychic. Or a genie," Reid said, his voice rich and warm and holding the tiniest thread of amusement. The warmth got to her the most, brought to mind all of those yesteryears she'd spent the entirety of the night trying to forget. "If any man on the face of God's green earth could use a cup of coffee right about now, that man would be me."

"Sorry. Not a psychic or a genie," Daisy replied, keeping her tone casual, confused by his. His warmth, his friendliness, his outward acceptance of her bore no resemblance to the man from last night. The question was…why? "Jinx tattled on you. Mentioned you were on the owly side, in need of sustenance and caffeine."

In truth, she'd been on her way to the kitchen when she overheard Reid's conversation with her dog. And she'd had to cover her mouth to stop from laughing out loud.

"That's…ah, rather perplexing," Reid said after a moment's hesitation.

"Which part?"

"All of it." Before she could blink, he was standing next to her, reaching into the cupboard for a couple of coffee mugs. "To start, I have no idea what *owly* means. To finish…your *dog* mentioned I wanted coffee and food? How does that work, exactly?"

"Owly means cranky." She shivered and wrapped her arms around herself, so Reid would think the reaction was due to being cold and not his close proximity. Too bad she couldn't fool herself. "And yes, Jinx and I have a method of communicating that defies logic."

"Uh-huh. Then why does she still hate men?" He looked around the room. "Where is she, anyway? Hiding out somewhere, ready to attack?"

"Nope. She's sleeping in the living room. Seems her quick sojourn outside this morning wore her out." Or maybe Jinx's feisty altercation with the man of the house had done that. Daisy could recall a few altercations—on the pleasant side of the equation—with Reid that had left her exhausted. "As to the other? I told you. I trained her to be that way."

"Right," he said matter-of-factly. "To protect you from the unwanted attention of men, I take it? Since you're a single woman living in L.A."

"Well, you know, can't be too careful." *Come on, coffee,* Daisy thought, staring at the ridiculously slow drip, drip, drip of the machine. She needed the distraction as much, if not more, as she needed the caffeine. "What about you?

Do you have a woman-hating dog waiting in the wings, to protect you from the unwanted attention of females?"

"Nah." Reid gave her a lazy, sexy sort of smile. She felt that smile all the way to her toes. Not good. Not good at all. "Haven't found the need."

"Gotcha." He hadn't found the need because he wanted female attention or...? Striking out that thought—fast— Daisy put a few inches of space between her and Reid. Just to simplify the mechanics of breathing. "Um. So, when do the girls usually wake up? Breakfast will be done soon. Baked French toast. Cinnamon. I hope they like cinnamon."

"Should be any minute. In fact—" Reid inhaled, as if drawing in strength "—we should probably have a quick discussion on how to handle their questions."

"Sure," she said, content to move into safer territory. "Shouldn't be too difficult. I'm their aunt, here to stay with them while their father recovers. But you'll still be here, so their schedules won't change too much in that regard." While this conversation didn't seem to be heading into the same danger zone as last night, she had every intention of standing her ground. "That is what we decided, right? Unless you've changed your mind about staying here?"

"Nope, can't say that I have." Reid grabbed the coffeepot and filled his mug and then hers. "But I thought we'd have some time while the girls were in school to talk things over. School's canceled for the day, though, so—"

"There's no school today?" a soft, tentative voice said from the other side of the kitchen. "And you're my aunt Daisy? Really and truly?"

"Hey there, peanut," Reid said. "And the answer is yes, to both of your questions."

Turning, Daisy took a good, long look at her younger niece, Megan. And her heart melted into a big, wet puddle. Megan's doe-brown eyes and fine light blond hair reminded Daisy of the girls' mother. Sweet and fragile and innocent beyond words.

"Morning, Megan," she said brightly. "And yes, I'm your aunt Daisy."

"I don't remember you." Then, shyly dropping her gaze, Megan said, "But I sleep with the doll you gave me for Christmas almost every night. I named her Holly."

"Holly is a wonderful name, and I'm happy you like her so much." Crossing the room, Daisy kneeled in front of the little girl and resisted the almost overwhelming desire to pull her close for a hug. "It's okay that you don't remember me. You were only two the last time I saw you. But I'm glad we can be together now, and I promise we'll have lots of fun."

Long lashes blinked. Ever so slowly, Megan raised her chin until her eyes met Daisy's. A small, hesitant smile appeared. "I like fun. Erin does, too." And then, as if worried that Daisy might not know—or remember—who Erin was, she said, "Erin is my sister. She's seven. I'm five. And she has hair that looks like yours."

"Does she?" Daisy knew this, of course, as Parker sent a photo of the girls with his Christmas card each year. "The red hair comes from your grandmother. My—and your daddy's—mom. Just like your beautiful blond hair comes from—"

Uh-oh. Was it taboo to mention Bridget? She glanced toward Reid, hoping he'd give her some type of a signal, but his attention was focused on Megan.

"My mommy," Megan elaborated, her voice carrying a note of pride. Sadness, too, but that was natural. "I…I don't remember her much. But Daddy says that all the time about my hair."

Daisy's throat closed in emotion. "Yes, that's what I was going to say. That you remind me of your mother," she said gently. "Ready for breakfast?"

Before Megan could reply, Reid—who had quietly watched their exchange while sipping his coffee—asked, "Is this a color day, peanut?"

A curious question. Just one more to ask later. And, not that she'd admit this, but her few seconds of talking with Megan had made it all-too-obvious how badly Daisy required Reid's input. She was even…grateful for any help he was willing to give. Now, more than ever, it seemed essential that she didn't screw this up.

Megan wrinkled her nose in thought before giving her head a decisive shake no.

"Well, then. A rainbow day it is," Reid said easily. "Why don't you run upstairs and get your sister while your aunt and I serve breakfast?"

"Okay." Megan started to reach for Daisy and then stopped, as if unsure. Daisy opened her arms and waited, sensing the decision needed to remain in Megan's hands. One second passed. Two seconds. Three… And then, all at once, the little girl pushed herself forward and hugged her tight. "I'm glad you're here," she whispered before letting go.

"I'm glad I'm here, too." After Megan dashed out of the kitchen in search of her sister, Daisy said, "That went better than I expected. She's a sweet little thing, isn't she?"

"Yup, she is." Reid began setting the table. Taking his lead, Daisy removed the baking dish of French toast from the oven. A few minutes of not-too-awkward silence ensued. Once he'd poured the orange juice, he said, "You were good with her, Daisy. And…well, I've reached a decision I feel is only fair to share with you."

"Um. Thank you." An unexplainable shiver of apprehension and foreboding brought a coating of goose bumps to Daisy's arms. "What decision might that be?"

"Well, it's like this," Reid said in a slow and purposeful cadence. "I walked in here this morning all set to make the best of this situation, and there you were, hunkered over the coffeepot in that flannel getup you're wearing. And I was smacked with a…profound realization."

Heat, instant and intense, appeared dead-center in her stomach. "Profound?"

"Significantly so." Facing her, Reid gently tipped her chin so that she had no choice but to look into his eyes. "To me, anyway."

Trouble. "Are we speaking of the coffee?" she asked, going for brevity. "Because while I agree that the first cup in the morning is important, to call it profound is—"

"No, honey. Not the coffee." While he spoke, he traced her lips with his fingers as if he'd done so every day for years on end, eliciting another series of shivers. From the touch itself, yes, but also from the waves of desire traveling through. "This is about us, Daisy. You and I."

She tried to think. Lord, did she try. "Our past? We can have that conversation. I mean, now probably isn't the best time, with the girls and breakfast and—"

"We will. But no, this isn't the right time." His voice held assurance. Confidence. "I'm speaking of now, not our past. And, sweetheart, you should know that in my opinion we—meaning you and I—are not done."

"Is this another game?" Swallowing, hard, she pulled herself free. "If so, I'm not interested in games, Reid. I told you last night that I'm here for Parker and my nieces, not to…not for any other reason."

"I'm not playing a game."

"Then what is this about?" Her heart hammered against her breastbone and her mouth went dry. "Because if you're alluding to—"

"Now see, that is exactly what I'm not doing." An easy, carefree grin lit his countenance. All innocence and charm. "My goal here is to be very clear about my intentions."

"And those intentions are…what?"

"The same as they were seven years and nine months ago." Determination firmed his jaw, straightened the line of his mouth. "If you recall, you mentioned in your good-bye letter—you know the one, from our wedding day?—that you still wanted to marry me, just not on *that* day."

Where could he possibly be going with this? "I thought we established that this wasn't the proper time to have this conversation. But yes, I…wrote something along those lines."

"Good, glad you remember." He leaned against the counter in a too-casual-to-be-truly-casual pose. "You also stated that you hoped—if fate was on our side—we might have a second chance at forever," he said, his tone quiet. Focused. "Do you recall those sentiments, as well?"

"Um…I…yes, but—" Syllable by syllable, his words crashed into her brain with the force of an out-of-control semitruck. "Why are you asking these questions?"

"Because what that letter boils down to is a contract. At the very least, a promise from you to me." Satisfaction and pleasure whooshed into his expression, his eyes, his very being. "You owe me a wedding, Daisy. And I plan to collect."

"Wh-what?" Huh-uh. Impossible. She'd heard him wrong. "I owe you what?"

"A wedding, Daisy. *Our* wedding."

"Is this a joke?" she asked, finding her voice. "Has to be a joke, right? Because no man anywhere would decide to marry a woman he hasn't seen for *eight* years."

Not to mention, marrying the woman who'd left him standing at the altar.

"Oh, I'm not joking." Reid pushed himself off the counter and strode to the large calendar hanging on the opposite wall. "How does April sound to you?" he asked, flipping the pages as he spoke. "Though, Cole and Rachel's wedding is the nineteenth. Is March too soon? Probably. I'd like Parker to be there. I suppose we could shoot for May again, but—"

"Payback? Is this a form of retribution?" When he didn't respond, when he did nothing but stare at her in a mix of pleasure and confidence, her knees wobbled enough that she had to move to one of the kitchen chairs to sit down. "What's the punch line, Reid?"

"Love," he said simply.

"Do you realize how insane you sound?"

"Marriage."

"Delusional, too. And there isn't any way I'm buying in to—"

"Maybe even a few children down the road." He let go of the calendar and took the chair next to Daisy. "I've always thought three kids was a nice, round number. What do you think?"

Love. Marriage. Children. Everything she'd once wanted with this man. Everything she'd once ran away from. Everything she'd long since decided wasn't for her.

"You can't really expect me to believe that you're serious. And…and this isn't funny," she said, speaking slowly and clearly. In order to get through that megathick skull of his. "You're joking. Or playing a game. Or you're out for revenge. Or—"

"None of the above," Reid said firmly. "I'm not only serious about this, Daisy, I'm committed. Guess I'll be working on proving that to you."

She had more to say. Much, much more, but the sounds of two little girls running down the stairs made any further discussion impossible. He was joking. He *had* to be joking.

But what if…what if he wasn't?

Chapter Four

The loss of Reid's sanity didn't feel as frightening as he would have expected. Odd, perhaps, but his sudden decision to pursue Daisy seemed almost inescapable. Pre-ordained by fate, even. *That* was the instinct he'd fought against all night.

Of course, he hadn't planned on stating his intentions quite so explicitly. Rather, he thought he'd announce his interest and his desire to get to know her again, and then go about the business of courting her. But in the blink of an eye, the details of her letter had appeared in his mind. *She* had declared it doubtful that her love for him would disappear.

She had written her hope that they'd have another chance. Those were her words, not his.

So, no, the idea of planning a wedding hadn't occurred to him until that second. But damn, he sort of liked the idea. Insane? Oh, hell yeah. High-risk? Yup, that, too. She could very well shoot him down from now until the actual wedding date and return to her life in California without so much as a glance over her shoulder. Or, he supposed, with or without a letter of goodbye. And hell, that would be rough, going through that mess all over again.

Truth was, though, he'd rather give this crazy idea everything he had and hope for a superior outcome than not try at all. Hope offered possibilities.

He wanted those possibilities. Because, whether he'd realized it until now or not, his gut told him they belonged together. And what better way to proceed than with purpose and intent?

Daisy wouldn't stick around forever. And, unless this aspect of her personality had changed, she didn't pay much attention to the subtle. A wedding, though? Nothing subtle about a wedding. That would grab and hold her notice—it already had—and while they were dancing around that topic, he'd begin tackling the obstacles, one by one, they'd need to confront.

And, if he had his say, move beyond.

Swallowing another gulp of coffee, Reid leaned back in his chair at the kitchen table and winked at Daisy, who was in the middle of a conversation with the girls.

She faltered, narrowed her eyes slightly, regained her focus and said, "Since there isn't any school today, I thought we could play a few games. How does that sound?"

Megan nodded enthusiastically but didn't try to talk through her chewing. Erin, on the other hand, shook her head and frowned. "I don't want to play a game."

"That's okay," Daisy said without pause. "We can do something else. Maybe…draw pictures for your dad? Or some get-well cards?"

"He likes our pictures and cards," Megan said. "He says we're artists."

"No. We colored pictures and cards for Daddy yesterday." Erin stabbed her fork into a bite-size square of her French toast. Glancing at Reid, she said, "Didn't we?"

"We did, but I'm sure your father would love more," Reid said, surprised by Erin's quick opposition to Daisy's suggestions. "Is there something else you'd like to do today, monkey?"

"Build a snowman," she said instantly. "With *you*."

Meaning, he guessed, not with Daisy. Hmm. "Well," he said, trying to figure out the reason for the child's negativity. Erin didn't easily warm up to new folks, so he'd expected some shyness on her part. But he hadn't seen this coming. "It's a little too wild out there for building snowmen right now. Probably best if we focus on indoor ideas."

"You can read us a book," Erin said, without looking at Daisy. "Or…or—"

"But I want to play with Aunt Daisy!" Megan said. "And books are for bedtime."

"Not always," Daisy said, her voice warm and relaxed. "Books are good for anytime you want to read—or hear— a story. So, Reid can read to Erin, and you and I—" Daisy pointed to Megan "—can do something else. Games or coloring or whatever you want."

"No!" Erin's mouth formed into a pout. "We always play together."

"That isn't true," Megan said. "So don't say it is!"

"Almost always, so it is true!" Erin vaulted from her chair. "I'm older and Daddy isn't here and I'm in charge. R-Reid is going to tell us a story and *she* can do something else!"

"Whoa, now," Reid interjected, taken aback by Erin's vehemence. Even so, he kept his tone calm, modulated. "First off, kiddo, you don't get to dictate what Megan does, and I think you know that." He waited for Erin to nod. When she did, he added, "Okay, good. Also, there isn't any call to be rude. Please apologize."

"Sorry, Megan," Erin said quietly.

"Okay," Megan said. "Just don't say stuff that isn't true."

"But we almost always—"

"Girls, let's not start a new argument when we're in the

middle of making up." Reid paused and looked at Erin. "Is there something you'd like to say to your aunt now?"

"Not really," Erin said, sounding far more like a teenager than a seven-year-old girl. "I just don't want to play with her today."

"You know that isn't what I meant," Reid said. "Please apologize to your aunt."

"Reid," Daisy said quickly. "She doesn't have to—"

"Yes, she does. Parker might not be here at the moment, but his rules still hold," Reid said, attempting to achieve the right balance of maintaining boundaries and showing compassion. "You tell me, Erin. What would your dad say if he was here right now?"

Erin's chin quivered. "That it is okay to show how we feel but it isn't okay to be rude or...or hurtful to other people."

"Yup, that's right," Reid said. "And what do you think he would want you to do?"

Blinking rapidly, as if to stop herself from crying, Erin looked from Reid to Daisy and then at the floor. "I'm s-sorry for being rude."

"It's really okay, Erin. This is new and sudden," Daisy said softly, looking as if she might burst into tears herself. "Thank you for the apology. And...I hope we can spend some time together later. If you want to, that is."

Shrugging, Erin spun on her heel and just about flew from the kitchen. Megan dropped her fork on her plate and started to stand, her intent to follow her sister fairly obvious. She hesitated and glanced at Reid with questions in her eyes.

He nodded and she took off. Sighing, Reid raked his fingers over his short hair. He wanted to sit down with Erin right now and reassure her that everything was going to be fine. But she needed to calm down some before she'd be willing to share whatever was bothering her.

So he'd wait. Not too long, though.

"She isn't normally like that, Daisy," he said. "I'll go talk with her in a few minutes, see if I can work out what the issue is." Daisy nodded and busied herself with clearing the dishes from the table. "She'll adjust, I'm sure. Just give her a little time."

"I hope so, and I will," Daisy said. "I…I almost see myself when I look at Erin."

"Not surprised. You resemble one another."

"The hair, yes. But she has her mother's eyes, like her sister, and the narrow Lennox nose." Now at the sink, Daisy began rinsing off the breakfast dishes. "If it wasn't for our red hair, I'm not sure anyone would see a physical resemblance. There was just something about the way she looked at me that seemed familiar."

"It's more than the color of your hair." Surprised that Daisy hadn't yet lit into him over his wedding proclamation, Reid gathered the drinking glasses and considered how to proceed. Go full bore or take a slower, gentler approach? "You share similar mannerisms and a propensity toward separating yourself from most other folks."

Daisy gave him a sidelong glance that suggested she was rearing up to clock him on the jaw. "Are you insinuating that my niece and I are self-absorbed?"

"Maybe. But only in the best possible light."

"Not quite sure how you can get 'best possible light' out of self-absorbed."

"Perhaps 'choosy' is a better description," he said, joining her at the sink. She continued to rinse and, as she did, he loaded the dishwasher. "Nothing wrong with that."

And there wasn't. Daisy tended to keep others at a distance until she determined if they could be trusted with her thoughts, dreams…that inner world of hers. Erin was the same. Most folks were to a certain extent, but some were more cautious, more particular, in who they let in.

"Honestly, I think she took one look at me and decided she doesn't like me." Pain and sorrow deepened the blue in Daisy's eyes. "I should've tried harder before."

"She hasn't decided anything as of yet." Reid didn't comment on the rest. There wasn't any reason to rub additional salt into the wound. He'd done a good enough job of that last night. "And you're here now. It isn't too late to build a connection."

"Maybe, but it seems I have my work cut out for me." Sidestepping him, she wiped off the table and resituated the chairs. When she finished, she faced him and arched an eyebrow. "And just to avoid any confusion, I want to be absolutely clear that I'm not going to allow you to indulge in some stupid game. I do not owe you a wedding. End of discussion."

Well, then. Full bore it was. "I believe I was already clear when I said that you did. And this discussion is far from over."

"Stop." Narrowed eyes met his. With a stubborn lift of her chin, she took one long step toward him. "This wedding talk of yours is nonsense. As I just said, I have my work cut out for me. I do not have time to deal with…with whatever you're trying to prove."

"We both have a lot of work in front of us," he said. "Planning our last wedding took close to a year, so supposing we settle on May, we still only have a couple of months." Unable to stop himself, he grinned. "March or April will leave us with even less time."

"There is nothing to plan!" Now the green in her eyes took precedence over the blue. From anger, no doubt, but desire had always had the same effect. "You are not due a wedding."

"We'll have to agree to disagree. A contract was made, a promise was implied." Shrugging, he said, "And, Daisy, you reneged on both."

"Is this because you want to *talk* about what I did? If so, just say that! We can talk. Right now, for however long you'd like. Otherwise, you need to…cease and desist."

"Sorry." He whisked his thumb along the soft curve of her cheek, her skin warming beneath his touch. "That's the one thing I cannot do."

"Assuming we went by your incredibly flawed logic," she said, flicking his hand off her face, "I still wouldn't owe you a damn thing. I returned the ring, which then signified the end of the so-called contract and my implied promise. Even if I hadn't, even if your argument held any weight whatsoever, the statute of limitations would have long since expired."

"Ah, well, I don't believe there is any such thing as a statute of limitation for affairs of the heart. Love, in my book, is one of those forever types of deals." Pushing his fingers into her hair, he gently tipped her head back. "Want to know what I'm thinking about right this instant?"

Her tongue darted out to lick her lips. A little move that just about killed him right then and there. "Oh, I don't know," she said. "That you should call a therapist?"

"For premarital counseling?"

"To have your head examined!"

"I'm compelled to kiss you," he said, allowing her the opportunity to shove him away. Slap him. Kick him. Or… agree to be kissed. "If you stay this close, I won't be able to resist."

"Why do you want to kiss me?" Neither her voice nor her gaze wavered, but the green in her eyes darkened another delicious degree. Anger or desire? "And why now?"

"I can't remember a time I haven't wanted to kiss you," he said, speaking the truth that was, depending on the day, a blessing or a curse. "As to why? Because you make me love you, Daisy. You always have, and I suspect you always will. I'm done trying to escape the inescapable."

"Sweet talk will get you nowhere. Other than proving you've lost your mind."

"I'm not arguing that possibility at all."

"Finally, we agree on something!" she said, yanking herself backward. "What is this really about? You couldn't wait to get me out of here last night, and now…now—"

"Kiss me, Daisy."

A pale pink flush stole over her cheeks. "You want a kiss?"

"That I do."

She stared at him. He stared right back, intrigued by where this exchange might lead, by the woman herself. This Daisy wasn't the exact same Daisy he remembered, and that was good—he wasn't the same, either. Not being able to predict what she might say or do held enormous appeal. More so than he would've thought.

"I'll kiss you," she said. "But only if you promise not to move. Not even an inch."

Okay, that seemed interesting. "Sure," he said. "I promise not to move."

Standing on her tiptoes, she brushed her lips along his jaw. Her touch was slow and seductive, potent and powerful. So much so, he had to use every ounce of his resolve to stand still, to let Daisy take control of…whatever happened next.

The warmth of her breath licked against his skin and a groan of pleasure, anticipation, caught in his throat. Her breasts were tight against his chest, her hands rested on his upper arms, and the softness—the light, flowery scent—of her hair tickled and teased his senses. His entire body resonated with awareness as her mouth skimmed the lines of his face, moving from his jaw to his cheek to his ear, before returning to his jaw to restart the journey.

Every second, every glide of her lips, every area their bodies met, was absolute torture. Absolute perfection. *Yes.*

This woman belonged with him, he with her, and nothing could alter that basic fact. Reid would, if necessary, drag the moon from the sky and wrap it in a solid gold, diamond-studded bow to convince her of this belief.

Daisy exhaled a breath and pushed away, putting far too much room in between them. Wiping her mouth with the palm of her hand, she said, "There. You got your kiss. Several of them, in fact. Can we end this ludicrous game now?"

"Again…this is not a game. Look," he said, carefully choosing his words, "I hadn't planned on this. When I found you in the living room with that crazy dog of yours, I wanted to feel nothing. I wanted to be able to send you on your way and get on with my life."

"And that reaction is totally logical. I understand why you might prefer my absence over my presence. I…I get that." She squeezed her eyes shut, pursed her lips and blew out a breath. "But if you're not playing some twisted game meant to shove me out the door, then I can't make any sense of your change in behavior or your sudden insistence to…to…"

"Marry you?"

"Y-yes."

"It's simple." Metaphorically, he reached for the moon and yanked it into his grasp. God help him, he really was going to risk it all. "I thought I had gotten you out of my system, that I was long over you. But the truth is, I love you, Daisy. Then and now. Still and forever."

Gasping, she shook her head in a physical rejection of his claim. Okay, not what a man wanted to see when he declared his love for a woman, but he figured she had the right to her shock and denial. He hadn't gotten over his own shock as of yet.

"I… You don't love me, Reid."

"But I do."

"You can't." Her already pale skin whitened a shade.

Maybe two shades. "You don't know who I am. You didn't know me before, either. You couldn't when…when I didn't even know myself. I'm not sure you loved me then, so to say that you love me now isn't…plausible."

"That's close to what I thought earlier, and if I were standing in your shoes, I'd feel the same." He wasn't an idiot. He knew he sounded as if he were off his rocker. How to explain what he didn't fully understand himself? He just…*knew.* "I might not know how you spend your Friday nights or if you still curse when you drive, but, Daisy…I know *you.*"

"You…you're caught up in the past or something. That's all this is." Dipping her chin, she focused on the tile floor. "I remember the way we were, and seeing you again has been intense. For both of us. So I think you're…stuck in what you—we—once wanted."

She could be right, he supposed, but he wasn't convinced. His intuition had swung into high gear, and he'd learned to listen when that happened. Doing so had saved his hide—and had helped him save other people's hides—on more than one occasion. Often in the middle of treacherous, life-or-death scenarios on the mountain.

Not everyone formed decisions the way that Reid and his family did. The Fosters trusted their guts, paid attention to their hearts, and would just as soon take the proverbial leap off a cliff based solely on these convictions. They did not sit idly by and do nothing.

Reid had sat idly by, though.

Seven years and nine months ago, he'd ignored his gut and had let Daisy go without a fight. Out of guilt and anger for his own poor, albeit well-meaning, actions. Out of pride. Out of his frustration and devastation over her departure and lack of trust in him…in them. Nope, he hadn't listened to his instincts then, but he damn well would now.

"I'm sorry you don't yet believe me, but I'm certain of

what I want. I won't be giving up, and I won't be walking away. Which means," he said, purposely drawing out the words, the moment, "I'm going to move forward and plan our wedding."

"Insane," she muttered. "Completely, unbelievably nuts."

"Possibly," he said. "But that doesn't alter my intent."

"Are you going to haul me to the church, whether I agree or not?" The bite was back in her voice, her demeanor, and energy snapped in the air between them. "Or do I have an actual say in this demented plan of yours?"

"Whether you show up or not is completely up to you, as it should be," he said, choosing to let the demented comment slide. "And naturally, you have a say in our wedding plans. I'm flexible on the details, darlin', so whatever you want will likely be fine with me."

"Flexible on the details? Whatever I want, huh?"

"We can run off to Vegas, if you'd like."

Irritation, irrefutable and complete, cascaded over her features. With a glare so heated it could melt every inch of snow currently covering the ground, she said, "Go for it, Reid. Spend your time, waste your money and plan a freaking wedding. But understand this—you can perfect every last detail, but you'll still be missing a bride!"

That, Reid knew, was the risk. Masking his concern, he went with a laid-back, no-big-deal sort of shrug. "Got it. Completely understood. I just happen to think you'll change your mind."

"Wow. Are you really that sure of yourself?"

"Sure enough." Reid removed the calendar from the wall and, like he had earlier, flipped through the pages. "Now, the only question I have is…what date—if you *were* to show up—works well for you? Or should I go ahead and choose the wedding date on my own?"

"You can't be—" She yanked the calendar from his grasp. A quick flip brought her to the month of May. "If you insist on continuing with this lunacy, let's dive head-first into the crazy pool, shall we? I choose May sixth."

May sixth. Their original wedding date. "Romantic notion."

"Isn't it, though?" She threw the calendar in the air toward him. He caught it, searched for and found the applicable month. With a slight toss of her head, she said, "There's a full-circle appeal, don't you think? Two weddings, same date, no bride at either one."

"Or you could marry me and we could be happy for the rest of our lives," he said, staring at the calendar. "Possible dilemma, though. May sixth falls on a Tuesday this year. Do you think that will present an issue for our guests?"

Tap, tap, tap went her foot. "I think 'our' guests will have a lot more to gossip about than having to attend a farce of a wedding on a Tuesday."

"Hmm." He pretended to mull over the idea. "Actually, this is supposed to be our special day, correct? If your heart is set on the sixth, we'll make it work."

"Reid," she said in utter calmness.

"Yes, honey?"

"Don't do this. Why complicate an already complicated situation?"

"Don't do…oh. You've already changed your mind about the date?" He scratched his jaw, feigning innocence. "That was fast. Still feeling May, or are you thinking a different month altogether? I hear June is one of the most popular months for weddings."

"You're…incorrigible and…and—" Snapping her mouth shut, she gave him a final withering glare and stalked from the kitchen. A few minutes later, he heard the slam of the downstairs bathroom door and, a few minutes after that, the rush of water through the pipes.

Whistling, Reid rehung the calendar on the wall. Most folks might consider what had just occurred as a dozen check marks on the con side of a pro-and-con list. But despite Daisy's aggravation, he felt lighter, more hopeful and content than he had in years.

Yup, she'd blustered and put up a fuss—who wouldn't?—and had, perhaps rightly so in this matter, decreed him a lunatic. What she hadn't done was outright say she no longer loved him. And that…well, he was about as sure as he could be that Daisy would not have hidden or veiled such a sentiment if she already knew her feelings.

Hope existed. For now, that was more than enough to keep Reid centered. After all, where hope lived, any damn thing on the face of the earth could happen. Even a wedding ceremony that the bride-to-be hadn't yet agreed to attend.

She had, though, set the date.

So May sixth it was. Perhaps this time, Reid wouldn't stand alone at the altar…waiting for a woman who never appeared.

Oh…just oh! How could she have forgotten about this side of Reid's temperament? She'd rarely argued with him in the past, but the very few times she had always resulted in Reid getting exactly what he wanted. Because she'd give in. Every single time.

But not on this.

Daisy dug out her hair dryer and plugged it into the wall socket in the bathroom. Really, who did he think he was, commandeering a wedding without her approval—without so much as a proposal!—and stating his love for her hadn't died? Then and now, he'd said. Still and forever.

Well. Okay. She couldn't deny the sweetness of that part of this entire fiasco. Couldn't deny the warm glow those words had given her. But, sweet or not, that didn't mean she'd bought in to any of his…ramblings. She hadn't. She wouldn't. She… Damn it, why was he doing this?

Powering on the hair dryer, Daisy bent her head and tried

to let go of the twist of anxiety tightening her stomach. If he weren't engaged in some form of payback, if this truly did not fall into the "game" category—and she no longer thought he was or that it did—then what was he up to? She just didn't know, and frankly, didn't want to waste any additional energy figuring it out.

There were other areas that required her attention. The areas that had brought her here in the first place. And she couldn't allow Reid—or anything to do with Reid—to cloud that purpose.

Okay, then. She couldn't control his actions, but she could control her *reactions.* No matter what he decided to do in regard to this ridiculous wedding of his, she'd maintain her distance, remain calm and wait for him to come to his senses.

He would. He *had* to. Because if he didn't, if he continued on in the manner he had this morning, she might begin to believe. In him. In his words. In…all of it.

And that could not, under any circumstances, happen.

As luck would have it, Daisy had her own mixture of confusion and memories creating havoc with her head, resurrecting all of those feelings she once had—and those that still existed—in her heart. Unlike Reid, though, after a full sleepless night of intense contemplation, she'd convinced herself that the rush of emotion, the strength of her attraction toward him, rested in the history they shared. None of it had to do with today.

Or so she hoped, because she did not do well with romantic entanglements.

She'd had a few relationships over the years, and each of them had ended in the same disastrous way. No, she'd never fallen for another man with the depth she'd once loved Reid, but she had cared for other men. Romantically. And with that care came her strong, strong desire to make them happy. To put their needs above her own.

Not such a bad thing, she supposed. Successful, loving relationships demanded give-and-take. For Daisy, though, she…lost herself in the giving, in the trying to be whatever she thought the other person wanted or needed her to be. Until she all but forgot who *she* was.

Easy to understand that this mentality came from her childhood, from all of her attempts to gain her father's love and appreciation. Comprehension, however, did not solve the issue.

So, several years ago now, she'd stopped dating. Entirely.

Without thought, she touched her fingers to her lips, recalling the flurry of small, light kisses she'd bestowed on Reid, the incredibly strong desire for their bodies to meld together in the way that they used to…for the completeness of being with Reid. A wholeness that held great appeal but had likely been false, based on *her* inabilities, *her* insecurities.

No. She wouldn't fall down that rabbit hole. Couldn't. *Memories* had induced her desire. *Memories* were to blame. Historical data that her body had pushed to the surface due to the intense force of being home, of seeing and dealing with Reid.

In a week or two, the turbulence would settle, their emotions would recalibrate into something less extreme and all of this crazy talk would end. Neither one of them would be worse for the wear, and she'd return to her life in California without any regrets. Old or new.

All she had to do until then was draw an impassable line in the sand and keep to her side. Well, that and let him do whatever he was going to do on his side…without reacting. As long as she didn't start to believe in his madness, she'd get through just fine.

A gurgle of choked laughter escaped from her throat. What in the hell was he up to?

Chapter Five

Pausing outside of the girls' bedroom, Daisy pressed her palm against her stomach—which very much felt as if she'd swallowed a handful of jumping beans—and silently counted to ten. The door was closed, but she heard the murmur of chatter easily enough.

Naturally, the deep timbre of Reid's voice proved the most distinctive, the most penetrating. A voice, Daisy believed, she'd recognize in the middle of a noisy crowd regardless of where she was, or if she expected him to be there.

She would just…know.

There were moments spread throughout her years in California where she'd hear a man speak, and something—his tone or the cadence or the manner in which a certain word was said—would have her think, just for a second, that Reid was nearby. Even as she'd searched the restaurant or the beach or wherever she happened to be, she would know that the voice she'd heard, despite its similarity in some context, did not belong to Reid Foster.

But she always looked. *Always.*

And, when she found the man whose voice had caused her breath to catch and her pulse to race—a man who was, of course, a stranger—she'd close her eyes and wait for the taste of bitter disappointment to fade. Maybe a few seconds. Maybe a few minutes. She would then continue on until the next time a man's voice captured her awareness.

Fortunately, this only occurred once or twice or, at the most, three times each year.

Annoyed with herself for thoughts she did not need to have, Daisy kneeled down to hoist Jinx into her arms. She'd cajoled the dog into following her for a couple of reasons. Mainly, she wanted the initial interaction between her nieces and Jinx to go well. In addition, she hoped her dog—who, unlike her feelings toward men, adored children—would accomplish what Daisy had not and create an instantaneous connection with Erin.

Kids loved animals, didn't they? Most of them, anyway?

"I need your help here," Daisy whispered to Jinx. "I need you to please, please ignore the man in the room and allow two little girls to love you. Can you do that, sweets?"

Jinx, sadly, didn't reply.

Twisting the doorknob, she walked into Erin and Megan's bedroom, and instantly loved what she saw. Pale-hued, multicolored butterflies covered the bottom half of the light mint-green painted walls. Billowy pink curtains framed the two long, narrow windows—one of which served as a centerpiece between the girls' beds—and a corner shelf displayed books, dolls and a small television set. Groups of stuffed animals, a child-size table and chairs, along with other various toys and activities were strategically scattered around the room. The framed pictures of rainbows and flowers and ladybugs added to the carefree joy the space evoked.

It was a perfect place for two little girls to call their own.

At the moment, Erin and Megan were stretched out on their stomachs on one of the twin beds, while Reid sat on the other with an open book on his lap. Ah. Reading time.

"Join us?" Reid asked with a smile. "I'll even let you read if you promise to use different voices for each of the characters. The girls insist, you see."

So confident. So freaking at ease. How could he sit there with that smile, that relaxed, almost satisfied attitude, after the exchange they'd shared?

For the sake of the girls, of course. And if he could pull off a laid-back, happy-with-the-current-world demeanor, then…she could, as well. Or she could try, anyway.

"Maybe later," Daisy said, striving for the same level of upbeat cheerfulness. Lowering herself onto the pink-carpeted floor, she smiled at Erin and Megan. They'd noticed Jinx right off, she knew, as their eyes were glued to the dog. "Her name is Jinx. Want to meet her?"

Nodding exuberantly, Megan slid from the bed and sort of half skidded, half tumbled into position next to Daisy. Jinx instantly freed herself from Daisy's hold and fell on Megan with all the love only a dog can give, without so much as a growl in Reid's direction.

It seemed the adoration of a little girl outweighed the annoying presence of a man. *Good.* Daisy had worried that Jinx might scare the girls if Jinx had gone after Reid like she had last night.

"Now I feel like chopped liver," Reid muttered, with more than a smidge of humor. "She really just hates men, huh?"

"Yep. And if you were chopped liver, she'd consider that a significant improvement," Daisy said, enjoying the look of pure delight on Megan's face. Then, glancing at Erin, who hadn't budged so much as an inch, Daisy gestured toward Jinx. "Feel like getting in on this?"

"No, thank you." Erin scooted across the bed for a pillow, which she squeezed tight to her chest. A yearning, so vivid that Daisy could identify the look from where she sat, swam in the girl's gaze. "Megan can play with...Jinx. I...I'm fine."

At a loss as to what to say or do, Daisy said, "Okay. There isn't any rush."

By now, Jinx and Megan were acting as if they were long-lost best friends. Megan's arms were wrapped around the dog, and Jinx continually nudged her nose into Megan's long, silky hair, bestowing the child's cheek with a sloppy kiss whenever the opportunity presented itself.

"Looks like your sister's having a lot of fun, monkey," Reid said casually. "I think you'd have a lot of fun, too. And...last I heard, you've been wanting a dog for a long while."

Erin shook her head and hugged her pillow harder, her despondency and stubbornness at not allowing herself something she so obviously wanted at war with one another.

"All righty, then," Reid said in concern. "The choice is yours."

The weight of it all—Megan's happy giggles as opposed to Erin's determined withdrawal, Reid's claims of love, her brother's accident and even her return to Steamboat Springs—combined to increase the invisible pressure on Daisy's shoulders.

She wasn't prepared. In any way.

True enough. But she had determined that her stance on Reid, and the reality of being back in her hometown, would both probably become easier within a few days. And okay, once she visited with her brother, her worries regarding his health would hopefully decrease. She might even glean some information that would help her better understand Erin.

Until then, the best she could do for Erin was to remain calm, positive, and to pay attention to her signals. In this second, what Erin needed the most was Daisy out of her bedroom.

"Okay, you goofs," Daisy said, rising to her feet. "I interrupted reading time, so I'll take Jinx downstairs and let you three get back to it."

"Stay!" Megan said, still giggling. "You and Jinx can listen to the story."

"That," Reid said, "is a great idea. No reason to run off."

Hmm. Was that an innocent, no-harm-meant gibe, or a planned one meant to remind Daisy of her transgression? With most folks, she would lean toward innocent. But with Reid, their past and his current state of madness—who knew?

"Oh, I'm not running off." She gave Reid a pointed look. "I still have to retrieve my suitcase from the car, and I have a few phone calls to make. Work and such."

Sort of true. The suitcase portion, if not the other.

Daisy worked as a freelance personal assistant, and usually only accepted short-term positions that appealed to her on one level or another. Some people required intense, hands-on motivation. Others required someone to function as a mediator between their personal and professional lives. She might help one client plan a social function, or assist another with organization, or manage an executive's schedule with the precision of a brain surgeon.

She'd even, a time or two, posed as a girlfriend.

What most of her assignments had in common was the similarity in clients, if not in job duties. Sure, she needed to earn a living, but whenever she could, she tended to work with people who were at a crossroads—either personally or professionally—and had experienced some type of an obstacle. People who were trying to get their life back on track.

Fortunately, in Los Angeles, the high demand for such a range of services never lessened. And the pay was good. When Parker had phoned, she'd literally just ended one such well-paying assignment. She had the free time available and the money in her bank account to see her through several months. Dumb luck…or a nudge from fate?

"What's another hour?" Reid patted the bed and winked. In a booming, carnival-hawker type of voice, he said, "Come on over, Daisy Lennox! Test your narrating skills! Engage and impress your audience! See if you can win the storytelling battle of the year against the amazing, the fantastic, the one and only champion of all narration, Reid Foster!"

"Please, please, please, Aunt Daisy?" Megan begged. "Read to us!"

Sudden laughter bubbled in Daisy's chest, causing her to momentarily drop her guard. Reading to the girls would be nice, especially if doing so eased some of the discomfort with Erin. But…reading the same book with Reid would require her to get close to him.

Close enough that they were sure to touch.

Their thighs, probably, since she'd have to sit right next to him. Or their fingers, as they turned the pages. Touching him, in any way, didn't seem terribly conducive to her goals.

But growing closer to her family definitely was. "That sounds fun," she said. "Just be prepared to lose your title, Mr. Champion. Because I'll have you know—"

"I'm really tired," Erin interjected, her words barely audible. "And I want to take a nap. Could you please go to the living room to read the rest of the book, so I can sleep? Please?"

On his feet instantly, Reid placed the back of his hand on her forehead. "You don't seem to have a fever. Anything hurt?"

"Huh-uh," she said. "I'm just tired."

"Ah. Well, a nap it is, then." Reid kissed her on the cheek, helped settle her on the bed and said, "Remember, there's a chance I won't be here when you wake up. If that were to happen, your aunt will take care of you until I'm back."

"Can't someone else make the mountain safe? I...I don't want you to leave."

"They need me there, kiddo. My job is one of my responsibilities, just like school is for you. If I don't show up, that makes it harder on everyone else I work with. Make sense?"

Erin squeezed her eyes shut. "I suppose."

Reid selected a plush, purple stuffed bear from the shelf, which he then tucked into Erin's arms as he perched himself on the edge of her bed. "I'll always come back, though. That's a promise you can count on. You know that, right?"

Nodding slowly, Erin pulled the bear close to her in a tight clutch. "B-but *she* doesn't know how we do things," she whispered. "You know how we do things."

This was hard. Seeing her brother's child struggle had a sobering, cold-bucket-of-water effect on Daisy. She wanted to help. She wanted to find a solution. But she had nothing.

"Here's what I think," Reid said, his manner gentle. "You know how we do things, and it would be really great if you could give your aunt some coaching tips. How does that sound?"

"I can help, too," Megan declared. "I know how we do things around this place!"

"Yup, you do. Both of you can help." Reid tousled Erin's hair. "Can you do that for me, monkey? I would really appreciate knowing you and your sister have everything under control."

"I guess, but I...I'm really tired." Erin yawned an impressive, and decidedly exaggerated, yawn. "I might sleep until you're done saving the mountain, so then Megan would have to help."

"That's quite the long while. You're sure you're feeling okay?" Erin nodded in reply. Sighing, Reid said, "Then maybe we should talk about what has you this tired?"

When Erin didn't so much as squeak, Reid glanced at Daisy and mouthed the word *sorry,* as he jerked his jaw toward the door. Daisy nodded in understanding and returned to her prior decision. Erin might be willing to talk, but not while Daisy remained in the room.

"Hey, Megan," Daisy said brightly. "I have an idea. Let's go to the kitchen and search the cupboards for cookie-baking ingredients. Maybe chocolate chip or peanut butter?"

The younger Lennox daughter screwed up her face in contemplation. "I know! I want oatmeal cookies with butterscotch chips. They're Daddy's most favorite cookie ever and we can bring him some when we go see him. Can we? Please?"

At those words, a childhood memory slid into being. Daisy and Parker had baked those cookies with their mother every year on their father's birthday and on Father's Day. They weren't only Parker's favorite, they were Charles Lennox's first choice in cookies, as well.

It was a bittersweet remembrance.

"Oatmeal scotchies are delicious," Daisy said to Megan, who was watching her with rapt attention. "We just need to make sure we have the proper ingredients."

Megan twisted in a half circle and bounded from the bedroom, her enthusiasm almost contagious. They would have fun, she knew, and she looked forward to spending the time with Megan. She just wished Erin would join them.

"Cookies it is," Daisy said to Reid and Erin. "If either of you decide to put on your baker's hats, you'll know where to find us."

"Maybe we will at that," Reid said. "Give us a few minutes here."

Before Daisy could leave the room, Jinx plunked her butt on the carpet in a single-minded, I'm-not-moving position. She stared in the direction of Erin's bed and whined. Loudly.

And that was when inspiration struck.

Leaning over, she picked up Jinx and carried her directly to Erin, who was watching them with curiosity. "I think Jinx is sleepy and wants to rest with you, Erin. Would that be okay?"

The child's eyes rounded and her mask of distance softened, replaced by the same deep yearning that Daisy had witnessed earlier. "She wants to stay with me? Really and truly?"

Laughing at the dog's near-frantic attempts to leap onto the bed, Daisy said, "Oh, I'd say she definitely, really and truly, wants to stay with you. If you're good with the idea?"

"Yes." A small smile tipped Erin's lips upward. "Jinx can rest with me."

Warmth and a sweetness that Daisy had never before experienced expanded within. No, a nap with Jinx wouldn't solve the core problem—whatever that problem might be—but they had to start somewhere. And this was somewhere.

Moving closer to the bed—and therefore, closer to Reid—Daisy carefully set down Jinx. And her smart, smart dog pressed her body next to Erin's, laid her head on the girl's stomach, let out a contented-sounding huff and shut her eyes. Completely at peace.

Slowly, almost reverently, Erin stroked Jinx's neck and back. "She's so pretty," she said. "And…and I think she likes me." A wistful expression appeared. "Do you think she does?"

"I can guarantee that she likes you." An ounce of the pressure on Daisy's shoulders dissipated. "Maybe after your nap, I'll show you some of Jinx's favorite toys? She especially likes squeaky toys."

Erin continued to lightly rub Jinx. Daisy waited through the silence, hoping that the promise of spending additional time with Jinx would propel her niece to agree.

Thirty seconds, maybe a little less, elapsed before Erin said, "I guess so."

That small, simple answer raised Daisy's hopes to the next level. "Then we have a date."

She turned to leave when Reid grasped her wrist, his touch gentle. Warm and solid. "A date, is it?" he asked in that annoyingly rich tenor of his. Humor sparkled there, as well. "I have a date for you. May sixth. Might want to mark your calendar, Daisy."

Several sarcastic comebacks landed on the tip of her tongue, but Daisy swallowed every one of them in favor of a graceful exit. Tugging free, she exited the room with her head held high. Egging him on would serve no purpose.

Little chance existed that she would ever forget that date, marked calendar or not. That was the day, every year since the year she left, that she'd reflect. Wonder. Imagine what might have happened if she'd ignored her instincts, if she'd stayed, if she'd married Reid.

And every year, she reached the exact same conclusion. She would not—even if given the opportunity through some magical means—alter that particular decision. Yes, leaving had been more difficult than she could have imagined. Yes, Reid had once given her a sense of completeness, wholeness and security that she'd lacked on her own.

A sense so strong, so all-encompassing, that it had taken her far too long to find herself, to wake up each morning and not feel the loss of something—someone—essential, and she wouldn't, then or now, surrender what she'd worked so hard to attain.

Her independence. Not needing anyone else to feel alive or content or…real.

The kitchen resembled the snowy white appearance of the outdoors. Somehow, and Reid didn't exactly know how, Daisy and Megan had managed to coat the counters and a large portion of the tile floor in a fine layer of flour. Their hair, clothes and noses were dusted in white.

It was, he decided, quite the charming picture.

"How's Erin?" Daisy asked, noticing his arrival. "Is she doing any better?"

Erin hadn't, despite Reid's efforts, opened up about the cause of her anxiety. She insisted she was tired, nothing more. But he figured most of her unease had to do with facing yet another change in such short order. Time, in that case, would make the most difference.

"She is. Due in no small part to that ornery dog of yours." The creature had the audacity to growl at him when he kissed Erin on the cheek. One way or another, he and that dog would become friends. "We can talk more later, before I take off for the afternoon."

With a quick nod of understanding, Daisy slid a cookie-dough-filled sheet into the oven and started the timer. Megan stood on a chair and spooned glops of dough on another baking sheet, seemingly happy and comfortable with the same change that had so upset Erin.

Pushing aside his concerns for now, Reid said, "Seems the baking is going well." He took one full step into the kitchen, and before he could process the teasing grins Daisy and Megan exchanged or their flurry of movement, he was met with two handfuls of flour in the face…causing him to sneeze. Not just once, but twice.

Well, that answered the question of the indoor blizzard.

Wiping off his face with his sleeve, he gave the woman and the child the sternest, I'm-not-pleased expression he could form. Neither of them bought it. Megan just about dissolved into a state of hysterical, breath-stealing giggles, while Daisy contented herself with a knowing smirk aimed in his direction. He figured he had two choices.

One of which involved a kiss. The other involved re-taliation.

Unfortunately, the kiss would have to wait until he and Daisy were alone. Retribution it was, then. Reid shrugged and, playing the you-got-me-good routine, walked toward the sink, saying, "How long were you two cookin' that one up?"

In between her giggles, Megan said, "It was all my idea! I got Aunt Daisy first, and then she got me, and then I got her again, and then I said we should get you."

"Oh, yeah?" In the second before he reached the sink, he pivoted, wrapped his arms around Megan's waist and hauled her up. Her giggles reached new proportions of hysteria. God, he hadn't heard her laugh like this since before Parker's accident. "Guess what, peanut?"

"Wh-what?"

Carrying her toward the open container of flour on the counter, he winked at Daisy. She grinned back. And he saw them—clear as day—several years down the road in their own home, with their own child, laughing and loving and living. *His* family.

The absolute rightness of this scene, of this potential reality, fused into Reid's DNA and became as permanent, as factual, as the dark brown shade of his eyes, the angled edge of his jaw…the strength and surety of his convictions. Some might call such a moment nothing more than déjà vu or groundless hope or…well, insanity.

Reid knew different. Such a moment could only be described as a gift.

A glimpse, he supposed, of what could have been. Of what could still be, if he played his cards right and everything aligned just so. Reinforcements couldn't hurt, though.

His family, in particular. Between Reid's two brothers, his sister and his parents—not to mention a pair of his siblings' significant others—he'd corral the support that a situation like this required. Soon, he'd arrange a meeting for the whole crew. They would be surprised by his intent, his plan, but they wouldn't let him down.

"Well, it's like this," he said to Megan, forcing his attention to the present. "You don't have near enough flour on your nose." Sitting the giggling girl on the counter, he dipped his fingers into the flour, which he then smeared on her nose. "Or your chin." He dabbed a dash of powder on her chin. "Or your cheeks. Or your—"

"Or your hair." Daisy slid into position on his left and reached into the container. Before he had the opportunity to react, she damn near dumped a fistful of flour on top of his head. The powder fell down his face, leaving him unable to see and sputtering white puffs into the air. "Why, look at that, Megan," Daisy said. "It seems we got to build a snowman today, after all."

Eyes bright with excitement, Megan gave her head a decisive shake. "Not yet, Aunt Daisy. His hair isn't white enough to look all the way like snow. I think he needs more."

"You do, huh?" Daisy reached around Reid, set to grab another handful.

Taking hold of her wrist, he tugged her toward him. He might not be able to kiss her, but he could certainly put the idea of a kiss into her mind. "I wouldn't do that if I were you," he said, keeping his voice steady and sure. Slowly, purposefully, he dropped his gaze to her mouth. "My methods of payback don't involve anything as simple as a bag of flour."

Like earlier, her tongue darted out to lick her lips. Like earlier, the minuscule motion jolted his body to full awareness. Of her. Of the many ways they could please each other.

Of the many ways they once had.

"Unfair," she whispered. "You don't get to make up your own rules. Not with this."

"When something this important is at stake, defining the rules is exactly what I get to do." Their gazes caught, held, and the heat between them became tangible. "Otherwise, I would be giving up without a fight. I already did that once, darlin'. I won't do so again."

"I don't have to accept your rules."

"Nope," he said, capitulating without argument. No reason not to when she spoke the truth. "But that will only inspire me to try harder. Increase my determination to succeed."

"It won't matter. Wouldn't have mattered then, either." One blink. Two blinks. "I don't regret my decision. You should know that now, before you take this nonsense any further."

Logically speaking, he'd long since assumed she'd found some version of peace, because she hadn't contacted him or reached out to make amends. Though, he supposed, he hadn't done so, either. But no remorse? Not one solitary wish to change any of what occurred?

That was a hard pill to swallow. Because Reid had plenty of both.

"You're telling me you have zero regrets?" he asked, directing all of his strength on shielding his shock. "None at all?"

"Not about the decision, no," she said, her voice catching slightly on the words, on the admittance. "I would make the same choice today."

The shock disappeared, replaced by pain. It slammed into him, and like a friggin' hacksaw, chewed through every muscle, every tendon, every cell and molecule, until the agony of her statement reverberated all the way through to his bones.

Hell, maybe it went as far as his soul.

"Without hesitation, Daisy?" he asked, his voice low.

"I…would have tried to talk with you, but yes. Without

hesitation," she said, each word ringing with pure, unrestricted honesty. "I enjoy my life, Reid. I like the person I have become far more than I liked the person I was. Think about that."

Oh, he would. For countless, sleepless hours, he was sure.

What he said, though, was "Well, I'd like the chance to get to know the person you've become. But, Daisy, I don't expect to stop lov—" All at once, he realized they were dipping into dangerous ground with a pint-size audience. Switching tacks, he winked at Megan, grabbed a large handful of flour and raised it above Daisy's head. As he opened his fist, he said, "I don't expect to stop loving…this look. White hair suits your aunt, don't you think, peanut?"

And in the wisdom only a child can have, Megan took in the scene and said, "When Erin and I don't get along, Daddy says we have to kiss and make up." She slid herself to the edge of the counter and jumped down. "You guys weren't getting along. So…kiss and make up."

"We're getting along just fine," Daisy said quickly. "We were just…talking."

"But we *were* in a disagreement, so technically speaking, I believe Megan is right." Reid stepped closer to Daisy and brushed some of the flour off her lips. "We really should make up. After all, whether Parker is here or not, his rules still apply."

"Yep!" Megan chimed in. "He wants us to be nice."

"Nice is one thing," Daisy said. "But technically speaking or not, I highly doubt my brother would expect us to—" The oven timer went off. Daisy blew out a breath, sending a cloud of white powder wafting around her. With a smug grin, she scooted to the side. "Well, there you have it. The cookies are done, so this conversation is over. We'll have to…make up later."

"Why would we want to do that?" Reid put himself in

front of her and draped his arm around her shoulders. One fast pull, and she was right there. Right where he wanted her. Her eyes widened, then narrowed. Her jaw clenched. And he figured he had five—maybe ten—seconds before her temper ignited and she slapped him. Nah, she'd kick him. "One kiss, Daisy. Just one."

Then, before she could put up a fuss, he kissed her. Not in the way he yearned to. Not in the way he would've if they were alone. But a kiss, nonetheless. Short and sweet, but real. And he felt the flicker of heat, the promise of more, in the meeting of their lips.

Just as he always had.

"That's silly!" Megan said. "Daddy doesn't mean we should really kiss, just that we should be nice and…and always remember that we love each other."

"Ah. I must have misunderstood. But still, that's real good advice, Megan," Reid said, keeping all of his attention on the woman he'd just kissed. "To be nice and always remember who we love. Don't you agree that's good advice, Daisy?"

"No regrets, Reid," she said, her voice firm. Her eyes, though, they weren't firm or hard or cold. They were warm and soft and…beautiful. "Remember that."

Oh, he would. But only for what it was. Painful information to absorb, yes, but also no more than a single, solitary component of the complete picture. A picture that contained many elements, including his hope. His belief. His unexplainable certainty at obtaining a future with Daisy. And, outweighing the rest, his love for her.

In Reid's mind, those were damn good enough reasons to continue on, to not give up, to go for the proverbial bucket of gold at the end of the rainbow. So that was what he would do. Without hesitation or…no, he couldn't state without fear.

That was fine. The thought of losing Daisy again *should* scare him.

If anything, the presence of fear validated his instincts, his convictions, and proved that he was fighting for something—someone—vital to him and to his life.

Chapter Six

Partly due to the weather, partly due to the reality of settling in and learning her nieces' routines, more than a week
passed before Daisy was able to take the girls to visit Parker.
Within those days, Daisy had continually attempted to
breach the distance between herself and Erin.

Unless Jinx was in the room or the topic of discussion,
though, Erin kept to her oh-so-polite approach. Daisy hadn't
decided what she thought of this. On one hand, how could
she complain about a child remaining polite? On the other,
this aloofness didn't offer any hint of the best way to proceed or help her understand the origin of the problem.

They were, for the time being, stuck on pause.

The same, in fact, could be said for Reid, whom she'd
seen less of in the past week and a half than she had in her
first twenty-fours in Steamboat Springs. His work schedule
had been intense, requiring him to leave the house early
and return late. He was not, however, too exhausted to forget about his love-and-marriage, we-are-not-done agenda.

There were the comments he'd toss her way, every one
of them referring in some form or fashion to May sixth.
There was that confident air he carried himself with whenever they were in the same room, and when the girls weren't

paying attention, that annoying-but-freaking-sexy grin of his, typically followed up by that devilish wink.

Small indications, yes, but when added with the random save-the-date cards she'd discover tucked in odd places—such as in the book she was reading or the silverware drawer—she had no doubt that Reid Foster's focus toward *marrying* her had not altered in the slightest.

And he'd kissed her—okay, more of a peck, but still—in front of Megan, and had then whispered that, later, he'd do a better job of it. When they were alone.

So, no. He had not thrown in the towel.

"Are we almost there?" Megan's chipper voice interrupted Daisy's never-ending, tumbling circle of concerns. They'd awakened to a beautiful and clear Saturday morning, and were now on their way to the hospital. "Does Daddy know we're coming?"

"Yes and yes," Daisy responded. She'd phoned Parker before they'd left to make certain he was prepared for a visit. He was. "And he's very, very excited to see both of you."

From what she understood, the girls weren't able to visit their father right after the accident due to their ages and the scope of his injuries. Parker had required several surgeries almost immediately, and hadn't been aware enough to interact with anyone for longer than a few minutes. Neither Parker nor Reid wanted to upset the girls with that visual reality, so they'd held off. The storm, of course, had caused another delay.

Now, though, the girls needed to see their dad.

"He's really going to be okay?" Erin's worry-laden voice brought forth a well of emotion. "When my mommy was sick, we went to the hospital to…to say goodbye. And Reid said that y-you might take care of us if D-Daddy died. I d-don't want to tell Daddy g-goodbye."

Megan instantly began to cry, and Erin followed suit.

Spying a convenience store to her right, Daisy flipped on her turn signal and yanked the car into the parking lot. No wonder Erin had seemed to dislike her on sight. She'd taken Daisy's surprise arrival as a sign her father was dying. And obviously, Reid had no idea he'd put that thought into Erin's head.

Once Daisy had the car stopped, she unbuckled her seat belt and pivoted. Both girls were sobbing. Megan's cries were louder, more vehement than the silent tears coursing down Erin's face. Didn't matter. Noisy or quiet, each were heartbreaking.

"This is not the same. Your father is still hurt, yes, but he is getting better. And the only reason I'm here is to help look after you until he can come home. Look at me, girls," Daisy said when neither Erin's nor Megan's tears subsided. "This is not a goodbye visit. This is a hello, we've-missed-you, we-love-you and we're-so-happy-to-see-you visit."

Erin's light brown eyes, just a shade darker than her sister's, watery and filled with fear, focused on Daisy. "Do you promise, Aunt Daisy? With your heart crossed and everything?"

"I promise. With my heart crossed and everything." Because she couldn't stand not to be closer to them in that second, Daisy climbed into the backseat. "I will never lie to either one of you. No matter what the question is, I will tell you the truth. Okay?"

"I can ask you anything, ever, and you'll never fib?" Erin asked, her curiosity at such a concept overruling her fear. "Always and forever?"

"Yes. Do you believe me?"

Erin studied her for a few seconds before dropping her chin in a jerky nod. She tightened her hold on her stuffed animal—the same purple bear Reid had handed her in her room that day—and said, "I won't fib to you, either. If you ask me something."

"Me, too, Aunt Daisy," Megan said. "No fibbing ever!"

"Well, then I'd say we have the start of a wonderful relationship." Daisy reached for and squeezed each of the girls' hands. "Ready to go see your dad now?"

The answer was, of course, a resounding yes.

Twenty minutes later, Daisy and her nieces stopped outside of Parker's room. Reid had already warned her and the girls what to expect when they saw him, but she thought a quick reminder might be smart. She kneeled down in front of them. "Remember what Reid said. Your daddy has some cuts and bruises. There will be machines near him that beep and make funny noises, but they're nothing to worry about. Okay?"

While Megan nodded immediately, Erin didn't. She opened her mouth, hesitated, and then as if recalling Daisy's promise, closed it again and also nodded.

Headway, perhaps? "Good. And if you have any questions, just ask."

Ignoring her jumpy stomach and her own bolt of fear over seeing her brother for the first time in so long, Daisy led the girls inside. Parker was half sitting on the bed, one leg hoisted above his body in some type of an uncomfortable-appearing mechanical contraption, and the other straight in front of him. Mottled bruises were on his arms—one of which was in a cast—his hands and his face. Beneath the injuries, he looked sturdier, more solid, than Daisy had expected. He was still her strong, confident older brother with the same sandy blond hair and friendly warmth emanating from his blue eyes. Some of her tension eased.

She'd missed him. More than she'd realized.

"Daddy!" both girls yelled at once. Neither moved forward, though. They were, Daisy assumed, caught in a web of longing and caution.

"Now there's the sight I've been waiting for," Parker said,

his pleasure and relief apparent. "Wow, have I missed you two. Come over here for a hug. I promise I won't break."

Erin made the first move, scooting to the edge of the bed. Carefully, as if truly concerned she could break her father, she eased in for a gentle hug. That was all it took for Megan to dash forward and propel herself into Parker's unencumbered, waiting arm. Parker began asking them questions about the past few weeks, and the girls happily answered.

As her nieces became reacquainted with their father, Daisy collapsed onto one of the guest chairs and released a pent-up breath. There were so many questions to ask Parker, so many possible topics they should—at some point— discuss, but she knew this wasn't the time.

They would need privacy, and perhaps, several easier-to-manage conversations first. So they could create a base-line, a new start to their relationship.

A sudden absence of noise drew her attention to the bed. Megan had crawled into position next to her father, while Erin had remained standing with her hand tightly clasped in Parker's. And her brother's contented expression, his absolute peace in this moment, reminded her again of all the time they'd wasted.

Family. *Her* family.

How stupid to forget—pretend?—that this connection no longer mattered, no longer held any weight or importance. What could be more important than family?

No, this wasn't the time to bring up past hurts or ask for Parker's input on Erin, or pose any of the questions that Daisy had wondered about for so long. They'd get there. She hoped they'd get there. Today was about…connecting. For the girls, for Parker. Maybe for herself, too.

"Hey there, big brother," she said when Parker's quiet, searching gaze finally landed on her. She forced her mouth into a teasing grin. "The mountain kicked your butt good, huh?"

"If you think this looks bad, you should see the mountain," Parker responded with his typical dry humor. "Fairly sure I managed to... Oh, who am I kidding? Yeah, the mountain kicked my butt. Did...ah...Reid mention he's the one who found me?" Now her brother's voice no longer held humor of any kind. "He stayed with me until transport could get me here, kept me talking and... Not sure where I'd be if it wasn't for him."

Gratitude and relief sank in fast. "No, he didn't mention he'd saved your life." Emotion, heavy and hard, settled in the pit of Daisy's stomach. "Though, I suppose that's just like Reid, isn't it? He isn't the type of man to—"

"Blow his own horn," Parker said, completing Daisy's sentence. "And nope, he isn't. Never has been. But I thought you should know."

"I... Yes, I should know that." She considered, briefly, telling Parker about Reid's wedding mandate, but decided not to. The girls were, after all, within listening distance. Later, she'd thank Reid. She might even kiss... No, a hug would serve well enough.

"Don't think I'll be skiing for a long, long time." Parker rested his jaw on top of Megan's head and squeezed Erin's hand. "If ever again."

"But you've always loved to ski," she said, her thoughts still on Reid. "And you know what they say—when you fall off a horse, the best thing you can do is get right back on."

"There are some things I love more than skiing."

"I understand. I'm just so glad that you're..." She let her words die off, not wanting to cause the girls any additional concern. "And I'm also glad I'm here."

"Me, too." He closed his eyes for a beat. "Very much so...on both accounts. And I'm looking forward to going home."

"I bet."

"Will be a while, I think," Parker said. "A month at the

soonest, from what the doctor says. If I don't—" He glanced at his daughters. "One more…procedure needs to happen first, and then physical therapy. Can you…I mean, will you be able to stay for that long?"

"Yes," she answered, mentally working out the logistics. Living in Los Angeles didn't come cheap, but she was careful with her money. She could manage a couple of months without issue. And, well, if her brother needed her for longer than that, she'd find a way to make it happen. "I'll figure it out, Parker."

"Thank you," her brother said. "I want the girls to know you better."

"I would like that," she said. "Things…should be different between us."

From there, the conversation changed tempo. In mutual but silent accordance, Daisy and Parker kept the mood upbeat and cheerful. Bit by bit, the girls became chattier, slowly morphing into the children they probably were before their father's accident. And, other than their natural hesitation when the visit came to an end, they remained talkative during the drive home.

"Aunt Daisy?" Erin asked from the backseat. "Can we all build snowmen after lunch? I…I want to try something special."

"Absolutely." Smiling, Daisy pulled into the house's driveway and shut off the ignition. "I think that sounds like a great plan. Perfect, actually."

The girls exploded from the car and raced toward the front door. Daisy sat still for a minute, allowing herself to savor the joy of this moment. Yes, everything would be okay. Yes, she was supposed to be in Steamboat Springs.

Not forever, no. But for now, there was nowhere else she'd rather be.

Saturday afternoon found Reid walking into Foster's Pub and Grill—one of the two local businesses his family owned and operated—with knotted nerves and tense muscles. He might have chosen to bring his family onboard, but that didn't negate his anxiety in the disclosure.

He had not a doubt that each of the Fosters would stand behind him in solidarity, but they would also be protective. They, of course, weren't aware that Reid might have been able to minimize the damage. Not only for Daisy, but also for himself. And he wouldn't share the details of the secret he'd kept today. Couldn't, really, when he hadn't yet told Daisy.

Reid stopped inside the wide double doors and appraised the room. While the pub's lunchtime rush had ended, plenty of folks still sat at the well-polished oak bar and the round, also oak, tables. Funny to think that in another week—two, tops—the city would begin to grow increasingly silent as the winter tourist season crawled to a close.

Nodding toward a few of the pub's regulars, Reid made his way to the kitchen at the rear of the building. He'd phoned his mother yesterday, had asked her to gather everyone together this afternoon. Margaret Foster had agreed without question or comment, though he figured she had plenty of both. Especially if she'd caught wind of Daisy's return.

Even if she hadn't, she—along with everyone else—would be mighty curious about his request. The Fosters typically held their business meetings in the middle of each month, so the March gathering wasn't scheduled for another week or so. And since these meetings—which were just as much social as they were business-oriented—tended to be held after hours, asking for everyone to find time in the midst of their busy day was unprecedented.

Waving at a few of the employees, he wound through the kitchen to the stairs that led to the now vacant apartment above the restaurant. All of the Foster siblings had lived there at one time or another, the most recent being his sister, Haley.

When she'd moved out, their parents had decided to turn the apartment into a large office area, complete with a conference table. And that was where today's meeting was set to take place. Reid paused at the top of the stairs and inhaled a calming breath. Stupid as all get-out to be so nervous. This was his family. He could count on them.

The truth of that thought steeled his resolve, so he opened the door to let himself in. And quickly saw that everyone had already arrived. Early, even, by a good fifteen minutes.

"Guess I made you all rather curious, huh?" he asked, walking directly to the table where everyone was seated. "Because I can't remember us ever starting on time for anything."

Haley grinned in apparent good humor, but Reid didn't miss the concern glimmering in her sage-green eyes. Her other half, Gavin—who stood close to six foot five and had a build resembling a linebacker's—sat beside her with a fair portion of worry in his own gaze. Glancing around the table, Reid recognized the same in every last member of his family.

Hell. He'd caused them stress. And that had not been his goal.

"Let me say this straight-out," he said, taking the empty chair next to his brother Dylan. "I'm not sick or moving away or becoming a monk. I don't have bad news to share. So whatever you all think is going on, chances are you're wrong."

"Good to hear," said Paul Foster, the patriarch of the family. He turned to his wife, who sat beside him, and patted her hand. "Your mother has been coming up with all sorts of outlandish ideas to explain why you might have requested this get-together."

Reid nodded but didn't reply. Looking at his dad was a lot like seeing a future version of himself. Reid and his brother Cole took after Paul the most in appearance, with the same black hair and dark eyes. Haley and Dylan more closely resembled their mother, with their reddish-brown hair and their chameleon—sometimes brown, sometimes green—eyes.

All of the Foster kids shared the long, lean frames of their father, and fortunately, the same high-powered metabolism that allowed them to eat whenever, whatever they wanted.

Pushing a long strand of hair behind her ear, Haley leaned forward. "Is someone pregnant? Am I going to be an aunt?"

"Nope," Reid said, chuckling. "No babies just yet."

"Hmm. My guess was monk," said Cole, the youngest of the brothers, with a wink in Reid's direction. "But you already ruled that one out, so I have no idea what's up."

One by one, the rest of the Fosters tossed in a selection of notions, some harebrained and some not. Resigned, Reid watched, listened and stayed silent. When his family got going, the best you could do was sit tight and keep your mouth shut until a lull presented itself.

When one did, he coughed to clear his throat. No reason to beat around the bush, so he dived right in, saying, "Daisy's in town, due to Parker's accident. She showed up the week before last, on a Tuesday night, and I...ah...hadn't known she was coming."

"Daisy's back?" Dylan shook his head as if the entire idea perplexed him. "Why... I mean, is she here to stay?"

"That was...*ten* full days ago!" Haley said. "Just like you to keep this news to yourself for so long. Geez, Reid. Why would... Oh. Has Parker taken a turn for the worse?"

"No, Parker's doing well. Daisy's here to temporarily help with the girls." And then, since Cole was attempting to whisper an explanation to his blond-haired, blue-eyed fiancée, Rachel, Reid said, "Daisy is the woman I almost married, Rach. I'm not sure if you remember her from when we were all kids or if you know what took place. If not, Cole can fill you in."

"I remember her, and I've heard a little," Rachel said, her voice quiet. "And wow, Reid, that must have been a shock for you, seeing her out of the blue."

A shock, yes, and a whole lot more. "It's been…interesting."

"How is Daisy?" Margaret asked. "And more to the point, how are you?"

"Daisy is fine. She—" Reid wanted to get to the heart of the matter, let his family absorb the information, and then return to Parker's house. So, without further ado, he said, "I still love her. And I've decided to plan another wedding and hope she chooses to attend."

An invisible tremor rocked the room at his announcement, silencing everyone. His mother closed her eyes and his father's eyebrows drew together in worry.

"Wait, wait, wait," Dylan said, breaking the quiet. "Let me get this straight. You've *decided* to plan another wedding and you *hope* she'll attend? I take that as meaning—"

"At this juncture, she has flat-out said no." Reid stretched his legs in front of him and tried for a casual, confident pose. "I plan on changing her mind, but I could use some help from all of you. Which is why we're here."

"So now," Cole said, focusing on Reid, his voice neither condemning nor accepting, "you're the one attempting to get the girl you love by means of…what would you call this? Trickery or game-playing or…hell, I don't know. What's your definition?"

"Neither. I'm not tricking Daisy, nor am I playing a game." In an effort to win Rachel's affections, Cole *had* resorted to a game of subterfuge. Reid had not approved.

"I've made my intent and feelings clear. She is well aware that I want to marry her. We've even set a date."

"Taking this a little far a little fast, aren't you?" Reid's father asked. "And why would Daisy set a date if she hasn't accepted your proposal?"

"Too far? No. Too fast?" Reid shrugged. "Probably, but I don't have a lot of time to waste. And I don't know why she chose a date, but she did." He tucked his hands behind his head. "I've decided to take that as a positive sign I'm heading in the proper direction."

Gavin chuckled half under his breath. "Or she couldn't stand up to the force of a Foster's will." He winked at Haley. "I know something about how that goes."

Haley snorted. "If I hadn't shown you the force of my will, you'd be hiding out in that house of yours, pretending you were happy without me. And we both know—"

"Wait. Everyone, just wait," Dylan said again. Tipping backward in his chair, he frowned at Reid. "I can't wrap my head around this. Why would you decide to marry a woman who has already proven she's unable to commit? Seems as if you're just asking for trouble."

Like Reid, Dylan had once lost the woman he loved. He'd married almost directly out of high school, and his wife had gone and fallen for someone else. Within a year of marriage, they were filing for divorce. Therefore, Reid was not surprised to hear this question from Dylan.

"I might be." He shrugged again. "Won't stop me, though."

"You're really this sure?"

"Yup. Can't explain it, really. It's this pure, absolute type of knowledge that stems from somewhere other than my brain. I love Daisy. And this time, I can't let her go without trying."

Resting her cheek on Gavin's shoulder, Haley sighed.

Of all of his siblings, Reid had figured his sister would come around first. She was chock-full of romantic notions.

"I'm on your side," she said, confirming this belief. "Whatever you need, I'll do."

"Me, too," Cole said. "I know where you're at right now. And…yeah, whatever you need. Just as Haley said. All you have to do is point me in the right direction."

Rachel murmured her agreement, as well, followed by Gavin. His parents and Dylan remained stoic in their silent regard. Still concerned, he wagered.

He started with his folks. "What are you two thinking?"

Margaret laced together her fingers and leveled her shoulders. "I don't know about your dad, but I'm thinking of those days after Daisy left. I'm remembering your devastation, Reid, and how long it took you to regain your footing. I don't…I just don't know if this—"

"Makes a lick of sense," Paul interjected. "Each of you kids have come up with one harebrained scheme after another. No wonder my hair is turning gray."

"They have, yes, but in the name of love," Margaret said softly. "I can't find fault in choosing love, even with my concerns."

"Um. Not me," Dylan said. "No harebrained schemes coming from this direction. In the name of love or not. Single. Staying so, too."

"Just wait until the day the perfect woman walks in your path," Haley said. "You'll change your tune soon enough."

"I most certainly will not."

Cole snickered. On another day, in another moment, Reid would've joined in with the teasing. Not today and not in this moment.

When the room quieted again, Paul said, "Like your mother, I remember the fallout, son. So I have to ask… have you two had an honest conversation about what happened back then? Do you believe—assuming Daisy agrees to your unique proposal and then manages to arrive for the wedding this time—that the two of you can create a stable relationship?"

"I'm as sure as I can be, but no, we haven't entered into a discussion about our history as of yet. We will, though. And, Mom, I won't lie. If this doesn't pan out the way I hope, I will be…upset. No way around that one." A lump the size of Texas manifested in Reid's throat. "However, I will be far worse off if I don't give this—me and Daisy— a go. That's just the way it is, so I'm asking for your trust and support."

Paul and Margaret exchanged a look that was decipherable only to them, and then, with slight shrugs and weary expressions, they both nodded. "If you're certain, then we're here for you," Paul said. "Just proceed with caution and preparation for a…less-than-ideal outcome."

"And of course, we trust you. You always have our support. But that doesn't mean I can snap my fingers and forget the pain that Daisy brought you," Margaret said. "If she doesn't purposely cause you additional pain, I can…well, I *think* I can forgive. I'll do my best."

His mother. So fierce, so loyal. He'd love her regardless, but he loved her, respected her, even more for those qualities.

"None of this is that simple." Reid selected his words carefully, thoughtfully. "There are details about what happened that you aren't aware of, and I'm not at liberty to tell you what they are right now. My history with Daisy isn't as clear-cut as you might think."

"I suppose that's fair." A brief pause and then the hint of a smile appeared. "It seems we have a wedding to plan. When…what's the date?"

"May sixth."

Margaret gasped. "The same date?"

"Yup." He didn't offer any additional clarification. No

reason to. "We're starting from square one, so basically everything from the ceremony to the reception needs to be worked out. All I ask is that no one mentions my house to Daisy, not even a hint of where I live."

Another secret that Daisy did not know was that, shortly before their original wedding date, he'd bought the house she'd adored as a girl. Her gingerbread house, a place she'd believed fairies had lived. It was meant to be a surprise, and well, he'd never considered living elsewhere. A sign he should've paid attention to long before now.

"Hold on here," Dylan said. "Don't get me wrong, I'm in. I'll help. But before we start digging into this—to use Dad's words—harebrained scheme, I have another question."

"Go for it. What's up?"

"You love the girl. Fine," Dylan said. "But does the girl love you?"

"I believe she does, though I don't know for sure," Reid admitted, again unsurprised by Dylan's forthrightness. "For now, let's proceed with the theory that she does. Or will again."

Though, even if Daisy's love hadn't died or could be resurrected, she might not forgive him when she learned the truth. That, Reid knew, was where his deepest fear resided. When she discovered that he could've saved her from that wedding-morning confessional-from-hell, chances were high she wouldn't require any other reason to walk away from the second-chance-at-forever wish she'd written in her letter.

He couldn't avoid the truth. Wouldn't choose anything other than honesty this go-round. Once he'd found the right time and place, he'd man up and do what he should've done before.

"Reid?" Haley's voice yanked Reid clean from his thoughts. "Are we planning a casual or a formal wedding? And what about the ceremony location? Or the reception? Or—"

"Let's keep it simple," he said. "Daisy would like it simple." Another thought came to him, so he turned toward Cole and Rachel. "I'm sorry about jumping in and stealing your wedding-day thunder. If I'd seen this coming, I would've warned you."

"Nothing to apologize for. Rach and I will be married and back from our honeymoon by May sixth," Cole replied with an easy, relaxed air. "And our wedding is set to go. Rachel's been a freak of nature in that regard. Compulsively organized, why you wouldn't believe—"

Rachel lightly punched Cole on his forearm. "And aren't you glad of that now? Other than final fittings and confirmations, we're done." She smiled at Reid. "So we have plenty of hands-on experience to offer."

"Thanks, guys," Reid said. "It's appreciated."

"May sixth, huh? So…nine-ish weeks from now?" Haley dug through her purse and pulled out a notepad and pen. "Let's do this! We need two lists. One for the actual details of the wedding, and another for helping Reid convince Daisy to…well, not abandon ship."

Everyone began talking at once, bringing up possibilities and ideas. This time, though, Reid joined in the conversation, secure in the knowledge that if this whole kit-and-caboodle went south, he had his family's support. Which was a relieving concept.

What this knowledge didn't do was make the haunting prospect of losing Daisy a second time any less of a weight to carry. Hell. It seemed that Dylan had perfectly and concisely summed up Reid's predicament. He was, in effect, just asking for trouble.

Chapter Seven

By the time Reid left the pub, almost two hours had passed. He was pleased with the afternoon's progress. Together, he and his family had conceived of a plan to keep the wedding wheels turning. Nothing outlandish. Nothing that involved trickery or subterfuge.

Mostly, they'd focused on simple reinforcement. Whether that would be enough or not remained to be seen, but he wasn't in this alone. That, all on its own, made a world of difference.

Reid first stopped at the hospital to see Parker, but his friend was sound asleep, so he'd gone home to retrieve a few necessary items. In particular, Daisy's engagement ring, which he'd never found the will to sell, trash or hurl from the top of the mountain. Once he had the ring in his possession, he returned to the road, whistling as he drove.

Not so much in optimism as in certainty of the path he'd chosen.

When he pulled his SUV into Parker's driveway, behind Daisy's car, it was to the sight of two lopsided snowmen, the beginnings of a third and…a snow dog?

Daisy and the girls were focused on completing the third snowman, and Erin and Megan were dressed appropriately for the cold weather. Jinx, he noted in some humor, wore a fuzzy, hot-pink canine sweater. But Daisy? She had on that blasted spring jacket, sneakers and—while he couldn't say for certain from his driver's seat vantage point—what looked to be neon orange socks masquerading as a pair of gloves.

In other words, she was all but begging for pneumonia.

Before his logical brain had a chance to function, he'd jumped from the vehicle and was storming toward Miss Sunny California. His irritation and concern at her seeming inability to…to…take care of herself becoming larger, more intense, with each step. She'd grown up in Colorado, hadn't she? Yup, she had. And that meant she knew better.

Fortunately, the sound of Erin's and Megan's happy giggles pushed in past his emotional stew, forcing him to stop midstride. Forcing him to rethink his approach.

Lecturing Daisy at all, but especially in witness of the girls, wouldn't earn him any points in the romance department. Besides which, whether she seemed so at this particular moment or not, Daisy was an adult. If she chose to risk illness by prancing in the freezing cold weather while attired in unsuitable outerwear, he supposed that was her call to make.

Not the smartest call, but hers.

And if she came down with a cold, he'd make her chicken noodle soup and hot tea and he'd…he'd take care of her. Whether she damn well liked it or not.

For now, though, he set his worry on the back burner, formed his mouth into a smile and relaxed his posture. "What do we have going on here?" he asked, approaching the group of adorably pink-cheeked females. "And why wasn't I invited?"

"You're invited, Reid!" Megan said, lurching toward him for a hug. "Look! We made a snowman for each of us, even Jinx. And when we go inside, we're going to have hot chocolate and cookies and watch a movie. And Aunt Daisy said we'll have pizza for dinner! But first—"

"Wow. Hot chocolate, cookies and pizza, all in the same day?"

"Pepperoni pizza," Erin said as she patted the head of the snowman into a less lopsided shape. "But Aunt Daisy says we have to eat salad with dinner."

"No way! She said we have to eat salad?" Then, ignoring Daisy's flustered scowl and amidst the girls' bubbling laughter, Reid pretended to give the snowmen a slow, indepth once-over. "I see Daisy's snowman, and Erin's and Megan's. I see Jinx's, too. But—" he scratched his jaw and stepped backward and searched the yard "—where's my snowman?"

"We waited for you." Daisy stuck her sock-covered hands in her jacket pockets and shivered. "Due to the rules of snow magic."

"Snow magic?" Reid said. "Uh…should I ask?"

"Aunt Daisy didn't know this, but I thought you would," Erin said, sounding somewhat flabbergasted. "If you want any snow magic in your snowman—"

"You have to start each of the snowballs yourself," Megan explained, her voice rising a pitch as she spoke. "With your own two hands."

"Uh-huh. We can help with the rest of the snowman, just not the start. That part was hard with Jinx," Erin explained. "We had to use her paws to smush the snow into small balls."

"And all of our snowmen have to be built on the same day, so you have to do yours now. Not tomorrow." Megan gave Reid a very stern look. "Or our snow magic might not work, and…and it *has* to work. So Daddy can come home soon."

In a soft, quiet voice, Erin added, "We might need some magic for that."

Aha. Reid didn't know where the notion of snow magic originated from, but it didn't take a rocket scientist to understand the heartfelt seriousness of the request.

"So you can see how important this is," Daisy said, her eyes bright from the cold. Also, Reid guessed, from emotion. "Besides, who wouldn't want some snow magic in their life?"

"I absolutely want—" Reid snapped his jaw shut as Jinx suddenly dove for his ankles with a whine-growl-yowl noise. Unbeknownst to Daisy, he'd spent the past few nights trying to warm up to her paranoid pooch. Obviously, he'd been less than successful. "Daisy?" he asked as Jinx dug her teeth into his jeans. "Can you...?"

"Can I...what?"

"Really?" When she didn't respond, he pointed at the dog attached to his body. "I'm not going to be able to build a snowman, magical or otherwise, with your dog yapping at my ankles."

"Of course." Daisy came forward and unlatched her dog from his pant leg. Picking up the unruly creature, she said, "But if you'll recall, I warned you right off that she won't stop so long as you're here. And, if you'll also recall, you said that you were fairly certain you could outwait a dog. Guess you were wrong on that account, huh?"

"Oh, I can outwait Jinx," he answered. "I can outwait just about anyone or anything if the need arises. Even, in case you're wondering, a reluctant bride. However, you and—"

"You think I'm *reluctant?*"

"However," he repeated, "you and the girls are cold. I would prefer to get all three of you inside sooner rather than later. Before that can happen, I need to build a magic snowman. But yes, Daisy, I believe you're understandably reluctant. Luckily, I'm a patient man."

"Obstinate, not patient. And here I was, feeling all warm

and gracious toward you, and then you…you have to ruin it!" Speaking in a lower volume, she said, "Thank you. For saving my brother's life. For…being there for him when I was not. I…just thank you, so much."

"You're welcome. It's… Well, I'm just glad I was there." Then, due to his discomfort at receiving attention of that sort, he grinned. "You know, I was thinking we could just drive to Vegas and skip the rest of the hoopla altogether. What do you think?"

Exasperation, quick and vivid, entered her expression and colored her cheeks a deeper shade of pink. "What you want," she said, keeping her voice low, so only he could hear, "is not happening. I keep hoping you'll come to your senses, but apparently, you have an obvious issue with admitting you're in error."

"That's a no on Vegas, huh?"

"You need to accept defeat, Reid."

"Sorry, that's something I just cannot do."

She opened her mouth—ready to light into him, he was sure—glanced at the girls' earnest expressions and promptly clamped her lips shut. Giving her head a quick shake, she said, "You're right. Everyone is cold, so I'll take Jinx inside and start the hot cocoa. But we're not done with this conversation."

"Nope, we're not," he agreed. "We have a lot of decisions to make before May sixth. Probably a smart idea to start those discussions soon."

Her mouth thinned in frustration but she remained silent. Tossing one last glare in his direction, she whipped around and stomped toward the house. Jinx, not to be outdone, offered a series of rumbling growls and short, yippy barks as she was carried off.

It was, Reid decided, a rather humorous scene.

The second the *reluctant* love of his life disappeared through the front door, Reid focused all of his attention on

Erin and Megan, saying, "We have several things to talk about, but first…tell me about this snow magic. Where did you hear about it and how does it work?"

"It's from a story," Erin explained. "If we all build our snowmen while thinking of one great wish—has to be the same wish for all of us, though, 'cause that makes the magic stronger—then at night, the snow fairies will sprinkle magic dust on the snowmen and our wish will come true. So our wish is for Daddy to be able to come home. Soon."

"But we have to think about the wish the whole time we're making your snowman," Megan said. "Or the fairies won't hear our wishing."

"And just because it's from a story doesn't mean it isn't true," Erin said, lifting her chin in that familiar stubborn way. "I asked Aunt Daisy, because she promised she'd never fib to us. Ever. And she said she couldn't say if there was snow magic or not, but that if we believed really, really hard, anything can happen."

"So we're believing really, really hard," Megan said, blinking several times in quick succession. "Really, really, *really* hard! For Daddy."

There wasn't a man on the face of the earth who could argue with the possibility of snow magic under such circumstances. "I think the same…that if you truly believe, anything at all can happen." Reid held out his arms and both girls piled in. Once they separated, he said, "Let's build this snowman. For your dad."

And so they did.

Inch by delicious inch, Daisy submerged her body into the hot bubble bath and sighed in relief when the water met her chin. Pushing a stray wisp of hair from her cheek, she let the warmth soak in, taking pleasure from the humble reality of no longer shivering.

March in Steamboat Springs could remain wickedly

cold, and today's romp in the snow had frozen her clear through. Even spending the rest of the day indoors hadn't erased the chill. Her hands and feet were chapped, her cheeks and lips were windburned, she had the beginnings of a headache and…and…all of it was worth the fun she'd enjoyed with her nieces.

Now that she and Erin had reached an understanding, Daisy believed their connection would continue to grow. Slowly, yes. But steadily.

Daisy cupped her hands and filled them with the honeysuckle-scented bubbles. Pursing her lips, she blew gently, sending a spray of foam fluttering into the air. She didn't give herself many indulgences in her current life, but bubble baths were—in a word—*heavenly.*

Her version of self-therapy combined with sheer relaxation and utter peace.

Resting her weight against the cool porcelain of the claw-foot tub, Daisy's lashes drifted shut. Tight muscles loosened and the slight, throbbing pain in her temples dissipated.

Her breathing deepened. Sleepily, a vision of Reid came to her. Beneath her closed eyelids, she could see him, his arms around her. Loving her. Misty water stroked along the length of her body, as she imagined what he would do, caressing her skin with its silky warmth.

With a long, drawn-out exhale of desire, Daisy feathered her fingertips from the flatness of her belly to the curves of her breasts, envisioning the trail Reid would take if it were his hands on her. A soft, barely heard moan slipped from her throat as she delved deeper into her private fantasy world. What would he do next? Knowing Reid, he'd kiss her. Fully, soundly.

She moved her fingers to her lips. Yes, he would definitely kiss her. Then he'd—

No, no, no. Jerking open her eyes, Daisy sat up straight, the suddenness of her movement sloshing sudsy water over the edge of the tub. What was wrong with her? Why was she thinking—*fantasizing*—about having sex with Reid? Not smart. Not smart in any way.

Her heart knocked against her breastbone in a too-fast, too-hard rhythm. So much so, she felt the pressure of the beat in her ears. Wanting Reid, desiring Reid, would lead her to possibly *loving* Reid, and along that path lay…disaster.

Never again would she lose even one piece of her identity to a man. *Any* man.

The bathwater suddenly became icy and uncomfortable against her flushed skin. Yanking the plug, she watched as the water noisily gurgled down the drain. From here on out, for the next little while, she was a shower-only gal. Cold showers, at that.

She then attempted to remove every last thought of ever again becoming intimate with Reid from her brain and stepped from the tub. She dried off, slipped on a pair of pajama bottoms and a T-shirt and then waited until she'd regained control.

The girls were in bed for the night, emotionally exhausted after their visit with Parker and physically so from the hours of outdoor play. Megan's eyelids had started drooping in the middle of her first slice of pizza, and Erin's yawning hadn't been far behind.

Reid was awake, though. And unlike the past week, he hadn't spent the entirety of the day working. Which meant he'd be alert and ready for action. If she walked downstairs with her body tingling from the mere *remembrance* of his touch, and he somehow clued in to this mental state of being, she couldn't guarantee…a damn thing.

Not what she would say or how she would feel. Not how she would react. And God help her if he decided that tonight was the night to make good on his promise to kiss her… really kiss her. If he did, she might as well start shopping for her wedding gown now.

So, yeah, she waited. For a good long while.

When her balance returned and with her sanity in check, she left the bathroom and slowly took the stairs. She had a plan now. Not the greatest plan, but one that should get her through the rest of the evening. She'd stretch out on the couch with a book and, no matter what Reid might say or do, she'd keep her face buried in said book.

Oh, she likely wouldn't be able to focus on the words, but the physical form of the book should serve well enough as a shield. Maybe enough of a shield that Reid would decide to call it an early night and go to bed. Without her, of course.

At the foot of the stairs, she heard his voice coming from the kitchen. She would've assumed he was on the phone except for the cajoling sound of his tone mixed in with the recognizable rumbling of Jinx's growling.

Ha. He was trying to make nice with her dog, was he? As if none of her male friends had already attempted the same...and failed. It was, she knew, a losing proposition.

Smirking, Daisy quietly walked to the end of the hallway and peered into the kitchen. Man and dog were at a standoff. Or, perhaps more accurate in this situation, a sit-off. Reid sat on the tile floor on one side of the room with a slice of deli meat—ham, she thought—dangling from his fingertips, while Jinx sat on the other side, her head held high in defiance.

Reid murmured persuasive words of encouragement. Jinx growled or whined—or both—in return. Her front legs trembled every so often, and her gaze remained frozen on the temptation in Reid's grasp. Easy to see that the poor dog desperately wanted the treat.

She just didn't want to have to cozy up to a man.

It didn't escape Daisy; the similarity of what had happened upstairs with what was occurring now. Only, she wasn't a dog and Reid wasn't a slice of ham. And the treat she yearned for came with a host of issues if she capitulated. Jinx would just make a new friend.

Mentally shaking the absurd comparison from her thoughts, Daisy back-stepped away from the kitchen and into the living room, where she retrieved her book from her suitcase, curled up on the couch and pretended to read. Her shield visibly in place.

Too bad she couldn't shield her heart with the same effectiveness.

Reid stared at Jinx in varying degrees of frustration and amusement. Yet another night of failure. Nothing he'd tried so far—squeaky toys, tennis balls, a chunk of rawhide or a friggin' piece of ham—had done the trick. The obstinate creature refused to let go of her disdain long enough to give him an opening. And he refused to give up trying.

His initial goal in becoming friends with Jinx was to prove to Daisy that he could. He'd gotten it into his head that if he were the man who managed to soften her dog's male-hating tendencies, her defenses toward him would relax some, as well. A dumb idea? Probably.

Somewhere along the line, though, his goal had shifted gears. He liked Jinx, and he disliked that she viewed him as a threat. And her behavior with him differed so greatly from her behavior with Daisy and the girls—all of whom she followed around as if they were covered in bacon grease—that he'd pretty much decided that some jerk had mistreated her at one time or another. Her aversion to men, Reid believed, was based in fear.

And that just wasn't right.

"Pig meat, Jinx." Reid waved the ham in the air, feeling about as idiotic as a man could get. "Bacon is tastier, I know, but ham is still a damn fine meat. This here is honey-baked, too. Good, right? If you come to me, it's all yours."

Other than a few anxious, needy twitches, the dog didn't

budge. Just alternated her gaze between his face and the ham, her dark, oval-shaped eyes filled with suspicion.

"Not happening tonight, huh?" Standing, Reid broke the ham into chunks and put them into Jinx's food bowl. He'd hoped the snack would be enough of a lure to draw her to him, but they'd been at it for a good fifteen minutes. Tormenting the dog into compliance was not on his agenda. "There you go, girl. Eat up. We'll try something new tomorrow."

He washed and dried his hands, leaned against the counter and removed the small envelope he'd stuck into his shirt pocket. Two messages for Daisy—one written, one sentimental—were tucked inside. He just had to figure out a good place to put the envelope.

A location she would come across naturally, but the girls would not.

The coffee canister, maybe. Or her purse, if he could get to it without Daisy seeing. Neither idea struck Reid as particularly original, though, and he sort of liked the notion of wooing her with a bit of creativity. He'd come up with something better.

Replacing the envelope into his pocket, he turned to leave, hoping to find Daisy in the living room. Earlier, he'd spoken to Erin and Megan about the likelihood of his moving out soon. It was time—or near time—that doing so made sense. For Daisy and the girls, so they could continue to grow closer without his presence acting as a buffer.

For him, too. As he and Daisy danced around one another—because he was far from giving up on her, on them—he thought a little distance would prove helpful. Hell, maybe he'd get real lucky and Daisy would actually miss him some if he weren't here every night.

At any rate, he figured enough fireworks were in their immediate future that having separate base camps would become a necessity. But he wanted to give her a heads-up and get her take on the option before he formed a final decision.

Jinx was now near her food bowl, licking her chops, apparently having finished her snack. His movement, slight as it was, caused her entire body to tense into stillness, and once again, he was met with a pair of dark and wary eyes.

Dog and man studied one another. Reid took a step forward. Jinx pivoted, so she had more space to maneuver, and retreated a few doggy steps. But she didn't growl. And she didn't seem all that interested in attacking his ankles.

Well. Perhaps he'd give this friendship thing another shot before seeking out Daisy. Sitting down, so he was somewhat closer to the dog's level, he said, "No more treats for the night, but how about a belly rub? Or maybe a scratch behind the ears?"

Tilting her head to the side, as if curious about where this conversation might lead, Jinx plopped her butt on the floor. So…they were back to sitting and staring, were they?

"You know," Reid said, "I don't believe you're really afraid of *me,* just my gender. At some juncture in your life, someone did something to you that made you fear men."

Little by little, Jinx's paws slipped forward on the tile, until her belly rested flat against the floor. She settled her long, narrow head on her legs and emitted a soft, keening sort of whine.

As if in agreement.

"Yup, that's what I thought. A man mistreated you, huh?" Reid frowned as he considered the many despicable methods a human being could use to inflict damage on an animal. "I gotta tell you, Jinx. That idea ticks me off. Makes me wish I knew that man's name and location."

Her left ear twitched and cocked in his direction, again forcing the thought that she wanted to make damn sure she caught every word of what he had to say. Nonsense, of course, but dogs were smart. Wouldn't surprise him in the least if she recognized his sincerity.

"But look, despite what this coward did to you, not all men are bad."

Offering a scratchy, gravel-coated grumble as a response, Jinx—without lifting her head from her legs—stomach-scooched forward a few inches. *Toward* Reid.

This seemed positive, so Reid continued to talk, keeping his tone in an easy, relaxed range. "If you give my gender a chance, I think you'll find that most of us are pretty good guys."

Another odd-sounding canine whimper emerged. In disagreement, most likely.

Or he could be losing his marbles. It was one thing to talk to a dog. It was another to believe the dog was an active participant in the conversation.

"I know. Difficult to believe when you've been burned once, but I wouldn't lie to you." And darn if the dog didn't ease herself forward another couple of inches. "I get being gun-shy, though. It's a natural state of being after someone has hurt you. And…ah…I respect your need for caution and vigilance, Jinx. I really do. You're just protecting yourself."

A visible shiver rippled along the dog's back. She kept her attention, her focus, solidly on Reid, and after a drawn-out huff, she edged herself toward him a little more. Now the distance between his knee and her nose spanned about six inches.

And Reid, sensing he was *this close* to crossing a barrier, held himself motionless. The last thing he wanted was to startle Jinx enough that she took off.

"Here's the problem, though," he said. "Remaining vigilant is smart only to a certain degree. There's a point where too much vigilance can stop us from experiencing a lot of good things. And—frankly speaking here, Jinx—missing out on the good isn't any fun. I guarantee—"

Elongated verbal sounds, rising and lowering in octave, erupted from the dog's throat as Jinx seemingly told Reid an impassioned story. He listened and nodded, as if he understood her, every now and then uttering, "Hmm" or "Is that so?" or "Really?"

This went on for two, maybe three, minutes, before she abruptly stopped and inhaled a long whoosh of air, and looked at Reid as if to say, "Well, now what?"

"Up to you, pooch," Reid said. "Whatever happens next is your call."

Without any further hesitation, Jinx pushed across the floor, erasing the remaining distance that separated them. Heaving a loud, breathy sigh, she dropped her head on his lap and bumped her snout into his hand.

"Friends, huh? Good choice," he murmured, stroking the dog's back. Emotion—entirely too sappy for a grown man's peace of mind—dampened his eyes, thickened his voice. "Thank you for the trust, girl. That took a lot of courage. I guarantee I won't let you down."

Jinx huffed a short and contented sound that, yet again, seemed to state she understood every word Reid said. And hell, maybe she did. Who was he to decree such a thing as impossible? He scratched behind her ears and under her collar, and it was then that an idea occurred to him. The perfect, creative place to put Daisy's envelope.

A place, he believed, she'd be sure to find both of his messages posthaste.

Chapter Eight

Close to an hour after Daisy had retreated to the sofa, Jinx stumbled into the living room. Reid wasn't with her, so Daisy assumed he was still in the kitchen or had gone to bed. She hoped for the latter. The dog, in a plea for attention, whined in a long and plaintive manner before resting her paws on the edge of the sofa.

"What's wrong, sweets?" Jinx exhaled what sounded an awful lot like a heavy sigh of remorse. "Oh, I see. You gave in, didn't you? Feeling guilty for the price of that ham, hmm?"

Another whine, even more protracted than the last, coupled with an unflinching, dark-eyed stare. If Daisy didn't know better, she'd swear that Jinx was asking for forgiveness.

"Well, look. There aren't many females who can resist Reid Foster's charm," Daisy said, petting the top of Jinx's head. "And this seems a lot like the morning-after regrets. My advice? Don't beat yourself up. You enjoyed the ham, so you got something out of it."

She kept patting and scratching Jinx's short-haired coat as she spoke, not feeling strange about holding a one-sided conversation. A huge portion of her reasoning in adopting Jinx was for the simple comfort of having company.

Besides which, Daisy wasn't entirely certain that their conversations were one-sided. Whippets were extraordinarily intelligent, empathetic dogs.

"So," she said, "are you feeling a little better now?"

And, as if proving the accuracy of Daisy's thoughts, the dog vehemently shook her head.

"Trust me, Jinx. You need to let it go. But I'll tell you this—" Daisy fingered the dog's collar, which she'd just noticed was askew and looser than normal. "Oh. You're not upset about surrendering, are you? Good for you. Stand behind your choices."

Unbuckling the leather band, Daisy started to tug it in a notch when her eyes fell on a small, gift-size envelope that someone—Reid, of course—had strung through one of the collar's holes using a garbage-bag twist tie. Lovely. He'd had ulterior motives for kissing up to Jinx.

Daisy freed the card and tightened Jinx's collar to the proper fit. "There you go, sweets. Should feel much better now."

Jinx wagged her head once more, as if ascertaining the issue had been corrected, and—apparently satisfied that was the case—loped toward the stairs. Lately, she'd been sleeping half the night with the girls before rejoining Daisy on the couch.

Alone again, Daisy stared at the still-closed envelope in a mix of abject curiosity and outright denial. Today wasn't her birthday or a holiday. So whatever existed inside the envelope would likely fall into the range of another save-the-date card or an appointment-reminder card or…well, something equally as frustrating. She *should* toss the sealed envelope into the trash.

She should *not* give Reid the satisfaction of opening the

damn thing. Of reacting to whatever he might have stuck inside. That would be the smart, the…independent move.

She didn't do anything other than stare and wonder and…obsess a little. Giving in to her curiosity—sort of—Daisy gripped the envelope at the top right corner and brought it up to the beam of light coming from the floor lamp. And saw nothing.

No. She would not allow Reid or this stupid, nondescript envelope to bait her into taking one solitary footstep in his direction. Satiating her curiosity wasn't worth the consequences. Her resolve strengthened, Daisy swung her legs over the side of the couch and stood.

In her rush to get rid of the temptation, she half tripped, half skidded along the smooth hardwood floor, dropping the envelope in the process. And it made a flat, hollow sort of a *ping* that a lightweight card encased in paper should not have made, even against a rock-solid surface.

Kneeling, she used the tip of her finger to press against the envelope, this time feeling the definite impression of a small, circular object wedged in the bottom crease. Oh, no.

He didn't. He couldn't have.

But she knew that was exactly what he had done. In a flash, her willpower evaporated and she crumpled the rest of the way to the floor. Once again, her heart thumped in that too-fast, too-hard beat, and a strong shudder of melancholy forced her knees tight to her chest.

Her ring. That freaking envelope held her engagement ring.

Of course she opened it. How could she do anything other than rip off the side of the envelope and pour the ring into her palm?

A riptide of emotion engulfed her and she shuddered again. Swallowing, she looked at the tapered platinum band, the sparkling square-cut diamond and the twist of the birthstone-embedded love knot—garnet for Daisy, opal for Reid—that elegantly framed the solitaire.

He'd had this ring specifically designed for her, for them. To celebrate their love, he'd said. Their unique connection and the joining of their hearts, their lives.

Now, as they had then, tears filled Daisy's eyes.

Damn him for this, for putting such a visceral reminder of how much she'd loved him in her hands. One blink and a fat tear, and then another, rolled down her cheek. A silent testimony to the girl she'd once been, the love she'd believed they'd shared, the precious beauty of the moment she'd accepted Reid's proposal and he'd slid this very ring on her finger.

She'd never forget that night. Ever. They'd returned to Steamboat Springs after her graduation, after a celebration with their families, and he'd been quieter than normal. Contemplative. Rather than immediately taking her home, they'd driven for a while, just talking and laughing and…well, being them, she guessed. The couple they were at that time.

And he'd stopped his car in front of *her* house. Not her actual home, not where she'd grown up, but the charming, gingerbread-style house she'd adored since she was a child.

Daisy smiled now, in memory. When she was young, she'd pretend that fairies lived in the box-shaped, country-blue-and-white-painted house, with its profusion of decorative, intricately cut details edging the windows and the doors, the steep roof and the narrow front porch. She'd believed that house was magic, and she yearned to live there. With the fairies.

And it was there that Reid proposed. He'd promised that someday, they'd live in her magical fairy house. Would raise their children there, would love and laugh and create a life—*their* life—in the gingerbread house she'd always adored. And as they grew older and grayer, would sit on its narrow front porch in rocking chairs and hold hands.

Still in love. Still together.

Nostalgia, her past dreams and desires, whooshed in and emptied Daisy's lungs with a sobbing gasp. She'd said yes. Instantly and without reservation. Oh, she'd been so in love.

And in less than a year of that beautiful, miraculous night, she'd…left.

"Daisy." Reid's voice came from behind, low and evocative. Compelling and sensual. "Do me a favor and read the card before you throw the ring in my face."

Grateful that Reid could not see her cry, Daisy reached for the card. The glossy red front contained no words, no pictures, no clue at what she might find written within. The sick, slick glaze of fear coated the inside of her stomach and clogged her throat. Yes, she was afraid.

Almost desperately so.

Not *of* Reid, but *due to* his insistence at achieving that which she did not wish to surrender. How stupid, to believe she could keep him at a distance, her emotions—past and present—at bay. Now, by the single gesture of his giving her this ring, she recognized how delusional those beliefs were. How could she erect a strong enough shield to withstand this?

She wiped her cheeks with her arm, straightened her spine and cracked open the card. Familiar, bold handwriting filled the small space, and almost at the same instant she began reading, Reid recited his own words to her.

"Once upon a time, a boy loved a girl and promised her the world," he said. "The girl accepted and returned the promise, and they were to live happily ever after." Before she could inhale another breath, Reid's hands were on her shoulders. "Nothing has changed, Daisy. I still love you, and I still want to give you the world. All you have to do is say yes."

Sitting down, Reid cradled her body with his legs and wrapped his arms around her, gently pulling her backward until she rested against the firm wall of his chest. And being there, with his warmth and strength surrounding her, felt good. Right.

Imminently so.

The word *yes* danced on her tongue, and how…how crazy was that? Each one of her reasons for staying clear of this entanglement, of him, remained valid and powerful. He wasn't asking to date her or get to know her all over again. He was asking to *marry* her.

After an eight-year absence.

"I can't say yes," she whispered. "The idea is ludicrous."

"Is it, though?" he asked, his hand now resting above her heart. "In here, Daisy—where it counts—does the thought of becoming my wife and spending the rest of your life with me really feel so preposterous that it's beyond consideration?"

No. God help her, the thought of marrying Reid—even under these whacked-out circumstances—no longer seemed as outrageous, as unthinkable, as it should.

Admitting so would put her into a vulnerable and unsafe position. But she couldn't outright lie to him, either. So what she said was "My home isn't here, Reid. My life isn't here."

"That isn't an answer to the question I asked, darlin'," he said, rubbing his thumb along the side of her cheekbone. "What I think is that you can see us together as clearly as I can, but something is holding you back. What's holding you back, Daisy?"

Oh, Lord. He had to stop touching her. Had to stop talking to her in that warm, wholeheartedly intimate voice. Had to stop… He just had to stop. Because each second that passed weakened the thin line of her defense. It was as if each word, each caress, sent a jolt of electricity straight into her brain, shaking her thoughts, her arguments and her beliefs.

If this kept up, they would collapse into a pile of mush, and she would succumb. Allow his thoughts, arguments and beliefs to filter in, where they would grow in strength until she wouldn't be able to see past them to her own. She *knew* this to be true.

Out of nowhere, an image appeared in Daisy's brain. Of Erin sitting on her bed, clutching that pillow to her chest, adamantly refusing to play with Jinx, even though that was so obviously what she yearned for. From stubbornness or fear or something else?

Daisy still didn't know, but the image, the memory, struck a chord that resonated deep within. Was she doing the same? Maybe.

She looked at the engagement ring and had to stifle a sob. As glorious as her memories were, she could not find a way to believe that Reid would have proposed to her prior self if she hadn't formed her personality, likes and dislikes, around his.

And that truth right there negated every last word he'd said since her return. Any love he might profess to feel toward her—then and now—could not be trusted or believed in, based on her past inability to be her real self *with* him. She couldn't change what was already done, but she could—if she found the courage and strength—change the present.

If she found a way to remain wholly herself, to not fall into her old habits, maybe…maybe a second chance could exist with Reid.

"Daisy, baby, talk to me," Reid said, his mouth close to her ear. "Tell me what's churning in that head of yours, because this silence is killing me."

Tightening her hold on the ring, she balanced each of her thoughts and emotions and worries against the other, untangling the knotted mess they had become so she could view them separately. And she chose strength, courage and…knowledge.

Of their past, of what could be. She chose to try.

"You're right in that there are lingering feelings here, between us," she said, her voice quiet. Clear, though. This admittance, she knew, was as vital for her to say as it likely was for Reid to hear. "I'm not agreeing to a wedding, but I am willing to consider the possibility that…that we are not done. And I'm willing to put some attention toward that possibility."

"Attention toward that possibility, huh?" His voice, the gentle pressure of his arms and the firmness of his hold, didn't waver. The only sign that her words had impacted him in any way was his quick intake of breath. "Be clear here, Daisy. What do you mean by that?"

"I mean…" Hell. What *did* she mean? "No guarantees or anything, but I guess you could say I'm interested in spending time with you on a…a personal level."

"So we're dating? As in bowling and movies and candlelit dinners?"

"Um. Yes? But we can skip the bowling," she said, going for lighthearted. In truth, her heart hung so heavy, it could have been an anchor. What was she doing?

Trying, she reminded herself. She was *trying*.

"And…shall I take all of this as a maybe, then?" He didn't have to explain the origin of his question. Not when his engagement ring lay in the palm of her hand. "Or are we still locked in a definite no for the time being?"

"Not a definite no, but…" Oh, God. Did she really want to go as far as a maybe? She shook her head. "Not a maybe, either. Somewhere in between, I guess."

His jaw brushed her cheek. "Any answer above a no is a gift."

"I just…I don't…I can't…" *Breathe and calm down.* "No promises."

"Okay," he said without qualm. "No promises. Just… hope."

Hope. Suddenly, the moment became a little too overwhelming, so Daisy scooted forward a few inches, out of Reid's arms. Twisting to face him, she opened her hand to look at the ring. And her deep, deep yearning expanded. "I think this is the most beautiful ring any man has ever given to a woman, but I can't keep it. Not unless…that is—"

"That ring has always belonged to you," he said, his voice and gaze intent. Serious. "And if you give it back, I'll just keep finding inventive methods to repropose. Over and over and over." Now he spoke in a light, almost teasing manner. "Could be fun, I suppose."

"I can't keep this," she repeated. "I haven't said yes."

"You can, and I believe we've already established we're at the not-yet-a-maybe stage." He moved forward, decreasing the distance she'd put between them. "I'm not asking you to wear the ring, Daisy. I'm asking you to…safeguard it. That's all."

Before she could decide whether she should argue or agree, Reid pushed himself even closer. Heat flickered to life, pumping through her entire body with a rush of sensation and longing. His intent, she knew, was to kiss her. Fully, soundly. Just as she'd imagined earlier.

And, oh, she wanted that kiss. Wanted his mouth to capture hers and take control. Wanted nothing more, in fact, than to feel that familiar pull of his body to hers and hers to his, the power of their desire, in the joining of their lips. More than a want.

She *craved* his touch, his kiss.

As if he could read her thoughts, his hands came to her face to cup her cheeks. His deliciously dark eyes, sinful and beautiful and filled with all of the promises she wished she could believe in, met hers. He bent his head downward and her lips parted in anticipation.

Currents zapped in the air—electricity of their own making, of the unique heat they created together—and her body, as if on its own accord, leaned toward him. In eagerness and hunger and a desperate, almost frantic type of need that stole her breath.

That last bit was what unclogged her circuitry and kicked her rational brain to life.

"Stop," she whispered, pushing her empty hand against his shoulder. Their lips were, maybe, separated by the width of a solitary strand of hair. So close she could almost feel him, taste him. She pushed again, harder this time. "No kissing."

A kiss would lead to sex. And sex would lead to falling too fast, which would then cloud her ability to coherently assess her feelings. Simply speaking, sex muddled everything.

"No…kissing?" His gaze, still dark and heated but steady, locked on to hers.

"No. No kissing," she repeated, forcing strength and surety into her tone. She didn't know how successful she was since the pounding of her heart reverberated louder than the volume of her voice. Space. She required space. She slid backward. "No touching, either."

Reid's brow quirked. "Are we setting rules now?"

Well, she hadn't thought of it that way, but… "Yes, that's exactly what we're doing."

He tapped his fingers against his leg. "Of course," he said, his voice smooth and rich, "you rightly pointed out that you didn't have to accept *my* rules. But I should accept yours?"

Flustered, from the almost kiss and the exchange, Daisy nodded.

"Not sure that's entirely fair," he said easily, without so

much as a bat of a lash. "How about if we compromise? We each get to set...oh, let's say three rules. And we each agree to accept and follow both sets of rules from the start."

She gripped her fist tighter. On the surface, his suggestion came off as logical. But she didn't have the slightest doubt that there was a catch. Something he wanted from her, maybe. Or something he wanted her to do that he didn't think she'd go for.

Of course, she could do the same.

"I don't know," she said after a deliberately long pause. "What if you set a rule that I don't like or vice versa? We need veto power. One veto each, no questions asked."

"So I lay out my three rules, you do the same and we can each strike one from the playing field. Why, we'd only have two rules each, and I really had my heart set on three."

"No, no, no." She almost laughed. *Almost.* "You state your first rule. I either agree and accept or I veto. Then it's my turn to state my first rule. We go back and forth until we've each set our three. But," she said, "we each only get a single no, so we have to use it wisely."

"Seems you've thought of everything." Reid stroked his jaw, as if in contemplation. "Fair enough. But you know that good manners—meaning, ladies first—dictate that you should start."

"Happy to." Her goal was to get him to veto right off, before she instituted her no-touching-or-kissing rule. And there was no way he'd agree to this. "My first rule is that you move out of this house. Tomorrow, after we have a chance to talk with Erin and Megan."

"It's a solid swing if you're angling for a veto," he murmured, his tone even and his features composed, "but you're forgetting a few key facts. You and the girls are accustomed to each other now. And frankly, now that we're dating, I sort of like the idea of picking you up and dropping you off. More traditional that way." He winked. "More romantic, too."

"So you're saying…?"

"I agree to your first rule."

"Are you quite sure?" she asked, shocked by his agreement. "What if this upsets the girls? I thought you were all about not changing anything else in their worlds right now. And Erin still isn't completely comfortable with me, so I'm not sure—"

"I already agreed, Daisy." Reid made a tsk-tsk noise. "But to calm your worries, the girls are fine with the idea of my moving out. We talked about it earlier, when we were outside with the snowmen." At her questioning look, he said, "It's time. And I'll still be around every day."

Ah. Well, then. And he was right, she supposed, but that didn't alter her surprise. Or the fact that she now had to come up with something else for him to veto.

"Okay," she said. "Your turn."

"*My* first rule is you have to help with the wedding planning, as if you have accepted my proposal." Before she could object or veto, he held up a hand. "Now, don't get all fretful. This won't equate to anything other than what I've said. There isn't a hidden agenda. I just want you to be a part of the planning."

"Wh-why?"

"Because, then, if your not-yet-a-maybe becomes the yes I hope it will, our wedding will actually be *our* wedding. Seems important, is all."

"I… That doesn't strike me as…" Aargh! Why couldn't she talk? Think? Or, for that matter, breathe? "What, exactly, do you envision this help entailing? Be specific, please."

"So businesslike." Quick humor darted across Reid's face. He reined it in and said, "You offer your heartfelt opinion, Daisy. On everything from the ceremony to the reception.

Select a wedding dress—I'll pay for it, of course—and…I don't know, whatever else a bride needs to get married. Basically, the whole shebang."

Trouble. Of the triple-shot-of-insane variety.

There were reasons—a gaggle of them—why this was so *not* in her best interests. Of greatest concern, though, was with how she'd reacted to the ring, to his sentimental card and the near-kiss. She feared—just by taking part in the preparations—that she'd become far too immersed in the situation, too attached to Reid's vision to see her own.

But damn it, if *this* was his first horse out of the gate, what were the other two? She couldn't chance losing her one and only veto on something so relatively straightforward.

"Fine," she said. "I accept rule one."

"That, my dear, is very good news."

Hmmph. He didn't appear disappointed. Rather, he had that satisfied, cat-with-a-bowl-of-cream glitter in his eyes. Possibly, she'd just made a mistake.

"Rule two," she said, thinking quickly, "is that…if my not-yet-a-maybe does not become a yes within a week of May sixth, you cancel the wedding. All of it, from beginning to end."

Probably, he'd nix this rule, and then she'd be able to institute her no-kissing-or-touching mandate. But if he didn't, she'd at least be secure in the knowledge that his mule-headedness wouldn't put him in an untenable, uncomfortable situation come May sixth.

She hated the thought of that scenario repeating itself.

"Veto," he said without preamble, causing her to inwardly wince. "That one's dead in the water. Come up with another."

"No kissing." Why, oh, why, was he so determined to see this wedding through? Shouldn't her agreement to date be enough for the moment? "Or touching of an intimate nature."

"What if you instigate the kissing or the touching?" he retorted. "May I then return the kiss or the touch, or…?"

"Yes, but I don't expect that to happen," she said with a hard swallow. Not for a while, anyway. "And it's your turn."

"Right." Rubbing his hands together, he said, "My second rule is that we will, at some juncture in the near future, have a no-holds-barred discussion about our past."

"That isn't a problem, Reid. I figured we—"

"There's more, Daisy," he said, his voice muted. "I will want to know every thought that led you to leaving that morning. And then—" he exhaled a constricted breath "—I want the opportunity to speak my piece."

Hmm. None of what he'd said seemed to be asking for too much, but goose bumps dotted Daisy's skin and pinpricks of alarm appeared. "Is that everything?"

"Yes, other than it's my call when we have this conversation."

"Okay. That's…fine."

"You accept?"

"Yes." Despite her unexplainable foreboding, she wouldn't deny either of them a conversation they needed to have. Besides which, she'd left him with a letter on their wedding day. This was the least of what she owed him.

"All righty, then," Reid said. "Your third rule is…?"

"No avoiding of the truth, fibbing or creating any attention-stealing diversions if I ask you a point-blank question," she replied. "You have to answer. Completely and honestly."

This, she hoped, would give her the ability to keep future surprises at a minimum.

"I'm committed to honesty, Daisy, and—"

"I'm not calling you a liar," she clarified. "I just don't want to show up for what I think is a lunch date, and find a roomful of people expecting us to get married. And don't tell me such a scheme is beyond you, because I know better."

He grinned. "See? You know me as well as I know you. But I'm fairly set on May sixth, so you have nothing to worry about in that regard."

"Right. Nothing to worry about," she muttered. From her perspective, she saw plenty to keep her awake with concerns. "Your turn. What's your third rule?"

"Pretty sure you'll veto this one."

"Try me."

"From now until May sixth," he said, his voice and demeanor very much that of a resigned man, "we talk for no less than thirty minutes each day. By phone or in person, I don't much care. But every day, I get thirty minutes of your time."

"That's it?" Narrowing her eyes, she sat up straighter. "Your final rule is to *talk* to me?"

"That's what I said, isn't it?" Leveraging his weight on the palm of his hands, he leaned backward and stretched his legs. "Not such a difficult request, I don't think. Though, I'll completely understand if you choose to pound your metaphorical gavel in outright rejection."

Why hadn't she prevented the freaking wedding-planning imperative? Leave it to Reid to start with his most significant rule instead of a red herring, accurately pegging her unwillingness to get rid of a veto too soon. This rule, on the other hand, meant nothing to him.

Unless…oh. Maybe he *had* saved his most significant rule for last, and he was using *this* rule as the red herring. Meaning, he had another rule, the one he really wanted to put through, one she would highly object to, waiting in the wings.

Not that it mattered. The request was simple and straightforward, so she had zero reason to kick it to the curb. "Good try, but I'm not biting."

"Biting? Not sure I'd object to *gentle* biting, but—"

"Drop the act, buddy," she said with a sniff. "I am not

saying no to this. You want to talk with me every single day between now and May sixth? Fine. I agree to the rule."

The satisfaction was back, all but oozing over his expression, making Daisy believe that *this* had been his goal all along. But why? What was so important about making sure she'd speak with him every damn day?

"Excellent," he said with his trademark wicked-grin-and-a-wink combination. "And just think, we might end up with a story worth telling our future grandchildren. Wouldn't that be something?"

"Yep. That would be something." Still irritated and confused by his last rule, she pulled herself to her feet. "Since we're done and I'm tired and this is the room where I sleep—until tomorrow, anyway—I'd appreciate some privacy."

He was off the floor and approaching her before she finished voicing her request. Despite her bout of irritation, she was captivated by the look of his long-and-lean, tough-and-rugged frame in motion. And with no warning whatsoever, her craving for him and his touch reignited

"Wh-what are you doing?" she stammered when he stopped in front of her. Far too close for any sense of self-preservation. "Do you…ah…need a definition of the word *privacy?* Because invading my personal space does not liken to—"

"Not trying to invade anything," he said, kneeling down by her feet. "But you dropped your ring. And while I could buy another, my greater preference is to not lose this one."

"That's… I didn't realize." She inhaled a lungful of air. "I'm sorry. I had no idea I'd—"

"Nothing to be sorry about. The ring is here, safe and sound." With that, he stood and pressed the ring into her palm. "Keep this, Daisy, whether you choose to wear it or not."

Again, she closed her fist around the ring. Again, she

shuddered in melancholy and loss. Right or wrong, she wanted to keep the ring. "If…if you're sure, I'll hold on to it. For now."

"I'm sure." Lifting his hand, he brought it as close to her cheek as he could without skin meeting skin. Her face warmed even without the physical touch. "May I kiss you, Daisy?"

Yes. "I don't… No. Not now. Not…yet."

"Okay," he said simply, his voice soft, his gaze securely holding hers. "I'm curious about something, though."

"What…um…might that be?"

"Why try to cancel this 'probable sham of a wedding' merely a week before May sixth? Why not outright cancel it altogether?" He paused, as if to let his words, his meaning, take root. And, oh, did they ever. "You could have, you know. After I vetoed, you had the control to stop all of this 'wedding nonsense,' and you chose not to. I find that…interesting."

The power of his statement rendered her speechless. She noiselessly shook her head back and forth as his words looped in an endless circle in her brain. Why hadn't she, indeed?

One more long, intense look—as if he were trying to peek into her mind—before Reid stepped away, giving her room to breathe. "Sweet dreams, Daisy."

Then he left her alone. With her thoughts. Her worries. Her confusion. Not the least of which was why she hadn't considered, even for a second, doing what he'd just suggested.

Because he was right. Absolutely correct in his assessment that she'd had the control, the ability to put an end to all of this wedding insanity tonight, the second she'd received his veto.

And she hadn't.

Chapter Nine

The following morning, Reid surveyed Parker's bedroom. He'd made the bed with clean sheets, vacuumed and even wiped off the light film of dust that had accumulated on the maple dresser and the nightstands. All of his belongings were packed and ready to go, and so far as he could tell, he hadn't forgotten anything. The room was ready for its new occupant.

And, after talking with the girls over breakfast—which had proved challenging food-wise, since Megan had declared today the color pink day—he believed they were also ready. Or, he corrected, as ready as they could be. A few questions were asked, a few sad looks were given, but Erin and Megan understood that Reid was not vacating their lives. He'd still see them every day. If they needed him, he was a phone call and a short drive away.

Sighing, he grabbed his two bags and went downstairs. He wanted to stop by his house and unpack, settle in a bit and—if he could fit in a shopping trip—hit the grocery store before his shift on the mountain that afternoon.

He deposited his luggage by the front door and turned toward the living room. Despite his belief that moving out of the Lennox household was the right step to take, he felt strangely lost and…deflated by the prospect. Waking up to-morrow morning without the chatter or exuberance of two little girls as his alarm clock would seem empty.

And lonely as hell.

Before he could sink too far into his gloomy thoughts, Jinx roared around the corner of the archway. Seeing Reid, she slammed on the brakes and slid to a skidding halt, just short of impact. She gurgled a yelp of surprise, but…that was it. No growling. No ankle tugging.

"Hey, girl," Reid said, hoping the peace they'd found in the kitchen hadn't evaporated. "Where were you headed off to in such an almighty rush?"

Her tail swished along the floor. And while she watched him with interest, there didn't seem to be the same level of wariness in her gaze. Good signs.

"See?" Reid said, petting the dog. "I'm the same guy today I was last night. Still your friend. Still won't let you down. Promise." Jinx snorted one of her canine replies and pushed her head upward, against Reid's hand. "You like that, huh?"

"Oh, she isn't picky. Any sort of affection makes her happy," Daisy said, walking into the entryway from the living room. Stopping, she crossed her arms over the navy-blue-and-gray sweatshirt she wore, eyeing Reid and Jinx with curiosity. "How'd you pull this off, anyway?"

"Patience." Standing straight, he grinned. "Perhaps a touch of that obstinate nature you continually accuse me of having. We also," he said, nodding toward Jinx, "had quite the conversation. She told me a story you wouldn't believe."

Daisy's lips quirked at the corners, and humor—as bright as the sun—glimmered in her eyes, over her expression. "Is that so? Which story did Jinx…ah…share with you?"

"If I told you, I'd be breaking a confidence. Sorry, can't do that."

"Uh-huh." She waited a beat, then said, "Seriously, I

have a few male friends, and they've tried everything to get Jinx to like them. Nothing's worked. So what did you do?"

Male friends? As in actual, platonic friendships or… more? Jealousy, swift and fierce, heated Reid's blood. Not a condition he experienced often, but the thought—the mere suggestion—of Daisy being romantically or sexually involved with another man did not sit well.

And that, Reid recognized, was a massive understatement. In truth, he had the sudden urge to stand over Daisy with a sword, protecting her from any man who might get it in his head to so much as *think* about looking at her. Ridiculous. Overkill. Way too cavemanlike.

But damn, that was how he felt.

Wasn't as if he'd give in to such an urge. Besides which, hadn't she described herself as a single woman on the very night she'd returned to Steamboat Springs? Yup, she had.

Once his blood cooled a few degrees, he shrugged. "Not much of a secret. I kept trying, kept reminding Jinx that I wasn't someone she had to fear."

"That can't be all there is to it," Daisy said in obvious doubt. "This is a huge accomplishment. Even the rescue agency stopped trying to retrain her. She… They called her a difficult-to-place dog. She required a female-only household."

"We reached an agreement, I guess." Reid scratched behind Jinx's ears, considering their exchange and then how similar his give-and-take with Daisy had progressed. Both scenarios had included talking, promises and…quite a bit of floor-scooting. He almost laughed. Daisy and Jinx had a hell of a lot in common. "Boiled down to plain old patience and the Foster mulishness."

"Well…whatever or however, thank you."

"Welcome. I was on my way to say goodbye to you and the girls when Jinx demanded my attention," he said. "Where are Erin and Megan? I expected they'd be with you."

"Upstairs. Going through the snow-magic book again, ascertaining they didn't forget anything." Daisy glanced toward the stairway. "They thought we'd hear from Parker by now, that he was coming home today. I told them that even magic can take a while to work."

"Ah." Reid had worried about this, but shooting down two little girls' hopes with the cold truth of reality was not something he would do. "I'll go on up and talk with them, see if I can find a balance between their belief in magic and honest expectations."

"I… That would be good," Daisy said. "Also, did you have some type of a conversation with Erin and Megan about who would take care of them if Parker died?"

"The night you got here," Reid said, thinking back to that evening. "The girls had watched this movie about orphans, and Erin had some concerns. She wanted to know who would take care of them if their father died. I mentioned you as one of the possibilities. Why?"

He listened as Daisy explained what had happened during their drive to the hospital. Why hadn't he connected the dots between Erin's behavior toward her aunt and the conversation he'd had with her? All of this time, she'd been suffering, scared that her dad might never come home, and Reid hadn't known. It made him feel about two inches high.

No. Shorter.

"I'll talk to them about that, too," he said, glancing at his watch. "I should probably do that now, before too much more time goes to waste."

"Wait! You don't have to move out," Daisy said, speaking so fast that her words merged into and on top of one another, and a rosy blush spread across her nose, her cheeks. "I hadn't meant for that rule to go through. I thought you'd veto it, and…"

"I know." Unable to stop himself, he moved closer to Daisy. "And if I didn't believe the girls or you were ready, I would've said no. But you are, they are, and I… With what's going on with us, leaving now is logical. Besides which," he said with a wink, hoping to lighten the moment, "if I stay, I'll have difficulty abiding by your no-kiss, no-touch rule."

Fine eyebrows arched in amusement. Or annoyance. One of the two. "You break that rule and I'll break one of yours. Or an arm. Which of the four is most important to you?"

"Go for the arm. The rules are far more important," he said, captivated by her eyes, her lips, her hair…hell, all of her. "Do you realize how astonishingly beautiful you are to me?"

"Um…no?" The rosy blush traveled from her cheeks to her neck to the glimpse of her collarbone. She rolled her bottom lip into her mouth before blowing out a breath. And all he wanted to do was pull her into his arms. "I'm just me, Reid. Nothing special."

"And that's where you're wrong. You're entirely special."

Blinking rapidly, she dropped her vision away from his. Embarrassment or pleasure? He hoped for pleasure, but guessed a combination of both. "I…well…um…"

"When someone offers you a compliment, the proper response is 'thank you.'"

"It's just that I—" raising her chin, she once again met his gaze with hers "—don't know if you see me as I really am. I'd like to change that. I'd like to…be myself with you and…um… What I mean to say is—" She stopped, breathed. "Thank you, Reid."

"Welcome," he responded. Where had she been going with that? He started to ask when he noticed a loose eyelash on Daisy's cheek. "I'm about to touch you," he warned. "But not intimately, so there isn't any call for slapping or kicking or fussing of any kind."

"Okay?" she said with another blink.

Approval enough in his estimation. Gently, he lifted the lash from her skin and placed it in his palm. Showed it to her and said, "Make a wish, Daisy." She swallowed, nodded. And he blew the lash from his palm into the air. "There you go. Hope the wish comes true, darlin'."

Rubbing her cheeks, as if to erase the pink glow she must know was there, she said, "You continually surprise me, Reid Foster. Sometimes, I think I'm ready to kill you."

"And what about those other times?" Probably, he shouldn't tease her, but the impulse was too great to resist. "Your thoughts have anything to do with kissing?"

A tremble of a smile appeared. Not all the way there, but damn close. "Maybe." The slightest of shrugs. "Maybe not. That's for me to know and you to…wonder about."

Oh, he would. Without a friggin' doubt.

"We're still good to go?" Anxiety, sudden and dartlike, pierced his gut and dried out his tongue. "All that we discussed…those rules and dating. Giving us a real, solid shot. Nothing's…ah…changed there, correct? No new qualms in the light of the day?"

"Morning-after regrets, you mean?" For some unknown reason, she laughed. "I meant everything I said. So, yes, we're still good to go." Another swallow, this one heavier than the last. "But no guarantees. That part hasn't changed, either."

Well, that was good enough for him. When he considered where they'd stood this time yesterday, a far sight better than just "good enough."

"Haven't asked for a guarantee. Don't particularly want one at this moment, anyhow," he said, speaking from the heart. "I'm…pleased enough with our current level of progress."

"Pleased *enough?* What more could you want from me?"

"Now that's a question." Reid ran his hand over his jaw. "Where to start? With a kiss or deciding some of the details for the wedding or straight to the honeymoon?"

"Did you have an accident sometime over the past eight

years?" she asked, her voice modulated and serious. "Something that might have caused…oh, I don't know, a brain injury?"

"Nope." He knocked his fist against the side of his head. "Rock-solid. All of us Fosters are blessed with hard heads. In fact, you might hear from my family soon. My mother or my sister or…hell, any of them might call or stop by."

Just that fast, her complexion went from pink to alabaster. "Wh-why might your family call or stop by?"

"They're helping with the wedding details, of course."

"They *know?*"

"I wouldn't think of getting married without telling my family, Daisy. Now that would be insane," he said. "You remember how they are. Can you imagine—"

"Possibly," she said with a temperamental flip of her hair, "you might have considered planning what I *have* agreed to before a freaking ceremony I have *not* agreed to. I said I'd date you, Reid. Not marry you. I can't believe you told your family! They…they…"

"Had to tell them. They'd have found out anyhow." True enough. They would've. Every member of his family had the ability to scent out secrets with the accuracy of a bloodhound. That being said, he wisely chose not to share he'd *asked* for their help. "And I have set up our first…odd to call it our *first* date. Friday, all day. I'll pick you up in the morning, after the girls leave for school. Haley will be here when they get home."

"I haven't said yes. I've said no. I've said not-yet-a-maybe, but I haven't said yes," Daisy mumbled, more to herself than to Reid. "And he told his family. His *family.*"

"Ah, Daisy? Still here. No reason to refer to me in the third person." She worked her jaw, but not a solitary sound emerged, and she squeezed her hands into fists. *Uh-oh.* "Guessing you need a little alone time right about now," he said. "I'll…ah…go talk with the girls. Make sure they know I'll be around tomorrow afternoon. Maybe we can all visit Parker together."

Eyes as green as they could get bore into him, but she still didn't utter so much as a syllable. So that, along with the smoke he could almost see pouring from her ears, made him think that he should, possibly—and just until she calmed some—get the hell out of Dodge.

Being a man who listened to his instincts, Reid blew Daisy a kiss—since he couldn't give her a real one just yet—and took the stairs to the girls' bedroom. Two at a time.

Pink day had started out easily enough with a breakfast consisting of strawberries-and-cream oatmeal. Lunch—with overly milky tomato soup, the final slice of ham and a tube of fruit-punch-flavored yogurt—had been managed. Dinner, however, was proving problematic.

Megan did not want any repeats, and there just wasn't one other food in the house that remotely resembled the color pink. Daisy knew this, as she'd scoured the cupboards, the pantry, the refrigerator and the freezer a total of three times.

"We might have to pick a second color, peanut," Daisy said, using Reid's nickname for Megan. "For this meal only."

Setting her mouth into a stubborn line, Megan gave her head a firm and decisive shake. "It's pink day. Pink clothes and pink food and *everything* is supposed to be pink."

"I realize this," Daisy said calmly. "But unless you're okay with oatmeal or another bowl of tomato soup, we're clean out of pink food."

"No. Don't want oatmeal or soup."

Both of the girls had reacted in different ways to Reid's departure. Megan's mood had slipped into the grumpy range, while Erin had returned to her withdrawn persona.

Believe it or not, until now, Megan's crankiness had been easier to handle than Erin's distance.

A well-placed tickle, for example, brought forth a squeal of giggles in the younger Lennox daughter. Erin, however, seemed uninterested in any and every type of activity Daisy had attempted. Including playing with Jinx. This time, at least, Daisy understood the crux of the problem—Erin missed Reid—and believed she'd adjust to the change in schedule once she saw that Reid would, indeed, be stopping in every single day.

Focusing on her older niece, Daisy said, "Any pink food ideas, Erin?"

"Don't know." Erin ate a bite of her macaroni and cheese. "Pink lemonade and pink marshmallows?" She wrinkled her nose. "Oh. Daddy sometimes eats pink fish."

Salmon, probably. "Don't think we have any pink fish lying around," Daisy said. "We could go to the store. Do you like fish, Megan?"

"Fish sticks, but they're not pink." Rubbing her tummy, she frowned. "And I'm hungry now, so don't want to go to the store."

Tomorrow, Daisy promised herself, she'd go food shopping and buy a veritable rainbow of selections. "I know you're hungry, and I'm sorry, but we either put off dinner and go to the store or you let me make you something to eat that isn't pink." When Megan neglected to respond, Daisy said, "Or you can skip dinner altogether, and—"

Sighing in frustration, she crumpled her hair with her fingers. Nope, she couldn't go that far. Could not let her niece go without a meal. Somehow, she was going to have to figure this out. God. How did parents manage this sort of stuff on a day in, day out basis?

"It's a pink day!" Megan said again, planting her elbows on the table and her chin in her hands. "And when I had a blue day, Reid didn't make me eat foods that weren't blue!"

Ouch. Blue? Okay, then. If common sense wasn't going to work, Daisy needed to try a different route. She was good at creative solutions. Certainly, there was one to be found here. Sitting down in the chair next to Megan, she said, "Can you explain how you pick a color day? When you got up this morning, how did you know that today was a *pink* day?"

"Some days are any color days, like rainbows. Other days aren't." Megan pursed her lips into a pout. "I just know it. Inside. And today *felt* like pink, so that's what it is. Pink, pink, pink."

Not all that helpful. "What does pink feel like?"

Light brown eyes narrowed. "Like pink."

Oh, good grief. In another set of circumstances—such as watching a similar scene on a sitcom—Daisy would laugh. Not in this situation, though.

"Right. But what does pink feel like—" she tapped Megan's chest "—in here? Does it feel sad or funny or silly or mad? Does the feeling make you want to sing or…go outside and play?"

"It's…happy. Being happy," Megan said slowly, grasping on to Daisy's intent. "But not just happy. Warm and… and it's like when I'm on Daddy's lap and we're both covered in a blanket and we're watching TV or he's telling me a story or he's brushing my hair."

Safe. Pink meant safe for Megan. Nurturing, too, Daisy guessed.

Why pink instead of yellow or green or purple didn't really matter. Somehow, her niece had connected that specific color to how she felt when she was with her dad. And since the girls had awakened that morning thinking about their snow magic and their wish for Parker to come home soon, then of course today was a pink day.

Little-girl logic, perhaps, but Daisy totally understood. Now to connect that feeling of safety and parental nurturing to something other than the color pink. If she could. "Tell me something, Megan. When your daddy is home, what would he make for dinner if he wanted to make you laugh?"

"Pancakes," Megan *and* Erin said at the exact same moment. "With smiley faces!"

"Sometimes, he'll cook them in different shapes, too," Megan added, her tone heading from grouchy straight to exuberant. "Like hearts or flowers or stars. And we get to pick what goes in them! Chocolate chips or bananas or—"

"Apples and cinnamon," Erin interrupted, also sounding more upbeat. "And he always puts on this really funny hat and apron. And then he'll dance all around the kitchen and try to flip the pancakes high into the air. As high as the ceiling! And try to catch them again."

Megan blinked. "He's not so good at that. Once…once," she said, her laughter spilling into her words, "a pancake landed on top of his hat! And he said—"

"That he meant to do that!" Erin blurted. Then both girls were laughing so hard they had tears in their eyes and were almost doubled over in their chairs. A solid minute of hysteria passed before Erin caught her breath. "He looked so silly, Aunt Daisy!"

"I bet he did." Daisy could easily imagine her brother in the scene her nieces had just depicted. Grinning, she said, "He's a pretty great dad, huh?"

"He's the best dad ever! The bestest of the bestest!" With a sigh that must have reached her toes, Megan collapsed against her chair. "I don't like that he's gone, Aunt Daisy."

"Me, neither," Erin said. "I wish he was here now."

"I know, and I know he wishes he could be here right now, too." Small words to offer real comfort for such an intrinsic longing. Too small.

Megan's stomach rumbled. Loudly. "I'm still hungry, and now I miss Daddy a lot, and…and…" Trailing off, she crossed her arms over her chest, and with her defiant expression firmly in place, said, "It's pink day."

"Yep, it is pink day," Daisy agreed. "So we can go to the grocery store and buy some appropriately pink food. Or... we can skip a pink dinner and make pancakes together. And instead of waiting until after we eat, we can call your dad while we're cooking. If we put him on speakerphone, he can help us make the pancakes just like he does. Your choice, sweetheart."

"I...I choose—" Megan scrunched her face in concentration "—pancakes and Daddy on the phone! That will be as good as a pink day, I think. Better!"

Which was exactly Daisy's hope.

"What about me?" Pushing her fork into her barely touched macaroni and cheese, Erin frowned. "I already have my dinner, but I want—"

"What dinner?" Daisy hijacked Erin's bowl and hid it behind her back. She gave her niece an exaggerated wink and said, "I have absolutely no clue what you're talking about, Erin. I see nothing that looks like dinner around here."

More laughter ensued, and oh, was there a better sound in the world than happy children giggling? Daisy didn't think so. Nothing she'd heard had ever come close, anyway.

They dug out the hat—an extra-tall, fairly hideous in the comical sense, lime-green chef's hat dotted with bright red-and-purple hearts—and the oversize matching apron, which the girls insisted Daisy wear. So she did. Proudly, even.

And when they got Parker on the phone, he talked them through every step he used to make the perfect pancakes. If he told Daisy to dance, she danced. If he told her to flip the pancakes high into the air, she did...and even caught them more times than not.

Not a one landed on her hat, though. That was fine. More than fine, really. Some memories, some moments, shouldn't be touched. And that particular remembrance belonged only to Erin and Megan and Parker. She'd prefer to let it stay that way. Intact and…precious.

After dinner, the rest of the evening progressed in a much smoother fashion. Even so, there was another absence that couldn't be ignored. An absence that went by the name of Reid Foster. Naturally, the girls missed him. Unless there was another reason for her near-constant searching of the house and occasional whimpers, Jinx also missed him.

Without thought, Daisy reached for the long, sterling-silver necklace she wore under her sweatshirt, running her fingers along the chain until they closed around her engagement ring. She couldn't wear the ring on her hand, but she couldn't *not* wear it at all, either.

So, yes, despite her hope to the contrary, Daisy missed Reid, too.

Chapter Ten

The first part of the week zipped by in a haze of activity. Sure, Daisy had already learned the basic ropes of her nieces' daily lives, but handling these myriad details without Reid's guiding presence—specifically, the morning routine—was almost an entirely new concept.

Something as simple as a misplaced shoe or forgotten lunch boxes or even the up-and-down moods of two little girls could throw an otherwise well-planned schedule into chaos. Evenings were easier, by a large margin. Reid would show up either just before or after dinner, and he'd jump in to help with homework, dinner or the girls' bedtime routines.

Strangely, perhaps, he didn't stay long once Erin and Megan were in bed. And, other than reminding Daisy about their all-day date on Friday, he didn't behave as if he were a man in love. He didn't try to kiss her or touch her or, hell, even converse with her beyond generalities.

A relief in some ways. Incredibly frustrating in others.

Probably, he was giving her space to come to terms with the agreement they'd reached on Saturday. Well, that or he was saving his energy for Friday, for whatever those plans entailed.

Regardless, by Wednesday morning, Daisy had decided to stop stressing over Reid's behavior and, instead, focus on what she could control. Starting with the practical, she wanted to clean the kitchen, deal with the laundry and respond to a few of the email inquiries she'd received from possible new clients. All of which were referrals from past clients.

But then, she wanted to visit with her brother.

While she had taken Erin and Megan to see their father the prior two afternoons, she'd yet to have any one-on-one time with Parker. His next—and hopefully, last—surgery was scheduled soon, this one meant to finish repairing the damage done to his leg. It was time, she believed, to have a conversation about their relationship, their family. A few apologies on her end, and a promise to be better, more involved, in the future.

And she didn't want to wait. Surgery was surgery. Anything could happen.

So, with this in mind, she hurried through her tasks and was almost ready to leave for the hospital when the chime of the doorbell rang. Not Reid, she guessed, as he typically let himself in. One of the neighbors, perhaps, wanting an update on Parker's health.

When she opened the door, however, the person waiting on the small front porch was not a neighbor. Rather, her visitor was none other than Reid's mother.

Margaret Foster looked much the same as Daisy remembered, with her straight, just-above-the-shoulders reddish-brown hair, warm sage-green eyes and smooth, lightly freckled complexion. Her petite and curvaceous frame carried a few extra pounds, and by sight only, she might be considered a soft woman. Daisy knew better.

Not only was Margaret physically strong from years of carting around trays loaded with dishes, but she was also, from the inside out, built of solid steel. She didn't mince words, she didn't disappear when trouble loomed and she'd go to battle for anything that mattered to her.

Especially her children. You didn't mess with the Foster kids unless you wanted to deal with their mama. And… well, Daisy *had* messed with a Foster kid. The firstborn, even. And she hadn't seen Margaret since the night before she was supposed to become her daughter-in-law.

Apprehension and, she wasn't ashamed to admit, fear solidified in her stomach. Even so, she metaphorically straightened her spine, and said, "Hi, Margaret. I… It's good to see you."

"Hello, Daisy," Margaret said with a small smile that didn't quite reach her eyes. "You don't look as if you were expecting me. Did Reid forget to tell you I was coming over?"

"He…mentioned some of his family might call or stop by, but—" She pulled in a breath. Oh, was he in trouble when she saw him next. "He didn't say exactly when."

The slightest touch of humor glinted in the other woman's gaze and teased into her smile. "Well, knowing Reid, I'm sure it was an oversight on his part."

Doubtful. More likely, this was his way of making damn sure Daisy was at home and not hiding out at the library or the coffee shop when his mother arrived. Because, yeah, that was probably what she would've done. What she said, though, was "Yes. Probably an oversight."

"I hope this isn't a bad time for you?" Margaret's voice, while not unkind, held the crispness of an under-ripe apple. "There are some basic details for the wedding that need to be settled before any other arrangements can be made. Won't take long, I don't think."

"No, no. Please come in. This is fine." What else was she supposed to say? Stepping to the side, so Margaret could enter, Daisy wondered what information Reid had shared with his family. "Did Reid tell you that I'm not... I haven't... That is—"

"That you haven't agreed to marry him? Oh, yes," Margaret said as she entered the house. "But he's also made it clear that we should proceed with the preparations." She regarded Daisy with a fair amount of curiosity. "I take it you're willing to help, despite your refusal?"

"In a manner of speaking, yes." Willing? Not so much. But if she expected Reid to abide by her rules, then she'd follow his. "Let's go into the kitchen and I'll explain. Over coffee?"

Margaret nodded. Then, seeing Jinx, who had finally poked her head around Daisy's legs, she said, "Why, hello there. Aren't you beautiful?" Kneeling, she held out her hand, and Jinx, always happy to make a new friend—of the female variety, anyway—rushed forward for love.

Several minutes later, once Margaret and Jinx had become properly acquainted, Daisy poured two mugs of coffee and brought them to the kitchen table.

"I'm not trying to muddle this...odd situation," she said, sitting across from Margaret. "But Reid is stubborn. He refuses to back down on this wedding idea, and I can't say yes. I—" she exhaled a breath, tried to steady her nerves "—*won't* say yes."

Wrapping her hands around her coffee mug, Margaret let out a soft sigh. "Ever?"

"I don't know." Daisy shook her head. "How can I know that? We... I've agreed to see where this—he and I—might lead. But I don't anticipate I'll have that answer by May sixth."

"And yet you're willing to assist in the wedding plans?"

"I don't really have a choice." She then attempted to explain the reasons why. The rules and how they came into being, his and hers. What she did not do was share the more intimate aspects of her feelings, her concerns...her fears. Those were private.

When she finished, Margaret chuckled. "He's a smart one, isn't he?"

"Too smart at times." Words, a million of them, crowded into Daisy's brain. Words she wanted to say. Words that Margaret deserved to hear. "I'm sorry for leaving the way I did," she said, allowing those words to spill from her mouth, her heart. "For whatever turmoil I caused. For hurting Reid. I was in a lot of pain that morning, and the truth is—" Daisy blinked to push away the sudden pressure of tears "—I just...I couldn't stay."

"Leaving him with only a letter was cowardly," Margaret said, speaking in a slow and steady beat. Still not unkind. Just matter-of-fact. "And yes, you caused him pain. He was devastated, nearly crippled by the loss of you. Ending your relationship in that manner wasn't honorable, Daisy. To you or to him, to all you'd built together."

"I'm aware of this now. Very much so, and I—" blinking harder, Daisy dipped her chin "—I wish I'd had the courage to do what was right then. I wish I'd somehow found the strength."

"Do you have the courage now?" Margaret asked, without even the slightest hesitation in her voice. "To do what is right, for both of you?"

"Yes," Daisy said, also with zero hesitation. "If similar circumstances presented themselves today, I wouldn't just run. I'd talk to Reid, face-to-face."

"And you won't accept my son's proposal unless you're absolute in that decision?"

"Correct. You have my promise on that, Margaret."

Silence, heavy with emotion, pressed in around them. Suddenly, Margaret reached over and grasped one of Daisy's hands. "I'm sorry, too, for what you had to go through that morning. Your parents made an unfair and thoughtless decision in the timing of that…confession. I had just as much anger for them, for what they did, as I had sadness for your choice."

This sentiment, and the truth behind them, shocked Daisy. Margaret was showing her grace and love when she could be—had the right to be—condemning and spiteful.

For a split second, she thought of her own mother, of the random attempts she'd made over the years to find some type of peace with her daughter. And how Daisy had not shown Clara Lennox the same grace that Margaret had bestowed on her. A troubling realization.

Shaking off the thought, Daisy said, "I mourned the loss, too. Of Reid. Of you and Paul, all of the Fosters. I couldn't wait to become an actual part of the Foster clan."

"We felt the same." Margaret squeezed Daisy's hand. "We loved you, too. All of us. And that, I think, made it more difficult to accept your choice. Or to easily forgive, because you were already a part of our family, yet you had hurt Reid so terribly."

"I understand," Daisy whispered, feeling every one of the regrets she'd claimed not to have. "I…would definitely handle that moment differently today."

"Well, then I think it's time for a fresh beginning." Margaret released her hold on Daisy's hand, and in the process, accidentally knocked over one of the coffee cups. The contents spilled onto the table and soaked Daisy's sleeve. "Oh! I'm so sorry. Are you okay?"

"I'm fine. Really." Fortunately, she'd dressed in layers that morning, so she unbuttoned and removed the wet shirt, displaying the powder-blue T-shirt she wore underneath. She grabbed a dishtowel from the counter, wiped the mess off the table and said, "The coffee wasn't hot anymore, so no harm done. Promise."

"I… Well, that's something, isn't it?" Margaret asked,

staring in the general direction of Daisy's chest. "You're wearing your engagement ring, Daisy. May I ask why?"

Crap. Just…crap. "Reid insisted I keep the ring, for safe-guarding." Tightening her fingers around the ring, Daisy searched for an explanation. "I didn't want to lose it, so…"

"Ah. Well, yes, that makes perfect sense." Margaret smiled, seemingly composed, but Daisy recognized the knowing gleam in her eyes. The same exact gleam she'd seen in Reid's eyes. Like mother, like son, apparently.

"I'd hoped to get to the hospital this morning," Daisy said quickly, in order to change the topic. "We should prob-ably talk about these wedding details now. If that's okay with you?"

"Of course." Reaching into her purse, Margaret retrieved a small, wire-bound notebook. She opened it to the first page, displaying a neatly numbered list. "We need to de-cide the venues for the ceremony and reception. We can't do much else until we know the locations."

"Right." Daisy swallowed past the lump that had mate-rialized in her throat and tucked the ring inside her shirt. Out of view. "I'm open to suggestions, so whatever you think is fine."

"It's what you think that matters here," Margaret said. "However, Haley and I did come up with several ideas, and I checked with the chapel you were to be married at before. They have room for a one-o'clock or a six-o'clock ceremony, but I wasn't sure how you'd feel about—"

"Not there," Daisy interrupted, her heart all but pound-ing straight through her T-shirt. She couldn't—wouldn't—allow Reid to stand at the same altar in the same church on the same date and…have the same outcome. "Actually, let's not repeat any of what was planned before. And I want to keep everything as low-cost, as simple, as possible."

Margaret's entire form stilled. She closed her eyes for a millisecond, as if in silent prayer. Upon opening them, she said, "Those are all conscientious considerations, but it occurs to me that if you were to change your mind, this will be your wedding day. Let's not go so far in the other direction that we lose any of the beauty that such a special moment should provide."

Oh, dear Lord. Somehow, Daisy now had two Fosters believing there would be—or, at least, *should* be—an actual wedding on May sixth.

"Please understand that this wedding is not—"

"Never say never, Daisy." The other woman's tone was once again crisp, but in decisiveness rather than coolness or uncertainty. "You don't know how you'll feel tomorrow, let alone by May sixth. Not with any clarity or certainty."

And there it was, Reid's bulletproof logic. Obviously, he came by it naturally.

"I suppose you're right," she agreed, mostly because arguing against the truth seemed illogical. She *didn't* know how she'd feel tomorrow, the next day or by May sixth. "But I still don't want anything planned that is too costly or extravagant."

"Agreed. Now," she said, crossing off several items on her list, "this might sound odd, but what about using Foster's Pub and Grill for both events? That will satisfy your low-cost requirement but allow me to—" she winked in a very Reid-like manner "—decorate with a wedding in mind. We'll be in our shoulder season, so can easily close to the public for the day."

Foster's Pub, from what Daisy remembered, had a somewhat old-world style of elegance and charm that shouldn't be overly difficult or expensive to transform for a simple wedding. More important, the place was familiar and safe, so when—if?—she did not change her mind, when—again, if?—she did not show up to marry Reid, he would basically be at home.

Surrounded by the people who loved him.

Which was probably the best, if not the only, way she could offer some form of protection, comfort, for whatever fallout he might experience.

"It's…a great idea." Perfect, really. "Let's do that."

"Wonderful!" Margaret said, beaming. "Morning or afternoon for the ceremony?"

"Um…I don't know." Overwhelmed, already picturing how the pub might look all decked out for a wedding, Daisy rubbed her arms to chase off her sudden chill of foreboding. "Seriously, I don't think it matters much. Whatever you decide is fine."

"I believe this is supposed to be your call." A brief pause. "So, morning or afternoon?"

Daisy focused on the wall calendar and recalled that May sixth fell on a Tuesday, then considered the practical logistics that any of Reid's guests would have to face. Giving in, she said, "Late afternoon. Four o'clock, with dinner after. But simple, all the way through."

Margaret nodded in approval and jotted down a note. From there, they discussed the reception in depth. Everything from food to entertainment to what freaking song should be played for Reid and Daisy's first dance as husband and wife.

As each decision was made, each detail set, Daisy forgot about the rule that mandated her input. She stopped thinking of the wedding as nonsense or as insane. She, instead, began to envision the wedding she'd truly want to have. *Her* wedding.

Not just that, but her wedding *to* Reid.

Almost without conscious thought, she took the rather large step from the not-yet-a-maybe stage into the maybe… just-maybe phase of possibilities. And for once, the overriding emotion that Daisy felt was not fear. It was hope.

Daisy sat across from Reid at the Beanery, Steamboat Springs' favorite coffee joint, in a billowy, scoop-neck

bluish-green blouse and with a quirky, almost mischie-
vous, grin on her face. She appeared pleased with herself,
happier than he'd expected, and remarkably, not annoyed
with him at all.

For five full days, Reid had done his level best to give
Daisy some distance, some peace and quiet, to consider all
they'd discussed on Saturday. Her admission that she still
had feelings for him had hit dead-center, and suddenly, the
stakes had shot sky-high.

To the point he'd considered calling a halt to every last
bit of this wedding mess he'd created in favor of simply
spending whatever time he could with her before she returned to California. In one instant, he'd wonder why he
ever thought planning a wedding was a good idea, and in
the next…well, he'd remember every reason he'd made the
decision to begin with.

Ultimately, he chose to trust his initial instincts and
keep the ball rolling.

And he'd done so by filling the first portion of today's
date with a visit to the county clerk's office for a wedding
license, which they couldn't actually file for another few
weeks, but Reid had all he needed now in order to do that.
Then they went to the florist, to select the flowers for their
ceremony, and the bakery, to decide on a wedding cake.
Both tasks were completed in shockingly short order. Daisy
had known exactly what she wanted.

At the florist's, she'd asked for wildflowers in an array
of vivid colors with something called silver brunia as a
"unifying element," and at the bakery—without tasting
any of the samples—she'd ordered white cake with lemon
buttercream icing and raspberries.

Sounded good to Reid. But then, he wasn't all that
choosy when it came to cake.

During their first nuptial go-round, he'd had one hell of
an issue in getting her opinion on any of the wedding deci-

sions. Mostly, he'd tossed out ideas until he'd seen a flicker of interest in her eyes or a smile of longing grace her lips. Indications he then used to narrow down the choices, until, eventually, their wedding and reception had taken shape.

That was fine then, and he'd deal with the same now if he had to. But he liked this change in Daisy. Liked that she felt comfortable, confident, to clearly and easily state her opinion. A sign she was becoming committed to him, this wedding, or one of maturity and self-assurance borne from the years they'd spent apart?

Could be both, he supposed. Would like to think that possibility held merit.

"So," Daisy asked, jumping clean into his thoughts, "what's next on the agenda? Your mother and I have the venues, reception menu and a few options for entertainment lined up. With the flowers and cake now taken care of, I'd say we're all but done."

"Oh, not quite yet," Reid said. Almost, though. Just a few more steps of the wedding-planning variety before they moved on to what he considered the real portion of their date. Well, the serious and hopefully romantic portion, anyhow. "Though, your willingness toward firming these details has come as a pleasant surprise," he said. "Are we to that maybe yet, darlin'?"

She tilted her chin, arched an eyebrow. "You asked—no, make that ordered—for my assistance. I'm good at getting things done quickly. Very good. And for this, I'd rather accomplish as much as we can, as fast as we can. Easier that way, since—" Here, she abruptly stopped and shrugged. "Just easier. Less stressful in the long run."

"Less stressful, how?"

Temper, just a flash of it, really, dipped into her expression. "I'm busy, Reid. With the girls and Parker, with arrangements for if...*when* I go home." She sipped her latte, her movements and body language tense. Quietly so, though, as if she were hanging on to her composure with every ounce of strength she had. "Uncluttering the nonessentials from the essentials reduces the stress. That's all I meant."

"Right. The nonessentials." Probably, he should be bothered by this claim, but her use of the word *if* in reference to returning to California held more weight, more importance, in Reid's mind. It also worked fairly well as a lead-in for some of what he'd hoped to talk about today. "What's it like, living in Los Angeles? Are you happy there, Daisy?"

"I'm…content. I enjoy my friends, my home. My job."

"Content is good," he agreed. "Content is, for most folks, more than enough, but I asked if you were *happy*. Do you wake each morning with the knowledge that you're where you're supposed to be, doing what you're supposed to be doing? Or are you…still searching?"

"Searching?" She gulped another sip of her latte. More as a delaying measure, he assumed, than from bona fide thirst. "What could I possibly be searching for?"

"Connections, maybe? You're all on your own out there, Daisy. Who has your back if you become ill or something in your life turns sour?"

"I'm not on my own. I have friends and…" When she looked at him again, the temper was alive and well, as evidenced by the bright green shade of her gorgeous eyes. Even so, Reid saw more than anger. He saw…loneliness. "What about you?" she blustered back. "Are you happy when you wake each morning, secure in your choices, your daily existence?"

"Depends on what aspects we're talking about. I love my work. Love living here, in Steamboat Springs, where my family and friends are."

"Which sounds awfully similar to what I originally said."

"Similar, yes. But, Daisy, unlike you, I absolutely have

regrets." He watched her closely, looking for a sign—*any* sign—that would state she'd missed him, longed for him, as he had her. "Decisions I wish I could do over, and—" Well, hell. There was Cole and Dylan entering the Beanery, a good thirty minutes ahead of schedule. "We'll have to finish this later."

Angling her head in the direction of Reid's gaze, she sucked in a breath. "Your brothers? Why am I surprised? I shouldn't be surprised." She returned her focus to Reid, and in a soft, tremulous voice, admitted some of what he needed to hear. "I wasn't entirely honest with you when you asked about... What I'm trying to say is that I am not without regret."

Damn it. He didn't want to wait until later, he wanted to hear this now. Sighing, he combed his fingers over his hair. A misstep, asking his brothers to join them. Hopefully one that wouldn't bite him in the ass before the day was over.

"Dylan and Cole are here to talk about the honeymoon," he said quickly, before his brothers reached the table. "And I meant for this to be fun and light. I'm sorry."

Just that fast, a mask of coolness slipped into being, replacing the conflicting emotions, the temper and the loneliness, that had been clearly evident. In a voice dripping with sarcasm, she said, "Oh, I can't wait. Our *honeymoon?* Really?"

"A mistake, Daisy." And damn it, after this he'd lined up what was sure to be another error. Well, he'd follow through and hope he could put them back on track before the day's end.

Now at the table, Dylan and Cole slid into the two remaining chairs. Dylan nodded in greeting and said, "Hey there, Daisy. Been a while, hasn't it?"

"Hey back, Dylan. And yes, it has." She flicked her gaze from one brother to the next. "Did you all phone each other this morning to discuss what to wear?"

It took a second for her meaning to hit, but when it did, Reid laughed. All three of the Foster brothers were wearing flannel shirts and jeans. "We have similar tastes. And you two," he said, directing his attention toward his brothers, "are early. Anything wrong?"

"Nah. Couldn't be helped, though," Cole said. "Mom and Dad need Dylan at the pub sooner than expected, so we thought we'd take a chance you'd already be here." He grinned at Daisy and waggled his eyebrows. "Nice to see you, Daisy."

"Nice to see you, too," she said, her tone friendly. Welcoming. "And congratulations! I hear you're getting married soon." She smiled in a sweet-as-saccharine sort of way. "I take it that you, unlike your brother, have a bride who has accepted your proposal?"

Dylan tipped his head back and laughed. Loudly.

"Yup." Cole's smile widened. "Rachel has, fortunately, agreed to become my wife."

"Well, that's really terrific. I'm happy for you," she said with a telling glance toward Reid. "And honestly? I *love* the concept of not planning a wedding until a proposal is properly given *and* accepted. Your brother could use some tips in that department."

"Sure," Reid said, not taken aback in the slightest. After all, the truth was the truth. "Maybe Rachel could give you some instructions in…oh, showing up for the wedding? Because I'd bet my last dollar that she'll be there, on time, ready to live up to her agreement."

"Whoa, guys. Chill." This came from Dylan. "Maybe Cole and I should take off?"

That, Reid thought, was a damn good idea. "Sorry for dragging you—"

"Oh, no. You asked them here. They get to stay." Daisy leaned the top half of her body across the table. Reid followed suit, so they were almost nose to nose. "Drop this now, Reid, before you spend another penny or waste any-one else's time."

"Not going to do that," he said. "So you might as well quit asking."

They stared at each for a solid thirty seconds before she withdrew and returned to her side of the table. "Stubborn fool of a man," she muttered, mostly under her breath. Then she held out a hand toward Dylan. "Might as well give me that file folder you're holding, so we can choose a honey-moon that will likely go to waste."

"Likely?" Dylan and Cole and Reid all said at once.

She blinked. Twice. "Just give me the damn folder."

Dylan, not having much choice in the matter, slid the folder to Daisy. She flipped it open, read through his list and looked over the various travel brochures tucked inside, seemingly uninterested in every last one of them. But Reid noticed that she stared at one for just a second longer than the others, and a glimmer of excitement, of yearning, ap-peared in her eyes.

Ah. He should've known. A tour, including overnight stays, in castles across Ireland. The magic and history of that experience would appeal much more to a woman like Daisy than a week-long ocean cruise or a hot and sandy beach in Hawaii or the Bahamas.

"Nope," she said, closing the file folder with a snap. "None of this is… I'm not choosing any of these destina-tions." She pushed the folder back toward Dylan. "A few days of camping and hiking will suffice well enough for this honeymoon, so…um…that's my decision."

Camping and hiking, eh? Sure, they could do that…in Ireland, in between castle hops.

"Sounds like a plan," Reid said, making a mental note to fill in Cole and Dylan on his true intent later, since they were handling the details. Hell. Maybe he could convince Daisy to go on a vacation with him, if not a honeymoon.

"Camping it is, then. Starry nights and sleeping bags and toasting marshmallows over a fire. Love the idea, darlin'."

"Of course you do." She rubbed her hands over her face and sighed. "One more item checked off the list. I'm almost afraid to ask what's next."

"Why, you should be able to figure that one out," Reid said with a wink. "There is one essential item that every bride needs, and that would be a—"

Chapter Eleven

Wedding gown! The dratted man expected her to try on wedding gowns. Worse, she'd have to buy one, otherwise he'd probably yank any old thing from the rack and have it delivered to her door with some sweet, sentimental little card that would make her all gooey-eyed and emotional and then she'd have a physical reminder of May sixth taking up space in her closet.

Daisy closed her eyes and pushed out a breath. In all of her considerations about what this date—this all-day, freaking date—might consist of, she had not, even once, arrived at the conclusion that they'd be spending a chunk of their time in this fashion. She should have, especially after the visit from Margaret Foster, but she hadn't.

Still, a rule was a rule, so she'd rallied. Initially, she'd sped through every decision put in front of her, trusting her gut and that annoyingly clear vision of *her* wedding to lead her through the maze. That had worked well enough, and she'd held it together. For the most part, anyway.

Until she'd had to choose a honeymoon destination.

Honeymoons signified love and romance. Fun, laughter, maybe some frivolity. And sex. A lot of hot, lusty sex between the newly married couple. And for whatever reason, being presented with a host of brochures of potential destinations had brought her to her senses, reminded her of the honeymoon she and Reid had originally planned. All of their hopes and dreams for the future swarmed in next, and that had been enough of that.

She refused to select a location for a honeymoon that she just did not believe could happen at this point in time. But if she did believe, if all of this was *real,* she knew exactly where they would go, exactly which destination she would've chosen. Ireland.

Since it wasn't and she couldn't, she thought of where they were—the Rockies—and went with camping and hiking. Cheap. Easy to cancel. No fuss, no muss. And, yes, she'd been quite pleased with herself for solving that not-so-little dilemma without breaking down or ripping those damn brochures into shreds.

Or reaching across the table to strangle Reid.

But now, while he was off doing God knows what, she was stuck in a bridal boutique with his sister, Haley, and Cole's fiancée, Rachel Merriday.

He'd literally walked her inside the boutique, ascertained that Haley remembered she was watching Erin and Megan after school, reintroduced her to Rachel—whom she'd met a few times when they were younger—and said he'd return in an hour or two. And then he'd left.

An hour or two. Awesome. Somehow, Daisy promised herself, she'd solve this ridiculous dilemma in far less time than that. She just hadn't yet figured out how.

"Stop looking so glum," Haley said, her attitude just as upbeat and bubbly as Daisy recalled. She'd always liked Haley. Still did, and under less weird circumstances, would've wholly enjoyed the reunion. "I know this isn't the most ideal of situations, but try to have fun…and, I don't know, let's look for a dress that isn't necessarily only meant for a wedding?"

Rachel, who reminded Daisy of a runway model, spun around in a circle with her arms spread wide. "Sure," she drawled, "because there are so many nonbridal gowns here to choose from."

"Maybe with alterations or…I don't know." Haley chewed on her bottom lip as she surveyed the shop. "We'll find something."

"Why are you two doing this?" Daisy asked, unable to keep the question to herself any longer. She'd stayed mute on this topic with Margaret, and again with Cole and Dylan, but now…well, now she wanted to know. "Why support Reid's insanity?"

"Because he loves you," Haley replied instantly and with full sincerity. "And I love him, and he asked. Reid never asks for anything from any of us. Plus…well, you could say that I understand where he's coming from. I…um, sort of followed a similar path not that long ago."

Rachel half snorted, half snickered. "Your path was far more convoluted," she said, still laughing as she scanned through a rack of gowns. "You followed Gavin home, went against most of what he told you, coerced him into a weekend alone and…hmm. I guess that about covers it."

Twirling a chunk of hair around her finger, Haley grinned, apparently not offended in the least. "And look where we are now. My methods were unusual but successful."

This, Daisy knew, was a story she'd like to hear. Not now, though.

"As for me," Rachel said to Daisy, "I've learned that the Fosters do not go to such extremes unless they are very certain of their feelings. And as long as I've known Reid, I've never seen him behave like this, which tells me he's serious. So that's why I'm helping."

"Rachel also has a better understanding of your side of the equation." Haley pulled out a long, frothy concoction of a wedding gown and went to a mirror, where she held it in front of her body. Shaking her head in rejection, she said, "Tell her, Rach."

"Let's just say that Cole wasn't entirely sane in his methods of pursuing me, either. And—" a light blush stole over Rachel's cheeks "—I sort of turned the tables once I discovered what he was up to, so I'm not exactly blameless in the playing-games department."

Okay, then. "I have no idea how to respond to...to any of this," Daisy admitted, feeling more overwhelmed than ever. "Other than I'm beginning to believe that every one of you is—"

"Crazy? Impulsive?" Haley offered with a light grin. "Don't worry, we're aware."

"I don't know," Rachel added. "I'd just go with...happy."

Happy. Reid's earlier question revived itself in Daisy's mind. Was she generally happy with her life in California? She'd thought she was. Had believed so until...well, until recently.

"What about this, Daisy?" Haley asked, holding up another voluminous, frothy gown. "Doesn't this look like something a Disney princess would wear?"

"It's pretty, but...not my style." The gown was beautiful, but had far too many beads and pearls for Daisy's taste. If she wore that gown, she'd feel as if she were the wedding cake. Of course, that shouldn't matter. Not unless she actually decided to be a bride on May sixth. "On second thought, that will work just as well as anything else. I'll take it."

"Um. No, you won't," Haley said. "Finding the perfect wedding gown is a process. I think Rachel tried on close to... Oh. Wow. Daisy, look at the dress Rachel found."

She was already looking. Already captivated.

The V-neck, crepe-backed gown that Rachel held was sleeveless with a light, delicately embroidered lace overlay that extended from the narrow straps at the shoulders all the way to the floor-length hem. If there was a train at all, it was short, perhaps two or three inches lower than the front of the gown. And there was not one bit of froth, not one inch of the ostentatious, not one pearl or bead or sparkly sequin to be seen.

Just simple and lovely and romantic and, yes, perfect.

She knew better, but she tried on the dress, anyway, and once she had, she couldn't leave the boutique without purchasing the gown, without allowing the bridal attendant to take her measurements for alterations. As fate would have it, the dress was almost a perfect fit, and would be ready for Daisy to pick up in a matter of weeks.

Which seemed to prove that this simple and lovely and romantic wedding dress was *supposed* to be hers, and, after very little deliberation, Daisy decided to trust those instincts.

Perhaps she was just as crazy as Reid, after all.

Yup, he'd definitely misfired.

When Reid returned to the bridal boutique to collect Daisy, Haley had already left to pick up the girls from school. Rachel and the love of his life were sitting on one of the benches outside the shop, and were involved in what appeared to be a somewhat deep conversation. Upon seeing him, both had clamped their mouths shut, looked at each other and, as if on cue, started talking about a host of rather inane, unimportant topics.

The weather. That white was the most popular car color. And something to do with Disney princesses and frothy concoctions that Reid couldn't make neither hide nor hair of.

So, after ascertaining that Daisy had, indeed, selected a wedding dress—though she refused to allow him to pay for it, and he'd yet to determine if that were a positive or a negative—he'd thanked and hugged his soon-to-be sister-in-law, and once they'd said their goodbyes, he focused on the remaining hours of his date with Daisy.

On the woman herself.

On the conversation they needed to have, and if that went well, perhaps some romance to round out the evening. Perhaps, if he were very fortunate, the kiss he'd been dying for since almost the moment Daisy had returned to Steamboat Springs.

And if none of what he planned went well, then what? Well, Reid wasn't quite sure on that front, but he figured he'd deal with that particular outcome if and when it presented itself.

Still, he'd misfired. He shouldn't have spent so much of their day on extraneous details that might or might not have any bearing. But what was done was done.

Now all he could do was step forward and hope for the best.

"Close your eyes, sweetheart," he said to Daisy, who was staring out the passenger-side window in utter silence. "I have another surprise, and this one has zilch to do with May sixth."

A small sigh emerged, but she faced front and did as he asked, and said, "In less than a day, we've planned the majority of a wedding, I've seen most of your family in one fell swoop, and seriously…I'm not sure I can take a lot more. I…might just want to head home soon."

"That's your call," he said, making a right-hand turn onto the street where he lived. "But if you can give me a few inches of additional rope here, my hope is you'll change your mind."

"A few inches? I've given you several feet of rope already."

She had. More rope than necessary to hang himself with, if he wasn't careful. Metaphorically speaking. "I agree.

And I appreciate your patience. Now, though," he said as he pulled his SUV into his house's driveway, "I want you to open your eyes."

With a soft whoosh of air, she did, and then…nothing. Her entire body stilled as if frozen, and several seconds later, a shivering type of shudder stole through her, shaking her shoulders, her arms, and when she lifted her hand to her mouth, her fingers trembled.

"This is my house. *Our* house," she said, her voice a mixture of confusion and emotion, desire and longing. "I…I don't understand why we're here, what you want from me, or… Why are we here, Reid? Is this… Are you trying to recreate the night you proposed? Or…?"

"This is where I live, Daisy," he said, his heart dancing a wild jig and his palms sweaty as all get-out. "I bought this place about three months before our wedding. Mom and Dad helped, and…well, it was to be a surprise. My wedding gift to you, to us."

"You *own* this house?"

"Yes. I have for just over eight years now." Unbuckling his seat belt, he twisted toward Daisy. "I told you when I proposed that this would be our home. The place where we would raise our children, and fate must have agreed, because the house went up for sale a few months later. As I said, my parents helped with the down payment, and I bought it. For us."

"But then I left, and…and…" Repeating his actions, she unlatched her seat belt and faced him. "You've lived here all this time?"

Clean forgetting about rule number two, Reid trailed his fingers along Daisy's arm. "How could I do anything but live here? This house represents everything I wanted with you, everything I wanted for us…and Lord, you loved this place. How could I get rid of it?"

Her aquamarine eyes grew shiny with moisture. "I'm so

sorry, Reid. So sorry for not trusting in you, in us, enough to come to you on that day. I was so…scared and alone and I couldn't see how I could marry anyone, even you, even the man I loved, when…when…"

"We can talk about this right now, right here in this car, if you want," he said, feeling every ounce of her pain as if it were his own, and wishing desperately that he could take the misery away. "Or we can go inside. Maybe have a glass of wine, make some dinner and ease into this conversation. Again, your call. Whatever you want."

One tear and then another dripped from her eyes and coated her cheeks, and it was all he could do not to wrap her in his arms and just hold her. For however long she'd let him. But he knew—or sensed, rather—that what Daisy needed the most was some space to…breathe, he reckoned. Find her balance and the strength he knew she had.

"I believe I would like to go inside and have that glass of wine, relax and…I don't know, Reid, just spend some time with you that doesn't revolve around anything other than us."

"Exactly what I was thinking," he said. "So what are we waiting for? Let's go inside."

Even that took longer than it should have. Every couple of steps from the SUV to the front porch, Daisy would stop and shield her eyes against the late afternoon sun and stare at the house, from the steep angle of the roof to the narrow porch, to the rocking chairs he'd bought that very afternoon and placed just so…as a silent reminder of what he'd once promised.

What he still promised, if she'd…listen and accept and, hopefully, forgive.

She waited silently while he unlocked and pushed open the door, and when he offered her his hand, she took it without objection, and he led her inside.

Over the years, he'd slowly updated and decorated the

place, trying to envision what Daisy might have chosen for furniture or paint color or… Hell, how had he convinced himself that he'd moved on and had built any sort of immunity in regards to her at all?

Nuts, that. 'Course, he also hadn't strolled around each and every day with her in the forefront of his thoughts, dictating everything he did and said. She'd been more like a… whisper in his head, his heart.

"That glass of wine or a tour first?" he asked, recognizing the jagged quality to his voice. He felt stirred up and shaken, unsure of the direction to take, of what made the most sense.

She tightened her hold on his hand, and a surge of confidence eased some of his rough edges. Thank God for that. "How about both, at the same time?"

So that was what they did. He poured them each a glass of wine, though he'd have preferred an icy cold beer, and room by room, he showed Daisy her fairy house.

Most of the rooms were painted in actual colors, rather than the basic off-white. In the living room, he'd gone with a shade called oceanside that was almost a perfect match to Daisy's eyes, and a medium, earthy brown for the trim. The kitchen was painted a clean, clear blue that reminded Reid of a cloudless summer sky, and the master bedroom held hues of dove-gray and a hazy sort of *almost* purple his mother identified as hyacinth.

To him, it just looked like plain old gray with a shot of color, but who knew?

The remainder of the house held varying shades of browns, greens and reds. His furnishings were on the simple but sturdy side of the equation—nothing flowery or frilly—and while he'd hung a few paintings and pictures on the walls, he'd gone easy there, not wanting to live in too cluttered or crowded of a space.

"You've done a really great job with this," Daisy said,

her voice as soft as her eyes. "I love how you've surrounded yourself with color, with brightness. And I…not that it matters, mind you, but I wouldn't change too much. Some more decorations, maybe. Flowers and plants."

"I'm glad you approve." Now they were back in the living room, standing on opposite ends, and damn, he wanted her closer. "Unfortunately, I haven't found one sign that any fairies ever lived here. Hope that doesn't disappoint you too much."

A small, sweet smile lifted the corners of her mouth. "Oh, they definitely lived here. They just took extra care when they left to ascertain no one could prove their existence."

"Maybe they did, at that. I…still think of this house as yours. Ours," Reid said, speaking from the heart. Plenty enough time to delve into the rest. Later. "I'm pleased you're here, Daisy."

In the smallest fraction of a second, the ease and relaxation they'd been building faded into nothingness. A zap of invisible electricity whipped through the air, changing the energy, the tempo, between them into something different. Something acute and complex.

And, unless Reid was way off base, something dangerous.

"Pleased? How can you be so sure, so confident, that you're *pleased* when I'm—" she bit her lips together and unshed tears once again filled her eyes "—scared. I'm *scared,* Reid."

Her pronouncement must have shocked her as much—if not more—than it shocked him. She slapped her hand over her mouth and took two steps backward. Her eyes became more watery, and his gut twisted and tied itself into knots. She was scared…of him? Of them?

Due to her physical retreat, he forced himself to stand still even though every instinct he had begged him to go to her. Begged him to offer her his comfort, his strength. But he knew, despite her current emotional state, that Daisy was a damn strong woman.

She didn't need his strength. She needed his…understanding.

So, for once, Reid ignored his instincts and stayed put. "Honey, what's going on here?" he asked, keeping his voice even-keeled and calm. "What are you afraid of?"

"There are a lot of things I'm afraid of." Wiping her cheeks, her eyes, she inhaled a shaky breath. "Helicopters being one. Mice. I'd rather face off with a ravenous bear than a tiny mouse. Because I can see a bear coming from a long ways off. Oh, I'm not that fond of overly loud thunderstorms, either. Or skydiving. I tried that once, didn't like it at all." She shuddered, swiped at her cheeks again. "But what I fear the most is…"

Her words faded away. He waited, to see if she'd find the strength he knew she had. The strength to tell him what had her so upset, so…fearful. A million possibilities came to mind, and frankly, he despised every last one of them. Anything that could fill her with fear, he hated.

Simple as that.

She leveled her shoulders, lifted her chin, and he saw strength and determination and fierceness had replaced her tears. And that was good. Just as he'd expected.

"What I fear most," she repeated, "is letting people down. In not being whatever person they need me to be. My brother. My nieces. Once upon a time, my father. And now that you and I are on this crazy, unpredictable journey, I'm petrified of letting *you* down."

"Impossible, Daisy." He started toward her but she held up a hand, so he stopped. "You can't disappoint me. All I want is for you to be…I don't know, you. Just you."

"Exactly," she whispered, turning away from him. "And therein lies the problem."

"I have no idea what that means." Frustrated now, along with concerned, Reid gave in to his instincts and went to her. He didn't touch her, though, didn't so much as reach a finger in her direction. He just wanted to be closer. Wanted *her* to feel his presence. "Trust me on this, if nothing else. I *know* who you are. I've always known you. How can you doubt that?"

"How can I *not* doubt that when for my entire life—even when you and I were together—I've pretended, put on a show…an act of who I am, what I like and don't like, and become someone else?" Her tears poured heavily, in a flood of self-recrimination and fear. "You didn't fall in love with the real me, Reid. You fell in love with a woman who didn't exist."

"Untrue," he said, his voice flat but definitive. "I don't know who put that outlandish idea into your head, but I loved—still love—*you*. The woman standing in front of me now."

"You're wrong."

"I am not wrong." Difficult, but Reid managed to hold himself steady. Controlled. "Why don't you give me some examples of times you weren't you, in regards to our relationship—past or present, I don't much care—and we'll see if we can untangle this misunderstanding."

"Examples? Um." She blinked. "College. You said we should go to the University of Colorado, even though you were a year ahead of me, so we could be together. And I just agreed. Never offered another option. Because I didn't want to let you down or…or lose you."

"Now, see, I remember this situation differently." Reid backed off and leaned his weight against the sofa arm. "We each wrote a list of the colleges we were interested in, and the University of Colorado happened to be number one on both lists. It was the logical choice, but not the only choice. And you couldn't have lost me, even if you'd gone to school in Timbuktu."

"We did write lists, but…okay. Maybe I've recalled that moment incorrectly."

"I think you might have." He waited a second. "Any other examples you have spinning in that brain of yours you'd like to bring to the table?"

"What about Portelli's? How did that become our favorite restaurant? Or the details of our first wedding…the date, the chapel, all of it. I didn't offer any input, not because you didn't ask, but because I just went with whatever you said, and I didn't want to disappoint you."

If this matter didn't carry such weight, such importance to the core of who Daisy was, he'd almost have laughed. Lord, the woman was blind when it came to herself, to him, to them.

"Well, look. We went to Portelli's because I loved seeing you happy. We'd walk in, and you'd get this warm glow that had nothing to do with their food. You just liked the ambiance."

Her jaw dropped but she didn't say a word. Not one.

"As far as the details of the first wedding? Think back for me, will you?" While he could supply this answer just as easily as the others, he sort of wanted her to see the truth on her own. "How often did I flat-out tell you we were going to do anything?"

Dead silence enveloped the room while she pulled the past to the present. He didn't prod her in any direction, just waited. In patience and in love. In support and in understanding.

Now that it was brought to the surface, Reid knew exactly where this mentality had originated, but he'd never— not once—witnessed Daisy behave in the manner she described with anyone other than her father. Not with Reid, not with her brother, not with her friends. What she did do, what he'd always recognized, was her stalwart protection of her thoughts and that inner, secret world she hid from most everyone.

That was the Daisy he knew.

"You never told me we had to do or go or be anything," Daisy finally said. "What you did… Oh." Her shoulders slumped as the fight began to drain out of her. "You asked questions, tried to determine what I wanted, what I liked, and took those things into consideration as decisions were made. Is…is that right?"

"Close," Reid said. "Our entire relationship was always a compromise. I just had to work a little harder to ensure that happened, since you stayed inside your head so often. I'd like to point out that you do not do that anymore, Daisy. Not to the same extent."

"No…I guess I don't."

"Damn straight," he said, pleased. "Hell, you've had zero issues clearly and openly stating your opinion from the friggin' second I found you in Parker's living room."

"You're right," she said, her voice somewhat stronger. "I've fought hard to get to there, to be able to do that."

"You've succeeded."

"I have a question now." She moistened her lips. In nervousness, Reid guessed. "A point-blank, straightforward question, and due to the agreement of rule number three— my rule, that is—you have to answer honestly."

"And I will give you a wholly truthful response," he said, wondering where they were now headed. "My word, Daisy."

Expelling a breath, she nodded. "You say you know me, so tell me, Reid. Who am I?"

So many descriptions came to mind. Beautiful. Funny. Intelligent. Warm and loving and strong. But Reid did not believe those were the words she needed to hear. She wanted proof that when he claimed he knew her, he really did.

And while she might not appreciate or even get the comparison he was about to toss her way, he had promised absolute honesty. So that was what he was going to give her.

"I know you, Daisy. Very, very well. That isn't to say I know everything *about* you, because I don't, and I shouldn't. Exploration is a part of any relationship."

"That sounds a lot like surface talk, but what I—"

"Now, give me a darn minute here. I know what you want, and I'm about to tell you," he said, laughing. "If a… oh, let's go with a turtle and a porcupine. If those two animals produced offspring, then the result would be a creature who is…well, frankly, pretty much you."

Daisy's chin set in an irritated line. "You view me as a hard-shelled, prickly, nonexistent creature? Wow. That's quite the…association you've made there, and if that's what you think of me… I don't know why we're even having this conversation. *Is* that what you think?"

"Yes and no." Reid mentally formed the explanation that had made perfect sense to him less than a minute ago. "I believe you're a very strong woman, but inside, you're vulnerable. Fearful of sharing who you are with others. In order to protect yourself, you've built this facade of being fully independent, of not needing anyone else to…I don't know, exactly, make you happy or whole." He shrugged. "Something along those lines."

Her eyelashes fluttered and the tightness in her jaw lessened.

"And that facade is the turtle's shell, in case you're wondering." Hell. All of this had sounded reasonable in his own head. Verbally, though, he wasn't so sure. "When someone begins to move in past that shell, your vulnerability grows. So you do one of two things. You either become defensive and distance yourself as quickly and completely as you can—that's the porcupine comparison, because who wants to be too close to a porcupine?—or you go the other route—"

"And throw myself in so fully, that I begin to feel lost. Afraid."

"Which leads us right back to avoidance. Distance. Keeping yourself solidly in your own world, both physically and emotionally." Reid pushed himself off the sofa's arm and approached Daisy. "When someone hurts you, like your parents, you recede so far into your shell you… well, you're kind of hard to reach. I give you California as an example."

"I… Yes," Daisy said, her voice muted, her expression stricken.

"Here's what makes you amazing," Reid said, needing to get out the rest. "You'll sacrifice your protection for other people, for those who need more than they can do on their own. You bring them into your world, share your—" he grinned "—turtle shell and porcupine needles with them, and all the while, you're working on solving *their* problems."

"It's a nice idea, but—"

"Nope. I'm speaking the truth here, as rule number three dictates. Might take you a while to poke your head out of that shell long enough to see what's going on, but then… well, then there's no stopping you." He stopped, inhaled. "Look at how you responded to Parker's accident, and how you are with the girls? And hell, from what Parker has said, it's pretty much what you do for a living—solving problems."

She reached for support, found the chair to her left and gripped on tight. "I don't see myself as kindly, but I can't argue with the distance or the avoidance or the…fear and vulnerability."

"Look a little harder," he said. "Or just trust in me, in what I see."

"I don't… I can't… Okay, I'll try," she said, giving a short, jerky nod. "I've wondered, needed to know, if you really loved me. The real me. And if you didn't see me, that real version of me I've tried to hide, if you would be disappointed. If you'd still insist we should be together."

"Daisy, look at me." She didn't, just kept her vision firmly planted off to the side. "I see you fully, all of you. And I did love you. I still do, baby. And you've only disappointed me once, when you left. Just that once."

"Quite the huge disappointment, though."

"Won't argue with you there," he said, allowing a layer of his defenses to retreat. "And I have questions, some residual anger and confusion. I hope we'll work all that out, because I do believe—"

"You should hate me," she whispered, interrupting him, her voice too heavy, too dark for his liking. "After what I did, you should despise me. *That* would make sense. Why… why don't you hate me, Reid?"

"The reason is simple." Since touching her broke rule number two, he shifted so that he could see her face. So she could see his. "I'd rather love you. That's what makes sense to me."

"What am I supposed to do with that?"

"Oh, I don't know. Maybe—and this is just a thought, darlin'—maybe *let* me love you?"

Chapter Twelve

Daisy couldn't breathe, literally, for a solid twenty seconds. All she could do, all she did do, was stand in statue stillness, and think of Reid's words, of everything he'd said.

Let him love her? Just…*let* him.

The thought was, at once, terrifying and electrifying, humbling and strengthening. But he knew her, he did, and that…well, that made the first step—*her* first step—a hell of a lot easier to take. Because that stubborn, stubborn man had been right all along.

She loved him. Had always loved him. Had never stopped loving him.

And, oh, Lord, the time they'd wasted, due to her worries and insecurities. Her lack of courage when she should have stood strong and believed, trusted, in their love. She didn't do that then, wasn't entirely sure she could do so now, but she could…*try.*

She looked at him, at this man she'd never been able to force from her heart, and he stood there, tall and straight and solid, so firm in his convictions.

He deserved the same from her. And so much more.

"Yes, Reid," she whispered, so afraid, so…*unsure,* of everything these words entailed. "I'll let you love me."

There wasn't a pause or a breath, just action. He came to her, pulled her into his arms and locked her tight against him. The softness of his flannel shirt rubbed against her cheek, the scent of him—rugged and clean and all man—surrounded her, and the strength, the blessed reality of his body pressed to hers, all served to calm her jumpy stomach and racing heart.

She'd yearned for, wished for, and had fantasized about this moment. And here it was…here *he* was, and she was so shocked, so damn grateful, she almost wondered if she were asleep in her bed and lost in one of her dreams.

"I have missed you so much, honey," Reid murmured, his voice soft and deep and sexy and sweet, all at once. "But I gotta ask about rule number two. May I kiss you now?"

A simple request, really, but a flash of heady warmth swept into Daisy's bloodstream, nearly buckling her knees with its potency. She looked up, and up some more, directly into Reid's eyes. They were dark and intense, searching and…well, beautiful. In so many ways.

She trailed her fingers along the angled edge of his jaw, felt the bristly roughness of his five-o'clock shadow against her fingertips and—standing on her tiptoes—brought her lips closer…closer…closer to his, and she kissed him. Fully. Soundly.

He groaned a needy, hungry sort of sound, and one hand came up to grip the back of her head, while his other lifted the hem of her shirt and found the small, tender area at the base of her spine. And the feel of his skin on hers dragged a moan from her throat, caused her temperature to rise another delicious degree. Or two or three.

Ever so slowly, Reid took control of the kiss she'd started, increasing the pressure of his mouth, his tongue teasing and tasting, savoring and exploring. And in no more than one combined beat of their hearts, pieces and parts of her soul she hadn't known were dormant shot to life. Along with this startling realization, the completeness she'd lacked for so long suddenly returned, filling her with absolute peace and now...now she understood what she hadn't before.

She could be, had been, *whole* without Reid, but she couldn't be, would never be, *complete* without Reid. The distinction between the two states of being was minuscule, perhaps, but profound. She belonged with him, he with her. Just as he'd said.

Also stunning was how her body recognized his, responded to his, instantly and without reservation. As they kissed, her nipples hardened and licks of desire, not so different from fire, swirled in her belly and between her legs, through and along and across every inch of her being.

She wanted him. Desperately and fully. In every way a woman could want a man.

Daisy was *this close* to unbuttoning, unzipping his jeans. *This close* to tugging the denim down, over his hips and off his legs. *This freaking close* to giving in to her hunger and her need and the bright, consuming energy that bounced and pulsated from her to him and back again, when Reid abruptly broke the kiss and stepped back.

Out of their embrace, away from...her.

The absence of him was immediate. Intense and heartbreaking. And, when she looked at Reid, he had a dark, haunted expression of...despair? Maybe. Maybe that.

Shudders of loss, of a different type of longing, replaced Daisy's desire. Confusion and uncertainty and fear rode in next, hard and heavy and unrelenting.

"Daisy," Reid said, his voice as ragged, as broken, as each breath he pulled in and pushed out of his lungs. "We need to talk. Before this goes any further, we need to have that honest, no-holds-barred conversation. Otherwise, we'll get too deep in for either of us to remain coherent."

Oh. *Of course.* "Your rule number two, I take it?"

"Yes. I wish we… Well, this has to be done. Simple as that."

Forcing her wobbly legs to move, she crossed the room and perched on the edge of the sofa. Her thoughts awhirl, her heart heavy, she delved in and spoke as quickly, as efficiently as she could, but with honesty. With all of her pain and remorse and sadness.

"I meant what I said earlier, about having regrets." A deep, cavernous sigh escaped as she considered her greatest mistake. "I should never have left in the way I did, and if fairies or snow magic could undo that choice, give me a second chance in that moment, I would handle that decision differently. Please believe that, Reid, if nothing else."

He sat on the chair across from her, leveraged his elbows on his knees and his jaw on his finger-laced hands. He seemed, she thought, tormented. And so, so far away from Daisy.

Impossibly far away.

"I do believe you, Daisy. I do." His brows drew together, his expression agonized and lost. Anger lived there, as well. She saw it, clear as day. "What I don't—can't—understand is how you were *able* to leave in such a manner, without an honest-to-God, real conversation. Hell, you didn't even call. How hard is it to pick up the friggin' phone?"

Strangely, as strong as her emotions were in that second, her eyes stayed dry. Her throat hurt from all she felt, though. And her chest had that hollow, frantic ache she remembered far too easily. Not as vivid or as sharp or as consuming, but there, nonetheless.

"Some of that has to do with what we've already talked about," she said. "After…after my mother told me the truth about my father, about her one-night stand, I tried so hard to believe in us, Reid. I did. But everything sort of collided in my head, and everything—even you and I—became this overwhelming mass of…confusion that I couldn't see beyond."

"One phone call, Daisy. One damn call and I would've been there, with you." Altering his position, Reid rubbed his hands over his eyes. "One call. That's all it would've taken."

A sob curled in the back of Daisy's throat as she listened, as she saw the damage she had done with her own eyes. "I just didn't know who I was, and I needed to figure that out, all by myself." Now, today, none of this sounded like enough of a reason to do what she had done, but it was the truth. Every last word. "So I could trust and believe in *me*. An identity that wasn't connected to my father or to you or to anyone else. And the reason I didn't call, couldn't call, was because I *knew* you'd talk me out of leaving."

He swore under his breath. "Would that have been so bad?"

"Then? I thought so. I believed the only choice was to start over."

"Without me?" Every muscle in his body tensed and grew hard. He snapped his fingers, saying, "Just bam, huh? Everything we'd planned, everything we were, you were able to throw it all out the window and run for the hills, *run away from me,* and start over. Wow, Daisy."

Oh, God. She found the chain around her neck, pulled it from beneath her shirt and held on to her ring—Reid's ring—as tightly as she could. For strength.

"Yes, I did that. In my confusion and shock over my mother's confession, nothing in my world seemed to make sense. And that included you. That included *us*." She tried to think, tried to find the exact right words, so he would understand. But she didn't know what else to say, other than, "I'm sorry. So sorry, Reid. I can't change this, and I can't go back in time."

Tension rippled and bobbed between them, around them, and all Daisy could do was wait and hope that somehow, in some way, Reid understood. That he would forgive her for her past mistakes, and remain true in his belief that they were meant for one another. A million years or merely thirty seconds might have elapsed, she didn't know.

Didn't care, either.

She was just grateful—eternally so—when he said, "Okay. I don't agree with that choice, will likely *never* agree, but I can and I do understand what you were going through, and how those emotions, that shock, scared you to the point you felt as if you had to leave."

"I would make a different decision today," she repeated. He needed to know this, believe this. "I *can't* promise I wouldn't leave, but I would talk to you. Let you know what was in my heart, and give you the opportunity to be a part of that decision."

"And that is enough. More than enough," he said. "I can let this go, Daisy. For us, for the future I hope we'll have, but there's something *I* have to tell you, and…" Yet again, despair and torment clouded his gaze. "This won't be easy, honey. And I'm sorry for that."

Warning bells screamed in her brain, and fear—cold and absolute—tarnished any relief she might have felt from his acceptance, from his willingness to forgive and move on. And she tried—Lord, did she try—to conceive of what he might have to say.

Of course, she couldn't. So she nodded and said, "I'm listening."

"Right. Here goes." A muscle tensed and then quivered in his jaw. "Not sure if you'll recall, but about a week before our wedding, we decided to take a day off and get away. We were going to hike, do some climbing at Rabbit Ears Peak, have a picnic and…just spend some time together, without the distractions of the wedding."

She nodded again. "I remember."

"You had some errands to run that morning, and something waylaid you—I don't know what now, can't put my mind on the specifics—but the point is, I arrived at your parents' house to pick you up before you'd returned. And…" He gave his head a hard shake, as if waking himself up or clearing his thoughts. "I let myself in, as I typically did."

Yes, Reid had been such a large part of the Lennox household, pretty much a member of the family, that he'd never had to announce his presence…not for years, anyway. That bit of what he said made sense, but her stomach twisted in apprehension.

She remembered that day. Remembered coming home and finding him in her room, sprawled out on her bed, with his eyes closed. And when he'd opened those eyes, they'd held the same look—the same freaking despair—she saw now.

"What happened?" she asked.

"Your parents were in the kitchen, arguing. They did not know I was there, based on the…volume of their voices. I… Well, I started to head their way." He paused, drew in a lungful of air. "I didn't know what I was going to do, exactly, but I thought they should know they weren't alone. I… Daisy, I didn't get that far. Wasn't able to do a damn thing before—"

"You knew," she said as her brain pieced together Reid's haunted look, what he'd already said and the time frame that this had occurred. "Oh, my God. You *knew.*"

"Yes. Not all of it, not every damn detail, but enough to know that Charles Lennox was not your biological father, that you had no idea, that he thought it was time to tell you and that your mother refused. I heard her refuse, Daisy." Reid cursed again, somewhat louder than before. "And I hightailed it to your bedroom to figure out what in the hell I should do."

"You did nothing. That was your choice."

"Only for that moment." He was up and out of the chair,

approaching her before she could so much as blink. Sitting next to her, he wrapped his hand around hers. "It was the week before our wedding, baby. And I didn't want you hurt. I...wanted to protect you."

"Right," she said, trying to find some type of balance to get her through. "So you decided to do what my parents had done for my entire life and *lie* to me. How...how could you do that?"

"Not forever. No." His voice was firm and unyielding, as was the pressure of his hand, his grasp on her. "I was not going to lie to you. I was just going to wait, until after our wedding and our honeymoon, so we could keep that time of our lives whole and unsullied. And the thought of hurting you at all, ever, just about killed me. So, yes, I kept the secret."

"You shouldn't have," she said. "That was the wrong choice."

"I know," he said, his voice quiet and resigned. "And I'm sorry."

So many things could have been different if he'd come to her with what he'd learned. Discovering she was not Charles Lennox's biological daughter still would not have been easy. She still would have been shocked, upset, scared and confused. The truth of her parentage *still* would have shaken her world and everything she'd known, believed to be true.

None of those facts would have changed.

But if Reid—the man who loved her, the man who was to become her husband—had told her everything he'd heard, she would not have doubted in *them*. She *knew* this. Because what was marriage if not an alliance? Two people standing together, arm in arm, for better or for worse, in sickness and in health. Marriage was, in essence, a team sport.

And that right there, his presence during the worst moment of her life, would have changed *everything*. They would be married now. They would likely have children now. And they would be living in this very house, together, right now.

She wasn't so far gone that she couldn't turn the tables, couldn't see that if she had talked with him before she'd left, the same scenario could also be true. Daisy knew this, as well.

But she had years of reflection behind her. Years of believing that she knew everything there was to know about that morning. The specifics of what led to her mother's confession and Daisy's resulting beliefs, behavior and, yes, mistakes. This news, though, came at her with the force, the strength and the unpredictability of a tsunami.

Worse, this confession of Reid's brought back every damn emotion she'd experienced almost eight years ago. Again, her lungs refused to take in air. Again, she had the frantic need to get away, to leave, to go somewhere she could breathe. So she could figure this out.

Figure out, exactly, what to do with this information. Figure out how to erase the hollow ache that, once again, had taken over her entire being—body and soul—so she could regain the core of stability she'd worked so hard to attain.

Damn it! This was a lot, maybe too much, to absorb in this minute.

She tried to reel in her emotions. Tried to view this— the decision Reid had made—in a logical, rational manner. Reminded herself of all the valid reasons she should let this go. He'd let her transgression go, so she should do the same for him, for them.

But she didn't know if she could.

If marriage was a team sport, then love was…what? The warm-up stage? Maybe. Regardless, eight years ago, she and Reid—for different reasons—had absconded from the team…from *their* team. They hadn't turned to or trusted in the other enough to hold steady, to stand arm in arm against the world and do what was right.

And…no, she just couldn't let that go. At least, not enough to allow her to move forward with Reid or with the future she'd been so close to believing in.

Squeezing her eyes shut, Daisy searched for the words she knew must be said, for even the slightest strand of strength to yank on and pull close, so she had something to hang on to. "I understand your motivation in keeping this secret, so I can forgive that, Reid. I can, and I do. And while I know this is unfair, I can't…don't think I know how to—"

"No," he said, his hand tightening over hers. "Don't say what I think you're about to say. Just wait. Consider… remember that I love you, that I've always loved you, and that all you have to do is take a step toward me. Just one step, Daisy. That's it. I'll do the rest."

He made it sound so simple. So effortless. As if he were merely suggesting she take a physical step, rather than a metaphorical leap of faith. The problem, though, was that some leaps were far too treacherous, too steep and precarious, to trust in faith alone.

And in this case, she couldn't find the will, the courage *or* the belief to jump.

"I can't," she said. "I'm sorry, Reid, but I just can't."

Chapter Thirteen

Spring had officially arrived in Steamboat Springs, date-wise, if not weather-wise, and the shoulder season had begun—meaning, the tourists had all but evacuated the city, and the residents were in relax-and-prepare-for-summer mode.

Reid hardly noticed the slowdown or the cool weather. In the twelve days following Daisy's rejection, he'd existed in an afraid-to-hope but afraid-not-to-hope state of mind. To counteract the negative side of the equation, he'd kept himself busy.

Today, as was the case most days, that included visiting Parker. He'd also been helping Cole and Rachel with their upcoming wedding. He was there for his family, personally and work-wise. And each day, he spent some time with Erin and Megan, as he wanted. As he'd promised. Those moments, though, were tough.

Not because of the girls, but because of Daisy. Even when she wasn't in the same room with them, he knew she was there, in the house somewhere, and while she wasn't exactly avoiding him, she had most definitely withdrawn into that tough-as-nails, prickly, turtle-porcupine shell of her own creation. And Reid did not know how to draw her out again.

Oh, he'd instituted rule number three—his rule, that was—and phoned her each night for their thirty minutes of conversation. But he did most of the talking. The first few nights, he'd tried to focus on them, on everything they'd already discussed, to no avail. Since then, he asked her questions. Almost any odd thing he could think of.

Parker and Erin and Megan, of course. Jinx. Daisy's life in California, her friends and her job. When they'd run out of air on those topics, he'd moved on to the sort of inane, unimportant subjects he'd heard Rachel and Daisy discussing at the wedding boutique.

And she answered every question posed, but only in the shortest method possible. She wasn't rude or unkind or even cold. Just abrupt and…well, sad. He thought she was sad. A thought that disturbed him to no end. *He'd* made her sad, and he wished to heaven and back that he knew how to change that status quo. To make her smile again.

Reid punched the appropriate floor level on the hospital elevator and waited while the doors swished shut, his mind still on Daisy.

Fortunately, he had some time left. A solid month before the wedding he hadn't canceled, the wedding he probably *should* cancel. Stupid to keep the thing going, especially because Reid didn't care if they were married on that particular day or not. Someday, whether on May sixth or ten years from now, he hoped Daisy would be his wife.

For now, he'd take whatever she'd give him.

But he'd gotten it into his skull that calling off the wedding would begin to shake his belief, his confidence in them, in all he saw for their future. So, no, despite his near certainty there would not be an actual wedding ceremony on May sixth, he could not, would not, turn away from the possibility. No matter how remote.

Daisy was here, in Steamboat Springs, and he figured she'd be here for a little while yet. Parker's surgery had gone well, but he'd still require a fair amount of support when he returned home. Reid did not have a shadow of a doubt that Daisy would stick around for the duration.

He had time, and that was the best thing he had going for him.

Clearing his thoughts, he stepped off the elevator and strode toward Parker's room, hoping to find his friend awake and in good spirits. Yesterday he'd seemed morose and out of sorts, clearly tired of being away from home, and ready to get back to his life.

Reid stopped in the doorway, looked in to make sure Parker wasn't asleep and grinned. Yup, today seemed better than yesterday. Not only was Parker smiling, but he also sat in a wheelchair near the room's large window. That was a good sign. Positive.

"I gotta say, this is a sight for sore eyes." Entering the room, Reid swung himself onto Parker's bed. "It's about damn time you got your lazy behind up and moving."

"Uh-huh. You're just jealous of all the attention I've received from the pretty nurses around here," Parker said, widening his smile. "But yeah, it's nice to be somewhat mobile."

"Understandable." Reid gave his friend a long look. "I've worried about you. Really am glad to see you're in a better frame of mind today."

"How can I not be? I am—" Parker mimed beating a drum "—going home soon. Possibly as soon as next week, depending on how quickly I can get up and maneuver without any help."

Now *that* was good news. "Well, then, I'd say your lazing-around days are over." Reid thought of the girls, of how excited they would be to hear that their snow magic, in a way, had worked. Their father was coming home ahead of schedule. "Do the girls know?"

"Yeah," Parker said, wheeling the chair closer to Reid. "They were here yesterday, and you should've seen them, Reid. With all their cheering and jumping, you'd have thought we were having a party that Santa Claus, the Easter Bunny and the Tooth Fairy were attending."

"They've missed you, so that's probably what it felt like," Reid said, imagining the scene. "Bet Daisy's pleased, as well?"

"She was. Is." An unidentifiable expression crossed Parker's face. "Though she wasn't thrilled when I mentioned our parents will be here soon. By the end of the month, or so. Once my father is given the green light for travel."

"Your parents are coming?" Reid inwardly winced. That would be difficult for Daisy. "Of course they are. I'm sure your mom's been a little nuts, not being here."

"Exactly." Parker gave Reid a long and steady look. "Works out well, in a way, since Daisy will be able to head for home once our folks have a chance to get settled."

"She's going home...at the end of the month?" Somehow, and Reid didn't know how, he managed to choke out the words. Daisy would be gone, back to her life in California, before May sixth. "I suppose that...ah...makes sense."

"No reason for her to stay, and my house isn't big enough to comfortably hold four adults, two kids and a dog. Besides," Parker said, "I've taken up enough of her time. I'm thankful she's stuck it out for this long."

"Right. Makes...ah...sense." Reid rubbed his temples. "End of the month, huh?"

"Yup, and you're repeating yourself now." Wheeling another few inches closer to the bed, Parker said, "You're also kind of green around the gills. Bother you, does it, that

Daisy's taking off somewhat soon? Anything you want to say about that?"

"Why would that bother me?" Reid said, not wanting to burden Parker with any of what he was thinking, feeling. "She has a life to get back to, and yeah, nice she's been here for you and the girls. Good for all of you, I'd expect."

"Has been, and I'm glad for that, too," Parker said. "I'd like to mention, just to put it out there, that other folks visit me. Neighbors. Friends. Your brothers have been by a time or two. Your parents stop in. Saw Haley earlier today, as a matter of fact."

Ah. Haley. That answered a few questions. "Well, my family is your family."

Parker reached for and grabbed an empty plastic water bottle, which he hurled at Reid's chest. Perfect aim. "You've been trying to convince my sister to marry you again, and we both know you've never gotten over her. What I want to know is…are you going to let her leave?"

"Only reason I haven't said anything on this front is I thought it should come from Daisy." Reid squeezed the water bottle, pretending it was a stress ball. "But to answer your question, I'm not sure I can stop her, nor would I want to. That's her call…."

"You love her, right?"

"I do love her." Reid tossed the water bottle back at Parker. He caught it with one hand.

"The woman I loved died, Reid. She's never coming back, and there's not one thing on this planet I can do to change that." Pain, fleeting but profound, deepened the blue in Parker's eyes. "You, on the other hand, still have an opportunity here."

"Do I? Doesn't seem that way." All at once, every damn doubt he'd tried to ignore surged forward. "Truth is, maybe I *should* give up. She took off, never once looked back, and I'm not blameless. I kept—"

"Well, not exactly. She did look back." Parker swore softly. "About a month after she left, she called you. I was there, answered the phone."

"Wait a minute. She called?"

"Yeah. You weren't doing well, and I was angry with my folks, angry at Daisy, worried about both of you. So I told her—" he cursed again, swiped his hand over his jaw "—to leave you alone. That she'd created enough havoc and that was the best she could do for you."

"Really wish you hadn't done that." He wasn't mad at Parker. Just stunned. This information sifted in with everything else, and rather than feeling pleased or relieved or…hell, hopeful, Reid was left with a sense of futility. "In a way, that's three strikes against us. Can almost make me believe that fate doesn't want us together."

"Three strikes? One is this, one is Daisy leaving, what's the third?"

"That I knew about her paternity and didn't tell her." Without mincing words, Reid related the facts of that situation. When he finished, he said, "Three decisions, three strikes."

Parker released a sigh. "If you hadn't so recently saved my life, I'd be honor-bound to kick your ass. You know that, right?"

"I know, and you still can," Reid said with a small, humorless smile. "Saving your life doesn't negate any of my mistakes."

"Why didn't you tell *me?*" Parker jerked his head to the side to stare out the window. There wasn't any true venom in his voice, just annoyance. "I love my mother and my father, but I hate that they did this to her. So yeah, wish you'd trusted in me."

"Couldn't," Reid said, speaking the simple truth. "If I was going to tell anyone, I would've told Daisy. She had to know before anyone else."

The men sat there in silence, considering what was versus what could've been. When Parker faced Reid again, his annoyance had vanished.

"Here's what I think," he said, his manner serious. "Perhaps you weren't supposed to marry Daisy eight years ago. Maybe these three strikes were meant to keep you apart *then,* for some unknown reason we can only speculate on. But then isn't now, and…if I had an opportunity to be with Bridget again, there isn't anything that would stand in my way."

Wise words, but Reid had already pushed against every barrier that Daisy had put in front of him. Now his instincts told him to step back some and give her room to breathe. He wanted Daisy to have the freedom to feel secure in the decision she'd already made, or—God willing—to come to a different decision and choose a new path.

One that included him.

So, he supposed he'd listen to another Lennox's wise words, and believe really, really, *really* hard that this time, Daisy would run toward him.

Standing in Parker's bedroom, Daisy stared at the lacy, romantic, simple wedding gown she'd picked up that afternoon—now altered to a perfect fit—and wished with every bone in her body she hadn't given in to temptation. She should not have bought this dress. What had she been thinking? Now this beautiful creation would go to waste, unworn and unneeded.

And that was just…sad.

Maybe, once she returned to California, she'd donate the dress. Maybe there was another woman out there who would take one look at this gown and declare it perfect. Already feeling the loss, Daisy carefully hung the dress in Parker's closet, where it would remain until she left for home. Another few weeks, maybe three. That's all she had to get through.

Parker would be home that very weekend, and her parents—God, her *parents*—would be here toward the end of the next week.

She pushed her palm against her queasy stomach in an attempt to vanquish her twisty nerves. Futile, she knew, while Reid remained in the house. He was downstairs with Erin and Megan, not to mention Jinx, right this very minute, and she'd…well, she'd chosen to hide.

Nothing had changed for her since that evening at her fairy house. She loved Reid. Now knew that she'd always loved him, and likely always would, but creating a life with him had gone from an almost yes—she'd been so freaking close—to a definite no.

Love did not necessarily equal a happily-ever-after ending.

Emotion, strong and overwhelming, came over Daisy in waves, but she did not cry. Could not cry. Sitting on the edge of the bed, she rubbed her temples and, for maybe the first time in her life, hoped for tears. Hoped for a temporary release of the empty, yawning ache deep inside that refused to dissipate. But, no. Nothing. Her tears, it seemed, had disappeared.

Or maybe, she'd simply used up her allotment. Maybe she'd feel this way for the rest of her life, with no respite, no peace. A horrifying thought.

Shaking her head to rid herself of that nonsense, Daisy pressed her hands against her eyes. Stood and headed for the stairs. She couldn't hide all night, and the girls needed dinner, and…as much as being around Reid hurt, she also yearned to stand in the same space with him.

Even if for only a minute.

Of course, later, she'd have his voice in her ear for *thirty* minutes. A shot of humor whisked in, dampening her anxiety and soothing her soul. Margaret Foster had been absolutely correct when she'd described her son as a smart man.

Due to that stupid, not-harmless-in-any-way rule, Daisy had to listen to Reid's voice—his ridiculously sexy, evocative voice—every evening. From now until May sixth. And, despite her sadness, despite the fact they talked about nothing of importance—he'd even stopped trying to convince her to change her mind—she craved these phone calls. Dreaded them, too.

It was in these moments, when there were no other distractions surrounding her, that she searched the hardest for the will, the courage, to take that jump. That freaking long and terrifying leap of faith, and every night as they said goodbye, she knew she couldn't.

So, yes. She craved the ability to talk with Reid, but at the exact same time, she dreaded the instant that, once again, she realized with crystal-clear clarity that nothing had changed.

On the morning of Cole and Rachel's wedding, Reid entered his brother's childhood bedroom in their family home to find Cole alone. And pacing. And sweating up a storm. All three symptoms likely caused by a giant, mega-size case of wedding-day nerves.

Not out of doubt, Reid guessed, but from the enormity of what was about to occur. And he got that. Remembered that anxious state pretty damn clearly, as a matter of fact.

As Cole's best man, Reid figured it was his duty to bring him down a few levels. So he started off by saying, "Look at you, in that spiffy tux. One might think you're about to be married." He checked his watch. "Rather soon, at that."

"I might be ill, Reid," Cole said in complete seriousness. "Can't seem to settle my stomach or stop pacing." He walked to one end of the room and back again. "See? Can't stop."

Hiding his humor, Reid approached his brother and as Cole made another pass, grabbed him by the arms and guided him to a chair. "There, you've stopped, no thanks required. Maybe you should talk to me instead. You're not having second thoughts, are you?"

"No! God, no. I've been waiting for this day for what seems like forever." Rubbing his hand over his forehead, Cole scowled. "I don't know why I'm nervous. I shouldn't be nervous. There isn't another woman I can envision spending the rest of my life with."

"Normal to be nervous, Cole." Reid poured his brother a glass of water from the pitcher their mother had brought in earlier. "Drink this. Since you're not having second thoughts, I'd say these nerves have nothing to do with Rachel. They're about…the step and all that awaits."

Cole gulped half the water down in one fell swoop. "Right. That's a good thing."

"It is, trust me. And while I can't swear to this," Reid said, "as I never experienced the moment firsthand, I'm thinking your nerves—every last one of them—will disappear the second Rachel takes her first step down the aisle toward you."

"She'll be beautiful. And, yeah, that's a positive image." Slamming his empty hand against his heart, Cole let out a long whoosh of air. "This feels an awful lot like when I was still on the professional skiing circuit. Right before a competition, I'd get this pumped-up, crazy exhilaration along with…yeah, this woozy slide of nausea and nerves."

That sounded about right to Reid. "Go with this for a second. How would you feel once you were at the top of the course, ready for the push-off?"

"The nerves would fade." Cole snapped his fingers. "And I'd just have that powerful exhilaration, the…anticipation and hope of how the next few minutes would go."

"Well, I think you can assume the same will happen

here, only instead of anticipating the next few minutes, you'll have an entire lifetime with the woman you love." A solid stab of jealousy struck Reid, smack-dab in the center of his chest. Not *of* Cole or Rachel, or even what they had, but all that awaited them. "You're a lucky man."

"I am." Happiness glittered in Cole's gaze. "I love her, Reid. So damn much it shocks me at times. Like we'll be in the middle of a conversation, or she'll be sitting across the room from me, and all of a sudden, this bolt of awareness hits, and I'll almost keel over from the strength."

"I know how that is," he said quietly. "Treasure those moments, treasure Rachel, and…I don't know, man, never let any of this, any of what you two feel for each other, become commonplace. And…ah…I wouldn't mind a niece or nephew down the road."

That broke the ice. Cole laughed and stood, grabbed his jacket and slung it on. "Yes, Mom," he said. Pulling in a deep, centering breath, he turned toward Reid. "What about you? Are you doing okay? I mean, this is probably tough for you. Because of what happened and…"

"I'm fine. Today isn't about me," Reid said firmly, emphatically. "Today is about you and Rachel and celebration. Focus on that."

But Cole wasn't about to be dissuaded. "You're still holding to the wedding on May sixth? No thoughts on canceling or anything?"

"Nope." On this, Reid remained resolute. Scared to death most times, not that he would admit so to another soul, but resolute. "I love her, Cole." He winked and repeated his brother's words, saying, "So damn much it shocks me at times. And I guess I'm just not ready to let go."

"I wouldn't give up, either," Cole said after a brief, considering pause. "And you should know, I'll be there for you, if…well, if this doesn't go down the way it should. We'll… ah…go fishing or hiking or something. Just us."

"That sounds good. Real good." Emotion, far too soppy for Reid's comfort, roared in and clogged his throat. Family. Where would he be without it? Then, with a glance toward his watch, he said, "It's time. Let's go get you married, shall we?"

"Oh, hell," Cole said, every one of his nerves reappearing. "Really? It's time? Now?"

Laughing, Reid led his wobbly legged, nervous-as-all-get-out brother to the door, to the car, and then, into the church. And yup, once Rachel started her trek down the aisle, her eyes focused on Cole, Reid saw only happiness, excitement and pride in his brother's gaze.

That was an experience he'd like to have, seeing his bride—Daisy, of course—coming toward him with love in her eyes, and the rush of emotion such a sight would evoke.

Yeah, Reid thought again, his brother was one hell of a lucky man.

Chapter Fourteen

Leaving Steamboat Springs was far more difficult than Daisy had anticipated. Partially because of the date—May fifth, a fact that struck her with no small amount of irony—and partially because everything that could have gone wrong on this day did.

Her parents had been continually delayed, and now they were set to arrive early that afternoon. Daisy wanted to be on the road by eight in the morning. Cowardly? Perhaps, but she saw no reason to put herself into an emotional spin before taking to the road for the long, fourteen-hour drive home. Besides which, Parker barely needed any help at this point.

Truthfully, she could have left a full week ago. She hadn't only because she'd enjoyed spending the time with her brother and the girls, and she wasn't entirely sure when she would be able to visit next. Well, Christmas for sure, but if possible, she'd like to make the trip sooner.

So, she'd awakened that Monday morning with a plan, and bit by bit, that plan fell to the wayside. First, she couldn't find her laptop. After close to an hour of searching, Erin had finally discovered it tucked in the linen closet, beneath a stack of towels. Parker said that Daisy had probably put it there accidentally, before her shower that morning, but…um…no.

Daisy did not tend to carry her laptop with her when her intentions were to stand in streaming hot water. Someone had hidden it, and initially, she'd thought one of the girls had done so in an attempt to keep her from leaving. They did not want her to go.

Neither admitted to the crime, and they were honest enough in their pleas that she began to wonder if the true culprit was her brother. Even so, she kept this thought to herself.

Then, after she'd completely packed her belongings and put her suitcases in her car, she was having a final cup of coffee with Parker. He stood, tripped, and her shirt was suddenly soaked clean through, requiring her to retrieve one of her bags and find a change of clothes.

Naturally, this solidified her belief that her brother was, for some unknown reason, trying to hamper her planned departure. She, again, decided to keep this to herself. Why leave on a sour note? But when her purse, with her car keys inside, also went missing, she'd had enough.

"What's going on here?" she asked Parker, her hands on her hips. "Because I know darn well where I left my purse, and now it's mysteriously vanished. Just like my laptop earlier."

Blue eyes blinked in feigned—she was sure—innocence. "I don't know, Daisy. Have you checked upstairs? Or maybe you stuck it in the trunk with your luggage? Or…" Pausing, he scratched his jaw and shrugged. "No clue. But we'll help you look."

The girls were home from school, due to a teacher in-service day, and they were more than willing to search the house. Another full hour of frustrated impatience passed before Daisy's purse was located by Megan. Under the kitchen sink, behind the extra-large bottle of dishwasher detergent and pretty much completely hidden from view.

And when the purse was found, Daisy saw her brother frown. What in heaven's name was he up to? She didn't know, but she planned on finding out. Posthaste.

"Hey, girls?" she said to Erin and Megan. "Can you take Jinx out in the backyard and play with her a bit, since she'll be stuck in the car all day? It would help me out a lot."

"We can do that, Aunt Daisy!" Megan said. "And we'll get her really tired, so she sleeps in the car and doesn't get scared."

"Since we won't be with her anymore," Erin added. "And she's used to us now."

"That would be perfect," Daisy said, knowing she was going to face a battle of emotions soon enough. Hers and her nieces. No, leaving them was not going to be easy. In any way.

The minute the girls were out of the house, she once again faced her brother. "I don't know what you're trying to do, but, Parker, I need to go home."

"Why?" he asked, settling himself on the living room sofa. His movements were slow and somewhat jerky, so it took him a minute to find a comfortable position. "I don't see why you can't stay for a few more days, or a week. Mom and Dad will be here. We haven't all been together since... well, since before you left the last time."

"I'm not ready for that, Parker," she said. "Mom alone, maybe. But Dad? He barely talks to me when I call to wish him happy birthday. I... No, I don't see how a face-to-face on the same day I'm leaving will do any good."

"Understandable. I just miss us all being a family, and with my accident—"

"We were never 'all' a family," she said tiredly. "You were, with Mom and Dad, and I was with you and Mom, but all four of us?" Daisy shook her head. "We weren't,

Parker. You know that as well as I do, and I don't believe you really expect that to change."

"Expect? Maybe not," he admitted, his voice low. "But I can hope, can't I? And Dad asks about you, Daisy. How you're doing, if I know if you're happy or dating anyone. I think he just doesn't know how to make that first move. So maybe if you were here...maybe that could change. It's worth a shot, isn't it? What's one more day?"

"You're such a great father, and I'm guessing a lot of who you are as a dad comes from our father, but, Parker," she said, trying to keep her emotions tightly in check, "I did not have that experience with him."

"Right. I know that, but come on. One. More. Day."

And she knew, in the snap of a finger, what was really going on. Tomorrow. The wedding. "This is more about Reid than Mom and Dad," she said, forming the statement as fact and not a question. "Why can't you let this go?"

"Because he loves you. And I've been living with you for the past few weeks, so it's fairly obvious that you love him, too."

"Sometimes," she said, "love isn't enough."

"That's cowardice speaking or...fear, maybe. Just go see him, Daisy. He has it in his head that he's pushed you too hard, so he's waiting, hoping you'll...just go see him."

She breathed in, deeply. Yes, Reid had pulled back significantly. He'd told her the same, that whatever happened, no matter what that was, remained in her hands. And that was good. Relieving. Empowering, too.

But she was still too afraid to take that damn step.

And she'd explained all of this to Parker in their many and extensive conversations on this topic. He'd made his stance very, very clear. And she'd done the same with hers. Simply speaking, she just did not have the energy to go into all of it again. Not with him. Heck, not even in her own head.

"I'm so happy you and I are becoming close." She went to him, sat next to him and rested her head on her big brother's shoulder. "And I will be here much more often. I love you, Parker. But part of this relationship means respecting each other's choices. And I can't stay."

Bringing his arm around her shoulders, he pulled her into a semi-awkward hug. "I love you, too, and okay," he said with a resigned sigh, "I'll respect your decision. Even if this particular one is…dead wrong." His fingers found her necklace and he gave it a gentle tug. "You're still wearing his ring, Daisy."

"Only because he refuses to take it back, and I don't want to lose it." Well, not the full truth. Close enough, though. Daisy stood and smoothed her hands down the front of her jeans. She wasn't wrong about this, about her decision. Couldn't be wrong. Not when so much was at stake. "Now, though, I need to get moving."

Goodbyes were said. Erin and Megan didn't cry, but when Daisy hugged each of them, they held on, their arms tight around Daisy's neck, for considerably longer than necessary. And no, part of her did not want to get in her car and drive away.

She'd done something important here. She'd built a connection with her nieces, her brother, and leaving felt odd and lonely and…sad. Incredibly, unbelievably sad.

But this, returning home, also held the lure of safety and comfort and stability. Three things she hadn't felt since her all-day date with Reid. She needed the comfort of home—*her* home—to find whatever peace of mind she'd lost. And, while she didn't quite comprehend the potency of the compulsion, her instincts were insistent that it was time.

That she had to go home, and she had to go home *now*.

"Okay, girls, listen up," she said, kneeling in front of them in the grass beside her car. "After I leave…if you go upstairs to your bedroom and look on your shelf, you'll find a present for each of you. Something special. And I hope that whenever you look at these gifts, you'll always remember how very, very much I love you."

For Erin, she'd purchased a small heart-shaped gold locket that contained two pictures, one of Bridget, Parker and the girls, and one of her and Jinx. With Erin's on-again, off-again need to have something to hug, she thought—hoped—the necklace would fill that requirement.

An idea she'd gotten from her own necklace and her recent propensity toward...well, hanging on to Reid's ring for dear life. The feel of that ring in her palm had given her comfort. She hoped the same would happen for Erin with the locket.

And for Megan, due to her color days, Daisy had bought a small charm bracelet. The band could be switched out for one of six colors, and the charms consisted of a locket with the same photos as Erin's. A miniature family, a dog, a pancake—yes, she'd actually found a pancake charm—a tiny doll and a few other mementos that she hoped would help Megan feel good, no matter the day's color.

Parker understood the reasoning behind both gifts, so he could explain that to the girls. And, she hoped by giving them something to focus on after she left, they'd be less sad.

"Thank you for the present, Aunt Daisy," Erin said in her oh-so-polite voice. "But I think I'd like it more if you stayed and just told us you loved us every day."

Megan dipped her chin in a definitive nod. "I think that, too. Please, please stay?"

Oh, Lord. She looked to Parker, but all he did was arch his brows and mouth the phrase, "One more day." Stricken with grief, with the acute sadness of two little girls she loved, she held out her arms, and said, "I'm sorry, but I really can't. Now come here for one more hug."

They piled in and she squeezed them as tight as she could, breathed in their scents and kissed them on their foreheads. One last hug with Parker while the girls fawned over Jinx, and that was that. Shortly after eleven, a good three hours later than her original plan, Daisy and Jinx were finally in the car, starting the long trip home.

And for the most part, Daisy felt…if not *good,* settled in her decision.

Jinx started whining about thirty miles out, a state of unhappiness that only increased the farther and longer Daisy drove. She pulled over several times for short walks and to give Jinx some extra attention, but none of that seemed to do the trick. All indications seemed to state—thankfully— that her dog wasn't ill. She just wasn't happy.

So Daisy talked with her as they drove. Tried to reassure her that everything was fine, that they were just going home. This calmed her for a little while, so Daisy continued with her constant stream of chatter. Well, about six hours into the trip, her murmuring words of comfort no longer had any effect, and Jinx's whining returned.

The eight-hour mark brought forth frantic whimpers, and ten hours in, Jinx began adding sharp, growling barks here and there between her whimpers and whines. At this point, all Daisy wanted was to get them home, so rather than stopping at a hotel, she pushed onward.

With less than two hours until they arrived at Daisy's apartment, Jinx's whimpers and whines dropped several levels in volume, and she curled up on the backseat. She did not fall asleep, but she quieted enough that Daisy could, finally, think.

About her departure from Steamboat Springs. About the looks on her nieces' faces as she drove off. About her conversation with her brother, and that her parents were now in the house that Daisy had considered her home since late February. And yes, she thought about Reid.

One by one, memories clicked into place, from their initial confrontation all the way through to their last. Every word, every look, every time he'd irritated her and every time he'd made her laugh. How he had somehow gotten through Jinx's defenses, and the absolute love he knew how to give—to Erin and Megan, to his family, to…Daisy.

All of it was there, available for her to consider, decipher, consider again and…at the end, revel in. As she did, a weight seemed to land on her chest, growing heavier as the miles went by, as she drew closer and closer to home. A desperate, almost clawing sensation began in her lower stomach, and by the time she pulled in to her apartment building's parking lot, she had gone straight from melancholy and confused to downright nauseous from emotion, from doubt.

In herself. In her decision.

Daisy parked her car and turned off the ignition. Closed her eyes and breathed deeply in an attempt to center herself. She was tired from the trip. Her head ached from the hours of Jinx's whining, whimpering and barking. Of course, she would be emotional.

Of course, she would have doubts.

Normal. Expected, even. She'd get a good night's sleep—in her own bed, thank goodness—and tomorrow all would seem better. Yawning, she clipped Jinx's leash to her collar for a quick walk before they went inside, and headed for the small dog park at the back of the building. The area was well-lit, the path easy to navigate, and as they walked, her dog continued to make soft, growly noises of unhappiness.

"Silly dog," Daisy said, unlatching the gate to the dog park. "We're home now."

Jinx gave her a look—a very human type of look—that seemed to state she couldn't believe Daisy had made such a ridiculous statement.

"Stop looking at me like that," Daisy said. "*This* is our home. Not Steamboat Springs."

With a snooty-sounding sniff, the whippet went to do her thing, and Daisy leaned against the fence to wait. The odd thought that this *wasn't* home crept into her consciousness, took root and expanded in size, increasing the sick jolt of nausea in her stomach.

As if in slow motion, Daisy pivoted to look at her apartment building. Three years she'd lived here. Three years this had been her home. And was, in fact, *still* her home.

But being here felt off. Wrong. And that strange, potent compulsion from earlier hadn't evaporated. The pull she'd ascribed toward needing to return home *now* was, if anything, stronger, more insistent, and…and…not about her physical residence.

Because this city, this building, no longer felt like home. *Reid.* Oh, Lord. What had she done?

Her legs weakened to the point that she sat down on one of the benches. Again, every moment she'd spent with Reid flickered to life in her head. He believed in her. He knew her, better perhaps, than she knew herself. And he still wanted her, still loved her, still believed they belonged together, and she…had run from him, from all of that, for the second damn time. *She'd* absconded from their team, even when he'd stood strong.

All at once, every tear she hadn't been able to shed in the past weeks came to be in a flood of emotion. But these tears were different in that they also came from a place of certainty. Every one of her fears now seemed ludicrous. Who cared how wide, how deep, how treacherous the leap was if, at the other end, she was with the man she loved.

The man who loved her.

Her doubts, one by one, disappeared. Because she understood, finally, that she did not have to take that leap alone. Reid would hold her hand and jump with her, and together they would not fall, they would…fly.

"Jinx!" Daisy said, unwilling to waste another second.

"We have to go, sweets. I…I have a wedding to get to. And barely enough hours to get there on time."

Her dog huffed and padded toward her, again with a very human type of look on her canine face. Something along the lines of "Duh. Took you long enough."

And then, without any sleep but with a blessedly happy and quiet dog, Daisy started the long journey back to Steamboat Springs, toward her real home. Toward Reid.

Chapter Fifteen

On the afternoon of May sixth, surrounded by his family and a group of his closest friends, Reid waited to see if his faith would be rewarded. Via Parker, he knew that Daisy had, indeed, gotten in her car late yesterday morning to return to California.

She hadn't phoned Parker since, and out of concern, he'd attempted to get a hold of her, to no avail. He'd mentioned her phone had gone directly to voice mail, so Reid was holding on to one last slender thread of hope. Perhaps, he'd told Parker, she'd changed her mind somewhere along her route, had turned around and her cell's battery had died.

He wasn't a fool. It was just as possible, if not more so, that she had shut off her phone in order to completely retreat behind her turtle-porcupine shell. But any strand of hope was better than none, so until he had no other choice, he was holding on tight.

If she didn't show, if today did not pan out as he desperately wanted it to, then Reid had decided he'd give her some time—a month, tops—and he'd go to California. Hell. He'd pick up his life and move there, if she asked. But if she shot him down…well, he'd have to give up.

For her and for himself. And he'd be okay, eventually.

But at this moment, in this second, a chance still existed. So for now, he chose to focus on that, rather than worst-case scenarios.

Didn't mean he wasn't nervous, though.

Pulling in a breath, Reid smoothed his suit jacket, straightened his tie and appraised the space his mother had created. There were a multitude of flowers—wildflowers with silver brunia as a unifying element—in the corners, on the tables, adding bright splashes of color and fragrant scents of spring to the room. Some of the flowers had been used, along with twisted vines of greenery, to form an aisle for the bride to walk down.

Long, billowy sheaths of white, gauzy fabric were strung with twinkling lights in a mystical, almost fantastical display from the ceiling, softening the normally rustic appearance of the pub. And, finally, there were small, round lanterns in muted, soft shades on the bar and the tables that illuminated the entire area in a hazy, romantic glow.

Margaret Foster had outdone herself.

Daisy, Reid knew, would agree. And damn it, he wanted her to see this, wanted her to walk in here and spin in a circle, delighted by all she saw.

He glanced at the clock and immediately wished he hadn't. Fifteen minutes until what was supposed to be the start of their ceremony. His gut kicked in another blast of nerves, and his jaw ached from clenching it so hard. Purposefully, Reid relaxed his muscles, forced a smile and took a stroll around the room. People were chatting and watching the time, watching him, with concern and curiosity. Most were likely wondering how long it would take him to shut this thing down. Hell, he kept asking himself the same damn question.

When he reached the corner where his siblings stood, he stopped. "I'm fine," he said as way of greeting, before anyone could pose the question. "A little anxious, but fine.

And I figure, either way this goes, we can have one hell of a party. So no gloomy faces."

"She'll be here," Haley said, her eyes and her mouth firm and steady. "I believe she will be here, so…you believe that, too."

"We all hope she'll show," Dylan said, his voice low. "But have you determined how long you're going to wait?"

"As long as he wants." Cole frowned at Dylan. "There isn't a time limit on this, and," he said, now looking at Reid, "I'll stand here for however long that is."

Reid nodded, too choked up to form any actual words. Having the support of his brothers and sister meant the world. Fishing with Cole, he reminded himself, if this went sour. Just the two of them. That would be good.

Finding his voice again, he said, "I see Parker and the girls, his parents. Think I'll go say hi, see how they're all doing or if they need anything."

"Sure. But I'm guessing if he'd heard from Daisy, he'd not waste time telling you," Dylan said, accurately pegging Reid's motivation. Or, at least, part of his motivation. "We could go upstairs, have a drink and just hang loose there for a while."

Nice idea, and Reid was grateful for the thought, the offer. But if Daisy walked in those doors, he wanted to know it instantly. "Thanks, but…rather stay here. Think I'll be more nervous if I'm in any other room. Better to keep moving, talking."

So that was what he did. No, Parker had not heard from Daisy, and no, he had not yet been able to reach her. He spoke with his father and his mother, both of whom were just as calm and supportive as he needed them to be. But every time Reid looked at the clock, a chunk of minutes had disappeared. Now it was four forty-five, and…well, much as he hated to admit it, he was beginning to lose what remained of his hope, his belief.

She had to show. He *knew* they belonged together.

By five-fifteen, he decided he'd hold off on the no-wedding announcement for one more hour. Longer, probably, than he should wait, but he kept thinking…couldn't get it out of his head, that if Daisy had driven all the way home before changing her mind, there was no way she'd have been able to do the return trip and be here by four.

He checked with the minister, a friend of his father's, to make sure he could wait that long. He could, he said, no problem. So. Six-fifteen, no later than six-thirty was Reid's cutoff.

'Course, if she showed at midnight tonight, he'd be good with that, too. Really, he just wanted her here. With him. Whenever and however and—

He heard the bark first. That strange, not-a-growl, not-a-yowl, not-a-yip bark that could only come from one specific, ornery-as-all-get-out creature. *Jinx.* And he knew, thank God almighty, he knew that his belief, his hope, his faith had not been in vain.

Heart galloping like a herd of wild horses, legs loose and wobbly, Reid made the slow, slow pivot to face the door. And there she was, standing in the entrance with that dog, whom he also loved, in her arms, wearing a wedding dress that was…a bit rumpled but still gorgeous, flyaway hair and tired but frantic eyes. To Reid, Daisy had never looked so beautiful.

Because she was here, for him, for them, and he'd waited for this one moment in time for…well, eight years. To the friggin' day.

All of his strength reappeared. His heart calmed, his legs steadied and he strode across the room, wanting her in his arms, his lips on her lips, and if she agreed, her hand in his from this day forward, for better or for worse, in sickness and in health.

"Reid," she said, the second he was in hearing distance.

"I'm so sorry I wasn't here on time. So, so sorry. I tried. Broke every speed limit, which, okay, probably not the best idea on no sleep, and had to stop to put on the dress, but I did not want you standing here, waiting for me. I did not want to be late, so—"

"Marry me, darlin'?"

Eyelashes fluttered and joy entered her gaze, wiping out the anxious adrenaline he'd seen but a second ago. "Yes," she said, loudly. Clearly. "Yes, I will marry you."

Whistles and cheers and applause filled the room, along with Jinx's yips of…happiness? Sure as hell sounded like it to Reid. And, frankly, he was done pretending that this dog wasn't more human than canine when, clearly, she was.

Everything happened really fast then. Erin came forward to claim Jinx, while Haley and Rachel and his mother stole Daisy into the back, to help set her hair and such to straights. He didn't see the sense in that, as she truly had never looked more stunning.

And then, amidst the flowers and the lanterns and the gauzy, romantic fabric, with his family and hers in attendance, the Lennox-Foster wedding, eight years after their original intent, finally commenced, and Daisy became his wife.

"Daisy Foster," he said with a grin and a wink. "May I kiss you now?"

He didn't wait for a response, sort of figuring that marriage superseded rule number two, and just gathered her close and lowered his mouth. When their lips met, a feeling of pure, perfect rightness settled in, filling him with a deep and satisfying sense of wholeness. This connection, the potency and power that existed between them, was intrinsic. Natural.

And sexy as hell.

Desire, hot and strong and alive, shot through him and raised his pulse, heated his blood. Never had any other woman had this effect on him. Never *could* another woman reach his body, his heart and his soul with such point-blank accuracy or completeness.

She was his. He was hers.

And he would protect her, love her, for the rest of his life.

Remembering they had an audience, he broke the kiss. "I love you, Daisy," he whispered. "Then and now. Still and forever. And I will never let you doubt that again."

"I have no more doubts, Reid. Not about us," she said, her eyes a tantalizing shade of green. "And I promise you that the only running I'll do from here on out is toward you."

"Aw, darlin', it's good to hear you say that, but," he said, unable to stop himself, "I'd like to remind you that I was right in this matter. I told you that I believed you'd change your mind, that you'd be here for this wedding. And it looks as if—"

That was all he got out before she kissed him.

Epilogue

"Hold still, you crazy dog," Daisy said to Jinx, who was hopping around as if she were a bunny rabbit. "I know you want to go outside and play with Reid and the girls, but we have to take care of this one little surprise first. Please?"

Quickly, before Jinx took off, she attached the small, gift-size envelope to her dog's collar, in the exact same fashion Reid had slightly over a year ago. Once the envelope was secure and Jinx's collar wasn't too loose, she led the dog to the back door.

"Okay, you know what to do," she said, opening the door. "Take that to Reid, sweets."

Off Jinx went, roaring through the grass to join Reid, Parker and the girls in their game of Frisbee. Smiling, beyond happy, Daisy placed her hand on her stomach and watched, hoping her husband would notice the envelope sooner rather than later.

She couldn't wait to share her news. They were having a baby. In December.

And she'd decided to tell him via a "We're Having a Baby!" card, similar to all of those frustrating save-a-date cards he'd left lying around Parker's house for her to find.

Seemed appropriate. And fun.

In the thirteen months since their wedding, she hadn't experienced a single regret in her emotional rush of a decision to turn around and return to Steamboat Springs. Life was good. About as perfect as a person could hope for, actually. She was madly in love.

Then and now. Still and forever.

All of her relationships were strong, or becoming stronger. She and her brother were rock-solid, and she adored her nieces with a wholehearted joy that continued to grow. The well of love she had for them seemed never ending.

She'd even, slowly and carefully, started mending the rift with her parents. Easier with her mother. Clara Lennox had profusely expressed her regrets, her apologies, and Daisy had accepted and forgiven. They were almost as close as they once had been, and for that, Daisy was grateful. Having her mother in her life again was a gift.

And her father…well, that would take more time, more caution, but she believed they were on the right road to becoming closer. Charles Lennox had apologized, as well. He'd even stated that his struggle in accepting Daisy was unfair, and that he hadn't realized how much he'd considered her his daughter until she was gone.

Would they ever have the type of relationship she'd once dreamed of? Probably not. Love existed between them, though, and she believed—or hoped—that given time, that love could help them form a nurturing, positive father-daughter relationship. As Reid liked to say, hope existed, and where there was hope, any damn thing on the face of the earth could happen.

So she chose to hope.

A series of barks pulled her from her thoughts, and her smile widened. In delight and in heady anticipation. Reid was almost sprinting toward the back door, with Jinx in excited pursuit.

Obviously, he'd found and read her card.

In less than twenty seconds, he was standing in front of her, his dark eyes intent, searching. Already concerned, she guessed, along with thrilled.

"A baby?" he asked, his voice holding every ounce of that concern, that thrill. "You're sure? No doubts on this in any way?"

"Hmm? Oh, the baby?" she said. "Absolutely positive. You're going to be a father sometime in December. Isn't that—"

"December? In the middle of the winter season, when I'm hardly ever here?" His concern grew, and she almost—*almost*—laughed. "So from early November on, you'll have to spend more time with my family. Or your brother, because I don't want you alone, and—"

"Maybe even a Christmas baby…wouldn't that be something?"

"We'll have to work out a system, so someone is with you when I'm not around. Dylan. He'd be a good choice." Reid closed his eyes and Daisy could just about see the wheels turning. "Parker, of course, but with the girls…no. Will have to be Dylan. Maybe he can even move in for the duration, or maybe your mom—"

And, as she had done at their wedding and many, many times since then, she walked up to her sexy, loving, protective husband, put her hands on his shoulders and kissed him.

Fully. Soundly.

He shut up and kissed her back. Also fully. Also soundly.

It was, she decided, the perfect arrangement.

* * * * *

NEEDED:
ONE CONVENIENT
HUSBAND

FIONA BRAND

For the Lord. Thank You.

I am the light of the world.
Whoever follows me will never walk in darkness,
but will have the light of life.
—*John* 8:12

One

Kyle Messena's gaze narrowed as the bridal car pulled up outside Dolphin Bay's windblown, hilltop church. The bride, festooned in white tulle, stepped out of the limousine. A drift of gauze obscured her face, but sunlight gleamed on tawny hair that was heart-stoppingly familiar.

Adrenaline pumped and time seemed to slow, stop, as he considered the stunning fact that, despite his efforts to prevent Eva Atraeus marrying a man whose motives were purely financial, she had utterly fooled him and the wedding he had thought he had nixed was going ahead.

Kyle had taken two long, gliding steps out of the inky shade cast by an aged oak into the blistering heat of a New Zealand summer's day before the ocean breeze whipped the veil from the bride's face.

It wasn't Eva.

Relief unlocked the fierce tension that gripped him.

A tension that sliced through the indifference to relationships that had shrouded him for years, ever since the death of his wife and small son. Deaths that he should have prevented.

The unwanted, brooding intensity had grown over the months he had been entrusted with the duty of ensuring that the heiress to an Atraeus fortune married according to a draconian clause in her adoptive father's will. Eva, in order to get control of her inheritance, had to either marry a Messena—*him*—or a man who genuinely wanted her and not her money.

Acting as Eva's trustee did not sit well with Kyle. He was aware that his wily great-uncle, Mario, had named him as trustee in a last game-playing move to maneuver him into marrying the woman he had once wanted but left behind. Confronted by the mesmerizing power of an attraction that still held him in reluctant thrall and unable to accept that the one woman he had never been able to forget would marry someone else, Kyle had been unable to refuse the job.

A gust of wind whipped the bride's veil to one side, revealing that she was a little on the plump side. Her hair was also a couple of shades lighter than the rich dark mane shot through with tawny highlights that had been a natural feature of Eva's hair ever since he'd first set eyes on her at age sixteen.

Kyle's jaw unlocked. Now that he had successfully circumvented Eva's latest marriage plan, he was ready to leave, but when a zippy white sports car emblazoned with the name of Eva's business, Perfect Weddings, pulled into a space, Kyle knew he wasn't going anywhere.

Eva Atraeus, dressed in a pale pink button-down suit that clung in all the right places, closed the door with an expensive *thunk*. Cell held to one ear, she hooked a matching pale pink tote over her shoulder and started toward the church doors, her stride fluid and distractingly sexy in a pair of strappy high heels. At five feet seven, Eva was several inches too short for the runway, but with her elegant, curvy figure, mouthwatering cheekbones and exotic dark eyes, she had been a knockout success as a photographic model. Gorgeous, quirky and certifiably high maintenance, Eva had fascinated gossip columnists for years and dazzled more men than she'd had hot dinners, including *him*.

Every muscle in Kyle's body tightened on a visceral hit of awareness that had become altogether too familiar.

A faint check in her step indicated that Eva had spotted him.

As the bridal party disappeared into the church, she terminated her call and changed direction. Stepping beneath the shade of the oak, she shoved the cell in her tote and glared at him. "What are you doing at *my* wedding?"

Kyle clamped down on his irritation at Eva's deliberate play on the "my wedding" bit. It was true that it was supposed to have been her actual wedding day. Understandably, she was annoyed that he'd upset her plan to leverage a marriage of convenience by offering the groom a lucrative job in Dubai. The way Kyle saw it, he had simply countered one employment opportunity with another. The fact that Jeremy, an accountant, had taken the job so quickly and had even seemed relieved, more than justified his intervention. "You shouldn't have arranged a wedding you knew couldn't go ahead."

Her dark gaze flashed. "What if I was in love with Jeremy?"

He lifted a brow. "After a whole four weeks?"

"You know as well as I that it can happen a whole lot faster than—" She stopped, her cheeks flushed. Rummaging in her bag, she found sunglasses and, with controlled precision, slipped them onto the bridge of her nose. "Now you get to tell me what you're doing at a *private* wedding. I'm guessing it's not just to have another argument."

He crossed his arms over his chest. "If you think you can kick me out, forget it. I'm a guest of the groom. I manage his share portfolio."

She took a deep breath and he watched with objective fascination as the flare of irritation was replaced by one of the gorgeous smiles that had graced magazines and posters and which had the power to stop all male brain function. "That's thin, even for you."

"But workable."

"And here I was thinking you were here to make sure I hadn't pulled off a last-minute coup and found another groom."

He frowned at the light, floral waft of her perfume and resisted the impulse to step a little closer. "It's not my brief to stop you marrying."

Her head tilted to one side. Through the screen of the lenses her gaze chilled. "No, it's to stop me marrying the man of my choice."

"You need to choose better." Out of an impressive discard pile during the last few months, on three different occasions, Eva had selected a prospective groom. Unfortunately, all three had been strapped for cash and willing to sign prenuptial agreements that spelled out the cutoff date for the marriage: two years to the day, the exact time period specified in Mario's will. Kyle had been honorbound by the terms of the will to veto the weddings.

"Jeremy was perfect husband material. He was attractive, personable, with a reasonable job, his—"

"Motive was blatantly financial."

Her expression turned steely. "He needed money to cover some debts. What is so wrong with that?"

"Mario would spin in his grave if you married a man with a gambling addiction."

There was a small icy silence, intensified by the strains of the wedding march emanating from the church. "If I have to marry Mr. Right according to Kyle Messena, then maybe *you* should choose someone for me. Only I'll need to marry him by—" she checked the slim pink watch on her wrist "—next month. Since now, thanks to you, I only have three weeks left to marry before my inheritance goes into lockdown for the next *thirteen years*."

Despite Kyle's resolve to withstand the considerable pressure he had always known Eva would apply, a twinge of guilt made his stomach tighten.

Women and relationships in general had always proved to be a difficult area for him. It was a fact that he was more comfortable with the world of military operations or the clinical cut and thrust of his family's banking business. He could do weapons and operational tactics; he could do figures and financial markets. Love and the responsibility—and the searing guilt that came with it—was something he would not risk again. "It isn't my intention to prevent you getting your inheritance."

Eva's serene smile disappeared. "No," she said with a throaty little catch to her voice. "It's just turning out that way."

Spinning on her heel, Eva marched back to her car.

Kyle frowned. Eva's voice had sounded suspiciously husky, as if she was on the verge of tears. In the entire checkered history of their relationship, he had only ever seen Eva, who was superorganized with a serene, kick-ass calm, cry twice. Of course, she had cried at Mario's funeral almost a year ago. The only other occasion had been close on eleven years ago when he'd been nineteen. To be precise, it had been the morning after Mario had hauled them both over the coals for a passionate interlude on Dolphin Bay's beach.

Memory flickered. A hot, extended twilight, a buttery moon sliding up over the sea, the clamor of a family party at the resort fading in the distance as Eva had wound her arms around his neck. He'd drawn a deep breath, caught the scent of her hair, her skin. Every muscle had tensed as he'd dipped his head and given in to the temptation that had kept him in agony most of the summer and kissed her...

If Mario hadn't come looking for Eva, they would have done a lot more than just kiss. The interview with Mario that had ensued that night had been sharp and short. As gorgeous and put-together as Eva had looked at age seventeen, she had more than her share of vulnerabilities. The product of a severely dysfunctional family, Eva needed security and protection, not seduction. Mario hadn't elaborated on any of those details, but the message had been plain enough. Eva was off-limits.

Until now.

He had no illusions about why Mario had done a complete about turn and made him a trustee, when for years he had treated Kyle as if he was a marauding predator after his one and only chick. For years Eva had stubbornly resisted Mario's attempts to find her a safe, solid husband from amongst the sons of his wealthy business associates. Mario, forced to change tack, had swallowed his objections to the "wild Messena boys," and had then tried to marry Eva off to both of Kyle's older brothers, Gabriel and Nick. When that strategy had failed because Gabe and Nick had married other women and Kyle's younger brother Damian had a long-standing girlfriend, in a last desperate move, Mario had finally settled on Kyle as a prospective bridegroom.

His gaze still locked on Eva, Kyle strolled back to his Maserati. Now that he knew Eva wasn't the bride, he should drive back to Auckland. Back to his ultra-busy, smoothly organized life. If he left right away, he could even make the uncomplicated dinner date he had with Elise, a fellow banking executive he had been seeing on and off for the past few months, mostly at business functions.

But as he approached the Maserati, which was nose to tail with Eva's white sports car, he couldn't shake the sense that something about the way Eva had stormed off had not rung true. It occurred to him that the tears he thought Eva had been about to cry could have been fake. After all, she *had* taken acting classes. She had been good enough that she had even been offered a part in a popular soap, but had turned it down because it had conflicted with her desire to start her own wedding planning business.

Suddenly positive that he had been duped, he dropped the Maserati's key back into his pocket. There could be only one reason why Eva wanted him to feel guilty enough that he bypassed the reception. She had already found a new candidate for groom and he would be attending as her guest. Since she only had three weeks to organize her final shot at a wedding, keeping her new prospective groom close made sense, because time was of the essence.

Certainty settled in when he caught the tail end of a conversation with someone named Troy. His jaw tightened. Troy Kendal, if he didn't miss his guess. A flashy sports star Eva had met less than a week ago in a last, desperate attempt to recruit a groom. Out of nowhere, the jealousy he had worked hard to suppress because it was just as illogical as the desire that haunted him, roared to life.

If Eva had been crying, they had been crocodile tears. She had been getting rid of him.

In no mood to leave now, Kyle waited until Eva terminated the call and dropped the phone in her bag. "We need to talk."

"I thought we just did."

Dropping her bag on the passenger seat, she dragged off her sunglasses and checked her watch, subtly underlining the fact that she was in a hurry to leave. Without the barrier of the lenses, and with strands of hair blowing loose around her cheeks, she seemed younger and oddly vulnerable, although Kyle knew that was an illusion, since Eva's reputation with men was legendary. "There's a solution to your problem. If you marry a Messena, there are no further conditions, other than that the marriage must be of two years' duration."

Her brows creased as if she was only just considering an option that had been bluntly stated in the will. "Even if I wanted to do that, which I don't, that's hardly possible, since Gabriel and Nick are both married, and Damian's as good as."

Kyle's jaw clamped at the systematic way she ticked his brothers off her fingers, deliberately leaving him off the list. *As if her fingers had never locked with his as they'd strolled down the dimly lit path to Dolphin Bay, as if she had never wrapped her arms around his neck and kissed him.*

"There's one other Messena," Kyle said flatly, his patience gone. "I'm talking you, me and a marriage of convenience."

Two

Eva choked back the stinging refusal she wanted to fling at Kyle. She didn't know why she reacted so strongly to him or the idea that they could marry. Mario's previous attempts to marry her off to other Messena men had barely ruffled her.

A year ago, when she had read the terms of the will and absorbed the full import of that one little sentence, she had been so horrified she had wanted to crawl under the solicitor's desk and hide. The whole idea that Kyle, the only available Messena husband—and the one man who had ditched her—should feel pressured to marry her, had been mortifying. "I don't need a pity proposal."

The wind dropped for a split second, enclosing them in a pooling, tension-filled silence that was gradually filled with the timeless beauty of the wedding vows floating from the church.

"But you do need *a* proposal. After two years, once

you've got your inheritance, we can dissolve the marriage."

Kyle's clinical solution contrarily sent a stab of hurt through her, which annoyed her intensely.

A former Special Air Service soldier, Kyle had the kind of steely blue gaze that missed nothing. He was also tall and muscular, six foot two inches of sleek muscle, with close-cut dark hair and the kind of grim good looks and faintly battered features, courtesy of his years in the military, that mesmerized women.

All of the men in the Messena and Atraeus families seemed to possess that same formidable, in-charge quality. Usually, it didn't ruffle her in the slightest, but Kyle paired it with a blunt, low-key insight that was unnerving; he seemed to know what she was going to do before she did it. Added to that, she wouldn't mind betting that he had gotten rid of some of her grooms with a little judicious intimidation.

The idea of marrying Kyle shouldn't affect her. She had learned early on to sidestep actual relationships at all cost. The plain fact was, she wouldn't have trusted in any relationships at all if it hadn't been for Mario and his wife picking her up when they'd found her on the sidewalk near their home one evening twelve years ago.

When they'd found out she was on the run from her last home because her foster father had wandering hands, they had phoned the welfare people. However, instead of allowing her to be shunted back into another institutional home, Mario had made a string of phone calls to "people he knew" and she had been allowed to stay with them.

Despite her instinctive withdrawal and the cold neutrality that had gotten her through a number of foster homes, Mario and Teresa had offered her the kind of quiet, steady love that, at sixteen, had been unfamiliar and a little scary. When they had eventually proposed adopting her, the plain fact was she hadn't known how to respond. She'd had the rug pulled emotionally so many times she had thought that if she softened and believed that she was deserving of love, that would be the moment it was all taken away.

In the end, through Mario's dogged persistence, she had finally understood that he was the one person who wouldn't break his word. Her resistance had crumbled and she had signed. In the space of a moment, she had ceased to be Eva Rushton, the troubled runaway, and had become Eva Atraeus, a member of a large and mystifyingly welcoming family.

However, the transformation had never quite been complete. After watching her own mother's three marriages disintegrate then at age seventeen finding out *why*, she had decided she did not ever want to be that vulnerable.

She caught a whiff of Kyle's cologne and her stomach clenched. And there was her problem, she thought grimly. Although, why the fiery tension, which should have died a death years ago—right after he had dumped her when she was seventeen—still persisted, she had no clue. It wasn't as if they had ever spent much time together or had anything in common beyond the youthful attraction. Kyle had married someone else a couple of years later, too, so she knew that what they had shared had not affected him as deeply as it had her.

Now, thanks to Kyle's interference, she had three weeks to marry anyone but him, and the clock was ticking…

Frustration reignited the nervous tension that had assaulted her when Jeremy had informed her he was backing out of their arrangement, but now that tension was laced with a healthy jolt of panic. Mario Atraeus couldn't have chosen a better watchdog for the unexpected codicil he had written into his will if he had tried.

She had been so close to marriage, but now Jeremy had run like a frightened rabbit. She couldn't prove that Kyle had engineered the job offer to get rid of Jeremy. All she knew was that he had used the same tactic twice before. Every time she got someone to agree to marry her, Kyle got rid of him.

Although why Kyle had stopped her marrying a man who had been eminently suitable, and whom she had actually liked in a lukewarm kind of way, she didn't know. Given their antagonistic past, she had thought Kyle would have been only too glad to discharge a responsibility that had been thrust on him, and which he could not possibly want.

Just like he hadn't wanted her.

Frowning at the thought of the brief, passionate interlude they had shared eleven years ago, she met Kyle's gaze squarely. "Thanks, but no thanks."

Dropping into the little sports car's bucket seat, she snapped the door closed. The engine revved with a throaty roar. Throat tight, still unbearably ruffled that he had actually had the gall to give her a *pity* proposal, she put the car in gear. Spinning the car in a tight turn, she headed in the direction of the Dolphin Bay Resort, where the reception was being held.

Her jaw tightened at the thought that even the location of the reception was tainted with memories of Kyle and the one time he'd kissed her. In starting her wedding business, though, she'd had to be pragmatic. The Dolphin Bay Resort was family run and offered her a great discount. She would have been flat-out stupid not to use the venue.

Still fuming, Eva strolled into the resort to oversee the gorgeous, high-end fairy-tale wedding she had designed as a promotional centerpiece for her wedding planning business. A perfect wedding that should have been hers, if only Jeremy hadn't cut and run.

Cancel that, she thought grimly. If only Kyle hadn't paid Jeremy off with a lucrative job offer in sandblasted Dubai! Taking a deep breath and reaching for her usual calm control, she checked her appearance in one of the elegant mirrors that decorated the walls. The reflection that bounced back was reassuring. Lately her emotions were all over the place, she was crying at the drop of a hat, she actually wanted to watch rom-coms and she was having trouble sleeping.

None of that inner craziness showed. She looked as calm and cool and collected as she wished she felt, her mass of tawny hair smoothed into an elegant French pleat, her too curvy figure disguised by a low-key skirt and jacket in a pastel pink that matched her shoes and handbag. The businesslike but feminine image achieved a balance between the occasion and her role as planner.

More importantly, it ensured that she did not compete with the bride or other female guests in any way. She had learned that lesson at what would have been her first wedding when the groom had gotten a little too interested in her and the bride had cancelled.

Eva walked through to the ballroom where the reception was being held and lifted a hand to acknowledge the waitstaff, all of whom she knew well thanks to the half dozen weddings she had staged at Dolphin Bay. She tensed as she glimpsed commiseration in the normally businesslike gaze of the maître d' as he mopped around an ice sculpture of swans she had recklessly commissioned because this was supposed to be her one and only wedding day.

The five-tiered extravaganza of a cake, snow-white

icing sparkling with crystals and festooned with clusters of sculpted flowers so beautifully executed they looked real, stopped her brisk movement through the room. Out of the blue, the emotion she had been working hard to stamp out grabbed at her. She had wanted to make this a day she would remember all of her life. Unfortunately, that had been achieved since it would be difficult to forget that her perfect wedding now belonged to someone else.

Stomach churning with a potent cocktail of frustration, panic and a crazy vulnerability caused by the fact that Kyle seemed intent on stopping her attempts to achieve a workable, safe marriage, she spun on her heel and made a beeline for the kitchen.

Bracing herself, she pushed the double doors open and stepped into a hive of gleaming white walls and polished steel counters. The cheerful clattering and hum of conversation instantly stopped. Eva's chest squeezed tight as waves of sympathy flowed toward her, intensifying the ache that had started in her throat and making tears burn at the back of her eyes. The jolt of emotion was crazy, given that she hadn't loved Jeremy in the least and marriage had not been on her horizon until Mario had literally forced her to it with that clause in his will. A clause designed to railroad her into the kind of happiness he had shared with his wife and which he had thought she should also have, whether she wanted it or not.

Until she'd started planning this wedding, she had thought Mario had been utterly wrong in believing he could make her want to be married. But every detail of planning her own wedding had confronted her, throwing together the stark realities of her life and cruelly highlighting the parts she couldn't have: the romance and the happy-ever-after ending that true love promised. Most of all, it emphasized the happy aftermath she would never experience: her own babies.

She had known since she was seventeen, thanks to a rare genetic disorder she carried, that she shouldn't have children. The disorder had proved fatal for her twin and two siblings, which had made her doubly wary about the whole concept of marriage. There was always the possibility that she could meet someone who didn't care about the disorder and who would be happy to adopt, but she had difficulty getting past the fact that she literally carried death in her genes.

In retrospect, it had been a huge mistake giving in to the temptation to design a wedding that patently did not go with a marriage of convenience. It smacked of wish fulfilment, and it had opened up a Pandora's box of needs and desires she had thought she had put behind her. She should have settled for a registry office ceremony. No fuss, no bother, no emotion.

Pinning a smile on her face, she breezed through the large bustling kitchen and waved at the head chef, Jerome, a Parisian with two Michelin stars. Jerome had designed the menu personally for her. He sent her an intense look brimming with passionate outrage and sympathy, even though he knew she had managed to sell the wedding on to a couple who had been desperate to marry quickly, owing to a surprise pregnancy.

Eva flinched at the concept that her pretty young bride not only had her perfect wedding, but was also pregnant. She could not afford to dwell on the painful issue that while she could not have children, other women could, and at the drop of a hat.

Keeping her professional smile firmly fixed, Eva fished her menu out of her bag and ran through it with Jerome. For once there were no last-minute glitches. Every aspect of this wedding appeared to be abnormally perfect. After dutifully admiring the exquisite mountain of cupcakes, which Jerome was decorating—her favorite forbidden snack—she escaped back to the reception room before he could toss his icing palette knife down and pull her into a comforting bear hug.

Kyle had proposed.

The kitchen doors made a swishing sound as they swung closed behind her. Eva stared blindly at the crisp white damask on the tables, the sparkle of crystal chandeliers and lavish clusters of white roses. She did not know why Kyle had the power to upset her so. It wasn't as if she was immersed in the painful, oversentimental first love that had gripped her at age seventeen. It wasn't as if she still wanted him.

As the wedding guests began to spill through the doors, she rummaged in her handbag, found and slipped on a pair of the most unflattering glasses she'd been able to buy. The lenses were fake, just plain glass, but the heavy, dark rims served to deflect the attention that her good looks usually attracted.

Fixing a smile on her face, she did a brisk circuit of the main reception room, which she and her assistant, Jacinta, had dressed earlier. Waiters were loading silver trays with flutes filled with extremely good champagne she had sourced from an organic vineyard. Trays of her favorite canapés from the five-star kitchen were lined up in the servery.

The reception was heartbreakingly gorgeous. Since it was supposed to have been her own, she had put a great deal of thought into every detail, no expense spared. The only consolation was that she would be very well paid. And, in three weeks' time, if she was still unwed, she would be in desperate need of cash in order to retain her house and keep her business afloat.

The doors to the kitchens behind her swished open as guests began to seat themselves at tables. Jacinta Doyle, her sleekly efficient personal assistant, came to stand beside her, a folder in one hand. Jacinta gave her a look laden with sympathy but, tactfully, kept things business-like. Halfway through a list of minor details, she stopped dead. "*Who* is that?"

An annoying hum of awareness Eva was desperate to ignore made her tense. Adjusting the glasses, which were too heavy for her nose, she frowned at the rapidly filling room. Her mood plummeted when she saw Kyle. "Who do you mean, exactly? There must be a hundred people in the room."

"He is *hot*." Jacinta, who was hooked into the sophisticated, very modern dating scene with a new man on her arm every week, clutched dramatically at her chest before pointing Kyle out just in case Eva hadn't noticed him. "I'm in love."

Irritation flared, instant and unreasoning. "I thought you were dating Geraldo someone-or-other."

"Gerard. His visa ran out, and his money." She shrugged. "He went back to France."

Eva pretended to be absorbed in her own checklist of things to do. "Don't let your heart beat faster over Kyle, because you'll be wasting your time. He's too old for you, and he's not exactly a fun type."

"How old?"

The irritation morphed into something else she couldn't quite put her finger on. "Thirty," she muttered shortly.

"I wouldn't call that old. More…interesting."

Something inside Eva snapped. "Forget Kyle Messena. He isn't available."

Jacinta sent her a glance laced with the kind of curiosity that informed Eva she hadn't been able to keep the sharpness out of her voice. "Kyle Messena. I thought he looked familiar. Didn't he lose his wife and child in some kind of terrorist attack overseas? But that was years ago." She pointedly returned her gaze to Kyle, underlining the fact that she could look at him any time she liked, for as long as she liked.

Even more annoyed by the speculation on Jacinta's face, as if she was actually considering making a play for Kyle, Eva consulted her watch. "We're ten minutes behind schedule," she said crisply. "You check the timing for service with the chef. I'm going to get a cold drink then have a word with the musicians. With any luck we'll get out of here before midnight."

With a last glance at Kyle, Jacinta closed the folder with a resigned snap. "No problem."

But there was a problem, Eva thought bleakly. The kind of problem she had never imagined she would suffer from ever again. For reasons she did not understand, Jacinta's interest in Kyle had evoked the kind of fierce, primitive response she had only ever experienced once before, years ago, when she'd heard that Kyle was dating someone else.

She needed to go somewhere quiet and give herself a stern talking-to, because somehow, she had allowed the unwanted attraction to Kyle to get out of hand, to the point that she was suddenly, burningly, crazily jealous about the last man she wanted in her life.

Three

Kyle strolled to the bar, although if he were honest, the drive to get a cold beer over settling for the champagne being served had more to do with the fact that Eva was headed in that direction.

Eva's expression chilled as he leaned on the bar next to her. The faint crease in her smooth brow as she sipped from a tall glass of what he guessed was sparkling water somehow made her look even more spectacularly gorgeous, despite the disfiguring glasses. It was a beauty he should have been accustomed to, yet it still made his stomach tighten and his attention sharpen in a completely male way.

She met his gaze briefly before looking away. An impression of defensiveness made him frown. Normally Eva was cool and distant, occasionally combative, but never defensive.

She placed the glass down on the counter with a small click. "I thought you had left."

The unspoken words, *now that you'd made sure I hadn't secretly gotten married*, seemed to hang in the air. Kyle shrugged and ordered a beer. "I decided to stick around. We still need to have a conversation."

"If it's about the terms of the will, forget it. I've read the fine print—"

"You've ignored the fine print." She had certainly failed to notice that he was her primary marriage candidate.

The faint blush of color in her cheeks flared a little brighter, sharpening Kyle's curiosity. Eva was behaving in a way that was distinctly odd. He was abruptly certain that something had happened, something had changed, although he had no idea what.

She sent him a breezy professional smile, but her whole demeanor was evasive. "If you don't mind, I really do need to work."

Usually, Eva was as direct and uncompromising as any man. The blush and the avoidance of eye contact didn't fit, unless... His heart slammed against his chest, spinning him back to the long summer days they had spent on the beach as teenagers. For a split second he wondered that he had missed something so obvious. But he guessed he had been so absorbed with trying to control the desire that had come out of left field that he had failed to see that Eva was fighting the same battle.

She tried to sidestep him, but the bar area was now filling up with people, lining up for drinks. Feeling like a villain, but riveted by the discovery, he moved slightly, just enough to block her in. She stopped, a bare inch from brushing against his chest.

Kyle's stomach tightened as he caught another whiff of Eva's perfume. He knew he should leave her alone and let her get on with her job. But the desire to evoke a response, to make Eva admit that she wanted him, was too strong. "The whole point of Mario's will was that he wanted you to marry someone who would actually care about you and who wasn't in it for the money."

"I know what Mario wanted, no one better. What I don't get is why you're so intent on enforcing a condition that is patently ridiculous?"

Kyle's gaze narrowed at the way Eva carefully avoided the issue of his proposal. "You're family."

"Distant and only on paper. It's not as if I'm a real Atraeus."

Kyle's brow's jerked together. "Your name is Atraeus."

Eva dragged in a breath, relieved that the unnerving sense that Kyle had seen right through her desperate attempt to seem normal and completely impervious to him had dissipated. "That doesn't change the fact that I'm adopted. I'm not blood." And that she could still remember what it felt like to wear secondhand clothes, eat cereal for dinner and fend off her mother's boyfriends. She was a very poor cuckoo in a diamond-encrusted nest.

"Mario wanted to help you. He wanted you to be happy."

She drew a breath. The clean scent of his skin deepened the panicked awareness that was humming through her. "I'm twenty-eight. I think that by now I know what it takes to be happy."

"And that would be paying some guy to marry you?"

Eva's brows jerked together. "Correct me if I'm wrong, but barely fifty years ago, arranged marriages were common in both the Messena and the Atraeus families."

"Last century, maybe."

"Then someone should have told that to Mario. And it underlines my point that a marriage of convenience is not the worst thing that could happen." And it wasn't as if she actually wanted to be loved. She had seen what had happened to her mother when she had become emotionally needy. Relationship train wreck followed by train wreck, the plunging depression and slow disintegration of Meg Rushton's life. It had all been crowned by her mother's inability to care for Eva, the one child who had survived the disorder.

A young man tried to squeeze in beside Eva. Kyle blocked him with a wolf-cold glance and a faint shift in position. In the process, his arm brushed against hers, sending a tingle of heat through her that made Eva even more desperate to get away. With grim concentration, she stared over Kyle's broad shoulder at the bottles of spirits suspended at the rear of the bar and tried not to love the fact that Kyle's behavior had been as bluntly possessive as if they had been a couple. That was exactly the kind of thinking she could not afford.

Kyle's gaze, edged with irritation, captured hers. "Let's put this in context. If a man is unscrupulous enough to take your money for marriage, chances are he won't have a problem pressurizing you until you give in to sex."

Eva's heart thumped hard in her chest at the thought that Kyle could possibly have a motivation that was tied in with caring about her, that in his own hard-nosed way, he had been trying to protect her. The next thought was a dizzying, improbable leap—that Kyle had a personal interest in stopping her from having sex with other men because *he* wanted her.

Annoyed that she should even begin to imagine that Kyle's concern was based on some kind of personal desire for her when she knew he regarded her as a spoiled, shallow good-time girl, she put the revelation in context. Kyle was gorgeous, megawealthy and successful, but the reality was that, like his older brothers and her macho

Atraeus cousins, shunt him back a few centuries, give him a sword and buckler and he would fit right in. Just because he was being protective to the point of being intrusive didn't mean he was attracted to her. It was just part of his DNA. "I know how to handle men. Believe me, sex will not be an issue."

Kyle's gaze dropped to her mouth. "Then, honey, you don't know men very well."

Her heart pounded a little harder, not at the implication that she was naive about men in general, but at the low, rough timbre of his voice and the sudden revelation that Kyle *did* find her attractive.

Eva swallowed against the sudden dryness in her throat. The fingers of her right hand curled tight against the childish urge to press the heel of her palm against the sharp pounding of her heart.

Someone else jostled her to get to the bar. Kyle said something low and curt, his arm curled around her waist as he pulled her against his side. The move was more courteous and protective than overtly sensual, but even so, another hot pang shot clear to her toes.

He released her almost immediately, but not before his gaze touched on hers, filled with unexpected knowledge. Another shockwave went through her. If she'd thought Kyle hadn't noticed that she was still crazily attracted to him, she was wrong. He knew.

"Damn, let's get out of here."

Taking her hand, he forged a path through the now-busy bar, and out of the blue, memories she'd buried flooded back. Kyle's fingers linked with hers years ago, the carefree flash of his grin as they'd escaped from the crowded party. The way the earth had stopped spinning and she'd forgotten to breathe when they had run down to the beach and long weeks of swimming and talking together had finally reached a flash point.

Breath suddenly constricted, she pulled her hand free and tried to ignore the heated tingling of the brief contact.

Kyle stopped, coincidentally, right beside the wedding cake. "You might think you can handle marriage to some guy you've only just met, but I know for a fact you've never even lived with a man."

The memories winked out with the suddenness of a door slamming. Her temper flared at the evidence that Kyle had been prying into her life. "Just because I haven't had a long-term relationship—"

"The way I heard it, you haven't had *any* real relationships."

She dragged off the glasses, her eyes flashing fire. "How can you know this stuff?" Although she knew the answer had to be Kyle's younger sisters, the Messena twins, Sophie and Francesca. Over the years she had become good friends with the twins, so of course they knew exactly how her life had played out. No doubt Kyle had engaged Sophie and Francesca in some kind of casual conversation, *gathering intelligence*. They would not have realized that telling Kyle she didn't go in for casual relationships would matter. "I knew it. You've been *spying* on me."

"Checking up on you. It's part of the brief."

And with his military background, Kyle had a certain skill set. When he had gone into the army, she had still been lovesick enough to keep tabs on him. Not satisfied with the rank and file, he had done officer training, then had gone into the Special Air Service, the SAS. When he had been sent on his first overseas assignment, she had lost sleep for weeks, wondering if he had been wounded or even killed. Then she had learned that he had come back from the mission just fine and gotten married on his days off. It was then she had decided she would never worry about him again.

She folded her arms across her chest, glad to have that salutary reminder about just how meaningless that long-ago holiday romance and kiss on the beach had been. "I am not a job."

"No." He stared at the monster cake with a faintly incredulous gaze. "You're a pain in the butt."

Her chin shot up. "Then why do the job?"

"Believe me, if Mario had chosen someone else, I would have been more than happy."

"Ditto."

A muscle jerked fascinatingly along the side of his jaw. Bolstered by the unmistakable sign of tension, Eva delivered the only ultimatum she had. "Then unless you want to keep tabs on me for the next thirteen years as my trustee, maybe you should let me get on with the business of getting married."

"Troy Kendal will never marry you."

She should have been shocked by the flat pronouncement, but in a weird way, after the relentless research he had conducted into all of her other grooms, she had half expected him to find out. "You don't know that."

The resolute quality of his gaze, as if he would let her marry Troy over his dead body, sent a forbidden little thrill through her. She drew a breath in an effort to still the rapid pounding of her heart. Something was definitely, seriously wrong with her. She should have been angry, desperate. She shouldn't *like* it that Kyle was systematically getting rid of her grooms.

She slid her glasses back onto the bridge of her nose, suddenly needing the camouflage. "This conversation is over. I have a business to run."

Kyle dragged his gaze from the mesmerizing sight of Eva walking away, gripping her official clipboard. His frown deepened when he noted a familiar figure giving him the kind of narrowed, assessing stare he had gotten used to over the past few months. Kendal was new on the list of men Eva had dated since Mario had died. He also deviated from the pattern of older, biddable admirers Eva had approached in order to find a manageable, paid husband.

Kendal was twenty-four, which made him younger than Eva by four years. He was also a well-known professional rugby player with a list of stormy liaisons behind him. Recently, Kendal had been sidelined by injury and had missed the cut for the new season, which meant his career was stalled. According to the research Kyle had done, he was also currently strapped for cash.

His jaw tightened as Kendal slung his arm around Eva's waist. He knew exactly where and when Eva had picked Kendal up, because he had conducted the surveillance himself. It was four nights ago at a trendy singles bar in downtown Auckland.

He relaxed marginally as Eva detached Kendal's arm with the kind of brisk efficiency that spelled out loud and clear that whatever bargain she had struck with Kendal, it was purely business. Which suited Kyle, since Kendal had the kind of reputation with women that sent a cold itch down his spine.

Kyle found a seat in the shadow of a large indoor palm, where he could keep an eye on Eva and Troy. Taking out his phone, he made a call to a contact. His family's bank poured a lot of money into sponsoring professional rugby. A few minutes later, after pledging a further personal donation from his own funds, contingent on a contract offer to Kendal, he hung up.

A waiter placed a plate of food in front of him. Kyle ate without tasting, intent on Kendal as the man took a call on his cell. Minutes later, Kendal left the wedding with a pretty blonde who had been seated at his table.

Kyle's phone buzzed. After receiving confirmation that Kendal had verbally accepted a contract offer, he terminated the call and sat back in his chair.

Eva wouldn't be happy with him. She was smart and would know exactly what he had done, but Kyle couldn't regret getting rid of Kendal. He was the kind of unsavory guy he wouldn't trust with any of the women he knew, family or not.

With Kendal now out of the picture, Eva's last marriage scheme had just collapsed.

The thought filled him with relief. If Eva had picked someone she could love, he would not have intervened. Instead, she had chosen a list of controllable men who really did just want money. Losers who were not immune to the fact that Eva was drop-dead gorgeous and distractingly sexy. Kyle knew exactly how the masculine mind worked. Platonic agreement or not, it would have only been a matter of time before Eva would have found herself maneuvered into bed.

His stomach tightened on a hot punch of emotion.

Over his dead body.

Kendal sliding his arm around Eva's waist had sealed his decision in stone.

Eva had turned him down, but in the space of an hour the game had changed. She wanted him. Up until now he had been content to keep his distance and let Eva exhaust her options, but now he was no longer prepared to stand back or let any other man enter the picture. She would accept his proposal; it was just a matter of time.

Eva was his.

Four

Eva shoveled a chunk of the gorgeous wedding cake onto a plate and for good measure snagged two of the ridiculously cute frosted cupcakes and a flute of champagne. It was an undisciplined decision and the calories would go straight to her hips, but it had been hours since she had eaten. Besides, since it was supposed to be her wedding, she figured she deserved a little comfort food.

Irritated with the glasses, which were pressing hard enough on the bridge of her nose to give her a headache, she dragged them off and tucked them in her pocket. The music was still pounding in the main reception room, but the bride and groom had departed, so there was no longer any need to look nerdish. Plate in one hand, glass in the other, she scanned the room for Kyle so she could avoid him. Although, since she had acknowledged the crazy, self-destructive fatal attraction that gripped her, she seemed to have developed an ultrasensitive inner radar so that, without looking, she knew exactly where he was.

When she couldn't find him, instead of being relieved, her stomach plummeted. Taller than most of the guests, he was normally easy to spot.

A wild suspicion formed that maybe he was with Jacinta, whom she had seen chatting to him on a number of occasions. The suspicion was allayed when she glimpsed Jacinta in animated conversation with the best man, who was considerably better looking than the groom.

She strolled down into the tropical gardens, where a few guests were sitting at tables, enjoying the balmy evening. The exotic plantings looked spectacular when lit at night. Kyle was nowhere to be seen, which meant he had probably left. Jaw firming against the impossible notion that the weird, plunging feeling in her stomach was disappointment, she belatedly remembered Troy.

The last time she had seen him he had been sitting with some blonde and drinking too much. Suspicious, because he had a definite reputation when it came to women, especially blonde women, she checked the dance floor. When she didn't see him there, she made a search of the hotel lobby and loitered near the men's room while she polished off the wedding cake and sipped a little more champagne. When Troy didn't appear, she strolled to the pool area.

The patio, which was fringed with palms and drifts of star jasmine that scented the night, was dimly lit and lonely. The enormous pool was empty of bathers, its surface limpid, the lights under the water giving it a jewel-like glow. Eva checked the bathing pavilion, which held changing rooms, showers and stacks of fluffy white towels. It, too, was empty. With the way her luck was running lately, she had to consider that either Troy had left with the blonde, or they had gotten a room together.

She should have been disappointed, but the plain fact was she had not liked Troy. Sitting down on a deck chair, she finished off the last of the champagne. Instead of leaving the flute on the pavers, where it could be knocked over and shattered, she decided to store it in her bag until she could drop it back at the bar.

She stared gloomily at the cupcakes. She was halfway through the chocolate one with fudge icing and pretty sugar flowers when a deep, curt voice cut through even that meager pleasure. "If you were looking for Kendal, he left."

"With the blonde?"

"With the blonde."

Eva slapped what was left of the cupcake back on the plate and tried to ignore the dizzying relief that while Troy had left, Kyle was still here. It was an odd time to note that while every man she had handpicked and tried to organize into her life—for just a brief time, and for money—had run out on her, the one man she had been desperate to avoid and who didn't need money, had stayed. "What did you say to him?"

Kyle emerged from the shadows of the palms, where she knew there was a shell path that led to the beach. Her stomach tensed. It was a path she could hardly forget, since it was the one she and Kyle had taken years ago when they had sneaked away to share their one and only passionate interlude. The awareness that was becoming more and more acute hummed through her like an electric current. A little desperately, she picked up the lemon cupcake with white chocolate icing and a delicate sprinkling of raspberry dust, although her appetite was gone.

Kyle dropped his jacket, which he'd slung over one

shoulder, over the back of a deck chair and walked around the pool toward her. "I didn't say a word to Kendal."

She tried not to be mesmerized by the way the pool lights glanced off the taut lines of his cheekbones and jaw, investing his skin with a bronze sheen as if he really was a warrior of old. "You've gotten rid of every other man, so why not Troy?"

He undid a couple of buttons and loosened off his tie, unwittingly drawing her gaze to the muscular column of his throat. Swallowing, she looked away from that fascinating triangle of tanned skin and ended up studying a scar that made a small, intriguing crescent on one cheekbone. For the first time she noticed that he had dark circles beneath his eyes, as if he hadn't been getting enough sleep.

Join the club, she thought, firmly squashing any hint of compassion. Just because an old attraction that should have died years ago had somehow reactivated, that didn't mean her brain had turned to mush. If Kyle had let her marry any one of the grooms she had chosen, they would both be getting plenty of sleep.

He paused just feet away. "Kendal's agent made him an offer he couldn't refuse."

There was a moment of weird disorientation, where ordinary sounds and sensations seemed to blink out, and yet her heart pumped so loudly it was deafening. She looked down and saw the lemon cupcake had turned to mangled chunks between her fingers. Dropping the remains of the cupcake on the plate, she grabbed the napkin that was folded to one side of the plate and wiped icing off her fingers.

Losing her temper wouldn't get her anywhere with Kyle. As long as she could remember, he had been utterly male, as blunt and immovable as a rock wall. Crazily, that was what had once attracted her so much. When her teenage world had been in pieces, he had seemed strong and disciplined in a quiet, steady way. Special forces had suited him down to the ground. "Money. I should have guessed."

He strolled to the edge of the pool. "Kendal's got a reputation. You wouldn't have been able to handle him."

"So you decided to handle him for me." She launched to her feet, too upset to stay. But in her hurry, she forgot that she had dropped her bag by the recliner, and in the dim light she didn't see the strap lying on the pavers. One of her heels snagged in the strap and she stumbled.

Strong fingers closed around her upper arm, steadying her. Her reaction was instantaneous as she jerked free and shoved at Kyle's chest. She had a split second to register how near she was to the edge of the pool. Kyle said something curt and grabbed at her wrist, but it was too late as the glossy surface of the water came up to meet her.

The cool water was a shock, but not as much as Kyle, whom she must have pulled off balance, plunging into the water beside her. Holding her breath, she kicked to the surface and tried to ignore the fact that she had left her shoes at the bottom of the pool. Pale pink to match her suit, and superexpensive, she had loved them with passion, but no way was she diving back in to get them with Kyle watching. She would wait until he was gone then fish them out later.

Swimming to the ladder, she climbed out, trying not to be aware of Kyle boosting himself over the side in one lithe movement. She was still angry with him, but it was difficult to sustain fury when her clothes were wet and clinging, her hair had collapsed into a bedraggled mess and every time she looked at Kyle, his wet shirt plastered to his chest, her mind went utterly blank.

Kyle dragged off his tie and peeled out of his shirt. Averting her gaze from his impressive torso, Eva walked briskly into the poolroom and retrieved two towels from the nearest shelf. Tossing one at Kyle, she kept her eyes averted as she dried herself off.

Instead of using the towel, Kyle draped it over a nearby lounger and dropped back down into the pool. Seconds later, he climbed back out with her shoes. Water slid off bronzed skin and dripped from his nose as he handed them to her. "I'm sorry I pushed you so hard."

Eva ruthlessly suppressed the desire to respond to the glimpse of humor since, technically, she was the one who had done the pushing. Grimly, she concentrated on drying the shoes. She absolutely did not want to start remembering all the moments they had shared all those years ago and start thinking of him as funny or sweet. They'd had their moment, and it hadn't worked out. "I'm glad I pushed you. You deserved it."

The quick flash of a grin almost stopped her heart. "Still the same old Eva."

And who, exactly, was that? she wondered a little bitterly. Years ago she had come to the conclusion that he saw her as a messed-up adopted kid. The kind of woman no Messena male in his right mind would date, let alone marry.

To cover up the fact that she was having difficulty keeping her gaze off his torso and a smattering of scars that looked suspiciously like knife or maybe even bullet wounds, she gripped the back of a lounger to put on first one shoe, then the other. She knew Kyle had been injured twice, the second time life threatening enough that he'd been medevaced from Germany back to Auckland.

That time, she had been concerned enough that she had rung the hospital to get an update on his condition.

When they had refused to do that over the phone, she had gone there herself, brazening her way onto Kyle's ward, even though visiting hours had finished. When she had finally found him, she had used her family connection to the Messenas and her celebrity status as a model to get into his room.

She had been shocked to see him pale and still and hooked up to monitors and drips, then a senior nurse had walked in and she'd had to leave. That had been just as well, because as she'd walked out the door Kyle's eyes had flickered open.

Dragging pins from her soaked hair and finger combing it out into some semblance of neatness, she couldn't resist the compulsion to sneak another glance at the worst of the scars and, inadvertently, found herself caught out by Kyle's gaze.

"I know that was you, all those years ago at the hospital."

She froze. "Maybe."

He raked wet hair back from his forehead. "I thought I was dreaming, but the nurse confirmed it."

She busied herself picking up her bag in order to drop the pins into it, but she wasn't paying close enough attention, so some of them scattered over the pavers. Crouching down, she began gathering them up. "It was no big deal. I was in town and heard you'd been—hurt—"

"As in, wounded." He handed her a pin that had skittered over by his foot.

She straightened and found herself uncomfortably close to his naked and still-damp torso. "I didn't want to say that, just in case you had that condition—"

"Post-traumatic stress disorder. Battle fatigue." His mouth quirked in a distractingly sexy way. "No chance, since I have no memory of being hit." He hesitated. "Why didn't you stay?"

Eva, still captured by the sudden intense need to know what exactly had happened, *who* had dared to shoot Kyle, took a few seconds to absorb his question. "You were critical—they wouldn't let me stay."

"I was only critical the night I arrived. I didn't see any family until the next day. So, how did you find out?"

Despite her clothes, which were steadily dripping, and which were now making her feel clammy and just a little chilled, she found herself blushing. There was no way she was going to tell Kyle that she had practically lived on the internet, tracking down Reuters reports, and that she had made a pest of herself by calling his regimental headquarters. "I had a modeling friend whose boyfriend was in the SAS." That part was true enough. She shrugged. "I just happened to mention that you'd been hurt and she…found out for me."

"But you didn't visit me again."

She straightened, hooking the strap of her bag over her shoulder. "I was *busy*. What is this? An interrogation?" Although something about Kyle had changed. The bad-tempered tension had gone and there was an undercurrent that made her feel decidedly breathless. She tried walking in her wet heels to see if they were safe. At the same time she surreptitiously smoothed her palms down the sodden, clinging line of her jacket and skirt to press out excess moisture. As a result, water tickled down her legs and filled her shoes.

Kyle stopped in the process of wringing out his shirt, his gaze arrested. "Maybe you should take the jacket off?"

"No." Eva had routinely taken her clothes off for lingerie ads, but there was no way she was going to take one stitch of clothing off in front of Kyle. She suddenly noticed the flatness of her jacket pocket. Her glasses were gone, which meant they were probably in the bottom of the pool.

"They can stay there," Kyle said flatly. "You don't need them. You've got the eyesight of an eagle."

"How would you know what my eyesight's like?"

"Remember the archery contests?"

Dolphin Bay, two summers in a row, when she and Kyle would go head-to-head at the archery range. "You always won those."

"I'd been practicing for years. You came second."

The sudden warmth in his gaze made her feel flustered all over again. She realized that the distance she had worked so hard to preserve, and which she had been able to maintain quite well if she was angry, had gone. Burned away in the moment she had realized that Kyle wanted her.

She walked to the edge of the pool and peered in. The glasses, with their dark rims, were easily visible. "I need the glasses for work."

"Why? They're not prescription, just plain glass." His face cleared. "No, wait, don't answer, I think I can guess."

Over seeing Kyle's buff, ripped, *hot* torso, she tossed his towel at him. A split second later the sharp tap of heels on tiles signaled Jacinta's presence a moment before she rounded the corner into the pool area.

Her eyes widened when she saw that Eva was soaked. "There you are, the bride's father wants to give you a check—" She noticed Kyle. "Oops. Sorry, did I interrupt something?"

"Nothing." Eva seized her chance to end the unsettling encounter and the crazy, suffocating awareness that had crept up on her out of nowhere. "Where is Mr. Hirsch?"

"In the lobby." Jacinta glanced at Kyle's washboard abs. "I told him you'd be right along."

But suddenly, Eva wasn't going anywhere. She took the one step needed to place herself squarely in Jacinta's line of vision, so that she had to stare at her, rather than at Kyle's bronzed, dripping skin. In the moment that she moved, it struck her that she was behaving like a jealous girlfriend. Kyle did not belong to her, and yet she was ready to fight tooth and nail to fend Jacinta off. "I'm wet and my hair's ruined. You need to go and collect the check."

Jacinta didn't move. "Did you fall in the pool?"

"We both fell," Eva said bluntly.

Jacinta made an odd little noise that sounded suspiciously like amusement quickly muffled then spun on her heel and disappeared back inside.

Kyle broke the tense little silence that developed in the wake of Jacinta's departure by tossing his towel on a recliner and picking up his soaked shirt. "At least you managed to sell the wedding on. I'm guessing right about now, you're getting concerned about money."

She met Kyle's gaze head-on. "Without the backup of my trust fund, all money counts."

And that was the other reason she found this whole process of having to qualify for her own inheritance so hurtful and undermining. All of the bona fide Atraeus and Messena family members who were born to wealth received vast amounts of money, and their right to do so wasn't questioned. She understood what Mario was trying to achieve with the marriage clause, but that didn't change the fact that the whole process made her feel separated from the rest of the family, and *different*.

Stung anew by what she saw as further evidence that, despite adoption, she had never quite fitted into the Atraeus family, Eva turned on her heel, intending to make a beeline for her car, where she had a pair of jeans, a T-shirt and sneakers stashed for the drive back to Auckland.

Kyle caught her arm, halting her. "I'm sorry. I shouldn't have mentioned the money."

The tingling warmth of Kyle's palm, even through the barrier of damp silk, sent a small, sharp shock through her. She jerked free. "I suppose you think I'm a money-grubbing gold digger who doesn't deserve—"

"I don't think that." His gaze dropped to her mouth. "You deserve your inheritance."

Her chin jerked up. "Then why have you been doing your level best to deprive me of it?"

"Money isn't the issue," he muttered. "This is." Bending his head, Kyle kissed her.

Eva inhaled sharply at the warmth of his mouth, stunned by the brief caress and the molten heat that exploded from that one point of contact. When she didn't move, Kyle's palm curled around her nape. The next minute she was pressed hard against the muscled heat of his body as his mouth settled more heavily on hers.

The passion was searing and instant and this time, Eva wasn't content to just be kissed. Palms flattened against the hard muscle of Kyle's chest, and all too aware that she was making a disastrous mistake, she lifted up on her toes and angled her head to increase the contact. His taste exploded in her mouth and the furnace heat of his body warmed her, so that she wanted to press closer still, to wallow in his heat and strength.

And suddenly, it registered just how alone and isolated she had been. Since her teenage fixation on Kyle, she had simply not allowed anyone else close. She had sidestepped relationships and sex. She hadn't thought she needed either, until now.

The strap of her bag slipped off her shoulder. She registered the thump as it dropped onto the ground, and the sound of glass breaking and dimly remembered the champagne flute. Her arms closed around Kyle's neck as the kiss deepened, and suddenly the cling of her wet clothes seemed sodden and restrictive, dragging against skin that was unbearably sensitive. His hand cupped her breast through the layers of wet fabric. Eva inhaled at the sharp beading of her nipple, but it was too late as heat and sensation coiled unbearably tight and splintered.

Kyle muttered something short beneath his breath. Eva pulled free of his grasp, her legs as limp as noodles, embarrassed warmth burning through her. Not only had she practically thrown herself at Kyle like some love-starved teenager, she had actually climaxed just because he had kissed her.

Dragging damp tendrils back from her face, she snatched up her bag and noticed that the champagne flute had broken at the stem and was in two pieces. Jaw set, she found the cake napkin and wrapped the base of the flute.

Kyle crouched down beside her and handed her the rest of the flute but, with her whole body still oversensitive and tingling, Kyle helping, Kyle intruding any further into her life was the last thing she wanted.

"Eva—"

She straightened, desperate to avoid him, but he rose lithely and blocked her path.

Too late to wish that she'd searched for her compact and checked her makeup. Her mascara was probably running. She must look a total mess—

"You wanted to know why I vetoed the grooms you chose. Two reasons. None of them were good enough. And I couldn't let you marry anyone else because *I* want you."

Five

Eva stared at Kyle.

I want you.

A small, sensual shiver zapped down her spine. Not good! She should be annoyed at the way Kyle had gotten rid of all the men she had chosen, not turned on and reveling in the fact that he had done so because he thought none of them had been good enough. "Let me get this right. You proposed because you want sex?"

Suddenly irritated beyond belief, she rummaged in her handbag, found her cell and stabbed a random icon. "Wait just one second. I'm sure I have an app you need called Sex Slaves Are Us."

Impatience registered in his gaze. "I proposed because you need a husband."

Somehow that was the wrong answer. "So sex would just be an optional extra?"

There was a small, vibrating silence. "Whether or not sex would be part of the deal is entirely up to you."

The anger that rolled through Eva was knee-jerk and confusing. She had been angry that Kyle wanted sex from her. Now she was even angrier because, evidently, he could take it or leave it. In her book, that brought them back to square one. She just wasn't that important to Kyle. And didn't that just feel like a replay of the past?

She jammed her cell back in her bag. Until that moment she hadn't realized how much Kyle's defection all those years ago still hurt. He had been a friend when she had needed one. She hadn't just wanted him at age seventeen; she had liked and trusted him. He had walked away without a backward glance then fallen in love with *and married* someone else.

She should have let this go a long time ago. It was neither healthy, nor balanced. But then, balance had never been her strong point. She had always been passionate and a little extreme. Of course, letting go of the hurt of Kyle's rejection was difficult, because in her heart of hearts she had felt sure that they had been on the verge of something special.

On the heels of that thought, suspicion flared. "Did Mario suggest you should marry me before he died?"

Kyle's gaze turned wary. "He did."

Now she really was embarrassed. Mario had been convinced that, despite her disorder, as an heiress she could have the same kind of happy married life he'd had with his wife, if she would only follow the old recipe and marry someone wealthy, trusted and close to home. He had relentlessly tried to marry her off in that way to Kyle's older brothers and, to her everlasting relief, he hadn't succeeded in raising even a flicker of interest. "I know for a fact that he asked Gabriel and Nick and they both turned him down."

Kyle shrugged. "That was a given, since they were both in love with other women."

Eva swiped at a renegade trickle of water sliding down her neck, suddenly incensed. "And who would buy into that crazy kind of medieval stuff, anyway?"

Kyle dragged his gaze from the creamy line of Eva's neck and the tantalizing hint of cleavage in the vee of her suit jacket.

He would.

Although, obviously, that did not reflect well on him. "If you're so set on a marriage of convenience, then I don't get why you're so against taking the second option in the will."

"And marry you?" Eva's chin came up. "Because, while Messena and Atraeus men may look and sound like modern twenty-first century guys, they aren't. Underneath that veneer every one of you is just as medieval as Mario was. And I don't want children. Ever."

The flat certainty of Eva's statement hit Kyle in the solar plexus.

Children. He had a sudden mental image of his small son, Evan, who had been just three months old when he had died.

His stomach tightened on the kind of grief no parent should ever feel as memory flickered. Evan, soft and warm on his shoulder, well fed and smelling of soap and milk as he had relaxed into sleep. The way he had used to crow with delight every time Kyle had picked him up...

When he spoke, he couldn't keep the grim chill out of his voice. "Children won't be an issue, because I don't want them, either. But in any case, we're only looking at an arrangement that will last two years."

He logged the flare of shock in her gaze. He had been

too abrasive. But when it came to the issue of marriage and kids, he couldn't be any other way.

His own family didn't understand him. But then, none of them had seen his wife and child disappear in an explosion that had killed five others and destroyed the barracks gatehouse. None of them understood that moment of sickening displacement, the knowledge that Nicola and Evan would be alive now if it wasn't for *his* insistence that they join him in Germany for Christmas.

The shock of their deaths and the weight of grief and guilt still had the power to stop him in his tracks. It was the reason he avoided friends who had kids and family occasions that, increasingly, overflowed with babies and small children. It was the reason he steered clear of anything approaching a conventional relationship, because he knew he couldn't be that person again. Just the thought of taking on the responsibility of a wife and child made him break out in a cold sweat. His oldest brother, Gabriel, who had arrived in Germany just hours after the explosion, was the only one who had an inkling about how he felt. He unlocked his jaw and tried to soften his tone. "If you agree to marriage, you set the terms."

She crossed her arms over her chest, her stance combative. "Let me see, everything but children, and you would prefer sex as an additional extra."

His gaze narrowed at the way she phrased the same kind of straightforward marriage deal she had personally negotiated at least three times in the past six months. Except for the sex. And he couldn't help a savage little jolt of satisfaction at that fact. "Yes."

She took a half step toward him. He registered the fiery glint in her eyes as she came to a halt in front of him and trailed her finger from a point just below his collarbone to the midpoint of his chest.

"Marriage to you? Now, let me see…" Her gaze locked with his, and he knew very well that she didn't intend to kiss him. "That would be a clear…*no*."

And with a shove she sent him toppling back into the pool.

The following night Eva prepared to go to a trendy singles bar with a couple of girlfriends. She hated singles bars and normally would never go to one but, after the debacle with Kyle, she was determined to make one more attempt at locating a husband.

Kyle's proposal was an unexpected goad. The fact that she personally wanted him had somehow made the situation even more fraught. Her response to his kiss had been a case in point. She'd never been able to resist him, and now he knew it. If they married, even if she said no to sex, would she be strong enough to hold out against him?

She flipped through her wardrobe for something to wear. She needed something that was sexy but reserved enough that she could attract a man who was reasonably good-looking, intelligent and down on his luck. She doubted she would find the type of man she needed at a singles bar, since most men who went there just wanted sex, but she had to try.

She chose a little black dress and pumps that weren't too high, because she was already medium height and she didn't want to narrow her options by being too tall. After putting on makeup, she combed her hair out straight so that it swung silkily around her shoulders. Affixing tawny earrings to her lobes, she spritzed herself with perfume and she was good to go.

The bar was packed. After ordering a drink, she sat at a cozy sofa and coffee table setting. Feeling like a wallflower, Eva sipped the iced water she had ordered.

Seconds later, she had her first approach, a handsome dark-haired guy who looked like a lawyer and proved to be. She sent him on his way when she found out he was married.

Two more conversations later with men who up front admitted they were married, but had left their wives—which meant they were utterly useless to her because they couldn't remarry until they were legally divorced—she scanned the bar. Depressingly, most of the men at the bar were either already hooked up with a partner or looked older, which from experience she knew probably meant they would still be married, even if they weren't living with their wives.

She caught a glimpse of the back of a guy's head as he disappeared into a shadowy part of the bar. Adrenaline pumped, because she was certain it was Kyle. He was the right height and his shoulders were broad. He half turned, giving her a clear view of his profile. It wasn't Kyle.

Unacceptably, disappointment deflated her mood even further. Of course none of the Messena men would be seen dead in a singles bar. They were too wealthy, too macho and too gorgeous. They didn't need to go after women, because women chased them. Jacinta's reaction to Kyle was a case in point. She had practically swooned over him.

A nerdy guy approached her and asked if she would like to dance. Eva checked out his left hand and saw the pale streak around his third finger. "Why don't you ask your wife to dance?"

"Uh—she's out of town."

"And I thought this was a *singles* bar. You should go home."

His face reddened. "Who are you? My grandmother?"

She gave him a straight look. "If I was, I'd be saying a whole lot more."

After biting out an uncomplimentary phrase, he spun on his heel and strode away. All pleasure was now leeched from the evening. In no mood to date, or marry, anyone, Eva pulled out her phone and checked an app that listed nearby nightclubs and bars.

She didn't want to go anywhere else. She would prefer to go home, make a cup of tea, curl up on the sofa and watch a movie, but she couldn't give up just yet.

She stepped outside of the air-conditioned bar into the hot, steamy air of a summer's night. It was like walking into a sauna. Glancing skyward, she noticed the heavy layer of cloud that had rolled in, blotting out the night sky. Because Auckland City was situated on a narrow isthmus with the Tasman Sea on one side, the Pacific Ocean on the other, the weather could change quickly.

Hailing a cab, she gave the driver the address of a bar she'd used before that was younger and a little wilder. She'd met Troy there, and that would have worked out if it hadn't been for Kyle.

He had vetoed every other guy she had chosen, and she couldn't help thinking that if she located a possible groom tonight, he would no doubt suffer the same fate.

Kyle wanted her.

She tried to dismiss the disruptive thought, but heat flooded her at the memory of the kiss and the way she had reacted, like a love-starved teenager on her first date! She breathed a sigh of relief as the driver pulled away from the curb and the cab's air-conditioning kicked in. Something made her glance back at the entrance of the bar. A tall, dark-haired man was just sliding behind the wheel of a glossy black sports car. Her heart slammed in her chest at the thought that it was Kyle, although she couldn't be sure. There were a lot of dark sports cars in town, which all looked the same to her, and maybe she was seeing the same guy she had noticed before?

If it was Kyle, that meant he was following her. A sharp thrill jolted through her at the thought.

Determinedly, she squashed the idea along with any hint of relief that despite her saying no, Kyle might not have given up on her. Keeping her gaze fixed on the city street ahead, she tried to remember all the reasons she had to be furious with him. Unfortunately, the reasons seemed hollow when she kept coming back to the stunning fact that he had actually asked her to marry him.

And she was wondering if the offer was still open.

Craning around, she looked through the back window. The car was following so closely it was practically herding the taxi, but the windows of the sleek sports car were too darkly tinted to reveal who was driving. The driver could see her, but she couldn't see him. Her heart pounded out of control. She was suddenly certain that it was Kyle.

The taxi pulled into a space and the sports car swept past. Eva paid the fare and climbed out, all the while giving herself a good talking-to. She should be frustrated and annoyed if it was Kyle—she should be furious—so why did it feel like the evening was suddenly looking up?

In the time it took her to close the door of the taxi, the sports car had disappeared. She checked in both directions, half expecting to see Kyle walking toward her. When she realized she was loitering on the sidewalk, actually waiting for him to appear, instead of going into the bar closest to where the taxi had parked, she quickly walked a little further down the road before spotting another random bar.

Pulse rate still high, she checked the street one last

time before walking in, only to find she had another problem. Now that she was here, she had absolutely no energy
or enthusiasm for finding a suitable husband. Her experience at the previous bar had literally been the last straw.

Kyle was right. She did not want a stranger for a husband.

She could still say yes to Kyle. But if she allowed the
attraction that sizzled through her every time she saw
Kyle to turn into actual love, where would that leave her
in two years' time?

The bar she'd chosen was an Irish pub, filled with
young people and a sprinkling of tourists. Feeling too
put-together and conventional amongst skin-tight denim,
shaved heads and psychedelic tattoos, she took a stool at
the counter, dropped her chin on one hand and ordered
a glass of wine.

The bartender, who looked ridiculously young and
was probably a student, instantly started chatting her up.
"Don't I know you from somewhere?"

Eva sipped her drink and logged the moment he recognized her.

He nodded his head, grinning. "Oh yeah. The buses.
The lingerie ad."

She groaned inwardly, but managed to keep her expression bland. She'd had a lot of practice handling these
kinds of conversations, since the lingerie company she
had worked for had plastered images of her on the back
of buses and on huge highway billboards. "That was a
while ago." Two years. Although it felt like ten.

"Cool. My mom used to buy your stuff."

Eva set her glass down and checked her watch. She had
promised herself she would stay for fifteen minutes. By
then, Kyle should have found a parking space and gone
inside the other bar and she could safely leave without

him seeing her. "I didn't own the company, I just modeled for them."

He grinned again. "Still…nice. Those billboards were *big*. Most of the buses in town had you on the back of them. Pretty sure some of them still do." He leaned forward on the bar, angling for a better view down the front of her dress. "If you're still into that kind of work, I've got a friend—"

"She doesn't do charities for school kids."

The rasp of Kyle's voice sent a hot tingle down her spine as he slid onto a stool beside her. Dressed all in black, a five-o'clock shadow darkening his jaw, his gaze wintry, he looked, quite frankly, intimidating.

Eva felt like banging her head on the counter. Former Special Air Service, an assault specialist who had once belonged to some hunter-killer squad with its own scary code name… Why, oh why, had she not known he would find her?

His gaze touched on hers and her fingers tightened convulsively on the stem of her wineglass. Taking a deep breath because her heart was suddenly racing, she dredged up a dazzling smile for the bartender who, predictably, was backing off fast. "Actually, I *would* like to speak to your friend. As it happens, in about three weeks' time I'll be in the market for some modeling work."

"Uh—my friend's more into *movies*, you know? Maybe, talk to me later." His gaze flickered to Kyle, the subtext clear. *When the boyfriend's gone.*

"He's not my boyfriend."

A nervous tic jumped along one side of the bartender's jaw. He glanced around, as if willing a customer to appear. "On second thoughts, I seem to remember my friend's getting ready to go overseas…"

And if she didn't miss her guess, the bartender was getting ready to run.

Drawn by a compulsion she couldn't seem to resist, she met Kyle's gaze and tried not to notice the instant little charge of adrenaline that shot through her at the laser blue of his eyes. Trying to ignore the tension thrumming through her, she ran her finger around the rim of the wineglass. "Do you have to ruin everything? Lately, I feel like I live in some kind of Mafia family."

"If you want modeling work, there are better places to get it than over the bar of some pub, like your agent, for instance."

"What would you know about it?"

"The bank has modeling agencies as clients. I don't know how they run their businesses, but I'm pretty sure it's not at—" he looked at the sign over the bar "—Irish Jack's."

She sent him a sideways glance that was supposed to be withering, then wished she hadn't when she caught the gleam of humor in his eyes. She squashed the sudden, almost irresistible desire to smile with him. "My agent still has clients lining up. I can continue my modeling career if I want."

"In movies?"

"I don't do movies. I just said that to annoy you."

"You succeeded."

Feeling a little panicky, because she did not want to love Kyle's dry sense of humor or the possessiveness, she slipped off the barstool. Maybe if she were standing, she would feel more in control. Unfortunately, Kyle also stood, towering over her, making her feel ridiculously small and feminine.

She made a beeline for the door but couldn't suppress her automatic pleasure at the small courtesy when Kyle held it for her. In her current state of mind, she could not afford to be charmed by Kyle's manners.

When she stepped out into the balmy evening air, she spun and confronted him. "Is the offer of marriage still open?" The words tumbled out sounding a whole lot more vulnerable than she'd planned.

His gaze sharpened. "Why? What's changed?"

She swallowed at the leap he'd made, his scary insight. Because something had changed. She'd felt it in the instant he had sat down at the bar and fended off the bartender. She didn't know exactly what had changed, just that she had *liked* it that Kyle wanted to protect her. "I'm not sure. I'm confused."

"The offer is still open." He was silent for a moment. "If you want, I can give you a lift home."

She frowned at the sudden switch from aggressive pursuit to coolness. The sense of hidden depth and layers abruptly made her aware of the abyss that lay between the teenaged Kyle she had once fallen for, and the mature, seasoned man who stood in front of her now. "Okay."

The lights of Kyle's Maserati, which occupied a parking spot further along the road, flashed. A short walk later, he opened the passenger side door for her. Taking a deep breath, careful not to brush against him, she settled into the luxurious seat, stomach clenching at the subtly masculine scent of leather. The door closed and seconds later, Kyle slid behind the wheel and the car accelerated off the curb.

As they cruised through town, stopping at intersections filled with tourists enjoying the restaurants and cafés, and loved-up couples strolling, she suddenly didn't want the night to end. "I don't want to go home. Not yet."

He turned his head, and she caught the glitter of

his gaze. The tension in the enclosed space seemed to tighten. "Where do you want to go?"

"The beach." The answer came straight out of the past and made warmth rise to her cheeks, because she belatedly realized the link to their long-ago tryst. It was just that the beach had been such a carefree place for her. She'd spent long summers at Dolphin Bay swimming and sunbathing and building late-night fires. Adoptive cousins, most like Kyle—second and third times removed— and extended family everywhere, and her old life with its trouble and grief left far behind.

Kyle took a turn in the direction of the marina. Traffic slowed. Ahead, Eva glimpsed a bus and hoped it wasn't one of the ones that still had the underwear ad. And, of course, it was.

Kyle sent her a neutral look. "That's one of the reasons Mario worried about you."

Eva studied the faintly battered line of Kyle's profile, the tough jaw and ridiculously long, silky lashes. She shrugged. She wasn't about to apologize for a highly successful modeling career. "Mario was conservative."

She switched her gaze to his hands on the wheel. A scar started at the sleeve of his shirt and ran the length of the back of his hand. "How did you get that?"

He frowned. "Don't change the subject."

"You always want to talk about me. Maybe I want to talk about you."

The minute the words were out, she wished she hadn't said them, because they sounded flirtatious and provocative.

"It's a fishing injury from a couple of years ago. Nick was casting and his hook caught me."

"I thought it might be from the military."

Amusement flashed in his gaze. "Disappointed?"

"No! That last injury putting you in the hospital was bad enough. You almost died." Her stomach bottomed out at the thought. It was almost four years ago, but she could still remember how frantic she'd felt. She hadn't questioned her reaction then, she had just thought it was a leftover of the crush she'd had on Kyle. But how long did crushes last?

Kyle changed lanes and accelerated smoothly. "When I woke up, Gabriel told me that if I didn't resign, he would join up. I knew he'd keep his word, and that the family and the bank couldn't afford to lose him, so I signed the discharge papers."

"You didn't want to leave? I don't know how you could have wanted to stay in after—"

"Nicola and Evan were killed?"

She stared ahead, the stream of oncoming traffic a colorful blur. "I'm sorry, I shouldn't have mentioned it. I know what it's like losing people you love. It's hard to believe they're gone."

She registered his curious gaze, as if he were waiting for her to elaborate. But she'd said too much already. She'd found that the less she said about her past, the better she fitted in. Ignoring the past didn't make it go away, but it sure helped her to feel more normal.

Kyle took an off-ramp and stopped for lights. "It was an attack on the barracks where we were based in Germany," he said quietly. "Unfortunately, Nicola was driving past the car with the explosives when it detonated. Evan was in his car seat. It was pure bad luck. If she had been a few seconds earlier or later, they would have avoided the blast."

There was a moment of silence. "If I hadn't insisted they come out to Germany for Christmas, they would still be alive."

The words, uttered flatly, nevertheless contained a rawness that riveted Eva. She didn't know why she hadn't considered that Kyle might blame himself for the death of his wife and child, but the flat statement made a terrible kind of sense.

Kyle was an alpha male. Testosterone aside, that meant taking charge and taking responsibility. To have lost the two people most intimately connected with him, the wife and child he had vowed to care for and protect, must be unbearable. In that instant a whole lot of things she hadn't understood about Kyle settled into place. Foremost was the fact that he had *loved* his wife and child.

A sharp ache started somewhere deep in her chest. The way she, all those years ago, would have loved to be loved. "You still miss them."

The lights changed, Kyle accelerated through the intersection. "Birthdays and important dates are the worst, but it's not as bad as it used to be."

"I'm sorry." As much as she had gotten used to loss and grief, the process of losing her family over a period of years had, at least, given her time to adjust. She could not imagine what it must have been like for Kyle to lose a wife and child, literally, in an instant.

He took the off-ramp for Takapuna Beach, his expression closed. "It's okay. It hurt, but it was years ago."

She stared ahead at the road as it unfolded, feeling suddenly incredibly self-centered. She had been viewing Kyle as controlling and intrusive—the big, bad wolf— but like all the men in his family, he was a family man.

Abruptly, she understood him in a way that was unbearably and intimately personal. As the oldest child in her family, she had said goodbye to her twin and two younger siblings. She could remember holding their hands and willing them to live. One by one they had died; there had been nothing she could do. It wasn't the shock of a bomb blast, but the sense of helplessness was the same.

Kyle turned down a side street then into a park, with the sea just a few yards from a small parking lot. Now that they were alone, and at the beach, she was out of stall time.

Panic gripped her. Given that she now knew she could not marry a stranger, she needed to decide whether or not she could cope with a temporary marriage to Kyle.

Six

Kyle tossed his jacket in the space behind the driver's seat and walked around the hood of the Maserati to open the passenger side door. Predictably, Eva already had the door open, but was still seated while she unfastened her shoes. He drew in a breath at the elegant line of her legs and the tantalizing glimmer of a fine chain around one slim ankle. "If you want to walk, I don't know how long we'll have. The forecast is for rain."

It was actually for a thunderstorm. He could already see lightning flashes farther north, and from the drop in temperature the rain could start any time.

"Don't care." She sent him a fleeting look that, half hidden by a tousled swath of tawny hair, was unconsciously sexy.

His stomach tightened as he was irresistibly reminded of a seventeen-year-old girl who had trailed endlessly along the beach at Dolphin Bay in a bikini top and a pair of ragged, cutoff denim shorts, driving most of the male population crazy.

She slid out of the Maserati, the gusting breeze plastering her little black dress against the lithe curves of her body as she closed the car with a brisk thud that made him wince.

She sent him a smooth, closed smile, the kind he'd gotten familiar with lately, as if he was one of her difficult clients. "I'm tired of the city and miles of concrete. I want to feel sand between my toes."

He depressed his key and locked the car before walking to the beach. Eva was already standing on smooth, hard-packed sand, just inches shy of the water, her expression oddly relaxed.

"I love it, especially when there's going to be a storm." She sent him a slanting sideways look as he joined her, as if she was trying to assess him in some way. She smiled encouragingly. "Shall we walk?"

His jaw tightened as he suddenly got it. After months of avoidance, Eva had changed tack completely. Every muscle in his body tightened when he realized that Eva's question outside the Irish pub about whether or not his offer of marriage was still open had been for real. And that some time between that moment and the drive to the beach, she had moved on to summing him up as a potential husband. When Eva began asking him about his work hours and his interests, he realized he was being interviewed.

In a weird way, it reminded him of when he was nineteen and had spent a whole summer getting to know Eva. In a lot of ways, the process had been the exact opposite of the usual pattern. She had started out so confident and self-contained it had been hard to get close to her at all.

One day, with the summer almost over and Kyle

pushed to his limits, he had saved her from an older guy who had cornered her at the end of the beach. The tussle had been brief, but when the tourist had beat a hasty retreat, she had stared at him and blushed. She hadn't said a word, just continued on as if it hadn't happened, but from that moment on her behavior had changed. In a weird way it was as if he had passed some kind of test.

She strolled down to the water's edge, wading in ankle-deep. There was no attempt to look sexy or alluring, just a simple enjoyment of the seaside. She turned, her gaze connected with his then dropped to his mouth before she looked quickly away.

Every muscle in his body suddenly taut, Kyle waited her out. He wanted Eva, and she knew it. Last night he thought he'd blown any chance of having her in his bed, but in the space of twenty-four hours, something had changed. Added to that, the beach setting was creating an unsettling sense of déjà vu, as if they'd been spun back years.

Lightning flashed, followed by a heavy roll of thunder. Simultaneously, rain pounded down.

Eva flinched at the sudden deluge, but the rain, though torrential, wasn't cold and, besides, she loved the wildness of it. Kyle jerked his head in the direction of the car but, caught up in the adrenaline of the moment, she grabbed his hand and pulled him toward the shelter of a large, gnarled *pohutukawa* tree.

She sucked in a breath as they stepped beneath the dense overhang of the tree. With the sound of the surf and the shift of shadows as dappled light from the parking lot flowed through the leaves, in a strange way it felt like stepping back in time to Dolphin Bay and that first kiss.

When Kyle reeled her in close and framed her face with his hands, the breath stopped in her lungs. She should have extricated herself in her usual smooth, sophisticated way, but ever since Kyle had slipped onto the stool beside her in the Irish pub, she had been subtly off balance. He had been tailing her for months and had ruthlessly gotten rid of any man who had gotten too close. Now he was making no bones about the fact that *he* wanted her, and against all the odds she loved that.

And suddenly she no longer wanted to resist him. Years ago she had loved Kyle and then lost him along with the whole future she had imagined she might have as a woman, a wife and a mother. He had loved another woman, but she'd had no one. Now she had a chance at... something. If she stopped to think— But right now, with the storm pounding all around them, all she wanted to do was feel.

When she ran her palms up over his chest to his shoulders, Kyle's response was instant. Hauling her closer still, he bent his head, his breath washing over her lips. "What is it with beaches," he muttered.

Lifting up on her toes, she wrapped her arms around his neck and kissed him, the passion white-hot and instant.

Long seconds later, she wrenched her mouth free and dragged at the buttons of Kyle's shirt. He muttered something short and sharp. Dimly, she registered the loosening of the fit of her dress as the zipper tracked down, a damp blast of cool air against her skin. A split second later the dress was gone and her bra along with it.

Bending down, Kyle took one nipple in his mouth. Dizzying sensation jerked through her in waves. When he lifted his head, she remembered his shirt, but he must have shrugged out of it at some point, because she found naked skin.

Kyle groaned. "Maybe we should slow down—"

Her palms slid down over washboard abs and found the fastening of his pants. He uttered a short, soft word. Moments later, she was on her back on the sand, her dress and what she guessed was Kyle's jacket and shirt beneath her.

Kyle's fingers hooked in her panties, dragging them down. Lightning flashed, illuminating the stark planes of Kyle's face as his weight came down on her. Sucking in a sharp breath at the sheer heat of him, she wound her arms around Kyle's neck, the fierce need to keep him close momentarily blotting out coherent thought.

"Babe—there's something I need to do first." He disengaged and rolled to one side. She logged the sound of foil tearing. A condom. Thunder detonated again and the rain pattered down through the canopy of leaves, splashing on bare skin so that she shivered.

Kyle hauled her close, sheltering her with his body, and in that moment it seemed the most natural thing in the world to hook one arm around his neck and lift up for his kiss. At the same time, curious about the condom, her fingers closed around him. She felt the smooth texture, the heated satin of his skin underneath.

A split second later, he came down between her legs. She felt the heated pressure of him. There was a shivering moment of sanity, when she logged Kyle's stillness, as if, like her, he had come to the sudden sobering conclusion of exactly what they were about to do. She should say no. Kyle would stop, she knew he would, and in a crazy way that in itself was freeing.

It was a plain fact that she didn't want to relinquish him or the burning, irresistible pleasure that held her in its grip. It wasn't love. She wasn't that silly, but when set against the shadows of her past and her present loneliness—the growing fear that she would never truly be cherished—it tipped an internal balance so that she no longer wanted to think, only to feel...

She felt him tense at the tight constriction and freeze in place. She thought he was going to stop, but when he lifted his head, she clung, unable to bear letting him go, arching against the burning pressure at the center of her body.

He groaned and a second later, shoved deep. She felt the drag of the condom, an uncomfortable pinching as with each downward stroke he seemed to push a little deeper still. Her hips twisted automatically, trying to ease the discomfort, but the restless twisting momentarily dislodged him.

He cradled her closer and the next downward stroke felt smoother, sleeker, more pleasurable, and she realized that something had changed. The condom was gone, but it was already too late as irresistible sensation gripped her, coiling tight, and the damp, heavy darkness shimmered into light.

Kyle stopped the car outside Eva's house. "We need to talk. Somehow, I don't know how, because it's never happened before, but the condom slipped—"

"You don't have to worry about contraception."

The words were out before she could call them back, but she couldn't regret them. She knew Kyle would probably think she was on the pill or had some other form of contraception, but that wasn't the case. She could get pregnant.

The thought made her heart beat wildly. It was the last thing she wanted, but maybe, just maybe, she could get lucky and it wouldn't happen. If it did... She drew a swift breath, unable to imagine a scenario that was so far out of left field for her.

Fingers fumbling in her haste, she unfastened her seat belt. She still felt damp, gritty and disoriented that the night had spun so far out of control that they'd actually had sex and, in the end, because the condom had come off, unprotected sex. She couldn't wait to say goodbye and escape into the quiet refuge of her home. "Thanks," she said brightly, throwing the car door open.

It was still raining. No problem, since she was already bedraggled and her dress was most likely ruined. Cheeks burning, she searched for her clutch, which had somehow managed to slide down the side of the seat. By the time she had retrieved it, Kyle was out of the car and it was too late to make a quick getaway.

Rain was cold on her bare arms as she jogged to her front door and searched for her key. Intensely aware of Kyle beside her, she jammed the key in the lock and somehow missed.

Kyle calmly took the key from her and unlocked the door. As he pushed it wide, the tinkle of glass made her freeze in place.

"Wait here," he said softly. Kyle stepped past her, flowing into the darkened interior.

A chill went down her spine at the quiet way he'd moved, his utter assurance, and despite her dilemma over whether or not to just give in and marry him, she was abruptly glad he was with her. Burglaries were common, but this was the first time it had happened to her.

Long minutes later, lights went on and Kyle reappeared in her tiny hallway. "I'll call the police. Whoever it was, they're gone now, out through the laundry door and over the back fence. The sound of breaking glass was a vase. They knocked it over on their way out."

Eva followed Kyle into her lounge. Drawers had been pulled out and emptied onto the floor. Her one framed family photo of her mother and father in happier days was sitting on the dining table, as if whoever had broken in had paused to look at it. Immediately, suspicion flared. Her last stepfather, Sheldon Ferris, had once tried to get money out of her, but Mario had threatened him with the police.

As she checked around the sitting room, she noted that her TV and stereo were still in place, but her laptop was gone.

Kyle terminated the call he'd just made. "A cruiser will be here in the next ten minutes." He frowned. "Did you set the alarm?"

"Before I left. I always do."

While Kyle checked her alarm system, she stepped into her bedroom. Her shocked disbelief was swamped by burning outrage. If her lounge was a mess, her bedroom was worse. Her closet and every drawer had been emptied. Clothes had been dumped on the floor with hangers still attached. Shoes, makeup and costume jewelry were scattered over the bed and the floor. She picked up lacy scraps of underwear and jammed them back in their drawer. She knew she shouldn't touch anything, because the police needed to see the scene of the crime, but she drew the line at having uniformed police officers claiming her underwear as evidence.

Until that moment, she had thought a burglary was about the scariness of a stranger, losing stuff and the inconvenience of insurance claims, but she knew now that wasn't so at all. Shock and anger that someone had thought they had the right to invade her privacy and rummage through her private things kept running through her in waves. They had tossed items aside and taken what they wanted as if she didn't matter.

She didn't know what was missing other than her laptop, but suddenly the laptop ceased to matter. A chill went through her, and she found herself rubbing her arms. Her home, her sanctuary and all of the personal things that were about *her* had been violated.

Kyle, who had been quietly checking through rooms, reappeared and looked annoyed when she told him the laptop was gone. "Anything else appear to be missing?"

She skimmed the room and tried to think, although when her gaze snagged on a broken music box, a precious keepsake from her childhood, her temper soared again. If it was Sheldon, a one-time used car salesman and inveterate swindler, he would know how precious that music box was to her. "It's a little hard to say with all the mess."

His gaze was cool and very steady as he noted the damage. "Made any enemies lately?"

She frowned. "I haven't had time. I work too hard."

"What about in business?"

"I deal with hotel groups and caterers. All they want from me is a confirmed date and a check, which they get."

She heard a car pull into her driveway. Trying to keep her emotions in check, Eva looked through the rooms of her house, relieved to see that the burglar hadn't managed to get to her spare room or the kitchen. Minutes later, she opened the front door for two police officers.

Absently, she noticed that the fresh-faced detectives who introduced themselves as Hicks and Braithewaite seemed dazzled, making her aware that her damp dress was clinging and her hair was tousled. It was a reaction she'd gotten used to over the years, and which she usually managed to ignore.

As Hicks flashed his ID, Kyle stepped into the hall, his hand settling in the small of her back. The small proprietorial touch in front of Hicks forcibly brought back the passionate interlude on the beach. But, given her shakiness over the break-in, she didn't mind the context. Messena and Atraeus men were naturally protective of the women in the family. Whether it was an elderly aunt or someone much younger, the small courtesies and the masculine backup were always available if there was a problem.

Kyle kept her close as Hicks asked questions and looked around. When they walked through the rooms, he even threaded his fingers with hers. They had made love, that was intimate enough, but Kyle's possessive behavior had shunted them straight into something scarily close to couplehood.

Eva's stomach lurched as, once again, she turned over her options: marriage or stay single and possibly lose her business and house, both of which were mortgaged. She faced losing everything for which she had worked so hard over the years. She would survive; she didn't have to have the silk cushion. What would hurt, though, with Mario gone and no inheritance until she was forty, was the feeling of alienation that would go with losing that essential link. Maybe that was a ridiculous way to feel, since she was still an Atraeus by name. But it was a fact that she had always had to strive to fit in, to feel good enough to be an Atraeus.

Whichever way she viewed the future, she kept coming up against one constant: she did not want to cut Kyle out of it. That meant marriage.

She drew a quick breath at a heated flash of their lovemaking. And if what had happened tonight was anything to go on, if they married, even if they started out as a paper marriage, she didn't think it would stay that way.

After taking photographs, Hicks asked a few straightforward questions and made arrangements for an evi-

dence tech to call in and dust for prints in the morning.
Eva gave him a description of the laptop and a serial
number, and promised to call in to Auckland Central Police Station with a list of anything else that was missing.

She decided against telling him right away about her
suspicion that the perpetrator could have been Ferris.
If it was, and he had left prints, the police would soon
know, anyway, and that meant she got to hold on to her
privacy. Mario had been the only member of the family
who had known the whole sad and sordid truth about her
past, and she preferred to keep it that way.

If Ferris had broken in, his motive would likely be
the same as last time. He wanted money, and he wasn't
averse to using blackmail to get it. Now that she was quite
well known, thanks to her modeling career, he would no
doubt threaten to release the details of her disorder and
her past to the press.

After closing the door on the detectives, she walked
through to the sitting room, where Kyle was examining
the photo of her parents where it lay on the table. "Your
mother and father?"

"Before they split up." Before her twin had died. Before her father, after finding out about the disorder, had
left for Australia and a new life. And before her mother
had remarried twice, having children who died to other
men who left. Before Eva had discovered that she carried the same rare gene as her mother, a disorder that was
lethal for fifty percent of children born to a carrier. In
Eva's mother's case, the odds had turned out to be even
worse, because out of four children, Eva had been the
only one who had survived.

Kyle rose to his feet. "Do you stay in touch with any
of your old family?"

The way he said old family, as if he saw her as part of

her new family, the Atraeus clan, was warming. "There was never much family to begin with. My mother was an only child." And the distant family that had been left hadn't wanted to know. "Why do you think I had to be adopted?"

Needing something to do, anything to take her mind off Kyle's large, distracting presence in her house and the tension that seemed to be pulling tighter and tighter, Eva began picking up cushions and stacking them on couches. Given that the cushions were cotton and linen, she figured there was no possibility that they would retain fingerprints. "I haven't seen or spoken with anyone from my mother's family since Mario adopted me."

Kyle began helping her clean up. Thirty minutes later, after picking up all of the loose clothes and underwear and putting them in a laundry basket so they didn't smear any prints that might be on the drawers or closet doors, Eva was satisfied they had done everything they could. She probably should have left everything as it was, but she had needed to restore as much as she could to reclaim her space and counter the creepy knowledge that someone had gotten into her house, even with the alarm turned on.

Kyle checked that the rear door was locked, then extracted his car keys from his pocket. "You can't stay here until you get the locks checked and your alarm upgraded. At a guess, the thief had a piece of equipment that could connect to your alarm wirelessly and give him the code—they're common enough. It would have taken him seconds to break in and then disable the alarm."

A shudder went down her spine at the brief description of how vulnerable she had been in her own home, even with the doors locked. Until she'd given the house a security upgrade, she wouldn't be able to relax, let alone sleep here.

Eva found her cell in her bag. Her first impulse was to ring one of Kyle's twin sisters, either Sophie or Francesca. Unfortunately, both of them had been out of town for a week or so. She checked through her contacts and found a number. "I've got a friend who helps me out at work occasionally. She'll put me up for the night." Annie had once had her own wedding event business, but had segued into special event planning for hotels and major corporations.

Her call went through to Annie's answering service. She tried again, with the same result. She tried Jacinta's number. Normally she never mixed business with her personal life, but she was desperate.

Jacinta's breathless *hello* was cut off by a lazily amused masculine voice, informing her that Jacinta was busy. Cheeks burning, Eva terminated the call.

Kyle lifted a brow. "No luck?"

She reached for her laptop then remembered it had been stolen. Luckily, all of her carefully managed business systems and contact lists were stored remotely so she could retrieve them, but it was still a major inconvenience. She picked up her phone and began looking online for a motel. "I could get a motel."

"Suit yourself. Or you could stay at my place. I've got a house just a couple of minutes from here. There's a guest room."

Tension zinged through her at the thought of staying with Kyle. *And continuing on with what they had started at the beach.* "I didn't know you bought a house." The last she'd heard, Kyle had lived in an ultraexpensive penthouse apartment in the Viaduct, an affluent waterfront area a stone's throw from the center of the city. Although, with all of the frustration of Mario's will and the times she'd had to spend trying to find a husband, she hadn't exactly kept up with family news.

"I bought the old Huntington place. It came up for auction a few weeks back."

Shock jerked Eva's head up. The Huntington place wasn't just a house. It was a fascinating Edwardian red brick folly situated on a rare acre of grounds that also ran down to a tiny private beach. She had caught glimpses of it from the road, through ornate wrought iron bars as she'd either jogged or walked past. But the ivy-festooned walls that glowed in the afternoon light and the lush garden possessed the kind of irresistible romantic charm that had drawn her like a moth to the flame. When she had seen that it was for sale, she had taken a risk and climbed through the gate. The overgrown gardens and the beach had been so beautiful that if she had been able to marry in time and obtain her inheritance, she would have bought it, regardless of what the house was like. "I can't believe you bought that house."

Especially since she had wanted it. From the first moment she had seen it, something had clutched at her heart. It was the most perfect family home she could imagine, even though she would not be requiring it for that, unless at some point she was able to adopt a child. Her most immediate purpose had been for her wedding business. It had everything for a perfect venue.

Kyle's expression turned wary. "What's wrong now?"

Jaw taut, Eva picked up the overnight bag she had packed and her clutch. Somehow, finding out that he was in possession of *her* house was upsetting. She couldn't quite put her finger on why. Maybe she felt so knocked off balance because for years she had been used to forging her own path, making her own decisions and doing things her way. Now, for the first and only time in her life, she had made love—with Kyle. Added to that, Kyle held the balance of power for the two things she wanted: her inheritance and the dream house.

As much as she wanted to say no about something, she couldn't deny the twisted desire to torture herself by looking around a house she knew would be beautiful and exactly what she wanted.

Seeing the house and knowing she could only have it on Kyle's terms would reinforce all of the reasons she should squash the incomprehensible, fatal attraction that had sneaked up on her.

What was wrong now?

She gave Kyle a cool stare. "Nothing much."

When Kyle tried to take her overnight bag, she kept a steely grip on it and marched to the door. "First you deprive me of my wedding. Now you've bought my house."

Seven

The crowded suburbs of Auckland seemed to disappear as Eva drove her car through the gates of Huntington House, with its stone gateposts and aged and stately magnolias arching overhead. Security lights came on, illuminating the thick tangle of rhododendrons and old-fashioned roses planted cheek by jowl with native *ponga* ferns and drifts of *reinga reinga* lilies.

The house was two-storied and peak roofed, with an array of chimneys that poked up against the night sky, adding to the old-world charm. Apart from more security lights, which illuminated the circular piece of drive before the front porch, the house sat in darkness, enclosed and secret with the thick press of overgrown trees and gardens.

Kyle drove into a garage off to the side. Since she was only here for the few hours that were left before she had to be at work, Eva parked near the front portico. By the time she had grabbed her things and locked the car, lights glowed softly in the downstairs area.

The scent of the sea and the sound of the waves hitting the shore nearby should have been relaxing after the tension of the break-in, except that it gave her another searing flashback of their passionate moments on the beach.

The portico lights came on and Kyle opened the front door wider, stepping out to take her bag from her.

Unwillingly loving Kyle's manners, Eva walked into the foyer, her heels clicking on the marble floor. Directly ahead a stairway curved away in a graceful arc. To one side there was an elegant front parlor and what looked like a series of reception and family rooms. On the other side of the staircase she knew, because she had peered through the windows when she had snuck into the estate previously, that a hall led in the direction of the kitchen and what had probably originally been the servants' quarters.

Eva let out a breath. "It's perfect." As a wedding venue. *As a family home.*

Kyle shrugged and indicated she should follow him. "At the moment it's a museum."

"You don't like it?"

"I wouldn't have bought it if I hadn't liked it. It just needs updating."

He walked into a huge kitchen, which was shabby and badly lit, but which already contained a selection of gleaming stainless steel appliances; fridge, cooktop, microwave and dishwasher. Kyle pointed out a kettle and toaster and a pantry that contained cereals and bread and a few food essentials if she needed to make a hot drink or get breakfast.

He indicated she should follow him up the stairs and showed her an array of bedrooms, finishing up with a large room with a king-size bed that was unmistakably his. He set her overnight bag down in the hallway.

Eva's cell beeped. When she took it from her bag, she saw Hicks's name flash up on the screen. When she answered the call, his voice was curt. Apparently they just had a call from a neighbor of hers to say that a man had been seen in her rear garden. They had just dispatched a cruiser to check it out. His main concern was that she was out of the house and safe.

When Kyle realized it was Hicks, he took the phone and had a terse conversation with the cop before terminating the call and handing her phone back, his expression grim. "You're not going back until whoever broke in is in custody."

"If they can catch him." She'd reached her limit for the night. She felt cold and shaky and couldn't seem to stop the tremor in her hands.

"Hicks is no slug. He's a member of the Armed Offenders Squad—he knows what he's doing."

She rubbed at her arms, which suddenly felt chilled, and couldn't keep the grumpiness out of her voice. "How do you know this stuff?"

"Quite a few former SAS end up in the AOS." He stopped. "Are you all right?"

She tried for a smile. "Of course."

"You don't look it."

A split second later she was in his arms, his hold loose enough that she could pull free if she wanted. As if sensing her tension, or more probably realizing that she was actually shaking, he wrapped her more tightly against him.

Eva took a deep breath, soaking in the burning heat that seemed to blast from Kyle as the horrible tension that had crept up on her finally began to unravel. "I guess that's what they call delayed shock. Interesting."

"You can be sure that whoever broke in to your house won't do it again," Kyle said coldly. "I'll make sure of it."

The soft, flat statement sent an electrifying shiver down her spine, and she had a moment to feel sorry for whoever it was who had broken into her house. She tilted her head back and met Kyle's gaze, and just like that her decision was made. Kyle was a powerful, in-control kind of guy, and right now that was exactly what she needed. She would probably regret it, but for better or worse she was going to marry him.

Kyle loosened off his hold slightly. "What is it?"

She drew a deep breath. "You were showing me to my room."

"You can have your own room, or you can share mine. Your choice."

She held his gaze unblinkingly. "Your room."

A hot pang went through her as he cupped her chin and bent his head, giving her plenty of time to pull free if she didn't want the kiss, and abruptly that was the final reassurance she needed. Kyle had already proved that he would never push her where she didn't want to go. Her heart slammed against the wall of her chest as his mouth settled on hers.

Eleven years ago, kissing Kyle had been the angst-filled, desperate risk of a teenager. Now it was an adult reaching for something that had been missing for more years than she cared to count, a hunger for warmth and closeness and for the no-holds-barred intimacy of making love.

Another long, drugging kiss later and she found herself being maneuvered through the door to Kyle's room and walked back in the direction of the bed. But when

Kyle tried to pull free, she coiled her arms around his neck, lifted up and kissed him again.

With a groan he pulled her close. He kissed her, his mouth firm, the feel of his muscled body pressed against hers, the shape of his arousal, the taste of him making her head spin. Another long, heated kiss and she felt her zipper open and the straps of her dress slide from her shoulders. "I'm still sticky and grainy from the beach."

"We can have a shower. Later." As her bra released, she tugged at the buttons of his shirt, dragging it open, but had to stop when he bent and took one breast into his mouth.

Her breath caught in her throat as a heated, aching tension gathered in the pit of her stomach. Somewhere in the distance she heard the lonely sound of a night bird, almost swamped by the slow sound of rain starting on the roof. She arched restlessly against Kyle's mouth, needing something more, but at that point he lifted his head and she felt the soft brush of the bed at the back of her knees. Sliding her hand down over the hard muscle of his abs, she found the top button of his pants, fumbled it open and dragged the zipper down.

Kyle's breath caught audibly, his hand stayed hers. Gaze locked with his, she lifted up and kissed him again. Attempting to step out of her shoes mid-kiss, she wavered off balance and ended up tumbling back on the bed. Kyle sprawled heavily, half on top of her, but when he would have moved, she wound her arms around his neck, tangling her fingers in his dark, silky hair and pressed herself against him.

Acting on impulse, she closed her teeth over the lobe of his ear.

Kyle's fingers closed around her wrists, his breath mingled with hers. "Babe, you don't know what you're—"

"Yes. I do." Dizzy with delight at the feminine power she had over Kyle, stunned by the sensations cascading through her and the careful way he held her close as if he truly cared for her, she kissed him again.

She felt his swiftly indrawn breath. "This time we're doing it right."

He disentangled himself and obtained a foil packet from his bedside table. After sheathing himself, he returned to the bed. A split second later, his weight came down on hers.

He cupped her face. "Are you sure you want to do this again?"

She lifted up for his kiss. "Why would there be a problem?"

She felt the scrape of lace as he peeled her panties down her legs, then his thighs parted hers. "Correct me if I'm wrong, but I think it's been a while since you've done this."

She hesitated, on the brink of telling him that before tonight she had never "done this," but then a quiet, instinctive caution gripped her. She had already given more of herself, and agreed to more, than she had planned. The urge to protect herself now was knee-jerk. Confessing that until tonight she had been a virgin would lay bare too much.

This time their lovemaking was more leisurely as he took his time kissing her, cupping her breasts and at the same time encouraging her to explore. Just when she thought she couldn't take much more play, she felt the press of him between her legs. Automatically, she shifted to accommodate him.

This time their joining was smoother, easier. She heard his indrawn breath, then his mouth came down on hers and he began to move and the heated tension turned molten.

Long minutes later, Kyle gently disengaged himself and rolled to one side, taking her with him.

There was a small vibrating silence. "The condom slipped the first time, but that's never happened before, so there's no risk of STDs" He propped himself up on one elbow. "But you also should have told me you haven't made love for a while."

She studied the stubbled line of his jaw, and the resolve not to reveal just how vulnerable she was with all things sexual settled in. She ran her palm over the damp skin of his chest, and evaded his gaze. "There wasn't exactly much time for conversation."

He cupped one breast, the intimate touch sending a tingling thrill through her. "It would have been good to know. We could have done things…differently."

She shivered as he dipped down and took her nipple in his mouth, her eyes closing as the heated, coiling tension started all over again. She tried to think, but her brain was fast becoming scrambled. "How, exactly?"

"I would have taken a whole lot more time."

Her eyes flipped open at the way his voice cooled, as if he was remembering the mishap with the condom. She summoned as much confidence as she could. "There won't be a baby."

Although the gravity of what had happened came back to hit her full force. The plain fact was that because she hadn't been sexually active, she didn't know a lot about where in her cycle was the optimum time to get pregnant. She had never before needed to keep track of her ovulation. She knew roughly when her period was, but that was about it. If by some remote chance she did get pregnant… But that wouldn't happen, she thought grimly, she would make sure of it. She would make an appointment to see her doctor tomorrow and get a morning-after pill.

And arrange contraception.

The decision made, she forced herself to relax about the whole issue of pregnancy. There was nothing she could do until the morning. "I'm sorry we didn't have a conversation before we made love, but I thought if we stopped you might…leave." She lifted up, pressing against his chest, and boldly rolled on top. "It's not as if you haven't done that before."

He tangled his hands in her hair, grinned lazily and pulled her mouth down to his. "You must be talking about leaving, since we've never made love before."

He kissed her and she felt him stir against her stomach. He rolled until they were lying comfortably sprawled, side by side.

It occurred to Eva that she had never felt so relaxed or so comfortable with a man, and she went still inside at the stunning thought that since Kyle didn't want kids then maybe, just maybe, he was the perfect man for her?

Just as long as she didn't get pregnant.

Eva woke to the sound of the shower. She blinked at the enormous old-fashioned room with its striped brown wallpaper and bare boards. She was presently the sole occupant of the huge modern bed, which sat in the center of the room.

Kyle stepped back into the room, wearing dark pants and a shirt he was in the process of buttoning. Feeling exposed, Eva dragged the sheet up to her chin before attempting to drape the sheet around her like a sarong.

Kyle strapped on his watch. "We need to have a conversation before we go to work."

Eva tried for a smile as if waking up in some man's bed after spur-of-the-moment sex was a very normal thing for her. "A conversation would be good in just a few minutes."

She found her overnight bag and lugged it through to the bathroom, which was still steamy from Kyle's occupancy. She quickly showered and dressed. There was no dryer, so she had to be content with combing her hair out straight. She quickly made up her face then checked her appearance. When she saw a faint pink graze on her neck, where Kyle's five-o'clock shadow must have scraped against her skin, the reality of what they'd done last night hit her.

When Kyle knocked on the door, she stuffed the sheet she'd worn into a laundry basket, hung up her towel and walked out into the hall. She was still barefoot, and Kyle, now fully dressed in a dark suit with a blue tie that made his eyes seem even bluer, towered over her.

She had hoped he might pull her into his arms and kiss her so they could both relax and have the discussion they needed to have, but he had his banker face on, cool, neutral and unreadable.

He glanced at his watch. "If we're going to get married, we should make arrangements."

Eva frowned at the way Kyle had casually leapfrogged the whole concept of a proposal. She guessed it wasn't warranted in her case, because she was the one seeking the marriage. Technically, Kyle was doing her the favor, but he had *checked his watch* as if he didn't even have time to talk about it.

Abruptly, she wondered if their lovemaking last night had meant anything at all to him. Annoyed enough to keep him waiting, Eva reached into her bag and found her cell, taking her time as she flicked through to her calendar, which she already knew was packed full of consultations that morning and clear for most of the afternoon, which meant she could book a doctor's appointment directly after lunch.

His gaze shifted to her mouth, and for a shivering moment the sensual tension was alive between them.

"What's wrong?"

"That would be the marriage thing. You haven't exactly asked me."

There was a vibrating silence. "I thought I had."

With careful precision, Eva checked the next month's appointments, of which, thankfully, there were a number. "I can recall something along the lines of a command, followed by a business-type proposition."

"Correct me if I'm wrong, but technically it *is* a business proposition. If you become engaged to me, the marriage can be approved immediately, since Mario made it clear his first preference for a husband was a Messena. You should have access to your trust fund within a couple of weeks. After two years, you receive the full inheritance."

When she continued to flick fruitlessly through her calendar, Kyle said something soft and curt beneath his breath. They both knew her answer had to be yes, but she was frustrated and terminally annoyed that after the searing intimacy they'd shared last night, he was now treating her as if she was an irritating pain in the rear again.

"Marry me, and you get the house."

She clamped down on the automatic burst of outrage that Kyle clearly thought she was so materialistic that he could buy her with the house. "I thought you bought the house for yourself."

He straightened away from the doorframe, but still didn't enter the bedroom, his expression oddly cagey. "For the short term. It's a good investment."

It occurred to Eva that after the passionate lovemaking last night, Kyle was now doing his level best to create some distance. Maybe it was just a masculine desire to compartmentalize. Whatever it was, it did not work for her. The last thing she wanted was to be treated as some kind of sexual convenience who could be bought.

She drew a deep breath. "Okay, I'll marry you. But what happened last night can't happen again. If you want a marriage of convenience then it has to be on the same terms I offered the others."

She hated saying the words; she had adored making love with Kyle, and she wanted to do it again but she couldn't do so under these conditions.

The hum of a cell sounded from his jacket. The cool neutrality of his expression, the same kind of expression she imagined he used at the negotiating table, didn't alter. "No sex. Agreed."

Kyle reached for his cell and slid smoothly into a business conversation, but Eva refused to let herself get either angry or depressed about it. Last night had been special in a way she hadn't expected, but this morning they had bounced back into the old, aggravated relationship. But perhaps the fact that Kyle had pressed her for marriage signaled that he wasn't as indifferent as he seemed.

It shouldn't be important, but she had to wonder exactly how Kyle had viewed their night together, her first and only night with a man. According to the gossip columnists, like all the ultrawealthy Messena and Atraeus men, he was hotly pursued and had enjoyed a number of brief liaisons. And, of course, she could not forget that he had been married. On his scale of things, having sex with her had probably barely registered.

Kyle terminated the call. "I'll apply for the marriage license today. How about having the wedding the week after next? Thursday?"

The date he wanted was twelve days away. She had already checked her calendar, so she knew that day was free. "Are you sure it has to be a Thursday?" Who got married on a Thursday?

She did. Giddy pleasure fizzed through her, which was crazy and dangerous, because she could not afford to project any kind of romanticism into this *business deal.* She could not afford to make herself any more vulnerable to Kyle than she already was.

Kyle leaned against the door, his gaze lingering on the rumpled bed. "You can change the date if you want. I'll just have to check in with my PA."

"Thursday will do." At least it would mean she would have more chance of getting a venue she liked, because all the good ones would be booked out on a weekend day.

"And Eva?"

She tried for her absentminded "I'm concentrating so hard on my schedule that I can't hear you" look, although from the piercing quality of Kyle's gaze she wasn't entirely sure she pulled it off. "What?"

"We need to keep the wedding low-key."

"What exactly do you mean by low-key?"

"I was thinking a registry office, two witnesses."

She stiffened as it occurred to her that while Kyle hadn't minded sleeping with her, he was not entirely happy at being linked with her in marriage. That maybe marrying a lingerie model did not fit so well with his conservative banker's image.

She tucked her cell back in her bag. "Maybe the word you should have used to describe the wedding is *secret*?"

"There's not exactly time for a big wedding."

"And why would we have one when it's only for two years?"

A pulse started along the side of his jaw. "Precisely."

She forced a smooth, professional smile. "No problem. We can get married *quietly*."

But it would not be in a registry office, and it would not be a hole-in-the-corner affair, as if Kyle was ashamed to be marrying her!

Eight

Shortly after nine that morning, Kyle's twin sisters, Sophie and Francesca, who had both recently returned from a buying trip for Sophie's boutique in Australia, cornered him at his favorite café. It was a neat pincer operation that could only have been spearheaded by his mother, whom he had made the mistake of ringing before he had left the house for work. Sophie, who was normally sleek and unruffled, looked haphazard in jeans and a cotton sweater, as if she'd left the house in a hurry. Francesca, the more flamboyant of the two, looked pale and still half-asleep.

Kyle braced himself. Both twins worked some distance away, and thus they did not normally frequent this café, which was close to his bank. He loved his sisters, they had stood by him through thick and thin, but they had a take-charge streak and a facility for winkling out the truth that tended to make things worse. "What do you want?"

Sophie lifted a brow. "We're family. Maybe we just saw you and wanted to say hello?"

Resigned, Kyle paid for his coffee and ordered a long black for Sophie, a latte for Francesca. "I repeat, what do you want?"

Sophie gave him a serene look. "Mom rang. We know you're engaged to Eva—we want to know why. You know we love you, Kyle. We also love Eva. Just answer our questions and we'll let you go."

Kyle paid for the coffees and joined Sophie and Francesca, who had commandeered a corner table. "Maybe we fell in love."

Neither of the twins showed a flicker of interest in his reply. Resigning himself to a longer conversation, Kyle sat back and worked on his poker face.

Their coffee arrived. After the waitress had gone, Francesca leaned forward and gave him a friendly smile. "You kissed Eva on the beach approximately eleven years ago, since then, nothing." She made a slitting motion across her throat. *"Niente."*

Kyle didn't allow his sister's Italian theatrics to do what they were designed to do—lure him into a discussion about his love life so they could really mess with his head. He had no idea how the twins had found out that piece of information, since he hadn't told anyone, including his mother. To his certain knowledge, the only people who had known had been Mario, who was now dead, and Eva. "Since I know you're not psychic, so you couldn't have spoken to Mario, I'm guessing you talked to Eva."

Sophie set her coffee down. "She rang me first thing. She needs a dress."

Kyle pinched his nose. The phone had obviously been running red hot.

A dress. That did not sound like a registry office wedding. "And since you supply a lot of Eva's brides, she called you."

"It's good business. I recommend Eva's wedding planning. She recommends my dresses. It's a marriage made in heaven," Sophie said smoothly, "while this one, clearly, is not."

Francesca put her coffee down with a snap. "We know Eva needs a husband to get her inheritance."

The hum of conversation in the café abruptly dropped. Heads began to swivel. Kyle's jaw compressed. "Eva told you that?"

Francesca blushed. "Not exactly. I saw Mario's will on your coffee table in your apartment one day. I couldn't help wondering why you even had a copy, so—"

"You read a confidential document."

Francesca's brows jerked together. "Maybe you shouldn't have left it out where just anyone could read it."

Kyle could have pointed out that his apartment wasn't exactly a public area, but he recognized a blind ally when he saw one. A little desperately he tried to recall the original thread of the conversation. "The reason I'm marrying Eva is private and, uh, personal."

A hot flash of just how private and personal they had gotten last night momentarily distracted him. He dragged at his tie, which suddenly felt a little tight, then realized his mistake when Sophie noticed the faint red mark on the side of his neck.

Sophie blinked. "You're sleeping with her. That changes things."

Francesca stared at him as if he'd just grown horns. "You're Eva's legal trustee and you're *sleeping* with her? Aside from being sleazy, isn't that against the law?"

Kyle kept a firm grip on his temper. "I'm not responsible for Eva. I'm a trustee of her adoptive father's will, that's an entirely different thing—"

Francesca gave him a horrified look. "Then she's pregnant."

"She can't be pregnant." Although the thought hit him like a hammer blow, despite Eva's confidence that she couldn't be.

He took a mouthful of coffee, which he suddenly needed. Although, Eva had not seemed to be worried about the possibility of a pregnancy, so he assumed that, like a lot of women, she was on the pill or had taken some other precaution.

Another thought hit him out of the blue as the strange dichotomy of making love with a sophisticated woman who had been at turns fiery and passionate then oddly awkward and uncertain registered. He had assumed the reason Eva had been awkward and uncertain was that she hadn't made love for a very long time.

Either that, or she was a virgin.

He drew a long breath and let it out slowly. He knew that Eva had never had a live-in lover; that was common family knowledge. They had all assumed it was because Mario was so old-fashioned and that Eva, out of respect for her adoptive father, was preserving an outward show of chastity. It had never occurred to any of them, least of all, Kyle, that she had been doing exactly what it appeared; keeping herself for marriage.

Although, technically, she hadn't saved herself for her wedding night.

"So this is going to be a real marriage?" Sophie picked up her bag, which she'd placed on the floor.

Kyle frowned as Sophie extracted her phone and made a call, speaking in the kind of low, flat voice that could have been lifted straight out of some B-grade thriller.

Apparently, something was green, not red, the 10-33 was over but in general it all still qualified as Alpha Charlie Foxtrot.

Kyle recognized code when he heard it, even if it was a crazy mix of the standard radio language used by the military for decades and the 10 Code that was in popular use by police and emergency services. At a strong guess she was relaying information to their mom, who had spent time volunteering for the local ambulance service as one of their call operators. "If you hand the phone to me, I can speak to Mom direct."

Sophie's gave him a faintly irritated look. "No need. She'll be in Auckland by this afternoon. You can talk to her at my apartment, since both you and Eva are invited to dinner at my place tonight. There's a lot to decide in a short time frame."

"Not that much, since the wedding is in twelve day's time."

Francesca gave him a pitying look. "You're marrying a wedding planner. They're Type As. And you know, Eva, she's like a double A."

Sophie set her cup down. "That means perfectionist. Aggressive. Even if you got married in a registry office, which will never happen because I know what the dress is going to be, it would be the most perfect registry office wedding imaginable. But, like I said, it's not a registry office, so you should brace yourself."

Kyle groaned inwardly. When he'd left Eva that morning, he'd been relieved that he'd gotten her to agree to the marriage. His concern had been to get the marriage done quickly and quietly. He thought he'd managed to convey that to Eva, but something must have gotten lost in translation, because now all hell was breaking loose.

But now he could see he had made a big mistake in

not factoring in the impact this would have on his family. Mistakenly, he had assumed that his mother, who had been pressurizing him to think about marriage again and find someone "nice," would be happy that he had finally decided to step back into relationship waters again.

The certainty that Eva had been a virgin when they had made love hit him anew. The anomaly of Eva choosing to give herself to him after years of celibacy and before they had even agreed to a marriage pointed to only one clear answer.

She wanted him just as badly as he wanted her.

An odd tension dissipated at the thought. At the same time, Kyle was aware that hell would probably freeze over before Eva would admit feeling anything at all for him. But then Mario had given him the distinct impression that Eva had suffered a lot of emotional difficulties as a child. He had assumed there was abuse in her past and had done what Mario requested and left her alone. He hadn't pried into Eva's history, but now that they were getting married, he resolved to find out exactly what had gone wrong.

A part of him was fiercely glad that Eva hadn't slept around, that she had waited and given herself to him. But he was aware that he would have to step carefully. He was cool, logical and disciplined. Eva was gorgeous and passionate, like rich, decadent chocolate, meant to be enjoyed in small, ruthlessly measured doses.

Francesca waved a hand in front of his face to attract his attention. "Just tell us one thing. Is Eva pressuring you to marry her?"

"No." The reason he wanted to marry Eva was cut and dried: it was the most efficient way of keeping her away from other men.

Sophie gave him a considering look. "But this is a marriage of convenience, right?"

Kyle decided there was no point prevaricating, since the twins had clearly made up their minds that it was. "Yes."

Sophie stared at him with her spooky eyes, the ones that interrogation officers would kill for and which sucked the truth out of you whether you wanted to tell or not. Clearly, she had just sucked something significant out of his brain, because she exchanged a look with Francesca. "Is there something wrong with a marriage of convenience?"

The twins gave him a pitying look.

Sophie sat back in her chair as if the case was concluded. "A marriage of convenience where you sleep with Eva? Sounds like a real marriage to us."

Eva rushed to her doctor's appointment only to find her last consultation had dragged on so long she had missed it and had to wait for an emergency appointment. Stomach churning, not least because she hadn't stopped to get any lunch, she sat down to wait.

At three o'clock, she finally got in to see Dr. Evelyn Shan, an elegant Indian woman with an impressive list of qualifications and a daughter, Lina, who had been a good friend of Eva's in her last year of school.

After a couple of minutes of catching up about Lina, who now lived in England, Eva finally managed to get to the point of her visit.

Evelyn's eyes widened ever so slightly at Eva's request for morning-after and contraceptive pills, before she began asking a crisp series of questions. "I'll prescribe the morning-after pill, and you need to take it today, as soon as possible. The results aren't one hundred percent, and given the time in your cycle..."

She scribbled a prescription. Eva, feeling about six inches tall, folded the piece of paper and placed it in her handbag. As she hurried out to pay for the consultation, her phone vibrated.

She took the call from Luisa Messena, Kyle's mother. Feeling frazzled, she agreed to meet Luisa, Francesca and Sophie at a nearby café in a few minutes, although she was certain "coffee" was a euphemism for what was about to take place. As much as she loved the Messena women and enjoyed their company, they were, each in their own way, formidable. It was also a fact that the twins knew about the clause in Mario's will.

She paid and filled her prescription at a chemist then hurried to the café. Sophie and Francesca were grinning like a couple of cats that had gotten the cream. Luisa hugged her with an odd smile in her eyes.

Feeling dazed that all three women seemed quite relaxed about the quick marriage, Eva ordered sparkling water. She intended to sip some now then cap the bottle, place it in her bag and, as soon as she got a chance, take her pill. She didn't want to risk taking the pill at the table, because she was pretty sure that if she took out the pack, the twins would recognize the medication and all hell would break loose.

Half an hour later, just as she was making her excuses to leave, Detective Hicks called. They needed to get into her house to dust for fingerprints, and they needed her to meet them there now.

After quickly explaining about the break-in to Luisa, Sophie and Francesca, she got up to leave, but Luisa wouldn't hear about her going on her own and insisted on calling Kyle.

She beamed as she disconnected the call. "He's more or less finished for the day and will drive you to your house."

Feeling just a little bit frantic because she needed a few minutes alone to take the pill, Eva found herself strolling across the road to Kyle's bank, an imposing old building with several floors and a plaster facade in a tasteful shade of mocha. She stepped through antique wood-and-glass revolving doors into the hushed echoes of a large reception area with marble floors and very high, intricately molded ceilings. She had been in the bank on a number of occasions before, but always with Mario.

Kyle stepped out of an elevator, and her heart did a queer little leap. He was dressed in the same suit she had seen him wearing that morning, *after she had gotten out of his bed*, but he looked…different. Maybe it was the understated richness of marble floors and pillars, the diffused light that shimmered through fanlights over the doors, but in that moment he looked utterly at home in the opulence and wealth of the bank and every inch the urban predator.

An hour later, they left her house, locking it behind the police team. After the short drive home, where they were changing for dinner because they were eating out, Eva finally made it to a bathroom.

Setting her bag down on the vanity, she took the morning-after pill out of her bag and read the instructions.

She needed to take the pill in the first twenty-four hours. She checked her watch. She was within the time.

Relief making her a little dizzy, she filled a glass with water, popped the pill in her mouth, took a mouthful of water and swallowed.

Nine

Ten days later, Eva walked into her office to find Jacinta rushing out, her normally magnolia cheeks bright pink. "Anything wrong?"

"Nothing." Jacinta waved her clipboard. "Just needed this. I must have left it in here by mistake. Oh, and some man called to see you. I actually found him in your office when I came in with coffee and shooed him out. I noted down his number on the pad beside your phone."

Frowning that someone had walked into her office while she'd been having a fitting for her dress at Sophie's shop, and without an appointment, Eva checked out the number, which was unfamiliar.

Eva sat down behind her desk. It was then she noticed that her handbag, which she'd left behind because Sophie's shop was just down the street, was gaping open. Mario's will was tucked inside where she had left it, but she couldn't remember it being folded open at the second page.

Feeling unsettled, she refolded the will and replaced it in her bag. It was ridiculous to think that the person in her office could be Sheldon Ferris. Picking up the phone, she rang the cell number noted on the pad.

A male voice picked up, and her stomach plummeted as she recognized her stepfather's voice. "What were you doing in my office?"

"Now, what way is that to talk to a relative? Especially with a wedding coming up."

The veiled threat in his voice made her tense. "You married my mother for a couple of years. That doesn't make you a relative."

"I suppose, now you're an Atraeus, and rich, you've got no time for the family you left behind—"

"If you want money, you can forget it." As far as she was concerned, Ferris had only ever been with her mother to benefit himself. He had lived off her sickness benefit and run up enough gambling debts that when her mother had died there had been nothing left.

There was a small silence. "You're not going to get rid of me this time." He mentioned a figure that took her breath. "If you don't want your story splashed all over the tabloids, you'd better pay up."

In that moment Eva noticed a message sitting on her blotter, from Detective Hicks, to the effect that they hadn't been able to make a positive ID on any finger-prints other than her own. She didn't care, she was now sure in her own mind who it was that had broken in. "That was you in my house the other night, wasn't it?"

The click of the disconnected call in her ear was loud enough that she wrenched the phone away. With shaky fingers, she set the phone down in its rest.

Sheldon Ferris. He popped up in her life at odd inter-vals, usually wanting money. Mario had frightened him off the last time, but Mario had failed to tell her what leverage he had used. All she could hope was that the fear of a police investigation would be enough to scare him off.

With the pleasure of trying on her wedding dress drained away by the nasty call, Eva deliberately tried to recapture her optimistic mood by checking through her wedding file.

Predictably, Kyle had not been happy when he'd discovered that Eva had not booked a registry office wedding and that she had involved Kyle's family in almost every aspect. Eva, on the other hand, had felt it was important that his family were involved, not least because in a more distant way, they were also her family.

She had invited the Messena clan to her last wedding, which hadn't happened, so why would she not invite them to this one, especially when Kyle was the groom? It just hadn't made any kind of sense to cut family out and in the process cause hurt.

It still felt faintly surreal that she was actually getting married, and that the toxic clause in Mario's will would be neutralized in just two days' time.

Two days until she became Kyle's wife.

The speed with which the wedding was approaching made her feel breathless and just a little panicky, which was not her. Usually she was in control and organized. She lived and breathed detail and was superpicky about every aspect of a wedding, which made her good at her job. She also had a huge network of contacts thanks to her family and her modeling days. She had thought twelve days was enough time to organize a small, intimate wedding, but it seemed the universe was working against her.

She'd fought tooth and nail over venues, food and music, and she was losing sleep. To cap it off, none of her bridesmaids of choice were available on a Thursday. Even Sophie and Francesca had had prior commitments that meant that, while they could come to the wedding, they just did not have enough time to do all the brides-maid things. She was starting to get desperate. The way things were going, the wedding *would* take place in a registry office.

Jacinta strolled back in with the clipboard in her hand, this time with a couple of sheets attached. Her dark bob was perfect and glossy, her vivid pink cotton dress, cinched in at the waist, made her honey tan look even darker and more exotic. "You said you wanted to talk to me about a new wedding."

Eva slid the page with the basic plan she had arrived at across her desk. "It's my wedding."

Her eyes widened with shock. "But, since Jeremy went to Dubai, you're not even going out with anyone—unless Troy Kendal proposed?"

"Uh-uh. Not Troy." Eva tried to look unconcerned and very busy shuffling pieces of paper as Jacinta flipped the sheet around and stared at the line that contained the groom's name.

"You're marrying Kyle Messena?" There was a curious silence. "Now I am confused. He's a babe, but I didn't think you even liked him."

Eva avoided Jacinta's curious gaze and tried to look serenely in love, which was difficult because nothing she felt for Kyle fell into the "serene" bracket. "*Like* doesn't exactly describe what I feel for Kyle."

That, at least, was honest. Nothing about any of their interactions had ever fallen into comfortable friendship territory. "We had a *thing* years ago, and when he knew how close I came to marrying Jeremy, he, uh…decided we should be together."

Jacinta managed to morph surprise into sparkly enthusiasm. "Sounds take-charge and...romantic."

Eva caught the subtext, *and so not like Eva.* She searched for a little enthusiasm herself. "Like I said, we go way back."

Desperate to quit the conversation, she checked her wristwatch. Happily, she had arranged to have lunch with Kyle, so she had a legitimate out. Jumping to her feet, she hooked the strap of the sleek handbag over her shoulder. "You know," she said vaguely, "the family connection."

Jacinta added the sheet to her file, her expression vaguely horrified. "Of course. If he's a Messena, then you're related."

Eva frowned at the way she said it. "The connection is hardly close. Mario was Kyle's great-uncle, and don't forget that I'm adopted."

"It's coming back."

Eva forced a smile. "Which reminds me, I have a favor to ask. We want to get married this week, and I was wondering if you could be my bridesmaid?"

"This week?"

"Thursday." She caught another little piece of subtext. "I'll supply the dress and shoes from Sophie Messena's boutique."

Jacinta's expression brightened. "Okay." She hugged the clipboard to her stomach. "I guess you must have both discovered you're crazy in love? Like a fatal attraction, since you didn't seem to even like one another at the Hirsch wedding."

Eva's phone chimed, negating the need to answer. Clutching the cell like a lifeline, Eva answered the call, which was from Kyle. She said his name with a pleased smile and waggled her hand at Jacinta, as if this somehow answered the question of whether or not she was in love. Happy to be free from the interrogation, she stepped out of the office.

"You sound happy."

The low register of Kyle's voice brushed across her nerves as she punched the call button of the elevator. She had stuck to her resolve that she and Kyle wouldn't sleep together, but listening to Kyle's voice, which was drop-dead sexy, didn't help. Neither did the fact that Kyle was exhibiting a kind of calm, measured patience with her that was downright scary. She shouldn't like that in an utterly male way he was waiting for her to get back into his bed. "It's lunchtime. I get to eat."

"And I intend to feed you."

Eva's fingers tightened on the phone. Why did that sound so carnal? She stepped into the elevator and hit the button to close the doors. "Where, exactly?"

"It's a surprise. I'll be waiting for you downstairs."

As she stepped out of the elevator, despite giving herself a stern talking-to on the way down, her heart skipped a beat when she saw Kyle. She was glad she had worn one of her favorite dresses, a cream sheath dress that made the best of her honey tan and tawny hair. Kyle was dressed in a sleek, dark suit with a snowy-white shirt and dark red tie and looked edgily handsome and just a little remote. She tried to look breezy and casual as she walked toward him, as if making love with him and agreeing to marriage had not been earth-shattering events but, even so, her stomach automatically tightened.

He held the door for her, and she stepped through, suddenly feeling ridiculously feminine and cosseted. Since the dinner with his mother and sisters, courtesy of living in the same house, they had spent more time together than she could remember since the Dolphin Bay days, and the tension was wearing on her nerves. "Where are we going?"

He opened the passenger side door of the Maserati and named an exclusive jeweler's. A glow of pleasure infused her. "You don't have to get me a ring."

His gaze touched on hers. "The ring's nonnegotiable. My family will expect it, and so will the media."

Her jaw squared at his reasoning and the quick little dart of hurt that went with it. Just for a moment she had felt that Kyle really did care for her and the engagement meant something more to him than a business arrangement. It was the kind of dangerous thinking she knew she couldn't afford, but which somehow kept materializing. As if it mattered that Kyle should care for her.

As if she wanted this marriage to be real.

Ten

Jaw squaring, Eva slid into her seat. "You don't have to buy the ring. I'll get one for myself, after lunch."

There was a moment of silence before the door closed with an expensive *thunk*. Fingers shaking just a little because out-of-the-blue anger had piled on top of the hurt and all over a piece of jewelry. Kyle slid into the driver's seat as she fastened her seat belt.

Somewhere behind them a horn blared. Glancing in the rearview mirror, she saw a delivery truck waiting for the space that Kyle had illegally commandeered. Her cheeks heated as she became aware that Kyle, aside from starting the car, wasn't moving. "We should go before you get a ticket."

"Not until we get something straight. I buy the ring."

Taking a deep breath, she forced her fingers to loosen on the buttery leather of her bag. "No."

The delivery truck gave another extended blast on its horn.

"I'm not moving until you agree."

She frowned at his steely blue gaze and the rock-hard set of his jaw. Not for the first time, she saw the defining quality that had seen him promoted in the military and which made him such an asset in the banking business: the cold, hard-assed ability to force his own terms.

It passed through her mind that living with Kyle would not be a cakewalk. He would be demanding, opinionated and difficult; she just bet that with his military training, he probably liked to make rules. Irritatingly, it also registered that she could never be happy with a man who didn't challenge her, that a part of her relished the battle. That in some crazy, un-PC way, Kyle suited her and that she would rather argue with him than agree with any other man she knew. "What if I don't want a ring?"

"Sophie said you wanted a dress. Why not the ring?"

She thought quickly. He was right, she did want the ring.

She guessed that, in her heart of hearts, it was tied in with the reason she wanted a real wedding in the first place. She liked the enduring conventions and traditions, the beauty and hopefulness, and she wanted to enjoy the occasion. Somehow, in going through the same process that countless other couples had entered into, there was a comforting sense of being a part of something time-honored and lovely, even if the marriage was a sham.

She decided the timing was right to mention another detail of the wedding preparations. "I'll have the ring, but on the condition that we get married in a church."

Kyle pulled out and let the delivery van take the space. "Let me guess. You've already booked the church."

"Since it's difficult to get one of those at short notice, I booked as soon as I had the date."

The extended silence that accompanied Kyle's smooth

insertion into city traffic underlined the fact that he wasn't happy with the idea of a wedding in a church.

Suddenly incensed, Eva contemplated telling Kyle to pull over so she could get out and walk back to her office. Her shoes were too high, her feet would hurt and she'd probably wilt in the heat, but it would be worth it. "If you think I'm going to stand in some dusty registrar's office somewhere, you can forget it."

Eva backed her statement with a fiery glance, in that moment prepared to cancel the wedding, cancel her very important plans for her business and the gorgeous house of her dreams—all disastrous consequences. It occurred to her that somewhere between sleeping with Kyle and agreeing to marry him she had lost her perspective and was hatching into a fully-fledged bridezilla.

Kyle muttered something curt beneath his breath as he accelerated through an intersection. "Are you always this difficult?"

Eva stared at oncoming traffic, barely seeing it. "You know I am. Mario would have wanted a church wedding. It's important."

"I guess I keep forgetting I'm marrying a wedding planner."

The easy way he said the words as if, ultimately, Kyle was relaxed with the whole idea of marriage and prepared to give her her way, doused the escalating tension. The dress, the ring and getting married in church might seem inconsequential to Kyle, but they mattered to Eva. Her upbringing with Mario had always included the church. In their small family, faith had been central, deep and important. She wouldn't feel married if it wasn't done in a church.

Kyle braked as traffic slowed. "Which church and what time?"

Kyle's sudden change of heart about the church, the ease with which he had adapted, sparked a suspicion. "You knew about the church all along."

"I didn't know the details, but the twins gave me a heads-up."

Which meant, since he hadn't mentioned it before, that he had more than likely saved the knowledge as a bargaining chip. In this case, to make sure she had the engagement ring he wanted to give her.

Feeling suddenly, blazingly happy that he had gone to so much trouble for her, she gave him the details. "It's the little church just down from the house. I was lucky enough to get it at short notice."

The vicar hadn't liked having his arm twisted, since he'd had to reschedule a regular session of the La Leche League, who had their monthly meeting in an adjacent room, but she had doubled the fee, which had smoothed things over.

A bus up ahead stopped for a set of lights. Eva winced as she recognized one of her last lingerie advertisements splashed over the rear of the bus.

The fizzing happiness died a death. Just what she needed, a reminder that Kyle was marrying a woman who was more recognizable to the general population half-naked than fully dressed. And in that moment it hit her what that would mean to a man who made his living in the ultraconservative world of banking. To say that she was an unsuitable wife for a man who dealt with the stiff etiquette of that social world was a massive under-statement.

A car peeled right and, as luck would have it, they ended up snug behind the bus, with her airbrushed, overly enhanced cleavage looming large. Eva's fingers tightened on her handbag, as any hope that Kyle had not seen the advertisement faded.

When she had been modeling, the profession had been so competitive that this particular lingerie shoot had seemed a good business move. It had certainly kept her in public view, but until now she had not noticed how tacky the posters were.

Even more on edge now, she stared at Kyle's profile, the clean-cut strength of his jaw and the way his broken nose made him look even sexier. "Maybe you shouldn't marry me."

Kyle's gaze captured hers. "What's wrong now?"

The mild, patient way he asked the question, as if she was a high-maintenance girlfriend *with issues*, made her stiffen. "Won't marrying me be a problem in terms of your career?"

Mario had thrown up his hands often enough at her decision to become a lingerie model. Added to that, over the years Eva had become sharply aware that her career, coupled with the Atraeus name, had guaranteed the kind of prying, intrusive media attention she hated.

Kyle pulled into a reserved space in the crowded, popular enclave that was the Viaduct, a collection of bars and cafés and apartments on the waterfront, just a stone's throw from the central heart of Auckland. Unfastening his seat belt, he half turned to face her, and suddenly the interior of the Maserati seemed suffocatingly small. "Is this about the lingerie ads?"

She met his gaze squarely. "It could affect your business. I mean, won't there be occasions when I have to socialize with some of your clients?"

"Honey, I part own the bank. I can buy and sell most of my clients. If they've got a problem with my wife, they can take their business elsewhere."

A curious tingling sensation riveted her to her seat. As Kyle exited the car, she registered what that sensation was: the recognition that in that moment something basic and utterly primitive had taken place. Without so much as the blink of an eye, Kyle had informed her that she was more important than his business. More, he had given her an assurance that he would uphold her honor and protect her unconditionally. An assurance that was guaranteed to melt her all the way through, because he had made her feel that she belonged to him.

Suddenly, it did not seem like a marriage of convenience to Eva.

Kyle opened her door and held out his hand. Still feeling electrified by the uncompromising way Kyle had stated his solidarity with her, his intention, on the surface of things, to treat her as a real wife, Eva put her hand in his. When she straightened, for a moment she was close enough to Kyle that she could see the crystalline clarity of his irises and the intriguing dark striations, the inky blackness of his lashes.

Only one other person had done the same, and that had been Mario.

She was aware that Kyle would know some of the details of her background, but only the parts that she and Mario had agreed could be known. He did not know about the genetic disorder, the deaths of her brother and sisters and her mother's depression; the constant moves to avoid one of her mother's violent boyfriends. He could not know or guess how difficult it was for her to trust *anyone*.

She had entrusted herself to Kyle, and now she knew why. Somehow, beneath the battle lines they had drawn for so long and all the tension and clashes, she had recognized that bedrock quality in Kyle. It was the same quality that had attracted her when she was seventeen and still raw from the disintegration of her family and being handed through a list of foster homes. It explained why she had never really forgotten him, even though he had walked away.

For a split second, his gaze rested on her mouth, and she realized that in his sharp, percipient way, he had picked up on the intensity of her thoughts and was going to pull her close and kiss her. She was so sure of it that she unconsciously rebalanced her weight to lean in close.

"Kyle! I saw you from across the street. I've been trying to get hold of you."

"Elise. I was going to call you."

Eva stiffened as a tall, narrow brunette with dainty features and a simple silk shift and jacket that she instantly recognized as Chanel, stepped up to Kyle and kissed him on the cheek. The extremity of Eva's reaction was easily recognizable; she was jealous. Why she hadn't considered that Kyle had a girlfriend she didn't know.

Kyle disentangled himself, his expression neutral. His arm came around her as he introduced Elise, a financial consultant with a rival bank. In clipped tones, he introduced Eva as his fiancée.

There was a moment of stony silence, and Eva found it in herself to be sorry for Elise.

Elise recovered fast. "I know you from somewhere."

That would probably be from the back of a bus, Eva thought.

Minutes later, Kyle unlocked a private entrance sandwiched between a high-end restaurant and an award-winning café. A few seconds in a private high-speed elevator, and they stepped out into the hushed foyer of a penthouse suite.

Opening a tall bleached oak door, Kyle indicated she should precede him. A little perplexed that Kyle had brought her to his apartment, rather than a café, Eva stepped into an elegant, spare hall that opened out into a huge light space. Beech floors flowed to a wall built almost entirely of glass, with sliding doors that opened onto a patio.

The apartment was vast and overlooked the bustling Viaduct with cafés and bars and a marina filled with colorful yachts. Further out the Harbour Bridge arched across the Waitemata Harbour linking the North Shore to Auckland City. To the right the quirky suburb of Devonport with its jumble of Victorian houses was clearly visible, and beyond, in the hazy distance, the cone-shaped Rangitoto Island.

A dapper man in a suit rose from one of the long leather couches grouped around a coffee table. "Mr. Messena, Miss Atraeus."

Kyle introduced her to Ambrose Wilson, the manager of a store that was very familiar to Eva, because a branch of her family owned it. Originally Ambrosi Pearls, the Auckland branch had recently expanded into diamonds.

Wilson indicated the long, low coffee table on which were placed several black velvet display trays that glittered with an array of diamond rings.

As Eva sat down, she fought a sense of disorientation that her wedding was in two days' time.

As she stared at the gorgeous rings, words she hadn't meant to say spilled out, "Was Elise important?"

Kyle, who had shrugged out of his jacket, tossed it over the back of one of the couches and loosened off his tie. "We dated a few times. Mostly at business functions."

And they hadn't slept together, she was suddenly sure of it. Relief flooded her. She let out a breath she hadn't realized she was holding. She didn't want to feel all twisted up and jealous, but lately she seemed unable to control her moods and Elise had pushed some buttons she hadn't even known she had.

Kyle frowned. "Does it matter?"

Eva forced a smile and picked a ring at random. "Of course not."

But if Kyle had been sleeping with Elise while he had been acting as the trustee of Mario's will, surveilling her and preventing her from getting married, all bets would have been off.

The thought pulled her up sharply as she considered where it was taking her. She could only ever recall feeling like this once before, and that had been years ago when Kyle had gotten engaged to Nicola and she had been fiercely, deeply jealous. But that had been because she had been in puppy love with Kyle, and she was not in love with him now; she could not be.

A little dazed, she slipped the ring onto her finger without really seeing it.

Kyle frowned. "That one isn't right."

"How can you know that?"

"I don't spend all my time with my head buried in stocks and bonds."

She examined the ring, with its delicate bridge of three perfectly matched diamonds. It was an expensive but very conventional ring, and he was right, she didn't like it.

Kyle picked up a ring that had its own velvet tray, a classic square-cut diamond that blazed with a pure white fire. The central diamond was large but elegant and framed by tiny white diamonds that glittered and flashed. The setting was platinum, which added to the clean, classical look of the ring. "You should wear something like this. It's pure. Flawless, wouldn't you say, Wilson?"

Wilson, who had been sitting at a side table with his

laptop open, strolled over to look at the ring. "That's correct. It was originally a ten-carat diamond, but we worked with it until we achieved an utterly flawless gem."

Eva met Kyle's gaze. He lifted a brow, and she suddenly realized what he was getting at with the ring. *He knew.* He knew that she had been a virgin when they had first made love. She went hot then cold. Normally when she had a fight-or-flight reaction, her instinct was to fight. This time running would have been the preferred option.

With an effort of will, she smoothed out her expression and replaced the ring she had picked up. When she would have slipped the ring Kyle had selected onto the third finger of her left hand, he preempted her and did it himself, the brush of his fingers sending tingling heat shooting through her.

Kyle's gaze was unnervingly intent. "Do you like it?"

She was trying not to love the ring too much, but it was as perfect as Kyle's unexpected gesture in acknowledging the gift she had given him when they had made love. She cleared her throat so her voice wouldn't sound thick and husky when she spoke. "Yes, it's beautiful. Thank you."

"Good." Kyle turned his head in Wilson's direction. "We're taking the ring."

Wilson produced another box from his briefcase. "Now would be a good opportunity for you to both try on wedding rings."

Reluctantly slipping the engagement ring off, she tried the platinum band Wilson handed her for size. The band, which had been made to match the engagement ring she'd chosen, fit perfectly, so in the end the choice was a no-brainer. Returning the band to its box, she slipped the engagement ring back on her finger.

Within minutes, Wilson had packed up the cases of rings and departed. Eva had no clue what the ring cost, although she could hazard it would run into the hundreds of thousands, if not more. No money had changed hands. But, since the Messena family were bankers for The Atraeus Group and related by blood, no doubt the transaction would take place in a more relaxed way.

Kyle checked his watch. "We need to eat then I'll take you back to work."

While Kyle was taking plastic-covered plates of pre-prepared food that had been delivered by one of the restaurants downstairs out of the fridge, Eva excused herself and went in search of the bathroom. She stepped into a wide spacious hall with several bedrooms opening off it.

The hall, like the rest of the apartment, was stylish, but bare, as if Kyle had no interest in creating a home. She had noticed the lack of artwork and family photos in the sitting room, so the two framed photos gracing the wall at the far end of the hall stuck out like a sore thumb and immediately drew her.

The largest one was of a woman with long, tawny hair and a striking tan as she stood on a street in a bright, summery dress, her arms bare as she grinned and waved at the camera. Eva instantly recognized Nicola, Kyle's wife. The second frame was much smaller and showed Kyle cradling a sleeping baby, his expression intent and absorbed as he studied the small, slumbering face.

Her heart squeezed tight as she looked at the baby, and she suddenly understood why the pictures were here and not out in the sitting room, or even placed more privately in his bedroom. It was as if Kyle couldn't bear that kind of constant exposure to his loss, but neither could he bear to not have the photos, so he had placed them in the hall, an area he didn't linger.

The look on Kyle's face as he held his son briefly riveted her and, for a splintered moment, the years spun back. Her own mother hadn't coped with losing her children. And suddenly, she understood that Kyle didn't just not want more children; after what had happened, he couldn't bear to have any more.

Eva had lost her brother and sisters and, ultimately, her mother. But she could not imagine the grief of losing a child.

Feeling subtly unsettled by the window into Kyle's past, she stepped into the cool, tiled bathroom. After using the facilities, she found herself staring at her reflection and wondering how on earth she could compete with the wife Kyle had loved and chosen, and who had *died*.

On impulse, Eva took the pins out of her hair and let it fall around her shoulders, much as Nicola's had in the photo—then, feeling foolish, recoiled and repinned it.

She wasn't Nicola and never could be. Nicola had been fresh-faced, cute and athletic, while Eva was curvy and sultry and city sleek. From everything she had heard about Nicola, they were very different. There was no way she could compete. But it was also true that Kyle had never forgotten her.

Heart beating too fast, mind working overtime, Eva reviewed every conversation, the clashes and the fights, the heavy-handed surveillance, the lovemaking and the one salutary fact that couldn't be ignored. After staying away from her for ten years, Kyle had come back. And he hadn't just blended into the scenery. He had been the dominant male in her life for the past year and had systematically gotten rid of every man she had chosen.

When Eva returned from the bathroom, Kyle had set out a selection of salads, cold meats and a savory quiche on the table. She met his gaze briefly. When his scrutiny dropped to her mouth, the undisciplined tumble of thoughts coalesced into clear knowledge. Kyle had honored her condition that they did not sleep together, but at the same time he had made no bones about the fact that he still wanted her, and not just sexually. She was certain now that he wanted *her*.

Delightful warmth suffused her. Until that moment, she hadn't realized how much that would matter. But since they had made love, she felt more intimately connected with Kyle, to the point that whenever he was near she hummed with awareness.

Conscious of the weight of the ring on her finger and the flash and glitter of the pretty diamond, Eva filled her plate from a tempting selection of salads. After choosing sparkling water, she followed Kyle out onto the patio.

While she ate, Eva kept glimpsing the diamond on her finger and couldn't help the rush of pleasure that, aside from the conventional need of a ring, Kyle had been so thoughtful. Under the circumstances, she hadn't expected a ring, let alone one that was so utterly gorgeous.

Kyle caught her gaze. "I ran into Sophie and Francesca this morning."

Eva almost choked on a mouthful of sparkling water. If Sophie and Francesca had chosen lives that did not revolve around the fashion industry, they would have been CIA, FBI or some form of Special Forces covert ops, no question. As it was, within the extended Atraeus/Ambrosi/Messena family, they were a force to be reckoned with. "You ran into them or they ran you to ground?"

Kyle's mouth quirked. "We work in different parts of town, so a chance meeting isn't likely. Sophie mentioned something about a bridesmaid and a guest list."

Eva set her glass down. "Your family need to be part of the wedding—"

Kyle set his fork down. "Babe, the wedding is two days away, there's not exactly time—"

"You don't have to worry, all you need to do is turn up. All the details are taken care of."

He lifted a brow. "How many have you invited?"

Eva put her fork down. "Just close family. I know you wanted to bypass all the fuss and frills and that you probably wanted to slide the wedding through before most of your family found out, but it is still *my* wedding, probably the only wedding I'll ever have."

Kyle's head came up. "Why won't you marry again?"

She kept her expression bland. "I'm not the marrying kind. I'm just not...suited for it."

Kyle frowned, but before he could reply, his cell rang.

Eva picked at her salad while Kyle walked to one end of the patio and conducted what sounded like a business call. When he came back to the table, his expression was thoughtful, but he didn't resume the conversation.

Relieved, Eva made an effort to eat a little more. Lately, with all the turmoil, she'd been skipping meals and eating sketchily, which was bad for her stress levels. Witness the off-the-register way she kept reacting to Kyle.

When Kyle was finished, she collected their plates and carried them through to the kitchen. Carefully taking off the ring, she set it on the counter, rinsed the plates and glasses and stacked them in the dishwasher.

Kyle, who had followed her in, replaced all the food in the fridge and wiped down the counter. When she dried her hands on a kitchen towel and went to pick up the ring, he beat her to it.

Automatic tension hummed through her as he picked up her left hand and slid the ring on the third finger. Despite trying to downplay the moment, a shimmering thrill went through her at the warmth of his hands, the weight of the ring and the sheer emotion of the moment. This was what he would do on their wedding day, and they both knew it would not mean what it should. But here in the mundane surroundings of his apartment kitchen, the small act seemed laden with meaning.

Kyle's gaze connected with hers. "You're right, it is beautiful."

For a blank moment, she thought he had said, "You're beautiful." She tried for a breezy smile. "Yes. It is."

When she would have stepped back, he kept hold of her hand. If Kyle had been any other man, she would have had no problem putting an end to the tension that had sprung up. But while a cautious part of her knew she should keep things businesslike, the crazy, risk-taking part of her wanted to kiss Kyle, to pretend for just a moment that the engagement, the wedding and *he* were the real thing. Without consciously realizing she had done it, she swayed closer. "We shouldn't."

"The hell with it," Kyle murmured. "We're going to have to kiss in church, and it's not as if we haven't done it before."

The vivid memory of the passionate night they had spent together, and further back to the long-ago necking on the beach at Dolphin Bay, sent a hot flash through her that practically welded her to the spot. Seconds later, Kyle's mouth closed on hers, her arms found their way around his neck and time seemed to slow, stop.

When he finally lifted his head, Kyle studied her expression for another few seconds, as if he was contemplating kissing her again then he released her. "We need to discuss something. Why didn't you tell me you were a virgin?"

Suddenly the choice of his very private apartment for the choosing of the ring and lunch made sense, when it would have been quicker to have gone direct to the jeweler. "It's not exactly something that comes out in casual conversation."

"I thought—"

"I know what you thought." The same thing most people thought. "That I've had more men than hot dinners."

"You don't exactly put across a facade of innocence."

Eva lifted her chin. "In the modeling business, if you're tough, men leave you alone. It's a way of keeping safe."

"Now you're making me angry."

"Don't be. The strategy worked." Until Kyle.

Walking out to the sitting room, she found her bag and hooked the strap over her shoulder, ignoring the question that seemed to hang in the air.

Kyle shrugged into his jacket and adjusted his tie. "I know you're probably not going to answer, but why me, and why now?"

"You're right," she said with a trademark breezy smile, as she headed for the door. "I'm not going to answer."

Eleven

Kyle woke, uncertain what, exactly, had pulled him from yet another restless sleep. Tossing his rumpled sheets aside, he paced to the window. Opening the curtains, he looked out over the now-smooth sweep of lawn to the bay and a delicate and beautiful sunrise.

His wedding day.

Memories cascaded. Another wedding day, clear and hot and filled with family and friends. Nicola, elegant in white. She had been sweet and smart, athletic and funny. Perfect. She had fitted seamlessly into the measured pattern of his life, and when Evan had arrived, that pattern had seemed complete. Until…Germany.

His stomach tightened. Now, a marriage of convenience.

Feeling tense and unsettled, he walked through to the bathroom and flicked on the shower. The problem was, every time he looked at Eva, convenience was the last thing on his mind and the guilt that he wanted her more than he had wanted Nicola, was killing him.

Unbidden, the hours they'd spent locked together in his bed replayed, along with the uncomfortable knowledge that there had been nothing measured about his response.

And that what he had felt had somehow sneaked up on him, eclipsing the past.

His head came up at the curious clarity of the thought. Peripherally, he was aware of the sound of the shower, steam misting the bathroom mirror, the steady beat of his own heart.

He drew a breath, then another, but the tightness in his chest didn't ease. It was an odd moment to notice that Eva had done something with the bathroom. There was a new mat on the floor in a soft shade of turquoise, and brand-new thick, white towels decorated the towel rail. A large glass jar filled with soaps decorated the bathroom vanity.

The feminine, homey touches should have reminded him of Nicola, but they didn't. Somehow, they were one hundred percent, in-your-face Eva.

Moving like an automaton, he stepped beneath the stream of hot water. He considered the moment of self knowledge that had hit him like a bolt from the blue, the guilt of wanting Eva, and that what he felt was different than anything else he had ever experienced.

It occurred to him that in the years since Nicola and Evan had died, he had done his level best to lock the past away but, in doing so, he had also failed to let it go.

And in that moment he finally understood what he needed to do.

Eva stepped out on the landing just as the front door closed with a soft click.

Frowning, she walked down the stairs and glanced through the kitchen windows just in time to see Kyle dressed in jeans and a T-shirt disappear into the garage.

It was possible that he had things to do in town before the wedding, but as it was barely six o'clock, nothing would be open for hours. Dressed so casually, there was no way Kyle was going into work, either.

Feeling unsettled, not least because after the incandescent moments in Kyle's apartment, she had half expected him to follow up with a suggestion that they break the rules and sleep together, and he hadn't.

She stepped out into the hall. The Maserati cruised quietly out of the garage. On impulse, she grabbed her car keys and decided to follow Kyle. It was a little crazy and a lot desperate, but Eva couldn't help thinking something was wrong, that maybe Kyle had gotten cold feet. Given the encounter with Elise the other day, she had to wonder if Elise was the reason. It would certainly explain the cool way he had seemed to shut himself off, as if he couldn't even be bothered trying to pressure her into bed!

Eva accelerated to the end of the drive and managed to catch the taillights of the Maserati as it turned left at an intersection. Fifteen minutes of nervous tailing later, and feeling certain that Kyle would spot her, she braked outside the gates of what was unmistakably a cemetery.

Relief that she had been wrong about Elise gave way to a sick feeling in the pit of her stomach. She had chased after Kyle in a fit of jealousy and had ended up intruding on what must be a very private moment. A moment that did not include her, because Kyle was not visiting Elise or any other old girlfriend. On the day of his wedding to her, he was visiting Nicola and Evan, the wife and child he had loved and lost.

Three hours later, hours that Eva had filled by first getting her hair and nails done then sitting in the kitchen sipping tea, she finally started to get ready for her wedding.

An odd, shaky relief filled her when she heard Kyle's Maserati return. After those moments at the cemetery, her imagination had run wild and she had half expected him to walk away from the marriage.

Although, why would he? she thought flatly. After all, to Kyle it was only a marriage of convenience.

The heat of the day grew more intense and oppressive as Eva changed into the dress Sophie had designed for the simple church-and-garden wedding. A strapless gown with a tight bodice and full, romantic skirt, the dress was made even more gorgeous by the fabric, which was a soft, pale-pink-and-rose-print silk with an ivory tulle overskirt.

Unfortunately, when she came to fasten the dress, which had about thirty tiny cloth-covered buttons at the back, she could get so far and no farther.

Taking a deep breath, she checked her watch. She was running to schedule, but she hadn't considered she would need help dressing and now she was out of time to call someone to come and help her. Another one of the little details she should have thought of, but which, in the rush to get things done, had escaped her.

She glanced out the window at the smooth sweep of lawn she had made sure was mowed and manicured, to where a group of men were setting up a white tent. Walking back to the mirror, she examined her reflection. Her hair was perfect, falling loose and tousled down her back, the soft waves held with hairspray. To match the dress, she had pulled a swath back from her forehead and fastened it with a clip studded with fresh flowers.

Turning, she tried to do up a few more buttons using the mirror, but when the silk-covered buttons kept slipping from her fingers and her arms began to ache, she gave up on the job. Ideally, Jacinta should have been here to help her, but her last text had explained that she'd had car trouble and would meet her at the church.

After checking the time again, Eva stepped out into the hall and went in search of Kyle, hoping against hope that he hadn't left for the church. A door swung open. Kyle emerged from his room and she drew a breath. In a charcoal-gray morning suit, with a white shirt and a maroon silk tie that subtly echoed the deeper color of the roses on her dress, Kyle looked breathtaking.

She half expected him to say that he knew she had followed him that morning, but instead his gaze simply swept her and lingered. She found herself blushing at the soft, intense glow that seemed to make his gaze even bluer.

"I thought I wasn't supposed to see you until the church."

"Jacinta's having car trouble, so I've lost my helper." She turned and showed him the buttons she hadn't been able to reach and tried not to sound too breathless and panicky.

She had always wondered why brides got so uptight and nervous. Now she knew. There were a hundred and one things that could go wrong. Right now she was beginning to wonder if anything would go right. "If you could do the rest of the buttons?"

"No problem. I was going to break the rules and come and see you anyway."

Swallowing at the intent way he was looking at her and feeling utterly confused because she had convinced herself that the attraction he had felt for her had fizzled out, Eva led the way into the sitting room where the light was better and waited for him to fasten the last remaining buttons.

Kyle gently moved her hair aside. The backs of his

fingers brushed her skin, the small searing touch making her breath come in. She closed her eyes and worked at controlling her breathing as he systematically fastened each tiny button.

When he was finished, she opened her eyes and remembered that she was facing a mirror and that Kyle had been able to see her face the whole time. She blushed and hoped like mad that he had been too busy with the buttons to notice that she was having a minor meltdown.

He met her gaze in the mirror. "I expected you to wear white."

She stiffened a little at the reference to her virginity. "I'm over the white dress. It would have reminded me too much of my last wedding."

"The Dolphin Bay extravaganza."

"Which, luckily, paid for the dress."

He produced a case that he must have set down on a side table while he dealt with the buttons. "You should wear these today."

Still off-balance at her response to Kyle, she opened the box and went still inside when she saw a pair of diamond studs and a pendant that matched her engagement ring. "I can't accept these."

"You're an Atraeus bride and these are wedding jewels, a tradition in the Messena and Atraeus families. Mario would have given you a set if he had been alive, and Constantine will expect it." His expression softened. "Aside from that, I want you to have them."

A blush of pleasure went through her that Kyle wanted to give her a special wedding gift, even if he had tacked that bit on the end. The mention of Mario and of Constantine Atraeus, the formidable head of the Atraeus family and CEO of The Atraeus Group, made her feel even more strained. Family was important and celebrated in the Atraeus clan, even if she had never been quite sure that she had been accepted.

Kyle took the pendant from the case and unclipped it. "You don't have to wear them for me. Wear them for Mario."

"That's not fair."

"It wasn't meant to be. Turn around."

She turned and found herself once again facing the large mirror that sat over the mantel of the fireplace. As Kyle fastened the pendant, her heart turned over in her chest. Framed by the carved gilt frame of the mirror, they could have been two people who belonged in another era, another time. She touched the pretty jewel where it hung suspended in the faint hollow of her breasts. Such a small thing, yet it added an indefinable air of nurturing and belonging that made her throat close up. Like the engagement ring, she loved the pendant, not because of its value, but because of what it said about hers. "It's beautiful. Thank you."

Feeling strained and a little misty-eyed, she took the diamond studs when Kyle handed them to her. After removing the pretty pearl studs she had inserted earlier, she fastened them in place. As she did so, she couldn't help being fiercely glad that the wedding to Jeremy had not gone ahead.

Kyle had been right. For all Jeremy's plusses in terms of a convenient marriage, he had been superficial and utterly self-centered. He would never have offered to buy her even a token engagement ring, and he had expected her to pay for the wedding rings and a new wardrobe for him. "This is turning out to be an expensive wedding for you."

Kyle grinned as he checked his watch. "Lucky for me I have a bank."

* * *

Half an hour later, the limousine Eva had ordered arrived. Still feeling flustered but relieved, she attached the ivory tulle veil that slid in just above her rose clip, picked up the bouquets for herself and Jacinta that she'd ordered from her favorite florist, grabbed her handbag with her cell and strolled out to the car.

A tall dark man was leaning down, speaking to the limousine driver. He straightened and half turned and she went into shock all over again as she recognized one of her Atraeus cousins. "Constantine. What are you doing here?"

Normally, Constantine was based on Medinos, the Eastern Mediterranean island that was home to the Atraeus, Messena and Ambrosi families. Occasionally, he and his wife, Sienna, spent time in Sydney, where The Atraeus Group had an office, but he seldom came to New Zealand.

Constantine grinned. "I heard there was a wedding, so I came to give you away."

She was glad she had thought to remember her handbag because now she needed a handkerchief. Juggling the bouquets, she found one and tried to delicately blow her nose so her makeup wouldn't be spoiled. "Who told you?"

"Kyle rang a couple of days ago, so I cleared my schedule. Sienna and Amber came with me. Lucas and Carla and Zane and Lilah were in Sydney, so they hitched a ride in the jet."

Meaning that quite a large chunk of the Atraeus family, with almost no notice, had dropped what they were doing in their high-powered, fast-paced lives to be at her wedding. Eva sniffed, abruptly overwhelmed. With Mario's death, she had been feeling more and more cast adrift, and her natural instinct was to cut ties and minimize the hurt. But it seemed that the more she tried to walk away from this family, the more they found ways to tie her to them.

When she tried to thank Constantine, he gave her a quick hug around the shoulders so as not to crush the flowers then checked his watch. "Time to go." He looked around. "Kyle said there was a bridesmaid."

Eva would have crossed her fingers if she wasn't holding the flowers. "Jacinta will meet us at the church."

When they arrived there, only five minutes' drive away, the cloud cover had increased, blotting out the sun and giving the day a murky cast. Praying that the thick cloud would blow over, Eva let Constantine hand her out of the limousine. There were a few stragglers outside the church, although Eva didn't recognize any of them. She groaned when she started counting children playing around the church grounds. The Vicar had clearly forgotten to reschedule the La Leche League meeting.

A car door popped open. Jacinta waved at her, and Eva's heart sank. Jacinta wasn't wearing her pale pink bridesmaid's dress. Instead she had on a bright, summery dress, one that fairly shouted cocktails on the beach.

Jacinta looked stressed. "I'm sorry. But when I tried to fix the car, I got oil down the front of my dress and had to change."

Sienna poked her head out the church doors. When she saw Eva, she rushed over with a pretty toddler in tow. Handing Amber to Constantine, she gave Eva a hug. "You look gorgeous. Are you ready? Kyle's going nuts in there."

Eva, who seriously doubted that Kyle was going nuts, retrieved the bouquets from the backseat of the limousine. "I'm ready." She nodded at Jacinta, who gave her a relieved grin as she accepted one of the bouquets.

Sienna took Amber off Constantine's shoulder, gave Eva a last reassuring smile and strolled into the church.

Constantine held out his arm. "Ready?"

Feeling a little shaky, Eva placed her hand on Constantine's sleeve. Jacinta remembered to pull Eva's veil over her face and they were good to go.

As the "Wedding March" started and they stepped into the cloistered shadows of the church, her heart thumped hard in her chest. Someone had taken the trouble to light candles in sconces around the wall, and of course the candles on the altar were lit, the flames lending a soft glow to the wooden pews and the vaulted ceiling. There were also flowers everywhere, white-and-pink roses dripping from vases, their scent mingling with the honeyed beeswax of the candles.

Kyle, standing tall and broad-shouldered at the altar, with Gabriel keeping him company as best man, turned, and time seemed to stand still as their eyes met: his tinged with a softness she hadn't expected to see, hers brimming. A little desperately, she reminded herself that she could not afford to feel this way, and neither could Kyle.

Kyle watched as Eva walked toward him in the soft, romantic dress, which clung delicately to her narrow waist, the skirt flowing gracefully with every step. When he'd seen her standing in the hallway of his house, for a moment he'd been stunned because the dress was the exact opposite of the sophisticated gown he had expected her to wear. But in an odd way, the dress summed up the Eva he was just now beginning to know: unconventional, gorgeous and packing a punch.

Gabriel, his eldest brother, and the obvious candidate for best man, since they worked together, caught his gaze. "Are you sure you want to do this?"

Kyle glanced at Eva, noting the way she clung to Constantine's arm. She had a reputation for being tough, professional and coolly composed, but with every day that passed he was coming to understand that the image she projected was as managed as the airbrushed ads she had used to pose for. Beneath the facade the seventeen-year-old girl he had kissed on the beach was still there.

And there was the root of his problem. Somehow, he had never been able to forget Eva even though he had stayed away from her for years, even though he'd married someone else. And Mario had known it. "Yes."

Eva came to a halt beside him and Kyle met Constantine's gaze, which was as male and direct as Gabriel's challenge. Only Constantine's version carried a different message. Marrying an Atraeus was not done lightly. Mario was no longer here, which meant now he would have Constantine to contend with.

As Kyle faced Eva, he should have been painfully reminded of another wedding day, another woman, but his first wedding, as important as it had been, was now viewed through the distance of time. At some point in the past four years, he realized, time had done its work and the grief and loss, while still there, had faded.

Eva took a deep breath as Kyle folded her veil back. A little disconcerted at the steadiness of his gaze, she said her vows steadily, although when it came to the part where they would care for each other through sickness and health, she almost faltered, because that was not in the plan. Kyle placed the ring on her finger, then Gabriel handed her the ring for Kyle.

She slipped the ring on Kyle's finger and experienced a moment of fierce possessiveness. The rings symbolized the vows, commitment, belonging and the exclusiveness of the relationship.

It was not the ideal time to consider the negative implications of her veto on lovemaking, but she was abruptly aware that if she wanted the exclusivity that the rings symbolized, then sex was going to have to be part of their bargain.

Over the past couple of days, she had been brought face-to-face with the unvarnished fact that Kyle might like to have sex sometime in the next two years. She also knew from her reaction to Elise that she would not cope well if Kyle slept around.

The thought that he might have a sexual relationship with Elise or some other unnamed woman made her go still inside. That could not happen. If Kyle was going to have sex, she needed it to be with her.

In a clear voice, the priest pronounced them man and wife. Kyle took her hands and drew her close. Eva met his gaze. "We need to talk."

"Not now." Then his mouth came down on hers, and for long moments her mind went blank.

The signing of the register was a confused affair, because the adjoining room to the chapel was filled with lactating mothers and small children.

Eva signed, then Kyle. When they stepped away from the desk on which the priest had spread the papers, Sienna almost tripped over an extremely interested little person who was clutching at the fabric of her dress.

"Sorry," a pretty young mother murmured, scooping up the little girl. "She thinks you're a princess."

Eva curtsied at the little girl, who giggled. "Then she should have this." Digging in a secret little pocket at the waist of the dress, she found the little blue silk flower she had tucked in the pocket as part of the "something old, something new, something borrowed, something blue" tradition.

When the young mother tried to refuse, she insisted, pressing the silk flower into the little girl's hand. "It's just a little thing and I'd love her to have it." Words she hadn't meant to say tumbled out. "I adore kids."

The young mother picked up the child, who was already demanding the flower be sewed onto her dress. She smiled as she started back to her seat, the little girl waving happily. "Now you'll be able to have some of your own."

Blinking at the sudden wave of emotion that hit her, Eva turned back to the wedding party to find Kyle watching her with an odd expression.

"This is different," Constantine muttered, detaching a toddler from his ankle and gently turning him around so he could crawl back to his mother.

Sienna picked up a pen and signed. "No, it's good," she corrected him. "It's like a day care at a wedding. Amber can play." She moved aside for Constantine and turned to watch Amber, cute in her polka-dot dress, who was busy martialling a group of babies.

As Kyle shook hands with the priest and handed him a check, Sienna chatted about Amber until it was time to walk back into the church.

As Eva bent down to pick up her bouquet, which she'd left on a seat while she signed the register, her stomach hollowed out and her head spun. Gripping the back of the chair, she waited for the dizzy spell to pass. However, when she straightened, she was still a little off-balance.

Kyle's arm came around, steady as a rock. His expression zeroed in on hers. "Are you all right?"

"It's nothing," she muttered, although her vision was still doing weird things. "I didn't eat last night—no time. And I didn't have breakfast."

In fact, she hadn't felt like breakfast, which was unusual. Usually, she woke up ravenous.

Sienna insisted she sit down for a minute, and once she was seated, handed her a wrapped candy. "Here, chew on one of these. I know it's sugar, but they're good when you can't keep breakfast down."

Eva unwrapped the candy and popped it into her mouth. The sugar rush made her head spin, but in a good way. "How did you know I couldn't eat breakfast?"

"The same way I know I can't eat it,' Sienna said. "You're pregnant."

Twelve

Kyle's gaze flashed to hers, his expression unexpectedly grim. "Eva?"

"I can't be." She shouldn't be.

Possibilities flashed through her mind, a mixture of joy and dread, with the dread coming out on top. She wanted no part of the grief and death that had disintegrated her family. As much as she would adore to be a mother, she could not be pregnant.

A chill went through her at the thought of what a pregnancy would do to Kyle. After years grieving for his wife and child, Eva giving birth to a child that would most probably die would literally make him relive the nightmare of his past.

Eva shook her head, regretting the sharp movements almost immediately. "I am not pregnant. No way."

She smiled brightly at Sienna, and Constantine, who was regarding her in a thoughtful way that made her wonder if he could see something she couldn't. Sucking in a breath to stop the roiling in her stomach, she called on the years of acting classes she'd taken, smiled and pushed to her feet. Luckily, thanks to the sugar, she was steady.

Relief and renewed confidence steadied her even more. "See, I'm not pregnant, just hungry."

And to prove it, she would do the one thing she had been shying away from doing as a double check that the morning-after pill had worked—she would use the pregnancy test she had bought and which was still in her handbag.

It would be negative: it had to be. Relieved that she had successfully dealt with the whole idea that she might be pregnant with a child that would most likely die, and which would break both her heart and Kyle's, she forced another smile. "I feel fine now. Really."

Kyle took her arm as they strolled back into the church to a smattering of applause and began their progress down the aisle. "Do you usually skip meals?"

"Only when I'm trying to get married on a twelve-day schedule."

"Have you done a pregnancy test?"

Eva smiled at an elderly Atraeus aunt. "Not yet, but I have one…just to confirm that I'm not pregnant." They stepped out into the vestibule. A cold breeze drifted in, making her shiver.

Briskly, she decided that discussing the whole situation about sex would have to wait until they cleared up the murky area of a pregnancy. "Getting pregnant the first time we made love would be huge bad luck," she muttered. "About as likely as lightning striking the same place, twice."

Lightning flickered as they paused at the top of the church steps.

Kyle inspected the now darkened sky. "What was that you were saying about lightning?"

Her reply was drowned by a crack of thunder, and a split second later the heavens opened. Rain poured down in a heavy gray torrent, drenching the photographer Eva had commissioned. Kyle pulled Eva back into the shelter of the foyer as the photographer collapsed his tripod, flung his coat over his precious equipment and ran for his car.

Lightning flashed again, although it was sheet lightning, she consoled herself, not the jagged fork lightning that would have been an uncanny reminder of the night they had first made love.

Luckily, there was a second venue for the photographs. After twenty minutes of snapping wedding shots at the photographer's studio, Eva dismissed the limousine driver and climbed into Kyle's Maserati.

When they pulled into the driveway of the house, which was lined with guests' cars, the extent of the storm damage was clear. A heavy gust of wind had obviously lifted a corner pole of the marquee clear out of the ground, collapsing half of the tent. The caterer's van was parked near the back door entrance, which opened into the kitchen, so he had clearly made a decision to operate from the house.

Appalled, Eva didn't wait for Kyle, but popped her door open. Dragging her skirts up, she dashed through the rain, which had dropped to a soaking drizzle, making a beeline for the kitchen entrance. As she stepped into the kitchen, which thankfully was a hive of activity and awash with lovely scents, she kept repeating the mantra that in the wedding planning business disasters happened, the thing was to have a backup plan.

Once she was satisfied that the canapés and champagne were already served and that the simple summer picnic menu she'd settled on would go ahead, just inside, she walked through into the sitting room just in time to see Kyle step through the front door. There was a thin smattering of applause, which quickly died away when the guests realized that Kyle was on his own.

Taking a deep breath to control the automatic tension and outright fear that hit her every time she considered that she could be pregnant, Eva claimed Kyle's arm. Calling on all of her acting skills, she accepted congratulations, which had been cut short at the church, and when she got the chance grabbed a glass of sparkling water and nibbled on canapés.

Kyle lifted a brow at her water. "No champagne?"

Eva immediately caught his drift. If she were pregnant, she would be avoiding all alcohol. Heat flushed her cheeks, along with another sharp jab of panic. She forced a smile and tried to keep things light. "Habit. I don't usually drink at all, I don't have a head for it, and I usually only ever drink sparkling water at weddings."

They were interrupted by Constantine, who had made himself the unofficial MC. After toasts and speeches, a late lunch was served. By that time, the summer squall had passed and the sun had come out. Jacinta, who had taken control of the indoor service, opened the French doors and dried off the outdoor furniture.

Kyle and his brothers carried over the tables from the wrecked marquee, which was now steaming in the heat; guests moved out onto the patio.

Zane Atraeus, Constantine's youngest brother, styled himself the unofficial bartender, and so the day took on a shape that kept putting a lump in Eva's throat. The things she had expected to go right had crashed and burned, but the unexpected presence of her Atraeus cousins, who had come a long way *for her*, gave her something unutterably precious; for the first time she truly felt part of her own family.

When she saw Carla, the wife of Lucas, who was the third Atraeus brother, struggling to eat salad from a plate while she held her baby boy in her lap, Eva set her own plate aside and offered to hold him.

With David in her lap, contentedly chewing on a teething ring, and listening to Carla chat about the alterations she and Lucas were making to their house in Sydney, she slowly relaxed. Although, holding David, the urgent question of whether she was pregnant or not kept resurfacing. As she talked interior decorating loves and hates with Carla, she determined that she would take the pregnancy test as soon as she got a few minutes to herself.

Kyle, who was caught in a cluster of aunts who were obviously grilling him, caught her gaze, his own ironic. The small moment in the midst of the noisy gathering was oddly heartwarming. Since the tension that had arisen over the question of a pregnancy, she and Kyle had not had one private moment together.

After the cutting of the cake, which was a pretty selection of cupcakes iced with white chocolate icing and pink sugar rosebuds and arranged in tiers, with one large cake on the top tier, someone put on a classical waltz.

Kyle held out his hand. "They're playing our song."

Eva set her plate down, pleased to do so, even though the cake was delicious. The faint nausea, which had continued, was spelling a death knell to her hopes. "I hadn't planned on dancing."

He shrugged as he drew her close, his hand warm at her waist. "It's a Medinian tradition," he said, referring to the Mediterranean island from which the Messena and Atraeus families had originated.

She inhaled, catching the clean scent of his skin edged with a tantalizing whiff of a cologne that was now heart-wrenchingly familiar. Feeling suddenly absurdly fragile and as if she had to soak up scents and sights and sounds before everything came to pieces, she placed her hand on Kyle's shoulder. Their closeness shunted her back to their night together and the shattering intimacy of lying in bed with Kyle. She could still remember the way he had smelled and felt and tasted—the way he had made her feel.

She concentrated on keeping her expression smooth and serene as heat from every point of contact zinged through her. As they began to dance to a well-known waltz by Strauss, desperate to distract herself from sensations that were just a little too intense, she breathlessly asked, "What did the aunts say?"

Kyle completed a turn as they reached the edge of the patio, in the process pulling her more firmly against him. "Apparently, Mario instructed them to make sure I gave you a proper Medinian wedding."

She frowned, caught by the oddness of the phrase. "Did they assume that you would marry me?"

He hesitated long enough for her to know that she was right. "Apparently, Mario discussed it with them before he made the will."

Thankfully now, others were dancing and the noise of the music and the general buzz of conversation was enough to create the privacy she suddenly desperately needed, when it seemed that nothing about their relationship was private in the family. She knew she shouldn't be upset, but the thought that Kyle was really only marrying her because Mario had put pressure on him struck a sensitive nerve.

Everything that happened with Kyle mattered, *because she loved him*.

She went still inside as the truth she'd been avoiding for weeks finally sank in.

Not only did she love him, she had always loved him, right from the very first moment. She had even loved him when he had dumped her, which was why it had hurt so much.

She stared at a pulse beating at the side of his throat, feeling even sicker than she had when eating the cake. "But when Mario suggested you should marry me, you didn't agree."

"I promised to see you married—"

"But you would never have chosen to marry me." A couple whirled past, Zane and Lilah, utterly absorbed in one another, both wildly in love, the complete opposite of her and Kyle. "You just had to in the end, because I ran out of time."

His hold on her tightened infinitesimally. "It wasn't exactly like that and you know it."

She stopped dancing and pulled free. "Then how was it?" She felt tense and on edge, her heart pounding. She wanted to believe that Kyle felt something more for her than duty and desire, but she also knew she had to try and be objective. No burying her head in the sand.

He caught her fingers and pulled her close again. "If I hadn't wanted you for myself, I would have let you go ahead and marry one of the men you chose." He paused. "You know I want you, and after that night on the beach, I think you know how much."

She drew a breath. "What about…love?"

His gaze cooled. "What about it?"

She tilted her head and looked into Kyle's face, the blue of his eyes, his Mediterranean heritage obvious in his olive skin, the clean cut of his cheekbones and jaw. "I love you." The words were flat and declarative, but she couldn't hide what she wanted. "The question is, can you love again, after losing your wife and child?"

Can you love me?

He did a slow turn into an alcove of the room that was private. "We need to slow this down. You agreed to a legal marriage," he said quietly, "one you stipulated would be without sex. That's not exactly a recipe for love."

Eva instantly regretted trying to lever some kind of confession of love from Kyle. She hated the enigmatic expression on his face, as if he needed to conceal his emotions in case she saw what he was really feeling. She had seen that look on the faces of social workers and foster parents when she'd been passed from home to home as a kid. It was duty, minus emotion, the exact opposite of what she wanted!

She met his gaze squarely. "Can you really separate love from passion so completely?"

"Eva—"

"No, don't say it. Don't say anything." The conversation had always been risky, but she had blown it completely, because while failing to obtain any admission from Kyle, he now knew that she loved him.

Her cheeks burned at the kind of vulnerability she had spent years avoiding. "Ask a silly question…" she said a little bitterly. "People separate love from sex all the time."

Only, she never did. She had only ever slept with the one man she loved.

Turning on her heel, she left the room. As she walked, she could feel Kyle's gaze boring into her back. As soon as she stepped out into the spacious foyer, she felt better. At times their relationship had felt like a game, but it wasn't anymore; it was serious and important, because she needed Kyle to love her. This morning it had felt as if they were balanced on the brink of that possibility, but now...

Lifting her skirts, she took the stairs to the upper level. She was hot, her feet were hurting and after possibly the most embarrassing conversation of her life she needed a moment. As she stepped into the dimness of the upstairs hall, she almost walked into Constantine who was quietly strolling along with Amber dead asleep over one broad shoulder. Eva stared at the picture father and daughter made then quietly escaped into her room.

Peeling off her shoes, she sat down on the edge of her bed. Tired of coping with the dress and its long skirt, she started on the buttons and eventually managed to ease out of the layers of silk and tulle.

She changed into a light silk shift in rich summer shades of berry red, with touches of pink, purple and leaf green. Hanging the bridal gown in the closet, she slipped on a pair of comfortable sandals that left her feet mostly bare.

After checking her makeup to make sure the dampness in her eyes hadn't smudged her mascara, she spritzed herself with perfume and walked back downstairs. As she reached the last tread, the front door, which was not locked, swung quietly open and a face from the past that she hoped she would never see again stopped her in her tracks.

Sheldon Ferris, his countenance deceptively average—the boy next door grown into middle age—smiled, his gaze taking in the rich foyer, "Nice house. You've done well for yourself."

Eva's fingers tightened on the banister. "I don't know how you found me, but you need to leave now, before I ring the police."

His gaze darted to either side, checking to see if anyone was about to disturb them. "And charge me with what? Knocking on your door?"

"I know it was you who trashed my house. I haven't given the police your name yet, but if I do, by next week there could well be a warrant out for your arrest."

Fear flashed across his expression, but it was replaced almost immediately by a hard-eyed determination. "And I know why you haven't given them my name. You don't want anyone to know about your trashy background—"

"There's nothing wrong with my background."

"Then why is it such a big secret? I checked. There are plenty of stories about your modeling success, but nothing about your past. But I guess if you don't care about your gutter upbringing, you won't mind if I splash it all over the press. I can see the headline now, 'Street kid, sex symbol rises to become Atraeus heiress.'"

"You know very well I was not a street kid, or a sex—"

"Give me what I want and I won't sell the story. I'll leave you alone for good." He named a figure that was even larger than the one he had quoted before. "Pay up, and I won't tell your new husband what's wrong with you. You'll never hear from me again."

Eva sincerely doubted that. She stared at the shifty gleam in his eyes, not for the first time wondering what her mother had ever seen in him. She guessed he had been younger and handsome in a lean way; now he was a little heavier with gray at his temples and his suit had seen better days. "I'm not paying you a cent. And if you think you can threaten me with telling Kyle anything at all about my past, you can forget it. Believe me, nothing you could ever say would make any difference to our marriage."

And that was nothing more than the truth.

The sound of footsteps made Ferris shrink back onto the front porch: the fear in his expression was palpable. Eva didn't wait to see who it was, no doubt strolling from the sitting room down the hall to the bathroom. She grasped the edge of the door and looked Ferris square in the face. "Mario had information about you. Pretty sure, if I look long enough, I'll find out what it was, and when I do, I'll take it to the police."

She closed the door firmly and held her breath as the shadow of Ferris's outline seen through the frosted glass disappeared. Feeling empowered that she had faced down her ex-stepfather, who had always been something of a bully, Eva walked back upstairs to her room and found her tote bag.

Extracting her phone, she rang Auckland Central and left a message for Detective Hicks to let him know that Ferris had called at her house, demanding money. She also stated that he had been harassing her and that she was certain he was the person who had broken into her house. The next call was to the PI she had retained. He didn't pick up, either, so she left a message asking him to forward any information he had found out about Ferris to Detective Hicks.

She hung up and considered the threat Ferris had made. She knew he would carry through and go to the press, which meant she was out of time.

Her heart squeezed tight as she considered what the disclosure of her dysfunctional background and her genetic disorder would do to her relationships with her adoptive family and with Kyle. Kyle wanted her sexually, and they had shared tender moments, but he had just not had enough time to fall for her. She had hoped they would have time, but if she was pregnant, her time had run out.

When she replaced the phone in her bag, her fingers brushed the pregnancy test kit she had bought.

As much as she needed to know if she was pregnant or not, she couldn't do the test right now, because to do so was to know the truth. And if she was pregnant, she would be honor bound to tell Kyle.

In retrospect, her decision to veto sex had been a huge mistake.

She loved Kyle; she had loved him for years. It was a depressing thought, but she had to wonder if she would ever fall for anyone else, or if Kyle was it for her. If that was the case, and she was beginning to think it was, then she couldn't let him go without a fight.

She was out of time. She needed to try one last time with Kyle, no matter how exposing or hurtful it was. She needed to change the rules and exploit the one power she did hold in the hope that Kyle would, finally, fall for her.

She needed to make love to her husband on their wedding night.

Thirteen

Kyle would have followed Eva if one of the aunts hadn't buttonholed him. After frustrating minutes of listening to a genealogy that went back to some obscure coastal village in Phoenicia, now modern-day Lebanon, his younger brother, Damian, took pity on him, clapped him on the shoulder and insisted he help him with the marquee.

Snagging a couple of bottles frosted with condensation, Damian handed one to Kyle and jerked his head in the direction of the tent, which was flapping gently in the evening breeze. "Aunt Emilia and the family tree," Damian's expression took on a hunted cast. "How far back did she get? The First Crusade?"

"Not quite. You interrupted her during the Third."

"Cool. You owe me one."

Damian bypassed the marquee entirely and stopped where the edge of the lawn dropped away to the small crescent beach below. "Although, strictly speaking, I'm in your debt."

Beginning to be annoyed, because he was certain Damian was referring to his marriage, Kyle watched the sun as it sank by slow increments into the sea, casting a brassy glow across the water. "You are not in my debt."

Damian gave him an, are-you-for-real look. "You did the deed," he said mildly. "I didn't think you'd let Mario pressure you into marrying Eva."

Kyle's jaw tightened. "Don't talk about my wife like that," he said softly. He met Damian's gaze. Damian, for all his youth, was something of a hard-ass, but Kyle had lived and fought with tougher men. "Mario applied pressure on all of us, but that wasn't why I married Eva."

"I don't believe it—you're in love with her."

Kyle frowned at the conclusion Damian had reached. What he felt for Eva was deep and turbulent. When other attractions had faded, somehow the fiery sexual connection that sparked between them when they were teenagers had held. For reasons he could not fathom, Eva was different for him. But he did not think the difference was about love.

For a start, because he'd spent so many years staying away from Eva, he didn't know about large chunks of her life. Come to that, he didn't know about almost any aspect of her life until Mario had adopted her.

His lack of knowledge about Eva made him frown. He had already engaged a security firm to put together a file for him. It was too late in the day to check with them now, but he would make it his business to check on progress in the morning.

Damian finished his beer, checked his watch and indicated they should walk back to the house. "I forgot that you once had a thing for Eva. After you lost Nicola and the baby, I guess I didn't think you'd marry again."

The mention of Nicola and Evan made Kyle's chest

tighten, although, like the conversation he'd had with Eva in the car the night they'd made love, he was actually able to think of them again without reliving the horror of the explosion. Somehow, the one thing he hadn't thought would happen had: he was finally beginning to heal.

Kyle let the still-full bottle of beer dangle from his fingers. "I miss Nicola and Evan," he said flatly. He and Nicola had had a good life together. She had come from a military family and had understood the life. They had traveled together and eventually made a baby together. "But they're gone."

He frowned as the conversation referenced the thought that had not been far from his mind for a couple of weeks now, the possibility, even if it was remote, that he could be a father again despite what Eva had said.

He examined how he would feel if she was pregnant and hit the same blank wall he had lived with for years. The raw fact was he just couldn't go there again. He couldn't be a father again.

Damian strolled onto the patio. "Nice piece of real estate."

Kyle scanned the guests, although he couldn't spot Eva. "The twins told me about it."

"I didn't know Sophie and Francesca were in the market for a house."

"They weren't," he said deliberately. "Eva was."

Damian shook his head. "I don't know why I was so worried." Shaking his head, he clapped Kyle on the shoulder and strolled off to join his girlfriend. Sky was a lean blonde, with ultrashort hair and dark eyes and who could ride a stock horse almost as well as Damian.

Kyle dragged at his tie, loosening it. Damian thought he had fallen for Eva and had bought her the house as a gift. He should correct him, but there was no way he could lay bare the truth that he had used the house as leverage in order to convince Eva that she should move in with him.

The whole business had involved a ruthless streak he had not known he possessed, although it was a fact that ruthless male behavior ran in the family. Constantine had kidnapped Sienna, and Lucas had decided not to mess with a successful formula and had done the same with his wife, Carla. Kyle's oldest brother, Gabriel, had proposed a fake engagement to keep his wife Gemma in his bed, and Nick had not been much better, luring Elena to the Dolphin Bay Resort under false pretenses then cheating on a bet to get her in his bed.

Frowning when he didn't immediately see Eva, Kyle deposited the beer he hadn't bothered to drink on a table and went to find her, but instead got caught up in a flurry of goodbyes as Constantine, Lucas and Zane, all with arms full of sleepy kids, made their way to their cars. The caterer had finished packing up his equipment and had left while he'd been talking to Damian and, thankfully, so had the bevy of aunts.

Damian, his jacket slung over one shoulder, his arm wrapped securely around Sky, lifted a hand in farewell. He was followed by the twins, who grinned, kissed and hugged him, signifying that the conclusion Damian had jumped to had spread through the family like wildfire.

By the time Kyle stepped back inside, the house seemed eerily empty, except for the kitchen staff who were busily tidying up glasses and bottles in the sitting room.

Jerking his tie from his shirt, Kyle walked to the French doors and began closing the house up for the night. As he locked the last door, he checked his watch. It had been a good thirty minutes since he and Eva had argued on the dance floor.

His stomach tightened at the thought that Eva might have been upset enough to walk out. And in that moment he realized that, despite his attempts to control the way he felt about her, he hadn't succeeded. It had been evident in his knee-jerk reaction when Damian had spoken about Eva and the way he had claimed her as his wife.

It was evident in the way he felt now. Tension coursed through him at the thought that Eva might have been upset enough after their conversation to leave him, then a footfall registered and he turned to see her walking down the stairs.

A van door sliding closed then the roar of the caterer's van heading down the drive sounded.

Kyle noticed the test kit in her hands and went still inside. "What's the result?"

Eva reached the bottom of the stairs, her face oddly pale. "I haven't used it yet. I guess I'm a coward, but the plain fact is I don't want to know until tomorrow."

She slipped the tube back into its box and placed it on a hall table and walked toward him. "There's just one other thing. I've changed my mind."

She stopped close enough that she could feel the heat emanating from Kyle's skin. She ran a finger down his chest. The heady masculine scents of clean skin and the subtle spice of sandalwood made her head spin.

Kyle's hand curled over hers, holding her palm to his chest. "What about?"

Lifting up on her toes, she boldly wound one arm around his neck, leaned in close and gently bit down on one lobe. "About the clause in the agreement that prohibits sex. If anyone is going to sleep with my husband, it's going to be me."

"There's not exactly a line." When she would have drawn back, his hands closed on her hips, holding her against him. "I'll get my lawyer to strike out the clause in the morning."

"But as long as we have a verbal agreement, the new condition is in effect."

"We could shake on it," he muttered, "but I've got a better idea." Lowering his head, he finally did what she had been dying for him to do ever since the wedding ceremony; he kissed her.

Long minutes later, the world went sideways as Kyle picked her up. When he reached the top of the stairs, instead of going into her room, he continued on down the hall and into the master suite, where he set her on her feet. The sun was down now, and the room was dim with shadows. Moonlight silvered the walls and threw light over the large bed occupying the middle of the room.

Kyle cupped her face and bending, he kissed her again. "Since we have a new agreement, this is where you'll be sleeping from now on."

She tried to both kiss him and start on the buttons of his shirt. When he finally lifted his mouth, she finished the buttons. "You won't get an argument from me."

"Can I get that in writing?"

"No chance." She caught the corner of his grin, as if he liked it that she argued with him, and out of nowhere hope flared, built on the foundation of a long-ago friendship and the mystifying strength of the connection that had always sizzled between them.

"Thought so." He shrugged out of the shirt and let it drop to the floor.

Closing her arms around his neck, she lifted up against him, loving the hard-muscled planes of his body held tight against hers. She felt his fingers at the zipper of her dress. Seconds later, it drifted to the floor. Her bra followed, and she shivered at the searing heat of his skin against hers. Kyle's fingers tangled in her hair, and she found herself walked backward in the direction of the bed.

He bent his head and took one breast into his mouth, and for long moments her belly coiled tight, the room seemed to spin and there was no air.

The first few times they had made love the sensations had been intense, now they seemed even more so and the awareness of the changes to her body settled in more deeply. She could not say for sure she was pregnant, but with every fiber of her being she felt it to be so and the knowledge added a depth and poignancy to their lovemaking, because every touch, every caress could be the last.

When Kyle lifted his head, Eva ran her hands down his torso and deliberately unfastened his pants. She heard his swiftly indrawn breath, felt his tension. A split second later, he had scooped her up and deposited her on the bed. She watched as he peeled out of his trousers, but when she would have expected him to come down beside her, he remained standing and she realized he had a condom and was sheathing himself. When he climbed onto the bed beside her, she wound her arms around his neck and pulled him close.

She felt the drag of her panties as he peeled them down and obligingly shimmied a little, helping him get rid of that last barrier. She felt his gaze on her in the dimness as he came down between her legs. Loving the weight of him, she clutched at his shoulders as slowly, gently, he fitted himself to her.

His gaze connected with hers again. "Okay?"

"I'm fine." Lifting up against him, she pulled his mouth to hers and kissed him, the passion white-hot and instant as they began to move together. Long moments later, caught in a maelstrom of sensations that were almost too intense to bear, the responses peaked, jerking through her in dizzying waves. Moments later, Kyle collapsed beside her then half rolled, pulling her into a loose hold.

The room had darkened further, so that the shadows appeared inky and the moonlight by contrast threw stark, cold light over the bare floorboards and the bed.

Kyle's fingers tangled in her hair, stroking the strands, as if he loved the feel of it. Emboldened, Eva propped herself on one elbow and studied the planes and angles of his face. She cupped his jaw, enjoying the abrasive roughness of his five-o'clock shadow. "How many times can you do that?"

Kyle's head turned into her touch. He caught her hand, bringing it to his mouth. "It depends. How many times did you want?"

"Once more, at least." Gathering her courage, Eva straddled him. Since the first night together, she'd made it her business to do some in-depth research about sex and had made some fascinating discoveries in the process. "But this time I get to be on top."

Fourteen

Eva got up just as dawn touched the sky with gray. Sliding from the bed, she walked softly to her room, found her robe and belted it at her waist. Still moving quietly, she walked barefoot down to the front foyer, retrieved the test kit and took it with her into the downstairs bathroom.

After she had used the kit, she set the stick carefully down on top of the cardboard box it had come in and washed and dried her hands. There were two windows in the stick. According to the instructions, if the smaller one showed a line, that meant she had done the test correctly, if the second window also showed a line, that was a positive result.

Taking a deep breath, she checked the stick. There were two lines.

She sat down on the side of the bath, her heart pounding. She was pregnant. The morning-after pill hadn't worked.

She had known it. Her period was late, and even though so little time had passed, she felt different. Her breasts were tender and she had gone off food. Her sense of smell had become acute, so that scents that hadn't bothered her before were suddenly overpowering.

She touched her abdomen, feeling a sense of wonder that there was a baby forming inside her. In the same instant, dread struck as she wondered if, in the lottery of genetic inheritance, her baby would lose. Her twin had died at age four. Her younger brother and sister had almost made it to five.

Just long enough for her and Kyle—if he agreed they should stay together—to fall hopelessly in love with their child before having to say goodbye.

Which was why she had to leave now. Kyle had already loved and lost a baby, but at least, as tragic as his loss had been, it had happened fast and unexpectedly.

If she left now, she could go through the pregnancy and birth alone. She could choose to have the baby tested while she was pregnant, or wait until after it was born. Once she knew the result, she would contact Kyle and let him know. If the child was healthy, she would happily share custody if that's what Kyle wanted. Given that this was a Messena child, she could not imagine that he would turn his back on his child. Kyle was an honorable man; when it came to the crunch he would be a father. But she was under no illusions about how he would feel about her for forcing the issue. She did not think they would have any chance now of a real marriage.

If the child was affected, it would break *her* heart. She didn't know how she would cope alone, but she would. Her mother had never recovered from watching three of her children die, but she was determined to be stronger than that. This child was precious. She would love it for every second that it was with her and if she was very, very lucky, maybe the baby wouldn't have the disorder.

Pushing to her feet, she put the stick back in the box and dropped it in the bin then walked quietly upstairs. She had packed last night, so other than changing into a pair of jeans and a soft cotton hoodie and slipping on sneakers, she was ready to go. Although, she needed to write Kyle a note first.

Berating herself for not thinking to do that last night, she looked for pen and paper. There were pens in her tote, but the only paper was the back of an envelope. Beginning to feel a little frantic, because it was almost fully light now and she knew Kyle was an early riser, she quickly scribbled a note, explaining that she was leaving him and that she relinquished all rights to her inheritance until she was forty and that he could have the house.

The plumbing gurgled as if the upstairs shower had just been turned on, which it probably had. Adrenaline pumped. That meant Kyle was awake.

She picked up her overnight bag and checked that the hall was empty. Walking as quietly as she could, she made her way downstairs, wincing as a tread on the steps creaked under the extra weight of the bag.

She placed the note on the hall table, along with her wedding and engagement rings and paused at the door to take a last look at the house. Throat aching, tears misting her eyes, she unhooked the chain then slowly turned the big old-fashioned key in its lock so it wouldn't make a loud clunking noise and pushed the door wide.

Cool morning air swirled around her as she gently closed the door, groaning at the audible click it made. Jogging to her car, which she had parked around by the garage so that wedding guests would have plenty of room out front to park, she loaded her tote and bag.

She glanced at the kitchen windows, her heart pounding because she half expected to see Kyle, then climbed behind the wheel, started the engine and backed out. Gravel crunched beneath the tires, preternaturally loud in the early morning air. Certain Kyle must have heard, she spared a last glance for the house, but the front door was closed and windows were blank. Depressing the accelerator, she took off down the drive.

Kyle wrapped the towel around his waist when he heard the sound of Eva's car starting. Cold knowledge hit him as he strode past her room and noted that the dressing table was bare. Cursing beneath his breath, he made it down the stairs and outside in time to see the taillights of her little sports car wink as she went down the drive.

Stomach tight, he strode upstairs, found his phone and called her. When he got her answering service, he tried again just in case she was stuck in traffic and hadn't had time to pull over and answer the call. He rang a couple more times then gave up.

He found clothes, pulled on a pair of jeans and a T-shirt then tried the phone again. Jaw tightening, he retrieved the keys to his Maserati from the top of his dresser and took the stairs two at a time. It was possible Eva had gone to work, although he didn't think so. He knew for a fact that she didn't have any weddings happening for a couple of weeks, and Jacinta was running the office meantime.

He yanked the front door open then stopped when something fluttered to the floor. He picked up the envelope, which was covered with scrawled writing, as if Eva had written it in a hurry, and read then reread the words. His stomach hollowed out.

Eva had left him.

She knew that meant that she would not receive her

inheritance, but she would manage without it. Without the inheritance she couldn't buy the house, so Kyle could keep it.

Except that Kyle didn't want the house if Eva wasn't going to be in it. He had bought it for her.

Correction, he thought grimly, he had bought it for them, in order to make marriage to him more palatable for Eva.

When push had come to shove, he had been just as manipulative as Mario in trying to entice Eva back into his life.

She had left him.

His heart was pounding, and he was having trouble thinking. The last time he had felt like this had been in Germany when he had lost Nicola and Evan, but at that point there had been nothing he could do.

He had to think. Something had happened. It had to be that Eva was pregnant.

In the moment he also understood that the secrecy about Eva's past—a past he had only just begun to probe—was somehow tied in with the pregnancy. He didn't know how, but it was a fact that Eva reacted to children in a way that wasn't normal. She adored them but had seemed to recoil from the idea of being pregnant and having her own.

Setting the note back down on the hall table, he decided there was no point in driving to Eva's house or her business premises. She wouldn't be at either place, because she knew he would look there.

He did a quick search of her room. The jewelry case with the pendant and earrings was on top of a dresser. All of the dresser drawers were empty. The wedding gown and the shoes she'd worn were in the closet, but nothing else. There was no sign of the pregnancy test kit.

He checked his bedroom and the bathroom, but the small trash can was empty. Frowning, he went back downstairs and did a systematic search of the rooms. In the first-floor bathroom, he found the pregnancy test kit discarded in the trash. When he pulled out the little stick, he noted the two lines. At a guess, that meant she was pregnant. He scanned the instruction leaflet, which confirmed it.

He stared at the stick with its positive result, took a deep breath then another. He felt like he'd been kicked in the chest. Eva was pregnant with his child. He was going to be a father. Again.

The thought filled him with a crazy pastiche of emotions—delight and the cold wall he'd hit when Nicola and Evan had died; horror and grief and self-recrimination.

One other salient fact registered. He loved Eva.

Correction, he was *in love* with her, because just saying the word *love* didn't seem to encompass the intense out-of-control emotions that kept gripping him. He was in love with Eva Atraeus, and if he was honest, by varying degrees he had been in love with her since he was nineteen. But Mario's complete veto of their relationship had closed that door.

She loved him.

There was no other reason for her to run. But he had been too concerned with guarding his own emotional safety—the protective habit that had dominated the past four years—to appreciate that love.

He had fallen for Eva, but he had ruthlessly suppressed any softer feelings and focused on the sex. He had played it safe, using the surface image Eva projected as his compass north, even when he knew it was just a facade.

Now there was a child, and in that moment, he knew that nothing mattered but Eva and their child.

The specter of the past and his failure to protect his wife and child was just that, a burden of guilt he'd hung on to for too long and which hadn't changed anything. Logically, he had always known that he could never have saved them. The terrorist attack had not been predictable.

But he would not fail again. Eva was pregnant. They were going to have a child. He needed to be there for Eva and the baby—if she would let him.

That long-ago conversation with Mario suddenly made him go cold inside. He had said Eva needed protection. Protection from what? He could remember asking Mario at the time and not getting a straight answer. He had assumed Mario had meant emotional protection, but what if it was protection from something or someone else?

Suddenly the break-in at Eva's house took on an added significance. A lot of items had been strewn over the floor, but a family photo had been set on the dining room table. Annoyed with himself for missing clues that should have alerted him to the fact that Eva had a problem, he walked through to the kitchen, picked up the phone and rang Gabriel.

Gabriel picked up on the second ring, his voice gruff.

Kyle explained he was taking a few days because Eva had run out on him. "She's pregnant."

There was a small silence. "And the pregnancy's a problem?"

Put like that, Eva running out sounded like a simple reaction to an unplanned pregnancy, but Kyle knew it was a whole lot more than that. "She knows how I feel about having a child. She's gone, Gabe. She's prepared to end the marriage and let the inheritance go into trust."

"I'm listening."

Kyle filled Gabriel in on the break-in and his suspicion that someone from Eva's past was putting pressure on her, maybe with blackmail.

Kyle heard a voice in the background, Gemma, and Gabriel's voice, muffled, as if his hand was over the receiver. "I had a conversation with Mario shortly before he died. Eva had a stepfather. Apparently, he stole all of Eva's mother's possessions shortly before she died. Not content with that, he tried to blackmail Mario. There was also a medical issue, although Mario didn't go into detail about it."

The thought that Eva could be sick made Kyle frown. She had seemed perfectly healthy, but plenty of illnesses were invisible until the last stages. "I need to know more about Eva's past. I think I need to access Mario's safe deposit box."

"Meet me at the bank in thirty minutes."

Kyle hung up. Until the moment he had seen her car disappearing down the drive, he had been able to fool himself that what he and Eva had was controllable and, for want of a better word, convenient for them both.

It wasn't. Control had been an illusion. He had wanted her from the beginning. But it was more than that now. Somewhere along the way, the wanting had turned to a need that was bone deep and inexplicable.

He had always thought that love between a man and a woman came down to a romantic cocktail of sex and companionship, but what he felt for Eva was raw and primitive. She had made him see *her* and not the savvy businesswoman, and she had stunned him with her capacity to love.

She loved him.

Until that moment, he hadn't understood what it must have cost her to say those words. Still locked into the failure and guilt of his own past, the goodbyes he had said at the graves the morning of the wedding, he hadn't been able to respond.

When he hung up, he remembered the note, which was written on the back of an envelope. Walking back to the hall, he found it and reread it then turned it over. All the hairs at the base of his neck lifted when he noted that the address on the used envelope was for a PI.

Walking through to his study, he found his laptop, Googled the PI and found that Zachary Hastings specialized in locating missing persons and covering domestic situations. Certain he was close to discovering exactly what was going on in Eva's life, he checked the time. Hastings's office wouldn't be open for an hour. Frustrated, he forced himself to make coffee while he tried to phone Eva again. When she refused to pick up, he left a message, asking her to call him.

He made one more call to the young detective, Hicks, who had been investigating the break-in at Eva's house. The information that Hicks provided, that they had a suspect and that Eva had made a statement to the effect that the same suspect had been harassing her, made his jaw compress.

Hicks wouldn't provide him with the name of the person they were investigating, because all of the paperwork was under Eva's name, but Kyle was willing to bet it was the stepfather. It was just another example of how Eva, with the self-sufficient streak she had, out of necessity, acquired as a child—and which he had seen as a hard, brassy confidence—was used to managing on her own.

Gabriel was grim faced as they stepped into the sterile vault that housed their safe deposit boxes. He produced the two keys required, and Kyle opened the box, which was filled with family jewelry and documents.

Kyle found the adoption papers with Eva's birth name and those of her parents. He made a note of all three names and their birth dates. He flipped through the documents, which were mostly investment portfolios. At the bottom of the box, he found an envelope addressed to Mario. It was filled with Eva's medical reports.

"Bingo," he said softly.

Suddenly, he was beginning to have a glimmer of what Mario had meant all those years ago by Eva needing "protection." Eva had a genetic disorder. He didn't know what the implications of the disorder meant, exactly, but by the end of the day he would.

In amongst the paperwork was a psychologist's report. Apparently, after years of trying to fix the dysfunction in her family, Eva had, at age fourteen, chosen to walk away from her mother and her latest husband, a petty conman, choosing foster care and survival, instead of hopelessness.

Kyle's chest tightened as he began to see Eva's abandonment of their marriage in its correct context. She wasn't a quitter. She was strong and resolute and she had thrown everything she could into their marriage in an attempt to get him to love her back.

For Eva to leave meant she had given up on him.

If he got her back at all, it would be a miracle.

An hour later, Kyle sat down opposite Hastings in a small, neat office on the North Shore. When Hastings refused to divulge what, exactly, he was doing for Eva, Kyle applied a little judicious pressure. Eva was his wife and she had disappeared. If Hastings wanted his bill paid, then he needed to give the report to Kyle.

With the report in hand and the addresses he needed, Kyle started searching for Eva. Two weeks later, after a series of dead ends, he abandoned trying to find Eva through her past connections.

Although, he would find her, it was just a matter of time. Eva was pregnant with his child, which meant she needed medical appointments. More important, within the next few weeks, she would most probably be having tests to determine whether or not the baby was affected by the disorder. It wasn't the avenue he would have chosen to find Eva, but it was the only one she had left him.

Fifteen

Two months later, Eva dressed in a soft cotton shift dress and a light jacket, both of which were comfortable to wear, given that her waistline was gently expanding. After locking the tiny cottage she had rented in a remote coastal village miles north of Dolphin Bay, she drove to a specialist appointment in Auckland.

As she drove, she noticed the same silver sedan had been behind her ever since she had left the small village and turned onto the main highway. An odd tension gripped her at the thought that Kyle had somehow located her and was keeping tabs on her, although she almost immediately dismissed the thought. For Kyle to go to the effort of finding her and having her followed would mean that he cared, and she did not think that was the case. Besides, she was on State Highway 1, heading toward Auckland, New Zealand's largest city. Most of the traffic in front and behind would be heading toward the same destination.

Thirty minutes later, her small car was swallowed up in city traffic. A small jolt of adrenaline went through her when she noticed that there was still a silver sedan two cars behind her at a traffic light, but as she accelerated across an intersection with light-colored cars stretching in several directions, she dismissed the thought that she was being followed.

Minutes later, she parked her car and took an elevator up to the specialist clinic where she had booked her appointment. She had tossed up whether or not to have her baby tested while it was still in the womb. There was a small risk of miscarriage, but she had decided that she needed to know sooner rather than later. Regardless of the outcome, she would love this child with all her heart. If the news was bad, it would tear her to pieces, but she would cherish each day: she would cope.

As she sat in the upmarket clinic, the classical background music that was playing changed to a soft, lilting tune. It was the waltz by Strauss that she and Kyle had danced to at their wedding, just weeks ago. Nerves already stretched thin, she searched for a tissue and blew her nose, relieved when the tune finally changed to a light and airy piece by Bach.

She checked her watch. Abruptly nervous about the long wait, she got up to get a foam cup of chilled water from the dispenser in the corner of the waiting room. The sooner she had the procedure done, the sooner she could get out of Auckland and minimize the risk that she might accidentally bump into Kyle or someone else she knew.

She drank the small amount of water she'd dispensed, grimacing at the fine tremor of her hands, a sure sign of stress. The sound of the glass door at reception sliding open attracted her attention. Shock reverberated through her when she saw Kyle, dressed in a dark suit with a snowy-white shirt and blue tie, walking toward her.

She was suddenly glad that, evidently, she was the first appointment after lunch, so no one else was in the waiting area. "How did you know I'd be here?"

"I know you're pregnant and that you would need a specialist appointment, so I hired a security firm to find out where and when."

And that wasn't all. "You had me followed!"

"That, too. It took me long enough to locate you, and once I did, I wasn't taking any risks." He came to a halt beside her, and she noticed the dark circles under his eyes, as if he hadn't been sleeping, and that his hair was ruffled as if he'd dragged his fingers through it repeatedly. "I know why you ran."

She crumpled the cup and dropped it in the nearby trash can as she desperately tried to work out how much Kyle did know. She tried for a smooth, professional smile. "I am pregnant. And if you'll remember, you expressly stated that you didn't want children."

"I said a lot of things I regret, especially that. Will you hear me out?"

Tensing against the too-rapid pounding of her heart and the one thing she had not seen coming, that maybe, just maybe, Kyle wanted to try again, she sat and listened.

In terse sentences, Kyle outlined the raw details of the grief and guilt that had consumed him, almost to the point of losing her. "You know how much I wanted you. It practically drove me crazy, but I couldn't seem to change the way I was wired until I lost you." He grimaced. "Gabriel probably thinks I went crazy. It certainly felt like it."

Grimly, he outlined how he and Gabriel had accessed Mario's safe deposit box and found her medical reports. That Kyle had even rung Hicks and found that she was having Sheldon Ferris investigated for harassment. He had also found Hastings and pressured him into supplying a copy of the investigation she had commissioned into her stepfather.

"You know about the disorder."

"And that we could lose our child."

Our child. She met his gaze fiercely. "I don't understand. You didn't want a pregnancy. You can't stand the thought of having a child, let alone one that could die."

"Couldn't. Past tense."

"What does that mean, exactly?" Against all the odds, the very fact that Kyle was here, that he had gone to a great deal of trouble to find her, filled her with wild hope. Hope that she couldn't afford because she had barely survived leaving Kyle and, now that she was pregnant, she could not accept the empty, convenient marriage he preferred. And she would not, absolutely not, terminate her pregnancy.

"I followed you to the cemetery the day of the wedding. I thought—"

His gaze connected with hers for a long, tense moment. "I was saying goodbye."

Kyle pushed to his feet and did a restless circuit of the room before crouching down and taking her hands in his. "I made a mistake, about you and the baby. And about myself. I thought I couldn't heal, but I did—it just took time." In grim, rough words, he told her about his hunt for her and the research into her past that had finally made him face his own demons. "When Nicola and Evan died I blamed myself."

Despite her determination to keep as much emotional distance from Kyle as she could while he spoke, her heart broke for what he'd been through. "You couldn't protect them from a terrorist attack."

"They shouldn't have been with me in barracks. I should have made them stay in New Zealand where it was safe." He was silent for a moment. "I was waiting for them as they turned into the barracks. One minute they were there, the next there was…nothing."

Appalled, she stared at the tight clasp of his hands. "I didn't realize you had seen it." And suddenly the small scars across his stomach and arms, the nick on his cheekbone made sense. If he'd been caught by a bomb blast, he would have had multiple injuries.

She touched her abdomen. "This baby could die." In terse words she told him the grim details of her childhood.

"I know," he said simply. "But the fact that our child may have the disorder, as bad as that would be, was never the issue."

And finally she understood. Kyle had blamed himself for the deaths of his wife and child, but it hadn't ended there. Guilt had seared so deep he thought he didn't deserve love or fatherhood.

She touched his clasped hands. "I thought you were incapable of loving either me or the baby." When the reality was that Kyle was exactly what she had first thought him to be when she had fallen for him as a teenager, a strong protector who loved deeply. The way he had responded to the loss of his family only underlined that fact.

Kyle gripped her hand. "I can love you and this baby, if you'll let me."

Dimly, she heard her name being called.

When she stood up, she pulled Kyle with her. "This is my husband," she said a little shakily. "I'd like him to come into the appointment with me."

Kyle sat with her while she had the procedure. When the clinician had finished, he ascertained the time it would take to receive the test results then made some calls. Normally it took two weeks, but a hefty donation to the lab facility, and the time was reduced to forty-eight hours.

When they left the clinic, on the advice of the clinician, Kyle insisted that Eva shouldn't drive and that she needed to spend the next couple of days taking it easy.

Kyle accompanied her down in the elevator. When they reached the shadowy environs of the parking garage beneath the clinic, Eva gestured in the direction of her car. "I could move back into my place for a couple of days."

Kyle's Maserati flashed as he unlocked it. "I want you to stay at the house."

Kyle was still looking at her in an intent way that made her heart beat faster, as if he couldn't bear to let her out of his sight.

She drew a deep breath, feeling breathless and on edge but oddly, crazily confident about Kyle for the first time ever. "Why?"

He cupped her face between his hands, and she let him pull her close, loving the soft gleam in his gaze. "Because I love you. I'm in love with you. I want you back, if you'll have me."

She felt weird and a little dizzy, but the feeling was oh, so good. "Yes."

A split second later she was in his arms. The emotions that rolled through her were too powerful and intense to even think of moving; all she could do was cling to Kyle, absorb the warmth and comfort of his presence, and the stunning fact that he loved her.

She drew an impeded breath. "I love you."

A split second later, he dipped his head, and finally he kissed her.

* * *

Two days later, Kyle, who had taken time off work to be with her, took the phone call from the clinic. He handed the phone to Eva.

Fingers shaking, she listened to the result then terminated the call.

Kyle pulled her close. "What did they say? Not that it matters. For however long we have this baby, we'll love it, and if you want more we'll adopt."

Eva swallowed, hardly able to believe what she'd heard after years of fearing the worst. "They think it's all right. There's no sign of any abnormality." Then she burst into tears.

Kyle simply held her, and when she'd finished crying, he pulled her outside down to the sunlight-filled cove at the bottom of the garden.

He loosened off his hold and handed her a clean handkerchief. "I just wish you'd told me about the disorder years ago."

"I didn't know I was affected until after Mario broke us up." She shrugged. "It was after that that he took me to a specialist and I had the tests done. I think he was afraid I'd run after you." She sent him a slanting glance, "And he was right. But when I understood I was a carrier of the disease, that changed everything."

Kyle's brows jerked together. "I would never have walked away from you because of a medical issue. Mario told me to back off. He didn't say why, exactly, but he gave me the impression you came out of an abusive home, that you needed protection, not sex."

She coiled her arms around his neck, loving the feel of him so close, adjusting by slow increments to the knowledge that her future and the baby's was going to be a whole lot different than she had imagined. "Secrets are hard to let go of—they become part of you." She hesitated, but it was time to let go of her own hurt. "Did I tell you that I love you, that I've loved you for years?"

"Not today." Dipping his head, he kissed her for long, dizzying minutes.

Eva drew a deep breath as Kyle finally lifted his head. In the time they'd been talking, the sun had slid down the horizon and the shadows were lengthening. "We should go back to the house."

"First, you need to wear these." He reached into his pocket and pulled out a familiar black velvet ring box. Holding her wedding and engagement rings in one hand, he went down on one knee on the sand and slid them onto the third finger of her left hand.

In the deep, steady voice she loved so much, because it was an expression of Kyle's character, that he, himself, was steady and true, he asked her if she would be his wife for richer, for poorer, in sickness and in health.

Her throat closed up. "I will. I love you."

When he rose to his feet, she lifted up for his kiss. As they walked back to the house together, Eva knew they would have difficulties to face but, finally, she was secure in the knowledge that whatever came, they would face it together.

Epilogue

Six and a half months later, in the midst of renovations to the house they had firmly updated while keeping all of the beautiful period features, Eva put the final touches to the nursery.

Maybe it was old-fashioned to want an actual nursery opening off the master bedroom, but since she would only be pregnant this once, she had decided she would have it exactly how she wanted. The renovation and redecorating had entailed planning, hours of online browsing and multiple shopping trips, but it had been a labor of love.

Kyle, who had arrived home unexpectedly, considering that it was only two in the afternoon and he shouldn't have been home for a whole three hours, leaned against the doorjamb and surveyed the room. "It looks good." He gave her a slightly wary look as he loosened off his tie. "Is it finished?"

Eva dragged her gaze from the electric blue of Kyle's.

Months into a marriage that had been more sublime and interesting than she could have imagined, because she had never had to share her space with a man, she was even more in love with her husband.

Her husband.

The words still gave her a thrill and filled her with a glow of happiness. She and Kyle had spent time on Medinos, a honeymoon gift from Kyle so she could get in touch with her Atraeus roots and get to know her Messena relatives. She had met more family than she could poke a stick at, but the experience had been filled with laughter and healing. Most of all, she had enjoyed doing up the house with Kyle—the house that he had bought for her—working together to create a home that was a harmonious blend of them both. They still disagreed; on occasion they argued, but Eva figured that was a healthy sign.

She critically examined the white-painted armoire stacked full of diapers, baby wipes and the one hundred and one essentials a modern mother needed. "I think it's finished."

But she had thought so before then changed her mind. It was part of the nervous tension humming through her, a bit like the bridezilla thing, only with babies.

Feeling suddenly breathless, Eva walked to the window—although with her very large bump, walking was more like a waddle—and pushed it wide, letting in the early summer air. It was so hot, she was burning up. She also felt as big as a bus, probably because labor was a couple of days overdue, and if she put on any more weight she would explode.

She tried to take a deep breath, but these days breathing deeply didn't happen, no matter how much she needed the oxygen. She attempted to give Kyle a serene, in-control look. "Why are you home early?"

"I thought I should be here, just in case." He frowned. "Maybe you should sit down, or better still, lie down."

Eva tried for a smooth, professional smile. The only problem was, deep down, she was a bundle of nerves. "I was sitting down before. I hate lying down." Who could know that even lying down would be difficult when pregnant?

Abandoning his relaxed position, Kyle came to stand at the window with her. Placing his arm gently around what used to be her waist, he leaned down and kissed her. As soft and tender as it was, it was a distinctly sideways kiss. Her stomach was so large now that any approach from the front was doomed.

"Is your bag packed?"

She shifted so that she was leaning back against Kyle, his arms around her. It was the only comfortable way to hug. She let out a breath, soothed by his presence. Somehow, when Kyle arrived, all of her fretful stressing melted away. "I've been packed for weeks."

"Good, because I'm taking you to the hospital. Now."

"You knew I was having pains?"

Kyle leaned down and nuzzled her neck. "Of course I knew," he growled.

She smiled delightedly at a phenomenon that still took her by surprise, and which she had never thought would affect a macho, manly guy like Kyle. She met his gaze in his reflection in the window. "You're having them, too."

"My secretary thinks it's hilarious."

She had a moment to consider that, as crazy as it was that Kyle was experiencing some part of her discomfort, it was just another sign of how well they fit together. She had expected to feel passion and desire and all the turbulent depths of being in love with Kyle; what she hadn't expected was the warm, close companionship that had steadily grown. They weren't just husband and wife, they were best friends.

She placed her hands over his, holding his palms spread over her stomach. Almost instantly there was a sharp kick and she held her breath, riveted by Kyle's absorbed expression. "I won't tell your family...for a price."

"Too late," he muttered grimly. "Francesca knows. That's the same as saying everyone in the family knows. Constantine rang me up today to say it was okay to feel pains. Apparently it runs in the male line."

She hesitated then decided to ask. "You didn't feel them...before?"

The look he gave her was surprised. "No."

Happiness filled her at the relaxed, neutral way Kyle had answered a question about the child he had lost, because that, too, was a sign of healing. Thankfully, the guilt that had seared him finally seemed to have been exorcised.

A pain that was sharper and more prolonged than the one before made her stiffen. Concerned, Kyle helped her to the bedroom, but she refused to lie down. The bed, as comfortable and gorgeous as it was, was her nemesis. Once she got on it, she felt like a beached whale. She practically needed a crane to haul herself out.

Another pain hit her, and Kyle went white. "That's it. I'm calling the hospital. We're going now."

It wasn't a hospital so much as a private clinic because, before the police had managed to charge Ferris after they had found her laptop in his house, he had sold a story about her to a Sunday paper, and now there was a media problem. When the original story had broken, Kyle had decided it was as good a time as any to do what they had planned and fund a charity for disabled children. Unfortunately, instead of neutralizing the story, it had only seemed to whet the appetite of the media. But in a good way, and they had begun actively following her pregnancy. Now, apparently, she even had an online fan club.

Eva tried to get comfortable in Kyle's Maserati as he drove through the gates of the clinic. Thick, subtropical plantings lined the driveway, closing out any view of the rolling hill country or the sea, which she knew had to be just a couple of miles away. They weren't that far from Auckland, but the isolation seemed eerily complete.

Kyle parked in front of the double doors of a facility that, situated as it was in a mass of towering tropical growth, looked more like the set for *Jurassic Park* than a hospital, and helped her out.

Feeling grumpy and emotional the closer she got to giving birth, Eva leaned on Kyle, because she now had weird pains shooting up her legs, although secretly she loved it that he fussed around her.

An orderly strolled down a shallow ramp with a wheelchair. Eva ignored Kyle's impatience when she didn't immediately maneuver herself into the chair. Instead, she concentrated on dragging her handbag out of the Maserati, annoyed that evidently Kyle didn't think she needed this last bastion of her femininity. Grimly, she noted that given that she was now shaped like a bubble, the bag was possibly the only verifiable sign that she was female. Hugging to herself the pretty pink leather tote with cute tassels and sparkling diamanté stuck to the side, she pretended the wheelchair was invisible and shuffled right by it.

Kyle kept pace with her, his expression carefully

blank, as if he was dealing with a mental patient. "You should have gotten in the wheelchair."

"I want to walk. I need the exercise."

A series of cramps hit her. She'd had cramps on and off for weeks now. Someone had named them Braxton-Hicks cramps, because they were supposed to be practice contractions that prepared the body for labor. The Braxton-Hicks episodes had been interspersed by two sessions of false labor but, so far, no result. As far as she was concerned, Braxton-Hicks was a liar, and she had been in labor for a month. Who knew if these were finally the real thing?

She shuffled a few more steps, aiming at the front door when one of her dizzy turns hit. Head spinning, she found herself veering into the large patch of tropical bush that loomed over the front entrance. Kyle caught her before she stumbled into the weird little forest and disappeared forever. He muttered something short beneath his breath that she was pretty sure was a curse word and swung her into his arms.

"You should put me down," she muttered fretfully. "I must weigh two hundred pounds."

"No sweat." She caught the edge of a grin. "I bench press that much most days."

She thumped his shoulder, but desisted when she almost dropped her bag. It contained her makeup, a magazine, some low-sugar snacks and her phone which, judging from this place, over the next few days could be her only link to civilization.

The front doors slid open. A cool, air-conditioned current washed over her. "Okay, you can put me down now."

"No."

Feeling disempowered because he wouldn't put her down and tired of being huge and heavy and vulnerable, she muttered the direst threat she could come up with. "That's it. You just lost any say in names."

Infuriatingly, that didn't seem to make an impact. "As long as it's not Tempeste or Maverick I can live with that."

She tried not to let the fact that he didn't care about the names get to her. "Why are you so happy?"

He lowered her into the wheelchair, which the orderly had anxiously inserted into the space below her body, but by now she was in too much pain to protest. She was beginning to think that her body had finally given up practicing and was actually going to give birth.

Kyle bent down, one hand on either rest, corralling her. His face was taut, and she dimly remembered that he was experiencing at least something of these pains himself.

He kissed her, surprising her into silence. "I'm happy because after today the waiting will be over, we'll finally be a family." His mouth twisted in a wry smile. "And because we don't have to be pregnant again."

Another sharp pain hit her as he steered the wheelchair to the receptionist's desk. The woman behind it gave Kyle a concerned look, but Eva was suddenly distracted by a suspicious warmth. She couldn't be sure, but she thought her waters might have broken. Either that or she'd had another one of those annoying little accidents. "I need to go to the bathroom."

Kyle gave her a narrow-eyed look, as if he suspected her of hiding something from him. *As if.*

He had a quick-fire conversation with the receptionist then finally wheeled her in the direction of the bathrooms. She pointed at the ladies, but he totally ignored her, wheeling her into the disabled bathroom.

She sent him an outraged look when he didn't leave. "You can't come in here."

"You're in labor. You need help."

"No. I want to do this one thing by myself."

She might have been talking to a rock. With easy strength he helped her out of the chair.

When he saw the wet patch, he said another one of his cuss words. "Why didn't you say your waters had broken?"

Face flaming, she let him help her out of the wheelchair. "How would I know? It's not as if I've ever had a baby before."

Kyle's expression was grim as he helped her in the direction of the toilet.

When she was finished, Kyle helped her back into the chair and wheeled her out into the corridor. Within seconds another pain hit, this one severe enough that she was finally glad to be in the chair.

When Kyle wheeled her into her room, both a doctor and a midwife were waiting for them. She was already in active labor, and the pain was quite intense. Eva did her best to ride through the pain, silently begging for the fastest delivery possible

It was forty-five minutes.

When Kyle, who had stripped off his suit jacket and tie and rolled up his shirtsleeves so he could pace better, realized that she was in too much pain to be even remotely interested in conversation, his face went white. Stepping out into the corridor, he snapped out a curt series of commands, including a demand for pain relief.

Within seconds the room was full of people. Another lightning examination, this time by the midwife, and Eva found herself transferred to a gurney and wheeled into the delivery suite.

With walls that were a soothing aqua, and soft background music playing, it should have been an oasis of reassuring calm, but Eva barely noticed her surroundings. All of her attention was focused on what was happening at the center of her body and how much it hurt. Somehow, all of the literature she had read had managed to gloss over this part.

Kyle's arm came around her, a hard-muscled band of strength that in those moments she desperately needed. A cramp gripped her that was so prolonged and intense she couldn't breathe. Kyle's gaze locked with hers and for a precious few seconds they were bound together in commiseration.

Her fingers tightened on Kyle's as a powerful tingling surge gripped her, wiping her mind clean of anything but the sudden, irresistible urge to push. There was a brief hiatus then another series of surges, which squeezed all the breath from her lungs until, in a rush, the baby was born.

Eva floated in exhausted silence, watching, dazed, as the midwife cut the cord, wrapped her tiny baby girl in a cuddly white wrap and placed her in Kyle's hands. His gaze bright blue and indescribably soft, Kyle cradled their daughter as if she was made of fragile spun glass and placed her in Eva's arms. Wonderingly, she looked into her baby's small, perfect face, the tufts of damp hair clinging to her head, and fell in instant love. The bed depressed as Kyle sat beside her. She felt the warmth of his arm wrap protectively around her shoulders.

Reaching out a forefinger, he gently touched his daughter's cheek. One tiny starfish hand latched around his finger, and Kyle froze in place. Eva's heart squeezed tight at Kyle's careful stillness, the way his gaze was riveted on the fierce grip of his daughter, and another wave of pure love and connection hit her, this time for Kyle.

He would be a wonderful father. She had seen it in his patience with her, his quiet tolerance of the mood swings that had hit her, his absorption with all the aspects of her pregnancy. It wasn't just that her hormones had been running riot. It had been an emotional time of processing the past, of letting go and forming a new future together.

Another contraction grounded Eva with a thump. The midwife hurriedly took their daughter. A few minutes later the unutterable gift that had shaken them when cheerfully announced by her doctor months earlier, their second child, was born. It was a boy.

The midwife placed their son in Kyle's arms and Eva gave herself over to joy.

Twins: a boy and a girl. Even though twins ran on both sides of their families, it had been so much more than they had hoped for.

Kyle called his family to let them know the good news. He asked everyone to give them some space, but that was like asking waves to stop pounding on the beach.

The Messena and Atraeus families were like a force of nature. They arrived throughout the day: Luisa with Sophie and Francesca; Gabriel and Gemma; Nick and Elena; Damian and Sky; and a little later on Constantine and Sienna, who had flown in from Sydney where they were holidaying. They had all admired and held the babies and showered her with beautiful gifts and filled her room with flowers.

Later on that evening, when everyone had left, Grace Megan woke up, her cry distinctively high-pitched. Benedict Mario soon joined in, although his cry was more of a bellow.

Kyle handed her Grace then cradled Benedict. Both babies were on the small side, around six pounds each, but they were perfect.

Closing her eyes, Eva whispered a prayer of thanks.

Somehow, out of Mario's well-meant interference, she had gained everything she had wanted and more: a perfect husband and a perfect family.

* * * * *

LET'S TALK
Romance

For exclusive extracts, competitions
and special offers, find us online:

- **f** facebook.com/millsandboon
- **𝕐** @MillsandBoon
- **◎** @MillsandBoonUK

Get in touch on 01413 063232

For all the latest titles coming soon, visit
millsandboon.co.uk/nextmonth

MILLS & BOON

THE HEART OF ROMANCE

A ROMANCE FOR EVERY KIND OF READER

MODERN

Prepare to be swept off your feet by sophisticated, sexy and seductive heroes, in some of the world's most glamourous and romantic locations, where power and passion collide.
8 stories per month.

HISTORICAL

Escape with historical heroes from time gone by. Whether your passion is for wicked Regency Rakes, muscled Vikings or rugge Highlanders, awaken the romance of the past.
6 stories per month.

MEDICAL

Set your pulse racing with dedicated, delectable doctors in the high-pressure world of medicine, where emotions run high an passion, comfort and love are the best medicine.
6 stories per month.

True Love

Celebrate true love with tender stories of heartfelt romance, fr the rush of falling in love to the joy a new baby can bring, and focus on the emotional heart of a relationship.
8 stories per month.

Desire

Indulge in secrets and scandal, intense drama and plenty of siz hot action with powerful and passionate heroes who have it all: wealth, status, good looks...everything but the right woman.
6 stories per month.

HEROES

Experience all the excitement of a gripping thriller, with an int romance at its heart. Resourceful, true-to-life women and stron fearless men face danger and desire - a killer combination!
8 stories per month.

DARE

Sensual love stories featuring smart, sassy heroines you'd want best friend, and compelling intense heroes who are worthy of
4 stories per month.

To see which titles are coming soon, please visit

millsandboon.co.uk/nextmonth

JOIN US ON SOCIAL MEDIA!

Stay up to date with our latest releases, author
news and gossip, special offers and discounts, and
all the behind-the-scenes action
from Mills & Boon...

 millsandboon

 millsandboonuk

 millsandboon

It might just be true love...

MILLS & BOON
MEDICAL
Pulse-Racing Passion

Set your pulse racing with dedicated, delectable doctors in the high-pressure world of medicine, where emotions run high and passion, comfort and love are the best medicine.

millsandboon.co.uk